Noble McCloud

Noble McCloud

A Novel
By
Harvey Havel

First Amendment Press International Company
uncut. unedited. quality literature

Published by First Amendment Press International Company
New Jersey, USA

First Amendment Press International Company, and the portrayal of
colonial, bell-waving man are registered trademarks.

Publisher's Cataloging-in-Publication
(*Provided by Quality Books, Inc.*)

Havel, Harvey.
     Noble McCloud : a novel / Harvey Havel.
     -- 1 st ed.
     p. cm.
     ISBN: 0-9670081-5-8

     1. Guitarists--New Jersey--Fiction
2. Alcoholics--New Jersey--Fiction
3. Twelve-step programs--Fiction.   I.
Title

PS3558.A779N62 1999   813'.54
                    QBI99-213

FIRST PRINTING

For Patrick Carroll

I looked across the river to the Jersey shore. It looked desolate to me, more desolate even than the boulder bed of a dried up river. Nothing of any importance to the human race had ever happened here. Nothing would happen for thousands of years perhaps. The Pygmies were vastly more interesting, vastly more illuminating to study, than the inhabitants of New Jersey.

Henry Miller, 1950

And the only thing that'll save them is to figure out a way to think about themselves and most everything else differently; formulate fresh understandings based on the faith that for new fires to kindle, old ones have to be dashed; and based less on isolating, boneheaded obstinance and more, for instance, on the wish to make each other happy without neutralizing the private self...which is why they showed up in New Jersey in the first place instead of staying in the mountains and becoming smug casualties of their own idiotic miscues.

Richard Ford, 1995

I don't want to give up. I promise I shall never give up, and that I'll die yelling and laughing.

Jack Kerouac, 1949

Book One:

Darkness

Chapter One

Tell me, sweet muse, the story of Noble McCloud. Come sit on my shoulder and sing into my ears of his plans, his visions, and his dreams. Time has given him the gift of youth, as he is a young man at the age of twenty-seven, still young and still unlearned in the ways of the world. He has an impression of how things work, but when asked, his mind wanders to another impression, another vague and outdated image, and these images speckled and dabbed with subtle colors approach him while laying in bed, his body supine, his arms supporting the back of his head, his eyes open in the darkness, waiting for his dreams to manifest themselves like flint sparks in the blackness.

As he lay in bed, he reached over next to him and turned on his small stereo. He preferred the stereo in the darkness, the blurred blue of the tuner, the red slit emanating from the CD player, and bouncing spasms of the equalizer. Gently he turned the amplifier louder, and from a small set of speakers came a drizzle of piano, the humble thump of bass, the knock of a snare drum, and the guitar.

For Noble the guitar held a special significance. Of all the instruments, it reigned like a king over its subjects. He paid immediate attention to the chords which moaned and giggled at precise intervals, up and down like hilly fields and open knolls overtaken by thunder. With each stroke of its strings he was transported from the dregs of reality into a flighty fantasy, as he imagined getting in his father's beat-up Oldsmobile, the windows down, the air tousling his hair, and moving along bare highways in the dead of night.

In his mind he headed for California, a place he knew little, only that the sun could be found there, a new beginning with blonde women in bikinis, and the prosperity which comes with being easy-going and laid-back. He envisioned the beach, sun-drenched with jogging women, the ocean against the shore charging the tranquility with an electric fire. He would find a job working on such a beach where the surfers tamed the waves and sailboats cut across the choppiness beyond the buoys.

The guitar took him to this warmer climate, although he lived in the dark of winter, the snow piling in the driveway, his piggy bank empty, the motivation lacking. And these visions of California came with another round of guitar riffs, which prolonged the inevitable drift to this land where reality escaped at the touch of a breeze. And maybe he would meet a woman there with eyes that reflected the ocean and an embrace which settled the anxiety of being dead broke and going absolutely nowhere.

The country remained in perpetual, aggressive, and self-induced hypnosis, working so hard as slaves to the greenback and its stored bullion protected by mighty warriors. He intimated he would find in California what could not be found in New Jersey, that he would be surrounded by musicians licking mean chords, banging bongo drums, and the women, especially the women, loving unconditionally. And then he heard a loud knock at the door which broke him from this reverie. Instantly his visions of the land drenched with continual sunshine faded as the guitar gasped for breath and died with a reluctant turn of the volume.

He lifted himself from his bed wishing only to be lost in his dreaming, and he answered the door with his hair standing on end and a three-day growth on his face. This other specimen standing before him with an angry look was Noble's father, McCoy McCloud.

Noble's father was dressed in a white shirt and khaki trousers, a set of plastic lenses from a by-gone era slipping from his nose, and a piercing gaze which meant Noble was in trouble. Noble had always wanted to please his father. He fell quite short of this goal. He had used the simple strategy of replying affirmatively to all his comments and criticisms while never acting upon them. This had been the routine for several months, and he could tell that his father had grown weary of it. He prepared for the worst, as some of his father's comments in the past had produced a hollowness and irregularity at the chest. To combat him with smart-aleck answers or vociferousness proved fruitless before, simply due to Noble's inability to raise his voice. His mind shut off. He understood that his fear only fed his father's remarks, and he braced for the tirade like shop owners before a hurricane. The gleam in his father's eyes intensified at the sight of him.

"Damn it, Noble! Why aren't you up yet?"

"I just thought I'd..."

"That's the problem with you damn it. Don't think, don't do anything. You lay in that bed of yours, your room's a mess. How many times have I told you to clean this place up? The garbage needs to be taken out, the car needs an inspection..."

"I'm sorry Dad."

"Sorry's not enough," as a sharp echo beat on the walls. "Sorry this, sorry that. Do you want to be a loser? And turn down that stereo, or I swear I'll rip the damn thing and crush your head with it."

"Dad, I think you're overreacting," as Noble turned off the amplifier.

"I don't think I'm overreacting," said McCoy McCloud. "Is this the way you want to live your life? Listening to that damn filth? At least listen to some good music for a change, could you at least do that right?"

"But I like this…," mumbled Noble.

"What was that, boy? Don't smart talk me, boy, not unless you want to be out on the street."

"I'm sorry, Dad. I didn't mean to…"

"Right out there on the street with all that crap. Someone has to teach you."

Noble had always wondered why his father never kicked him out sooner. Perhaps old and stocky McCoy McCloud had a reason for keeping his son within yelling distance.

"Now there are two things you're doing today, Noble, two things. First, I want this place clean, top to bottom. That means the dishes, the garbage, the floors, the carpet. If you're not doing anything, at least make yourself useful. Downright lazy. No common sense. Is this why I sent you to college? To do nothing but lie on your ass all day? A waste of time and money, that's what I think…"

Noble nodded in his usual way, his heart fluttering, and his father's steely blue eyes poking him like sharp tacks. He had seen his father this way before, a long, continuous rant just before work, and he would be thankful when he left.

"Now I've got a long day ahead of me, and I want this stuff done before I get back."

"When are you getting back?"

"You don't have the right, you hear me, the right to question me about anything. Do as you're told, and if it's not done, you will leave, is that perfectly clear? Can you understand a direct order?"

"Yes, Dad, it'll get done."

"Good. That's what I like to hear. And stop listening to that crap. Do something with your life. And also I want dinner waiting when I get home, and if you cant find anything in the fridge, go out and get something from the Food Stop."

His father collected a few papers from the small kitchen and departed. Noble caught his breath, closed the door, and relieved himself of his father's orders for later in the day.

He looked from his window. The snowflakes conspired with the wind and brought a deep freeze to the region. He lay in bed again, turned the stereo back on, and resumed listening to a guitar which turned melodic and sad. His foggy mind captured his father's angry gaze, but as the guitar wailed and cried, he again envisioned his challenging escape.

The world was an impression, most people struggling and fighting for a home or vacations, this same world where no one liked what they were doing, undertaking their tasks because they had to, not because they wanted to, and after conforming to their pressurized tasks, these same people changed their molds like snakes molting, and became unregulated beasts with an assertiveness and aggressiveness that circumvented courtesy and affability, humility and altruism, all in the name of what a simple system demanded: work and more work, a course in how to become a self-serving machine in the pursuit of pleasure stored within burning muscles lifting heavy cargo. And these machines which result from years of prolonged labor skew the genes, as genes are malleable, and reproduce replicas so exact in form and content that the slivers of humanity dissolve at childhood. The offspring grows into a similar mechanical beast more disturbing than the first, stepping over hyacinths in bloom and other men of misfortune. The process begins anew with hopes that this pattern leads to a beast more capable and controlling of the uncertainties which give creation its charm and purpose. Instead, the machine works harder and longer, discarding its capacity for kindness, filling its own wardrobe of self-interest and disturbing vanity for an end which is never fully realized. The humanoid is crushed by a simple system, all in the name of some false freedom enslaving the populace.

The sadness of the guitar transformed into a hurried strum, shifting Noble's outlook and mood. The gloom he projected blanched. His spirit recovered from haunting images of people ripping each other apart for bread crumbs, water, oil, and precious stones. He thought of things more rationally. Perhaps this wasn't a system which forces its participants to work. Work it seems only lasts for eight hours, and then the night is free to do whatever one wishes with the money he has earned. Or a man could choose from a variety of employment, as there were many listed in the classifieds. And within work one could find meaning as well as subsistence, identity as well as accomplishment, friendship with his fellows, respect and self-esteem if the product should benefit another. Or he could develop certain skills which make him complete and knowing, because without work one surrenders his chances to grow and learn of himself, and what would one do all day without work? One would isolate in a room and become boring and insular, mentally masturbating to death; an atrophy of mind and muscle crippling the connections with any working person. People in China work just like people in New Jersey do, and work must be the way of the world, the essential outcome of trading goods and services, and green money only a currency to facilitate such a system, paper which equalizes the man reaping grain and the man selling toilet brushes, so they may trade on a common footing. Labor produces tangible results like the roads which cut across the nation or the diamond ring placed on the hand of a comely woman. Without work what would there be, and aren't we lucky to choose the work we do? We can't eat without planting a seed which requires a bent back and two hands, nor can a woman be impressed by a sparkling toilet without a brush. And if there were little work to be done, there would be more time to bash our heads against a wall and flog those who cross us. We would starve, as an apple needs picking before being eaten, and the actor must perform while on the stage...

From its logical twang, the guitar then joined the other instruments to complete the selection, and the reprise brought with it more thoughts of escape.

Noble envisioned a wide green field stretching for miles, girdled by craggy mountains with snow-covered peaks. The sunshine bathed this field in a brilliant light and warmth, and at the head of the field stood a giant stage with rafters holding enormous speakers blasting the same sounds he heard on his stereo. On this sunlit field flocked thousands of women wearing scanty clothes. Noble mingles with these celestial beauties, and he spots one with blonde hair gracing her breasts. Her precious skin is tan against the sun's rays, and she wears a bright, polka-dotted sun dress. Her nose is faded pink and symmetrical with her features, the foreskin worn and peeling from the sun's intensity. He sees her from afar and moves closer, the guitar continuing its established rhythm. He smiles and dances towards her. Once at her side his blue eyes connect with hers and they begin the dance, and within her eyes he sees an unencumbered clarity and truth, and in her body he sees sinewy waters pouring from mossy cliffs, and from that moment when the guitar chants to it conclusion, he knows that this woman will care for him and never leave, even though her beauty frightens and subdues the most cold-hearted men.

He takes her into his arms and feels her firm and curvaceous back. He finds it inviting, and while he feels her, she wraps her arms around him, and they sway gently, wiping away years of their common uncertainty. And the music stays with them, the guitar so loud that it makes the dead rise up and dance along, and the entire world is dancing, the living and the dead, grinding to this one guitar bellowing hysterically.

He remained in bed for some time, the field and the stage disappearing, and a slow orange sunset setting over the sky, and soon the sun looks like a

match in the darkness, and the vision fades with the reminder of McCoy
McColud's commands.

Noble's room was in shambles: compact discs scattered like
minefields, some of them without covers, a warped pizza box in the corner, a
pile of laundry near the door, old magazines left open to pages unread, soda
cans crushed and discarded to the side. The task of cleaning proved so
daunting that Noble found himself paralyzed. He imagined the process of
cleaning before rising out of bed, and this same intimation kept him there. He
had the entire day to clean, and he flirted with the idea of listening to more.
But he recalled the words of his father, and with the immediacy of an alarm
clock he picked himself up, retrieved a garbage bag from the kitchen and
threw away the artifacts which littered his room. He pulled a damp towel
from the laundry pile and stuffed the remainder under his bed. He peeled off
the clothes he had been wearing for several days and darted to the bathroom.
The mirror, spotted with dried toothpaste, told the story of his
mismanagement, but he liked the way he looked at these times. He took
pleasure in being totally disheveled and unkempt before showering.

He shaved once every week and showered every other day. The
process of cleaning himself took on a ritualistic importance. First, he sat on
the can and cleared his digestive tract. Second, he applied a thick lather to his
face and shaved so painstakingly close that not the slightest stubble was left.
Third, he hopped in the shower, the hot current pelting his skin. He stayed
there for at least forty-five minutes, soaping and shampooing himself.
Between these two events his mind wandered to the guitar he had heard, to
the visions which had joined it. He emerged from the shower in a daze, beads
of sweat at his brow, his face burning. Fourth, he dried himself thoroughly,
and vacated the steamy bathroom to cool off, only to return five minutes later.
He then applied the deodorant to his underarms, and wiped alcohol swabs
over his face to prevent unsightly acne, a stage of hormonal imbalance from
which he never recovered. Finally, Noble was clean, and the sixth step
involved cleaning his ears and navel with cotton swabs. Occasionally Noble
tumbled into an annoying seventh step: the clipping of fingernails and
toenails, twice every month. After a close inspection, he chose not to.

His clothes were kept in piles on the floor, mostly unfolded, the clean
clothes separated from the dirty ones. On this wintry day, he discovered only
a pair of briefs and a blue-collared shirt in the clean pile, the rest of his
clothes under the bed. He pulled out a pair of faded blue jeans, a cotton
sweater, and a pair of worn socks. He dressed quickly and performed the

duties for his father nonchalantly, as though only his room mattered and not the rest of the house.

The single floor house stood tiredly on a property sandwiched by other houses similar in structure and appearance. From Noble's room, one could see directly down a narrow hallway to his father's room on the opposite side. A living room, the small kitchen, two closets, and two bathrooms rested in between these two poles. Noble likened it to a trailer.

His main task now was to flee the house. The home beyond his musical sanctuary suffocated him. He checked his room before leaving, making sure all of his electronic equipment was off, (should his father later complain about the utility bill). He grabbed his gray coat, which was much too thin to withstand the winter and rushed down a long snowy lane which led to the center of town.

He passed quiet homes covered with snow, utility poles draped with ice, and swaying streetlights with their yellow signals flashing. The gusts of wind penetrated his coat, but he was determined to make it to the center of town.

Upon arrival, Noble noticed how the winter took on a cheery quality. People abated winter's severity. Compared to the lane, the town bustled with activity. A busy road ran through its center, a long strip prepared for slow-moving vehicles, their tires slipping. On either side of the main road stood shops of all kinds, very fashionable shops such as a jewelry store, a quaint cinema, a couple of classy Chinese and Italian restaurants, suit shops, an august bank, a travel agency, the diner with a hundred varieties of flapjacks, a family pharmacy, and a couple of coffee houses. Noble often felt refreshed after leaving the shadowy lane and entering what he often termed the hoi-polloi area, the rents high as well as the property taxes. He never understood how his father made it to a town such as this, and on occasion he would see the latest sport sedans cruising by, or luxury sport utility vehicles, a trend at which he secretly scoffed, as he was old enough to remember the gas crisis of his youth. The main road ended at a train station which carried commuters to and from Manhattan, and two parks graced the town: one near the train station, the other at the midpoint of the strip.

At first Noble wandered aimlessly, window shopping and people watching. He tried to find women, preferably older, with shopping bags dangling from leather gloves; they had husbands who worked for large, multinational corporations, most likely at the office, those sorts of women, and certainly he found a few of them parading near the shops. Their demeanor amused him. He often imagined their worlds filled with dinner parties and social functions, a daughter attending private school, a beach house along the shores of Long Island. He was intrigued mostly by where these women lived. He noticed how they entered town and surreptitiously left at the end of their shopping sprees. He had only heard about their houses. Not once had he set foot in one. He assumed they lived in a region far removed, the part of town which turned bucolic and exclusive. An hour wandering the town made him shiver, and he knew it time to visit his good friend Shylock Winston who worked at one of the coffee shops near the park.

The coffee shop, housed in a brown brick building, stood at the corner of an intersection across from the family pharmacy. Although the shop was small, Noble admired the aesthetics of wrought-iron tables and chairs lining the wall, the island where skim, half-and-half, and whole milk waited in cylinders, the posters of famous impressionists, and especially the impeccable calligraphy on the blackboard listing the many varieties of coffees and teas. Before entering he scoped the place out through the large windows which offered a view of the entire shop. He spotted Shylock at the register counting money. He knew that his shift ended soon.

The aroma hit him as he walked in. He knocked on the register table and broke Shylock's concentration.

"Don't do that!" yelled Shylock thumbing through dollar bills. "Now I've lost count."

"Sorry, Shy. Didn't mean to startle you."

"At least it's not one of these damn customers. All day, I tell you, all day. It's been so busy. They come in and out, and I'm sick of coffee, I tell you. If I smell another bean, I'm likely to puke."

"Want me to come back later?"

"Nah, stick around. I'm here at least for another hour. Have a seat and listen to some tunes."

He sat in the corner and stared at the passersby on the street. The snow had picked up considerably and in the distance bulky trucks cleared the snow and sprinkled sand. Although Shylock had said the shop was busy, Noble found little proof of that. The sidewalks had mysteriously emptied as the snow grew heavy.

"Noble, Noble, Noble McCloud," sang Shylock.

"That's my name, as you are Shylock Winston."

"Yes indeed. Sorry I was so short with you back there, but counting the money has to be the worst part of this job."

"It doesn't sound like you're happy here. I've noticed that change in you."

"You think so?"

"Yes, I do. Every time I see you, you say you aren't happy here, and it's true, you're mood changes each time you're on the job."

"Is it really that noticeable?"

Noble paused for a moment.

"I don't know," said Noble finally, "I don't know about anything anymore."

"Don't sound so down, Noble. It isn't that bad. Imagine if you had to work here five days out of the week, serving coffee and being polite. You have it good, Noble, damn good. I wish I were in your shoes- No responsibilities."

Noble found this surprising. He envied Shylock. He was independent, had his own place on the outskirts of Waspachick, his own finances to manage, and remarkably his own car which was essential to having any life at all. Noble could have responded, but he chose not to, fearful of Shylock's bitter mood. Shylock usually complained after the long shift, and Noble took it upon himself to be his personal punching bag, as this was the routine. Shylock finished his counting and filled two cups of house blend.

"Noble, Noble, Noble McCloud," sang Shylock again, "tell me, how's everything in la-la land?"

"It's not exactly a dreamworld," said Noble.

"Yeah right. I hate this job. Nothing but work for the rest of my life. It gets so monotonous, the same customers come in and out, and what do they pay me? Peanuts. That's exactly what they pay me- no health insurance, retirement plans, nothing but bags of beans. Damn it, I want out of this town. Hey, how about this? Let's go out and have ourselves a few drinks?"

"I don't think so," said Noble, "I've got too much stuff to do."

"Like what?"

"I have to cook dinner for my father. He's getting home in a few hours."

"God, your old man, eh? I've never met anyone so pissed off at the world. I don't know how you handle him."

"It takes practice like anything else."

"In other words, he tells you what to do, and you do it. He asks you to jump, and you jump. God, Noble, you have to get out of that house. You're father is like a drill sergeant."

"I can't help it. If I don't listen to him, he'll kick me out."

"Maybe that's the best thing for you. You'll get kicked out, and you'll have to find a job like everyone else on the face of this planet."

They sipped their coffees slowly, and Noble recalled his great escape through the heartland, only to arrive where the sun hung above the horizon.

"I've got a few plans in the works," said Noble.

"Like what?"

"Believe me, when I say that something's gonna change mighty soon. I can feel it."

"Oh bullshit, Noble. You're not going anywhere, and either am I. We're both stuck here, forever wearing this apron, locked up in Waspachick, headed nowhere but behind this counter serving mocha to a bunch of addicts. They're addicts, Noble, plain and simple. Let's do something about it. Forget your father tonight. I'm really in the mood for a few drinks, relax, meet some women."

Noble initially liked the idea, but froze at the dreary consequences. His father would beat him with both criticism and a belt buckle if he even thought about neglecting dinner. He turned against the idea.

"I mean, what do you do all day? Sit around and mope?" asked Shylock with more alacrity.

"I do lots of things."

"Like what?"

"I read the newspaper and music magazines. I listen to all sorts of music, and I'm really getting good at that..."

"In other words, you do nothing at all. The least you could do for your best pal is go out with him, out of town lines, mind you, for a drink or two. You can tell your father anything. Tell him you've been searching for jobs."

"That will never work. And besides, how would it look searching for a job in the evening? All the shops are closed."

"C'mon, Noble. Don't be such a woos. One of these days you're going to have to stand up to dear ol' dad. And you've got enough weight behind you to give him a few blows."

"I'd never do that," said Noble sharply.

"Okay, but you're coming with me tonight. This is one thing I do know."

Noble pictured his father yelling at him. He weighed the decision carefully: either anger his friend Shylock or enrage McCoy McCloud. And his father wouldn't stop with one round. McCoy McCloud would continue for weeks, pounding the lapse into him. But then again, he would enjoy an evening away from Waspachick. He imagined women of all kinds hanging over him while a loud guitar blew from the speakers. At this single image, Noble found it difficult to reject Shylock's persuasion. He gulped his coffee, as most of it had cooled. He looked out the window as pedestrians with shopping bags fled the harrowing snow.

"Noble, you've got to stop thinking about your father. I know you love him and all, but the time comes when you step out of his shadow and build your own life. Going to this bar means a lot more than wine, women, and song. It's your fight for autonomy and self-reliance, not in defiance of your father, but to gain that one ounce of respect from him, that you have friends and a life apart from his silly requests. He can cook dinner on his own, he's a grown man, and one night out never killed anybody. I know what you're thinking: that your father will yell at you and never let go, but really, Noble, you have to think of your own needs."

"You really think so?" he asked searchingly

"Yes, me and every other bone-head in Waspachick. Let your father have the night away from you. Maybe a better relationship will happen if you're not stuck in your room the whole time. Believe me, things will get better with your father, only if you're away from him."

"Y'know, Shy, you're absolutely right. Damn it, I'm going with you tonight, and I don't care if my dad yells at me."

"That's the spirit, Noble!" said Shylock patting him on the arm. "See, I knew you had it in you. I know of this place a few miles down the road, in the next town, and right now it's happy hour, and all these gorgeous women flock there."

"They say that about all the bars," he grinned.

"This bar is special. I know so many people who get laid from going to this one place."

"What kind of music do they play?"

"Not exactly sure, but if all the women go there, and I mean wealthy women too, the music can't be that bad."

They left the coffee house shortly thereafter. Shylock had a used Honda, and he drove through the slippery streets in a hurry. He set the tuner to the popular music station which rehashed the same tunes so much that the songs were liked, not because of their quality, but more due to a psychological conditioning, until each weak chord, every lyric was pummeled into memory, something akin to brainwashing, or at least Noble thought of it this way. He admitted he liked some of the new songs, but found more meaning in the ones he listened to at home. The music on the popular station turned horrifically meaningless after a while, as though meaningful riffs and jams demanded too much effort in a world drained of energy. Any lyric too critical, any riff too deviant contributed to a mind-blow intense enough for a man or woman sitting in a lonely car to change the station and continue their meaningless ways. Noble thought there was one exception to this theory: the meaningless melodies stored in a vault, only to be brought out twenty years later, zapping the listener to the past where these tunes first took hold. A constant deluge of meaningless music, and his friend in the driver's seat had been captured by its spell.

"Let's change the station," suggested Noble.

"Why? And listen to the crap you listen to? Forget it."

"It's not crap, Shy."

"Sorry, but the old stuff is outdated. Don't you get sick of listening to the same tunes over and over again?"

"I have a first class record library," said Noble.

"Yes, and I bet the dinosaurs had one too. Wake up. Smell the coffee. No one listens to that music anymore. Get with the times. All the music you listen to doesn't exactly attract the women."

"What are you talking about?" he asked heatedly.

If there were one item Noble was passionate about, it had to be his music. Passion comes in different forms: a man's passion for a woman, a passion for cooking gourmet meals, a passion for building model airplanes, a passion for the Dow Jones Industrials, or a passion for healing the sick. Noble had an intense passion which ought to be differentiated from ambition. Ambition without passion is a V-8 engine running overdrive without oil, while passion without ambition is a brand new, multi-valve, formula one race car that won't start at the turn of a key. Noble was full of passion but lacked ambition. He never had the inclination to pursue his day-dreams, but cared so much about music that it ruled his days and nights with such fantastic fervor that nothing could interfere with his idolatry of the guitar and the instruments which added to its vitality. And when anyone, especially Shylock, argued against his music, he felt his blood rise and his heart pound. But he couldn't find the words to defend his tastes. Instead he sat motionless while the synthesized drum beats from the popular song filled the car with a hopeless dread. His anger turned in on itself, like a mouse devouring its young. Shylock continued:

"I'm sure of it. No one in their right mind listens to that kind of music anymore. It's so passe' like the hoola-hoop or that Trash-80 your father had."

"I disagree," mumbled Noble.

"And why shouldn't you? You keep listening to that same old stuff, and I have no idea what pleasure you get from it. See, now this music here," as Shylock turned up the volume, "is the music of today. Don't you like any of it?"

"Not really," yelled Noble over the music.

"Well, how the hell are you supposed to get a woman, when you can't connect with them on a musical level?"

"I'm sure lots of women like what I like. You underestimate them."

"Whatever. You like the kind of music my mother listens to, only that my mother refuses to hear it anymore. She stopped listening to it a long time ago. But don't worry, Noble my boy, because tonight I'm gonna fix you up with a woman, yes sir," as Shylock grinned. "Just pretend that you dig the music. That's the first step. Once you let the music take control, and add to that some women, maybe some dark mysterious lights, and some beer, you'll be all set."

Noble went along with these high expectations. He even succumbed to the industrial music on the radio. They sped along the inanimate roads of North Jersey, the snow flakes grazing the windshield like galactic stars. Noble hid his slight fear of the night turning into a complete flop, as no one would be out during a snow storm, and at a few intersections the lightweight car skidded on the road; He quickly buckled his seat belt.

"Relax," said Shylock, "I'm a good driver. You should know that by now. Take it easy. This thing has gotten me through plenty of storms. The cop-ers are all at the doughnut shop."

An anxiety clutched him at these cock-sure remarks. Shylock egged on the small car despite the conditions. They drove for a few miles and parked behind the night club, its neon light a beacon for the entire town. Noble was reassured by the other cars in the lot, and while walking to the front, his shoes caked with snow, he could hear a rhythmic thumping through the sturdy walls, and a chatter which suggested laughter and inebriation.

"See, Noble, you should trust me."

The bar was crowded, almost jammed, and at the head of the room a small space was filled by a set of drums, large amplifiers, and to Noble's delight, a guitar and bass resting on silver stands.

"You didn't say there'd be a band," he said while waiting on line.

"See, I'm full of surprises tonight. And I know you have no money. You can pay me back later."

"And how am I supposed to do that? I barely have enough to eat."

"Don't worry about it. Call it friendship. I'll even pay for your drinks."

"That's all right. I won't drink tonight. Besides, we have to get home, don't we?"

"Worry about that later. We must celebrate the blessings of life and partake in the divine elixirs of wine and women."

"You're crazy," he laughed.

They waited on line for a few minutes, paid the cover, and walked into the place excitedly. Shylock headed for the bar quickly, and Noble tagged along like a bewildered younger brother. He handed him a cold beer, and he sipped slowly. All around him delightful women mingled with confident men. He could only watch at first. Then he felt detached, as though socializing with the opposite sex was impossible. He couldn't say he was jobless, without a car, without a career, relying on his father for his livelihood. He noticed how some of the men, very clean-cut and athletic, kept these women laughing as though they had known each other before. He knew, however, that certain men were able to turn on their charm like a light switch. They lent humor to simple statements. It pointed to some astronomical intelligence and aptitude which Noble lacked, and due to this terrible misfortune he thought lesser of himself and greater of these men.

"Hey, Noble, over here," yelled Shylock who had gravitated towards the denser area. While side-stepping the sweating bodies, he excused himself at every opportunity and approached his friend with a look of consternation.

"I hear the band is quite good. They have a wicked guitar player; They should be playing in a few minutes," yelled Shylock.

"But it's only Happy Hour," he yelled. "How long are they playing?"

Shylock didn't hear the question, and Noble dropped the issue. Instead he leaned against the oak-paneled wall, near the busy bar, and continued his slow sipping until he spotted a long, languid woman wearing a black, sleeveless dress. She held a glass of red wine; her flaxen hair tinted a similar hue. She was alone, and her expression featured a dreary urbanity. She was stuck in a small town just like Noble. At first the woman intimidated him. She looked far too classy, even blasé, and Noble consulted with Shylock who was already chatting with a woman by the doorway.

"Hey, Shy, sorry to interrupt, but you see that woman over there, don't you dare point, but you see that woman in the black dress?"

"Yeah? Go up to her and introduce yourself."

"What do I say? She seems so, so, so sophisticated."

"Tell her you're working in Manhattan."

"Doing what?"

"I don't know, make something up."

"But that would be lying."

Shylock pulled his bewildered friend to the side.

"Listen, man, you weren't born yesterday. You know what to do. Say something that will make you attractive, that's all. Don't lie, just bend the truth a little. Wait. In fact, lie Noble, lie your guts out. Do you really want her? Do you find her attractive, I mean so attractive that you are forced to confront her in some way?"

"I think I do."

"Don't think, Noble. Go up to her and say you work in Manhattan as an investment banker of some kind, and see if she falls for it. It's lying, I know, and you don't like lying, but guess what? Everyone in this joint does the exact same thing, and the one who lies the most gets the women; It's that simple. Now go up to her and say you work for a bank, and if a relationship forms, fine, then bend the truth, and if she falls for you, then be honest, but right now go up to her and lie like a rug, and don't bother me for another twenty minutes. I've got work to do myself," and he pushed Noble towards the woman in the black dress.

He needed an opening line and thought of all the possibilities but came to no firm conclusions. He would offer her a refill, but he remembered he was dependent on Shylock for the drinks; so he scrapped this idea. She seemed sad in an imperceptible way. His heart pumped faster, and he moved directly in front of her, his beer close to his chest.

"Hi, I'm Noble McCloud. What's your name?"

He knew this a terrible first line, as he could not think of anything funny or witty. Her expression made him even more nervous as he wasn't much of a conversationalist, especially with women.

"Alexandra," she said curtly.

She didn't look at Noble while saying this. Instead she looked towards the bar area.

"What brings you here? I come here some of the time."

"Listen, are you going to buy me another drink or what?"

He hated to make negative assumptions about people, and this in turn contributed to his ingenuousness, but he could have sworn she was wasted on something besides alcohol. And although she acted wasted, it somehow contributed to her overall attractiveness, as being beautiful and being stoned at the same time passed his erotic test.

"I can buy you a drink, sure. What will it be?"

"How about a shot?" as her speech stretched, right on the verge of slurring.

"I can do that. Will you wait here a minute? I'll be right back."

Noble went up to Shylock.

"Shylock," as he pulled him aside, "I need some money to buy her a drink."

"That's the first mistake, Noble. Never spend money on a woman you really don't know. But I'll allow it, but just one drink, okay?"

It took Noble a little while to get the drinks. The bar was crowded, and he raised his hand instead of pushing through layers hugging the bar. He wasn't seen by the bartender at first, but a man moved out of the way, and Noble sneaked into the empty gap. He ordered a red wine, a beer, and two shots, and returned to the woman who continued her condescending air.

"Thanks. What's your name again?" she said while taking the glass.

"Noble, Noble McCloud."

"What brings you here, Noble?"

"A night out. It's been a really long week for me," he said with effort.

"It's only Monday."

"I've been working all weekend, and it's so nice to encounter a friendly face."

"Well, whaddaya do?" she asked.

"I'm an, an investment manager for a bank in Manhattan."

"Really? Don't find too many of you here in New Jersey. You probably live in Waspachick, right?"

"Yes, I just moved there," he lied again.

"Anyway, cheers," and they slammed down the shot of bittersweet liquid.

The shot warmed his innards and after a few moments his mind swam and all of his inhibitions about meeting a woman surrendered to a loose fog.

"Yes, I manage several funds in other countries, you know, an international conglomeration and amalgamated fund yielding interest in emerging markets at low inflation. You know how it is."

"Which firm do you work for?"

"Ummm, many different ones actually. You can say that I'm a no-load mutual investor with funding from Asian business, that and holdings in Europe and the Middle East, a closed shop really, but the market is so volatile, that stability comes every quarter, and the futures are good, you know, very international funds and investments."

"It all sounds very complicated," she said with a grin.

"Well, the market trend is so uneasy, as they are saturated with supply and demand, and price fixing on the municipal bonds are yielding the same as a Treasury note at a good low interest rate. Basically, I'm making lots of money now, despite a growth in the blue chip, penny stock ventures."

"Can you tell me who you work for? Or is it something private?"

"Yes, First...First Imperial on Wall Street."

"You don't look like the Wall Street type."

"Well, what is the Wall Street type really? No, but I do work across the street from the exchange."

"Any good stock tips?"

"I'm not on that level. I'm actually trading different futures and options from various sectors, so I don't deal with stocks, just bonds and conglomerates."

"It all sounds very interesting," and her keen interest in Noble's station in life dissipated. She returned to her languid self.

Noble had little idea where to take the conversation. For a few moments they simply stood there while the house music played.

"Would you like to dance?" asked Noble suddenly.

"No thanks," she said. "I don't see anybody else dancing."

She had a point.

"So what about you?" he asked.

"I'm a student."

"Oh yeah?" What's your major?"

"Fine Arts."

"Wow, that's terrific."

"It doesn't pull in much money, but I'm surviving."

"You look like an artist."

"Thanks," she said weakly.

The conversation died at this point, and Noble searched for words but came up empty. He liked the way she spoke, a tone which suggested she had seen it all, and that nothing surprised her. Her demeanor reeked of an apathy and ennui. Stricken by the silence between them, Noble slipped away as she turned her back. He didn't want to interrupt Shylock, so he moved closer to the band's equipment and marveled at the dormant ensemble bathed in blue light, as though the equipment would suddenly spring to life by talented hands. He was disappointed with the conversation. It was the first time in a very long while he had found a woman so striking, a woman who, with a little persistence, could get her picture on the cover of the magazines.

He had heard before that women who were too beautiful have a rough time finding men, as most men are too intimidated by them. Noble wasn't intimidated any longer, due to his warm inebriation, but his lack of words touched upon a hopelessness he usually encountered when mingling with the opposite sex, as though beautiful women were never looking for the man of quiet responsibility and assiduity, but the man who was handsome, dangerous, reckless, and aggressive. Noble thought of himself apart from both types of men, a lingering mass taking up valuable space. He fit into the category of those who didn't fit into any category. He had an affinity for his music: heavy and powerful riffs and long, swinging distortions, the impetus for his journey into a fantasy filled with the most revered guitarists of his day, appearing on the stage, the crowd on its feet, the lighters notched high, the illumination transforming a dark arena into a million brilliant halos. And when the musicians appeared for their first set, as the alcohol numbed his lips and soaked his brain, as the chatting ceased and the listening began, Noble forgot of his disappointments over the woman and found solace within the band.

He concentrated on the guitar player, not his appearance, but the way he cupped the long neck of his six string, how he utilized an every day quarter to pick at the tension gathered beneath his fingers. And at the touch of them the lights hanging above winked and danced, sending a neurotic shiver through his entire body, and once a rhythm was established among this trio of guitarist, bassist, and percussionist, he drifted once again to areas beyond the Jersey borders, away from the cold which crippled his spirit, and such a flight forced him to stand and stare while the many around him swayed. He cared neither for his position nor status in life, nor for his father's wrath which would pour upon him. Finally he lived for the moment, the exact moment when the coin touched the chords. The band played like this for three sets, and during the brief intermissions he returned to the bar area where he saw Shylock and a woman kissing in the corner.

He chose not to interrupt. Some men are lucky this way. They know exactly what to say at the right moment. Noble then craned his neck in the hopes of finding his Fine Arts major in the swarm. He spotted her to the side of the amplifiers laughing, smiling, giggling with the guitarist, as though a renewed charm captivated her. He searched for a drink in her hand but found none. She flirted freely with the guitarist, as though she had known him. She put on airs to attract him. Perhaps she knew him from some forgotten bar, or maybe she adored his music, the dexterity of his callused fingers. Whatever it was, she flirted with him openly, and Noble wondered what the guitarist said to her. She touched his arm repeatedly. She appeared to be enjoying his company, her laughter more constant and spontaneous, a solid sign that she had immediately disliked a trait in Noble which all comely women disliked. And instead of concentrating on having a good time, Noble turned upon himself and searched, with an angry determination, for what he lacked, and he discovered his personality was one entire defect that repelled attractive women. He knew his standards were somewhat high and couldn't understand why he fell for women who were out of his reach. He fell for those women instantly like a house of cards, and at every opportunity they shunned him. He could have been the richest man on earth, with a bank account full enough to purchase the entire neighborhood, and still they would turn away, the sentencing mandatory, an ingrained ritual as the goddesses on their planet decreed. He took another drink, his brain swimming.

He would leave, that's what he would do, head out on some generic interstate to a land where the beautiful women of the highest standard were plentiful. The odds of attracting one would lessen exponentially with each mile. He would leave tonight, yes, steal his father's car and follow the sun, away from this woman. His anger towards her seethed. He exculpated the guitarist who charmed her. His anger took the form of voracious gulps.

Noble sailed closer to the instruments. While keeping a polite distance, he heard what the guitarist said to her. The guitarist would score, he determined, and this fair actress had chosen a pitifully ugly and unappealing guitarist at that: his hair greasy and long, his sunken cheeks scarred with old acne, nothing compared to Noble's looks- a face he recalled instantly.

Although he thought he was the better man, he had not a shred of proof. And with this last effort of defending himself to himself, he balked and was overwhelmed instead by an immense sorrow. These women told him things he already knew to be true, and they did so by their silence and subtle avoidance. Alexandra was just one example among many, as though these women belonged to the same battalion marching upon Waspachick neither to rule nor plunder but to turn their backs and pass him over for ugly guitarists. He felt a hand on his shoulder.

"Hey Noble, Noble, Noble McCloud," sang Shylock.

"Hi, Shy. What ya been up to?"

"You having a good time?"

"It's interesting."

"You don't look like it. Is something the matter? Lots of women around here."

"Yeah, I saw you hooking up."

"Damn straight. What do you think of her?" asked Shylock of his latest conquest. "She's hotter than the others, eh? What happened to the one you were working on?"

"The conversation fizzled. I have no idea what to say to these women. It's like I get up to them, and then something stops, my brain stops, and nothing comes out, like it's taking too much effort."

"Did you tell her about the investment banking?"

"I tried that. She's not interested."

"Noble, you have to make her interested. Women will never flock to you. You have to go out and get them. Be aggressive, and turn on the charm."

"It would help if she weren't talking to the guitarist."

"Stop building obstacles. If you really want her, you'll get her. Now go! Go up to her," and Shylock pushed him in their direction.

He stood in a no-man's land: too far away to be recognized, too close to go unnoticed. The two glanced at him for a moment and then resumed their conversation, as though he were a fly buzzing about their heads. He stepped closer, almost tip-toeing, his heart pumping through his chest, and he searched for correct words. He looked behind him, and Shylock had disappeared. Noble refused to move closer and retreated to the bar area away from the musician's space. He had an intense desire for the woman, a desire like never before, and his anger rested in his inability to take action, as desire and action were mutually exclusive concepts.

He considered being alone for the rest of his days, leading a monkish existence without women, only admiring them on magazine covers, only watching them from afar. He would keep to himself and listen to sad songs, occasionally walking about the town, eyeing the women with bulky shopping bags and laughing the same laughs of a man imprisoned by solitude.

Noble remembered his first and only girlfriend, a meaningless relationship several years ago. She was short and plump, nothing terrific. Noble's standards were so high that he never considered this woman anything but a good lay, and he arrived at that point by accident.

The two were paired together for a class project, and they worked in her dormitory room late at night. They took a break from their work and relaxed on the sofa. And there it happened, right on the sofa in the darkness.

For the several months which followed, Noble continued this sexual relationship but never moved beyond that. The sex satisfied his own erotic longings, and towards the end of the relationship they barely talked, only fucked with regularity, twice a week at appointed times. Throughout their relationship which spanned nearly two long years, the girl wanted more, not just sex, but something too substantial, like a conversation, or taking walks about the campus. Noble couldn't comply and brushed her off in search of women who were unattainable, women like Alexandra, never the woman who cared for him or could offer more than her body, but a woman deemed beautiful by conventional standards, the beauty of an elite few. Even though Noble had little feeling for her, she definitely had feelings for him, and at every opportunity he squashed these feelings by avoiding her, even making her cry on occasion. After their first night together he wanted to end it, but he didn't have the heart to tell her. Noble knew how he had used her, and at the bar he found himself drunk and unforgiven.

Noble never discovered beauty for himself. Instead he relied on magazines at the check out counter and the occasional movie, as though a handful of wizards decided for him what was beauty and what was not, while the overwhelming majority of women never had a chance of fitting these tight standards. Instead they put fingers down their throats or even practice self-mutilation with razors and lit cigarettes, all in the name of a rigid beauty no one rightly possessed.

No wonder some women refuse to shave their armpits and leg-hairs. These same women, however, are still prisoners no matter how defiant they seem. They will forever be haunted by the gaze of those like Noble McCloud, and despite his high standards, he quietly appreciated and admired these organic apes, as his mind wandered to them.

He found their rebellion attractive, not as individuals, but as a tribe, strong and proud, destined to do without the male species. He saw none of this tribe here, but this ex-girlfriend may have already joined their ranks. The band members collected in the small space and readied for another set which was to be their last. Noble was so preoccupied with thoughts of his old girlfriend that he had forgotten the band would play for an hour more, and he rejoiced. The bass strings vibrated, and the guitar and drums followed this subtle introduction until all at once these instruments were played together, not as an overwhelming collective force, but as individual instruments interdependent on one another: the bass keeping a rhythm, the drums adding the weight, and the guitar singing plaintively, as though each instrument had its duties, and if one faltered, the tune would be incomplete, a body without a soul.

In front of the guitarist danced Alexandra, her arms dangling, her face directed towards her beau who played with an alarming accuracy. A few members of the audience danced without partners. They twirled under the soft light, their hands swirling, their bodies carving their own space on the floor. Noble found himself nearly alone at the bar as he watched these dancers twirl and swirl, lost and oblivious to the world around them, living in their own imaginations and sharing a strange partnership with the sound, leaving them devoid of rationality and logic, their minds suspended in an amniotic fluid at the scientist's lair, the remainder a collection of mellowing bodies graced by eternity and bliss, captured neither by intellect nor hunger, but by an electric guitar guiding them like tourists through a sun-drenched land of double rainbows. And Noble envied them. He envied the guitarist who commanded Alexandra's attention, he envied the plump man next to him, his hands writhing in the air, even Shylock to some extent who had found someone to kiss after a hard day's work. Noble did not want to go home. He took some sort of pleasure from being completely miserable.

He considered walking up to her, turning her around and planting a firm kiss on her mouth. But this approach was too risky as she danced in front of this guitarist who fed her with artistry, and he tried to discredit him in some way, but he knew already that this guitarist had succeeded in his art while Noble succeeded at nothing. He was a non-entity, a face you see for an instant and then forget instantaneously, as Alexandra must have forgotten him by now, her arms becoming more expressive with each chord and her Ledaen body swaying to strings in tune. Noble contemplated the inevitable nights of loneliness without a woman to call his own, as though he moved within impenetrable walls, and within this small space of scratches, nicks, and markings lived a man dying to connect with someone on the other side, only to find the walls too sturdy and the spirit too weak. The dancers in the bar take on the form of floating nymphs, smart enough to warrant attention, but imaginary enough to ignore.

Perhaps he needed a few more drinks or a little taste of the herb he stashed under the mattress for those late nights with his stereo, but he knew he could no longer handle this loneliness. Somehow a woman was the answer to all of this, yes, the woman Alexandra whose heart belonged to this unsightly mess playing a mean and accurate guitar. And suddenly Noble did what he thought only the crazy men did. He laughed aloud, a fit of cackling which attracted the bartender who calmly told him he was cut-off for the night.

Noble demanded another drink and a shot and bargained towards that end. The bartender gave him a beer on the house and called it even. The end of the tune marked an exodus of hot, sweating bodies from the dance floor to the bar. This included Shylock who approached him hurriedly.

"That was the most amazing set! These guys are really good. See, I told you you'd have a fun time."

"I think I'd better go home, Shy. I'm suddenly not feeling too well."

"Now? You want to leave right now?"

"Kind of. It's getting sort of late, and you know, my father's probably pissed at me."

"What about the woman?" asked Shylock.

"She obviously shows little interest in someone with huge amounts of cash."

"Listen, Noble, if you want to leave, that's fine, but I need to stay. I've got this fine looking woman I've been working on, and I'm going home with her."

"I thought so. Good job, Shy. I'm sorry I've been such a dud, but I gave it my best shot, and as usual I'm going home without anyone."

"Listen man, I know from experience that it happens all the time. It used to happen to me. I used to sit in these bars waiting for some dream-girl to waltz by, and our eyes would connect, and soon enough we would start talking, the conversation would go nowhere, and I'd end up leaving early. Hey, it happens to everyone, and I'm sorry it had to happen to you, but that's the breaks. And, hey, she's only one girl. Think of how many women there are in Waspachick alone. Man, don't look so down. Every guy has an off-night, and if I were a woman, I'd jump your bones, that's exactly what I'd do, 'cause you're my best friend, man, and my best friend can't go without a woman for that long."

"Yeah, it's just that women are somehow turned off by me, and I can't understand why. I mean I think I'm a pretty good guy. I'm not a saint, but I'm not a complete sinner either."

"When was the last time you got laid?"

"I don't think..."

"Just tell me," said Shylock seriously.

"Well, it has been a very, very long time, let's put it that way."

"What? One year? Two years? Three? Four? Five? Oh my, Noble. That's kind of a shame, I mean not to put you down or anything, but you're a good looking guy, I mean more than five years? Man, in all that time you didn't once come up to me and say something? We could have found someone for you on the professional level. We could have started some savings plan at the bank or solicited donations for your cause among men of conscience and good will, because no man should ever go that long without a good lay..."

"I'm not concerned with getting laid, Shylock. I want something more than that."

"That's it. Hold it right there. That's exactly it," said Shylock excitedly. "See, that's what the women see. They see a man who wants some kind of terrible, long relationship, when all they want is to get laid themselves."

"I don't think that's true, I mean, isn't that a positive thing? Not wanting to get laid but having a relationship? See, it's something else, and I'm not sure what it is. Maybe it's my physique, or perhaps I should join a gym, oh I don't know what the hell it is, but whatever it is, it's pissing the shit out of me..."

"Noble, have faith. You should pray to get laid."

"I'm not about to ask God for a good lay. I think he has his hands full preventing people from killing each other, so I'm not about to ask him for that."

"So then what is it?"

"They see that I'm afraid, that I'm lacking self-esteem. They see through my lines and lies and half-truths and whoppers to that part which begs for a woman, and they see this timid man who wouldn't know what to do if he ever had the chance of holding her for only a second, if that were the case. I mean there are so many theories I've developed, and one of these..."

"Listen, man, stop working up all that bullshit and act. Action is what counts when it comes to women. They want action, not a man of thought. And with that, I see my woman walking this way. What do you think of her?"

"She's beautiful," said Noble downing his drink, wondering how in creation Shylock had nabbed her.

"Listen, I've got to take her home. Would you care if I took her home, and you called a cab?"

Noble knew it would come to this. Not only was he deserted by women at his time of greatest need but also by his friend who dragged him out in the first place. He looked at him incredulously for a moment, making sure he wasn't kidding, and when he determined he was serious, he asked him for another drink so the inebriation would last until he found his way home. Shylock agreed to the deal and bought him a shot, then a beer to wash it down. Noble surprised himself by standing straight.

"Are you sure you don't mind? Because I could call it off and take you home instead."

"No, Shy, don't be ridiculous. I'm a grown man. I'll find my way home."

Shylock left with the woman after he bid his final farewells, and Noble stayed a bit later, milking his beer. A scattering of people remained. The band members dismantled their equipment as the house lights heralded forth unwelcome spikes of sobriety. Shylock had given him cab fare, but Noble spent the money on an extra beer and an accompanying shot. He persuaded the bartender who stood behind the taps in disbelief.

The lights made little difference in Alexandra's appearance. She gleefully chatted with his arch-enemy the guitarist who looked utterly repulsive. The bartender and he shared the same level of incredulity: the bartender marveled at how much Noble could put away, while Noble wondered how a man so ugly could be going home with the prettiest woman in the joint. It didn't make sense, like those dancers lost within their reptilian movements or the manner in which Shylock left him there to rot, or discovering that he had to walk home, a good five miles in frigid weather, only to be yelled at, if not beaten, by his father upon arrival. He sat at the bar until most of the patrons left. He didn't want to move, didn't want to think. The entire evening seemed pointless, the liquor acting as a strange medication which left him unsatisfied.

He swallowed what was left of his drink and left the bar quickly. He didn't notice the cold. The road to Waspachick was dotted by street lamps, and he followed them like bread crumbs. He couldn't concentrate on any one idea for too long, but the one that kept recurring was the image of his father cursing at him. This gave him the motivation to move faster down the road, although he wouldn't be arriving any time soon. Even though the wind picked up and the cold penetrated his jacket, he would have rather gone anywhere but home. He would have much rather preferred the company of a woman, any woman at all, and he reasoned that these women all hid from him, perhaps deliberately, and to find a suitable one he would have to journey beyond Waspachick to some town where the bars never closed and the guitar solos never ended. This was the extent of his utopian vision, a place where everything was for free, paid for by that minority who took pleasure from labor. He didn't go beyond that, only wished that the dormant gas station he passed were some café where the women sipped cappuccino and stared at him through the windows. 'I'm not made for this world,' he thought suddenly. Shylock fit right in. He had a good paying job, women constantly surrounding him, a place of his own, an automobile. Why couldn't Noble do the same?

It's not like Noble never worked before. In fact, at one time he had the curiosity and drive to do just that. He envisioned starting his own business, as most students of his day thought of doing. In order to secure a loan, he had to amass some sort of capital, which his father refused him. He targeted the financial sector, an immediate stream of cash changing hands over martinis and shrimp cocktails. And this seductive impression lured him into applying for jobs at banks and brokerage firms in Manhattan.

After months of sending resumes, usually with no response, he received a brief phone call from an investment firm. He interviewed for the position of assistant cafeteria worker. This was how far two semesters and no connections took him, but he was more attracted by the job's potential. He could get to know one of the managers by cooking his lunch and move through the company, and since there were no other opportunities, he took the position and envisioned a vertical move through the ranks of rich and talented money-people, all so he could start a simple business and live just as simply.

As an assistant cafeteria worker he slaved long hours at minimum wage. He was assigned to a small room with meat slicers, an industrial fridge, warming trays, serving tables, and steel trolleys. This small area of heat was proportional to the size of the investment firm. His boss was the cook himself who prepared meals to suit individual tastes. While obsequious to the managers, the cook barked commands at Noble who did most of the prep work. Noble didn't mind taking orders. After all, he was a new face and didn't possess the faculty of barking back when the orders seemed too abrasive. He put up with it for the time being, waiting for the beneficent fund manager in an Italian suit to rescue him from the drudgery of lifting heavy boxes, slicing lettuce, and pleasing the cook. And for the first week he worked without breaks despite his aspirations. He did everything the cook asked of him. He mopped the floors, took out the garbage, washed most of the dishes. After the lunch rush he even tried talking to the cook. The cook, however, refused conversation.

A week had passed at the cafeteria, and Noble searched for ways to meet those working upstairs. The office was divided into two floors, and the ceilings were thin enough to hear the telephones and the shouting on the sales floor. Noble knew it to be a hot-bed of activity. He knew he must make it up there somehow.

One slow day, he asked the cook for a break. He complained of cramping in the lower leg, so the cook let him go for five minutes. He took a six-pack of soda from the refrigerator and headed upstairs.

"You can't go in there with that," said the receptionist who stood guard, the door behind her leading to the sales floor.

"One of the managers requested it," lied Noble.

"Which one?"

"I'm not sure. We just got the order downstairs."

"Doesn't Louie usually handle this? Maybe he knows," as she picked up the phone.

"Ah, I wouldn't do that. He's real busy down there preparing for the lunch rush and all."

"But it's after lunch," she said.

"Well, you know, the post-after lunch, early dinner rush. Lots of work down there."

"I don't mean to sound picky, but we all leave before dinner time. See, if I don't do my job, I may lose my job, so it's important I know who this is for."

Noble was about to crumble but kept a straight face. His insides warmed. He could have retreated, but he couldn't stand working with the cook. And in a flash of brilliance he recalled him speaking over the downstairs phone: 'Mr. Cuthbert, sure right away.'

"I think it's Mr. Cuthbert," said Noble finally.

"Oh. See, it wasn't that hard now, was it? He should be on the floor."

With relief he walked through and encountered an environment he had never before seen. The astonishing sight swept him to the corner of the room. The traders and salesmen sat among a complex of desks without barriers, so they could see and yell at each other. An electric board displayed stock prices, strange numbers and symbols filled a ceramic board, and at the head of the room stood an elevated platform where high-level managers sat in quiet contemplation, while the salesmen below scurried about. The cafeteria was a cage where he slaved over condiments and fixings, but the sales floor seemed like a larger cage where nicely dressed animals clawed and fought with computer terminals. His feelings were mixed. He appreciated the fast pace but thought it entirely uncivil, almost bestial and oppressive. He wanted to be part of the action, but the pressure would have paralyzed him. Nevertheless he grew accustomed to this incredible scene, the six-pack dangling from his hand.

His white uniform and apron appeared like a bright neon light, but no one noticed. They ran passed him or shouted across the room. Noble, however, spotted a silent woman in the corner, looking into her terminal with a quarterback's aplomb. He cautiously approached her as she seemed harmless and disconnected from the frenzy. He prepared a greeting. Her brown, crinkled hair fell to her shoulders. Her hazel eyes darted to him as though interrupted from a pleasant dream.

"Can I help you?" she asked calmly.

"Hi, I'm Noble McCloud. I work downstairs with Louie."

"And?"

"Well, I just thought I'd bring some of you guys some soda. You want one?"

"No," she responded flatly.

"It's kind of crazy around here. I mean I wonder how you handle it. Everyone shouting and yelling, it's so exciting. I was wondering, how do I go about becoming one of you guys, a stock broker and all? I'm willing to learn, and I thought you could help me out. I know this seems sudden, but it would help me out, if you could…"

"First of all, I'm not a broker, I'm a trader," she said.

"Or a trader," he smiled. "I mean I'd like to work here in that capacity?"

"Listen, I don't mean to be rude, but I'm working here."

"I know, and I'm working downstairs, and I'm just so sick of the job, and I'd like to be up here with you guys, trading or brokering."

"Noble you said your name was?"

He was fired that afternoon by the unit manager. He wandered the lower end of Manhattan in disbelief and despondency, a charging bronzed bull on a concrete island, men in suits and leather portfolios headed for the subway and women with white sneakers chasing taxis, the tall buildings crowding the stretch of blue sky above. 'We have to let you go,' the manager had said, and Noble couldn't defend himself properly. He walked around Battery Park for a couple of hours, his eyes following his shoes, and the world was somehow against him, the beautiful day a travesty, a mockery, and his career plans dashed. He formulated his defense to the unit manager while wandering Battery Park, his own mind combing the entire scene as a reflection; And he would sue them, that's what he would do. He would hire a high-priced lawyer, and the lawsuit would attract the press, and the company would go down, and they would be indicted on charges, the brutal price for firing a then younger Noble McCloud. But soon this faded, and he found himself near South Ferry, a herd of commuters passing him with stoic glances like automatons unable to empathize with his plight, only concerned with their own worlds, and if a young man had a heart attack in front of them, they would trample him while racing for their seats.

While walking towards Waspachick in the early morning he felt the same way; everything was meaningless and disappointing, and no one cared whether he faded away or vanished. Shylock would care for a little while, but he too would be an automaton, a robot with superficial needs, his visions narrowed to crisp dollar bills from a cash machine and a new set of duds, because this is what it comes to, and Noble was somehow excluded from this process, as though the way of the world went one way and he another, like taking a fork in the road and ending up alone and lost. The prospects of this solitary journey didn't make him vomit or hang his head, but it made him angry.

On the road towards Waspachick he searched under the snow where smooth stones hid between the sidewalk and the curb. He picked up a few and threw them one by one at a parking sign a few feet away. He wound up as a pitcher does and hit the sign a few times sending sharp clangs into the air, and each pitch became harder and faster, the clanging almost like church bells through the sleepy road. He threw until his arm hurt. He never noticed the police car standing behind him. The red and blue lights flickered when the officer had enough of this recklessness. Noble was fearless, drunk and fearless, and the officer put a flashlight to his face, his two-way radio belching static and distant voices.

"What do you think you're doing?" asked the officer, an automatic at the hip.

"What does it look like?" snapped Noble.

"Let me see some identification.'

Noble sighed and furnished a laminated card purchased at an arcade in Manhattan. The officer studied it carefully, verifying his photograph, and keeping his reactions to himself in a silent, officious manner indicative of most county cops.

"Is this all you have? How about a license?"

"Does it look like I'm driving a car? Don't you think I'd be driving home in this shitty weather if I had a license?"

"Let me give you a little friendly advice," said the officer sternly, "if you don't change your tone real fast, I'll haul you down to the station for drunk and disorderly and lock you up for a night, you got that? Now you better start talking with a little more respect, you got that?"

Noble was confused, but the message got through, and he stood limp, his anger dissipating, a renewed self-pity overcoming him. He didn't know whether to run or to weep, but strange notes, musical notes, played in his mind, speaking to him in a melody and cadence no longer angry but child-like and apologetic.

"Now it's obvious you're drunk, but you're also damaging town property. Where have you been all night? You coming from the bar down the road?"

"Yes, officer," replied Noble glumly, his bladder full.

"If I ever catch you out here again, throwing rocks at the signs, I will haul your ass to the station."

He pulled a black leather binder from his back pocket and wrote him a ticket. Noble couldn't tell how much it was for.

"Now you're over in Waspachick?"

"Yes, officer."

"Well, it's cold out here, and it's a good three or four miles to the town line. You can keep walking, or you can ride with me. It's your choice."

Noble missed the officer's face, but his voice sounded much milder, almost soothing, as though he felt guilty for acting tough. Noble's feet were wet with slush, his fingers numb, his ears stinging. The wind tunneled down the road in the direction of Waspachick. He acted on his first impulse and rode with the officer.

"I don't want to go home," said Noble as they rode.

"Where do you want to go then? Not many places open at this hour." And then: "Go home, and get some rest."

Noble's vision blurred, and the lights on the squad car's console, the radar, the radio, the speedometer, even the officer's dark profile melted and bled into the night, and Noble passed out in the back seat of the officer's car.

His eyes opened all of a sudden. He was in a room with gray lockers. He lay on a loveseat. The woolly texture wrinkled his face. A spot of drool leaked from the corner of his mouth, and his back hurt, his upper torso twisted to the right, his lower to the left. He didn't know where he was, only that his head pounded and swam in a liquid nausea.

His initial response was to sleep for a few hours more, but then the foreign environs caught him, and he regained consciousness with a start. He checked the locker room and the shower stalls but found no one. An eerie silence coated the place, and a sense of profound dread filled his stomach. He knew neither the time nor the day, only that he had gotten shit-faced the night before. What he did afterwards remained a devastating mystery, and he feared the worst, that he had killed someone or had gotten into a brawl.

He walked down a long, green-tiled hallway, opened the door, and discovered to his horror that he was in a police station. At the desks sat two blue-uniformed policemen typing reports, and the African-American officer stood from his chair and gave Noble a wry smile. He was well-built and tall with a jutting chin and muscular jaws. Noble was about to faint, but the officer told him not to worry.

"How are you feeling?" he asked.

"Where am I?"

"Welcome to the East Waspachick Police Department. As you can see from my badge, I'm Officer Comstock. I'm the one who picked you up last night."

"What happened? Did I do anything wrong, because I don't remember a damn thing, I don't recall anything but this children's music, and the bar, I remember that, but other than the bar, I don't remember a damn thing. Where's Shylock, my God, is he alright..."

The officer explained the events of the previous night. They had brought him to the station since there was some question about going home.

"Oh, shit. I'm in deep trouble, deep trouble," said Noble.

"Only a ticket," said Comstock.

"No, it's not that," he stammered, "it's, it's my father, he's probably looking for me, and once he finds me, he'll kill me. He'll take my head and chop it off, right at the neck..."

"Those are pretty serious allegations," smiled Comstock. "I'm sure it's not that bad."

"Oh no, it is. It's very bad. Where am I? East Waspachick?"

"That's right."

He thought he was better off at the police station. He could live in the locker room with the two officers guarding the door. He needed only a small boom box, no, a hand-held transistor radio, and he would need nothing else. He could eat leftovers and take showers once in a while. No need for new clothes. He could wear the same clothes for the rest of his life.

"You're free to go," said Comstock with a smirk, "but pay that ticket."

"What if I don't want to go?"

"We only house criminals, and besides, don't you want to go home? This place is kind of boring, don't you think?"

He left the police station and encountered a bright white spot where the sun should have been. The snow slowly melted, and by each house water trickled earthwards from the roofs and trees. Fear and dread accompanied him five miles to the town center, and the roaming pedestrians no longer filled his curiosity and amusement. They were hollow shells without faces, floating over the pavement, looking at their feet, floating like spirits who had lost their lives as Noble was about to lose his. He tried hard to remember the events of the preceding night but only recalled fragments of himself in a drunken stupor, watching the blurry bodice of a woman with a long-haired man.

His head pounded with each step. He approached the coffee shop where Shylock worked, and he peered into the wide window. Shylock wasn't there, even though he was scheduled to work.

Noble needed him but found nothing but icy waters streaming through the gutters into grilled basins. Water had it easy, he thought. It endured the germ of life. It ruled it. It presided over crustaceans, fish, and tiny plankton and prickly sponges, and he wished he could be inanimate like water, or a simple brick or concrete slab, unable to think or to dream or to project far into the future, but exist without a problem. Sure, even water had to evaporate, but it returned to earth as rain, and this cycle was assured, unlike the spontaneity of bad luck. He mused to himself in this manner, as though the objects in the town were better alternatives.

He walked the lane which led away from the strip. This desertion and desolation represented the middle class area which he knew as his home. The world had its way of separating its inhabitants into similar sets, alike in appearance, like the houses which grew uniform, and their drab colors. With each house he grew more afraid, and he looked ahead to see if his father's Oldsmobile was parked out front. He saw a speck in the distance but still wasn't sure. He wanted to run towards it, like the mad scream before an execution, but then he thought more sensibly, as he could sneak into the house through the window of his room which was probably unlocked. Or maybe he could pass the house and keep walking, never to return. Some people do this, he mused, but everyone who does ends up in jail, out on the street, or hooked on heroin. This happens when any young man ventures beyond Waspachick, a town which gripped its inhabitants with a curse and surrounded itself with an impermeable force field. No one got in, and no one got out, and it was rumored that the curse would lift by urinating on the town statue. Noble considered this approach.

While walking along the slushy lane, he suddenly remembered the woman he met at the bar, what was her name, yes, now he remembered her like a psychedelic flashback. It was Alexandra, the long, languid, surreal Alexandra whom had given him looks of innate snobbery, not overt, but subtle. In the shops and on the street corners, the women collectivized against him and emanated this terrible attitude, as though he smelled of strong body odor. This same attitude made them all the more attractive. These women shunned the money, because it went against their artistic values, and yet to converse with them one had to have loads of it, enough to buy a home on the Northern side of town, those brick, isolated palaces. Women in Waspachick, however, walked all over town, and he feared they saw him as a misfit, a pariah, especially on Saturday nights when wine-sipping women jammed the sidewalk restaurants.

And their male counterparts seemed so normal, normal in the sense that they had giant egos tastefully revealed. He wasn't too self-conscious, but around women he never played the game, and women sniffed him out as much too serious, perhaps a man devoid of pleasure. And he really wanted the chance to be worthy of a woman such as the fair Alexandra, the woman who discriminated against his awkward flannel shirts and garage pants, his worn shoes and tube socks. He needed a woman who would shun him completely, the type that goes for a man and then laments over his testosterone level, his action flicks, his childish competitiveness, and above all, his insensitivity. It's never the lonely, humble man who lands the women, thought Noble, no, it's the loud, loose, and lusty animal who captures by force and ferocity the gentle woman, the Andromeda chained to a rock longing for Theseus to free her from the claws of a bestial, roughhewn monster, and this has been so since the beginning of time, and absolutely nothing has changed.

We may call progress what we like: these technological breakthroughs which supposedly make life easier, and yet the relationship between the sexes resumes its traditional course. Sure there have been advancements for the individual woman, but not in Waspachick: a dystopic stagnation in the Northern section of New Jersey where the women suffocate behind panels of glass like mannequins inside expensive apparel shops, the jewelry stores no one enters, the expensive furniture shop where a simple throw pillow costs his entire monthly allowance. The man who analyzed and took his music seriously never had a place.

He did not hate Waspachick or its women, however. These discriminations kept him occupied and allowed him to complain. And he wondered what Shylock had that he didn't have (besides a car, an apartment, and a high-profile job). But Noble loved melody, rhythm, and rhyme: sounds which united the most disparate elements, the symphony of guitar which made the women sway and acquiesce to his clandestine fantasies. But what happens when he only listens to these melodies but fails to produce or create them? His constant consumption of music rose above the level of that greasy, long-haired musician. What was it that attracted this fair maiden to this slime? She must have went home with him, as these women opened themselves to rebellious intruders who cared little for them. The shy one in the corner only looks upon them with desire and self-ridicule. Enough of these women, thought Noble. He had enough of their condescending stares and conspiratorial neglect. And yet he could not quench the desire burning in his chest, tearing apart the tissues, scalding the brain. He desired them beyond desperation, to a point where he severed communication and drifted, with the aid of a steely guitar, into his imagination where a kiss was feasible; the frog who metamorphosed into an exiled prince.

He planned for solitude with his CD collection and a yellowing ceiling above, and in his solitude he would be driven mad and blind by chronic masturbation, and in this self-imposed exile from the land of woman he would discover a darkness which slowly overtakes him like mosquitoes biting at flesh, ticks burrowing into skin, horseflies stabbing at pores, and when there is nothing left but bone and a permanent grin, he would be relieved and at rest, finished with his demise.

His mind drifted in this fashion as he approached the house padded by melting snow, the driveway vacant. He silently rejoiced. He could now sneak in, nurse his nausea, and listen to songs which triggered a catharsis.

Dishes from his father's breakfast were dropped into the basin, and crumbs from burnt toast littered the counter. The floor of the long hallway was still as stained.

His urge was to retreat to his room and barricade the door with heavy objects, but he came to his senses and knew he should meet his irate father head-on, only with tact and dignity. And then a marvelous idea sprang from the loins of necessity and pressure.

He checked the fridge and found an untouched Cornish game hen his father had been saving. Should he surprise his father with the miniature chicken? He would have to do it quickly. He wasted little time towards its preparation. He boiled some vegetables as well. He thought it an amazing idea, and he watched the game hen turn brown and wet in the oven, and from his room he blasted fast and abrupt power chords which contributed to this sudden burst of optimism and delight. Four aspirin and a few vitamins aided in his recovery. He brushed his teeth and shaved painstakingly, as per his routine, and by that time, the game hen was cooked, and the vegetables simmered to flaccidness.

This would work. It had to work. His father would come home after a long day and enjoy a hearty meal, as good as those restaurant meals, perhaps even better, and the hen and the vegetables would line his stomach and induce a drowsiness. His father would lumber into bed and watch the news, exculpating Noble. Noble could then attend to his guitar-worship and daydreams.

During this preparation he took the view that labor produced tangible results, and he appreciated the workers of the world, and found a reason for belief in work, as though the positive aspects were many, not the drudgery and the monotony, but doing work for its own benefit, for the saving of his own skin, for the freedom of choice which comes from competing products and prices. He had the power of choice, never in the hands of some politburo, those old men with cold stares, red stars pinned to their epaulets, and a fleece of ribbons at their chests. No sir. Where else could one find such a delectable, plump, and detailed bird along side these mixed vegetables? Next time he would choose broccoli and peas or leeks, provided some capital is available.

At this point his newfound delight transmogrified into a guilt, for he recalled the village idiot, or that's what all the townsfolk labeled him- a man in his fifties who stood with a smile in front of the family pharmacy. An iron fence surrounded the area where this man used to sit and observe the timid women. His pants were faded and torn, his jacket wrinkled and thin. He too needed food, and perhaps Noble was a bit too extravagant. The town bum represented the side effect, as town hall's primary motivation sprung from the old money, not the desires of the village idiot whose one vote had the salience of a gnat hovering around an electrified lantern. So Noble came up with the idea of breaking off a leg and giving it to him someday, but who knew where that piece of hen would go. His father would be happier with the leg, and how would it look with part of it gone? The town idiot would hock the leg for a sip of schnapps. The leg is necessary as the village idiot would attack a shopper if faced with starvation, and there Noble lost himself. He forgot he stared into the oven for some twenty minutes, his eyes sore and the hangover returning.

He often over-thought in this manner, utilizing his inductive powers, flaying a big picture into detailed images, a cooked game hen into frozen flesh and bone, everything backwards. No wonder. The CD was skipping.

His father returned once Noble's initial optimism waned. The meal had grown cold. He stood near the doorway and feigned delight in receiving his father. McCoy McCloud's eyes burned through him. He carried a hard, plastic briefcase and wore a threadbare herringbone coat.

"What? You've come back?" asked McCoy McCloud.

"Yes, I had a long night last night, and…"

"And what?!" he shouted.

"Well, I had some errands to run…"

"Don't lie to me boy. Don't you dare lie to me."

"I'm not lying. I had a long night, and a friend of mine had an emergency, and I had to see him last night."

"You expect me to believe that? Not only are you a fool, but you're also a terrible liar. Get out of my house. Take your stuff and get out. You don't live here anymore."

"But Dad, if you'd just…"

McCoy moved closer, his smoldering breath grazing Noble's face. His father had said this many times before, and at each instance Noble had wiggled free from this ultimatum. But he never encountered a tone so solemn and fierce.

"Get out of this house. I'll give you twenty minutes," and he stormed into his lair and slammed the door.

Noble wiggled. He warmed the food and set the table. He was afraid his father really meant it. But he had thought so before, and continued plan A: the meal. Plan B: he would retire to his room and wait for the sunrise until his father's anger cooled. Plan C: or the worst case scenario, he would call Shylock and stay at his apartment for the night only to return in the morning when his father was in a more forgiving mood. He had never used Plan C, but this evening he came close.

"Well, why aren't you out yet?" asked McCoy, startling him in the kitchen.

"Dad, look, I'm sorry. It was wrong of me, just plain wrong, and for my penance I cooked this wonderful meal- your favorite, a Cornish game hen and veggies. It's real tasty. Try some. It's the least I could do for a hard working man like yourself. Please, sit," as he pulled out the chair.

McCoy looked at the presentation for a moment. Noble's heart raced, and he immediately thought of Plan B. McCoy picked up the plate and threw it to the floor, the plate breaking into bits.

"Pick it up!" he yelled.

Noble got on all-fours and slowly sifted through the mess in an attempt to make sense of the sudden confusion. And then he heard leather passing through belt loops and the weary sound of a loose buckle. The first whack upon his rump came hard and fast, and each whack thereafter grew more painful, dreadfully painful, but even more painful was McCoy's words which he heard sporadically:

"You fucking girl…you little piece of shit…this will teach you a…sound…proper…lesson…never…to fuck with me…Don't you ever…touch my…food…without my permission…you hear?…You fucked up…no good son…of…a bitch…"

Warm fluid filled his eyes, and soon his rump throbbed with pain, and his tears flowed.

"…lazy…good-for-nothing-bum…you think…everything…is for free…well, I'm here to tell you…nothing is for free…Stop crying…You hear me?…You little piece of…Now pick it up…Clean this fucking mess…You're just...like your mother...a little sissy...a little girl...crying to his Mama...no good...bitch...she was..."

With each strike Noble could think of nothing but the next one and the next one, yearning for the end of his father's snide comments. And when it did end, he collapsed, his chest nailed to the kitchen floor, and the immediate intimation of purchasing a revolver and blowing the old man away. His ideas diverged into two roads, one leading to this permanent solution, the other understanding he could never carry out the action and get away with it. He hated the man and wished him dead, and he prayed for this transgression.

He remained on the floor for nearly twenty minutes, the blood returning to his buttocks, the excruciating pain, like countless nails, rupturing his broken dermis. His father's door slammed shut, and the beating ended for the night. He hadn't been beaten that badly for several months. He would leave, that's what he would do, he would leave, take all of his CD's and head for the sun-drenched shores, those pink, sandy beaches where the women smiled, the seagulls hung motionless in the wind, and the tender waters lapped at the sand. And from these two roads, there appeared a third road, this entity known as the imagination, a nonsensical, unconscious arena which heals the most troublesome duels between extremes of thought, a savior which fills the gaps of dislocated deductions and meaningless calculations, a sublime goddess amidst temples of rubble, a soothing balm to a swelling and burning rump.

Noble staggered to his room and fell to his bed, but before doing so he listened to a melancholy selection, sad enough to sustain his self-pity. His tears of pain transmuted into tears of great sorrow, the acoustic guitar commiserating and touching a deep part of him rarely revealed, something broken and buried. He felt under his mattress for his bag of marijuana. He lit the roach and singed his bangs in the process, but the sudden head-rush pacified him. Instead of escapism, Noble remembered his mother from long ago, the same woman to which McCoy had referred.

Chapter Two

The herb chipped at his pain and refunded him with pleasant, mysterious memories. After twenty-two it all went down hill, the narrow concave rut where there was little opportunity for change or growth, a no-man's land between adolescence and adulthood, as though he had encountered a developmental glitch at childhood which led to his present misery. But the weed adopted a smooth effect. Memories flooded him, mostly memories of his mother, a frail but comely woman with golden hair and thin, sallow cheeks, which were signs of malnutrition and self-sacrifice. He thought of her when his misery hit a nadir, and from this lowest point these gentle memories thrust him suddenly to a zenith, a view of magnolias and orchids from on-high, these same flowers within a strange garden vanishing and appearing with the cycle of seasons, and upon this peak he envisioned this wonderful garden, these flowers sunning themselves, and young children of different ethnicities dancing hand-in-hand, a collection of rainbow streaks over them, and the band playing in a continuous melody, not a rant, but a chorus of angelic song and praise, a utopian vision neither feasible nor reliable, but a product of his imaginings. And somehow these random impressions of joy and beauty served as the only representation of what his mother meant.

"Noble? Noble? Are you awake?" he heard in the distance.

The young Noble, who lived in the same room, felt a soothing hand upon his back. His mother's hand did not erase what he dreamt. It assisted his transition from the unconscious realm to that moment when the hand stroking his back brought him gracefully to her voice, a gentle Eurydice tempting an impatient Orpheus.

"Awww, mom."

"You wanted to go to the park today, didn't you? It's Saturday and a very gorgeous day. Do you still want to go?"

"Let's go then," he said weakly.

He wore pajamas with action figures on them, his bed sheet one sprawling cartoon. His school books were piled on a small desk, his clothes in a chest of drawers. This was Noble before his obsession with music. He was a simple child who walked on weekdays to the elementary school which catered to the old money, and teachers who examined carefully some students but not others.

His mother packed a basket of cold-cuts and soft rolls for this particular outing, and after he had dressed and bathed, he walked with her to the park in the center of town. At the park's center stood a statue erected in the mid-nineteenth century of the town's first mayor. His mother spread the' blanket near this statue. They sat for some time, curious of the people around them, the bright sunshine asking nothing in return.

"Mom?" he asked while munching on a sandwich, "I don't wanna go to school no more."

His mother smiled, as she had had the same thoughts once.

"What's the matter with school?"

"I don't like it. Miss Drudgeson always yells at me."

"That's because you're not doing well. If you improve, she'll stop yelling at you."

"I don't wanna go back. I don't wanna learn arithmetic anymore. It's so bad and boring."

She pat him on the head a few times and laughed.

"Is Daddy sending me to military school?"

"Your father just says that, because your grades are so low. He won't send you away. About you're father, he's under a lot of pressure lately."

"He's mean to me," said Noble.

"That's because he loves you. He's only trying to do what's best. He may not show it, but he does love you."

"But you love me more than he does."

"Never compare our love for you, Noble."

"Do you love Daddy?"

She wiped off a gob of mayonnaise below his lip.

"You shouldn't be asking these questions, but I'll tell you, only if you act like an adult about it."

"Do you love Dad?"

"Yes, I love him," she said. "He's a good, responsible man, and he takes care of us."

"I don't love him. He never says anything. He makes angry looks and stuff, and I hear you fighting all the time. You don't love him neither, especially when he yells and stuff."

She looked into the cloud spotted sky, sighing, confronted by his persistent curiosity and precociousness.

"Noble, it's never easy," she said. "You're father and I have disagreements like any couple, but that doesn't mean we don't love each other. When we first met, we were very young, and very much in love."

"Even when he hits you?"

"He doesn't hit me."

"Then what's all that noise?"

"Well, we exercise a lot, and sometimes it makes a lot of noise."

Noble believed her, although he had never seen them exercise before.

"Love is a wonderful thing," she continued, "but also very hard, and your father and I were very much in love. He was twenty-two, and I was seventeen when we married, and ever since we loved each other, and although he doesn't show it at all, he loves us, and when we had you, our love grew stronger."

Her words sounded good. He was paying attention, not to the meaning of her words, but her elocution, her soft and patient tones akin to her hand stroking his back, her palm patting his head. He didn't care so much about his father's anger and neglect. His mother filled that void, acting as both mother and father. Her love for her son never gushed or overflowed with sentimentality. She became firm and resolute when his discipline wandered, when his room was messy, when he refused the main entre'e and craved only the desert, when he didn't brush his teeth, or when he vehemently declined trips to the barber. And this duality weighed upon her, to Noble innocent ignorance, because she hid sweetness in favor of a more aggressive and disciplined approach. Rarely did she answer his many questions with avidity as she did in the park that morning. Noble was too young to recognize the distinction. Ironically she understood her limitations as a disciplinarian, unlike McCoy McCloud. She buried her anger like a hatchet in a log. She raised her voice only to her husband, never to her child, and as a result she paid the price both physically and emotionally, as her husband served as a vent which belched back a greater, more damaging heat.

Noble admired her. He trusted her, the only person he could trust. Besides she cooked a mean fried chicken, and at these special meals she relaxed and let the young Noble lick his fingers.

Their meals were solitary occasions, McCoy McCloud noticeably absent. He spent his time after work at a local tavern on the North side of Waspachick, far enough from his wife who couldn't intrude with any convenience. Noble and his mother would sit in a comfortable silence, their conversations spent but their mutual affections lingering. His mother seemed more severe inside the house than outside, as though the poor relationship with her husband was revealed on the yellowing walls, the sofa where a sharp spring poked through the cushion, and the wall-hangings layered with dust.

On occasion she helped Noble with his homework. She wasn't employed in the conventional sense, so she had many an opportunity to read her romance novels purchased from the supermarket. Noble, after school, watched his mother sprawled on the sofa, patiently reading.

Noble had just learned how to read, but did not include books among his few activities. He would have rather played in the mud, or drink cola, or stare at the black and white television screen for hours, as though these shows reflected the truth and not the jolly, shiny, and downright fake values of fantastic liars who espoused values no one on this planet ever adhered to, but a steady stream of false happiness which encouraged him to act properly while hiding valid feelings, forcing him to dislike himself amidst these men built by factory engineers and these women who were the products of plastic, silicone, airbrushing, and cosmetics thicker than icing.

Reading took too much effort, and television very little, so little that his brain cells burned. The activities he found most enjoyable led him closer to stupidity, insanity, and death. Noble's mother knew of his affinity for the television, and when he watched for too long, she would shut the chatterbox off. She sat him on her lap and read passages from the latest romance novel, words which her child could not comprehend. He was soothed instead by her inflections, the way she pronounced the multisyllables, the diphthongs at each consonant which flowed from her mouth like an instrument rich in tone, as though each word were a note, and the combination of words a symphony played by vibrating vocal chords. These chords showered him with riffs and landscapes.

After a chapter or two he grew tired of her speech due to his intense but futile effort to understand. And the information received only elicited song. He used these words out of context, as though establishing sound instead of sense, and he regurgitated these complex sounds in the classroom.

For some time his second grade teacher thought him bright, advanced, and learned, until she read his compositions which didn't make any sense at all. And so Noble listened attentively when his mother read. He smiled with her during the romantic interludes and cried when tears rolled down her cheeks.

He returned to the television after these readings, as though the people within these compartmentalized boxes, inducing a thirty-minute resolution to conflict, kept him company in a way his mother could not. He witnessed perfect families- the wise and gentle father smoking a pipe in his study, the mother who prepared gourmet meals and mopped the floors with a friendly, bald-headed bodyguard wearing a gold earring, the brother who broke a window with a baseball, the cute toddler who smiled but said nothing. In short, the television and even the few films he saw reflected everything Noble was not, the result being a generous dearth of reality, and when thrown into the ordinary world, things seemed drab and boring, and his young fantasies grandiose, his ambitions high as a dramatic overachiever, a status which resulted in his inability to handle the simplest arithmetic and most lucid paragraphs. He could not concentrate on anything for a reasonable period of time, the remote control pressed every few seconds, searching and eventually finding anything to entertain him.

He relaxed with his mother at the town statue and ate the sandwiches, but drew little pleasure from it. He wanted more. Every day had to be a carnival. He had little idea of the work involved to create a ceaseless and steady stream of fun. He merely watched and then dreamed without taking any action, a characteristic which haunted him to this day.

"Simple pleasures," said his mother in the park. "That bird over there…"

"Where's the bird?" he asked.

"That red bird hopping over there- his life is spent gathering worms and feeding his young. And when the day is sunny and warm, he enjoys it, all within his working life, and one day school will end. It doesn't continue forever. What do you want to be when you get older, Noble? Have you given it any thought?"

"I don't know," he said sheepishly.

"If you could be anything you wanted, what would it be?"

"I wanna be a movie star," he said suddenly.

"A movie star? Do you know I wanted to be a dancer on Broadway?"

"That's for girls."

"Oh, really? I knew a lot of men who were dancers, good dancers too."

"Why aren't you dancing then?"

"Well, life has this special way of knocking things down to size. I mean, if I were a dancer, I'd never have had you."

"Did you buy me in a store? That's what Shylock says."

She smiled gently, even though she had little idea how to respond.

"A stork delivered you," she said, "right to our doorstep. A huge bird with a big sack under his beak, and the bird carried you from the bird world into Waspachick, and he delivered you on your birthday."

"Where's the stork now?"

"Delivering other babies."

This sounded plausible enough, until the intimation of stardom returned.

"I wanna be on television."

"Why television? Do you like acting?"

"Acting?"

"Sure. One has to act in order to be on television. You can't just wander on the set and play a role without practice and training. Are you sure about this? I wanted to be a dancer, a great dancer, the most famous dancer like Anna Pavlova or Isadora Duncan. And I dreamed about being on the stage, and my father took me to dance classes everyday after school. And I practiced and practiced. I ate only fruits and vegetables, and soon enough I wore away."

"Huh?"

"I grew very skinny, too skinny, and Mommy had to go to the hospital, because she wanted to be a dancer so much, and only a precious few make it out there. There are so many who try so hard, even at the expense of their own lives. Actors are the same way. So are painters and sculptors. They want fame and fortune, and they use their artistry as a big boat carrying them to glory and recognition, but when one uses art in that manner, one always fails, as I failed. I realized, after I went to the hospital, that dancing was only a way of making me noticed, so that more people would pay attention to me, admire me, comment that I was beautiful. Do you feel the same way? Do you want more attention from Daddy and me?"

"I don't like Dad. He always yells and stuff. I want to become an actor like you said."

"Acting isn't easy. Maybe the top one percent get famous and live off they're acting. I'm not saying that you don't have a chance, Noble, I'm not saying that at all. You can do anything, anything you want, as long as you work for it, pay taxes, and the rent, utilities, and the food. Nothing's for free. Everything has a price, and the arts has an enormous price tag, so large that even the rich folk on the North side avoid it. The best thing, Noble, is to do well in school for now and not worry so much. Enjoy your youth, because it only comes around once. It's not easy being young, but it's a lot harder being old."

"And then we die? Where do we go, mom?"

"Wherever you want, wherever you believe you should go, be that heaven or hell, outer-space, back to earth, or even eaten by worms underground. It's all up to you."

"I'd go to the movies."

"And I'd be on the stage, dancing with Nureyev and Barishnikov," as she giggled and ruffled his hair.

At these rare moments Noble connected with her. The days and nights of solemnity and austerity were eviscerated for her laughter and genuine happiness at letting herself smile and giggle. She became another woman when she discussed dancing. She kept this simple dream. Noble had little conception of this, and understood little of what she said, only that she was at one point a dancer, and it was partially his fault that she gave up.

"If I wasn't here, you would dance still?" asked Noble.

"Having you is ten-times better than dancing. Things change over time, and it changes for the better. Without you, my life would be, would be, not the same as it is now. Do you get it?" she asked as though seeking affirmation.

"When I'm grown up, I'll buy you a dance place, and you can dance all day, and I'll also get a room with my friends and see you dance."

She kissed him on the forehead, the young Noble vindicating himself for obstructing her dream. They lay on a white sheet as the park filled with random villagers. A young group of men tossed a Frisbee, the locals on disability sat on the benches along the strip, the neighborhood middle schoolers conversed loudly, a couple on an adjacent bench necked, all of these events under the auspices of the sun, as though the end of the outing constituted a crime.

After the lunch, his mother said:

"Listen, I have to visit a friend of mine. He lives a few blocks away from us. Now, what I want you to do is run home, and I'll be back in an half-an-hour."

"Can't I come with you?" he asked excitedly.

"I'll meet you at home, Noble."

"Pleeeez, mom? I won't bother you. Pleeez can I come?"

She pondered his plea for a moment.

"Alright," she said finally, "you can come, but you will sit in the living room and not make a sound. I'm seeing a very important client, and you are not to disturb me, is that clear?" her austerity returning.

"I'll be quiet. I'll watch TV."

"No, not even that. You will stay in one place downstairs and just sit there, like a fly on the wall, is that clear too?"

"Okay, mom, I'll be quiet. Like a fly."

They left the park shortly thereafter and walked hand-in-hand passed their house and further South. His mother didn't say a word on the way. Noble didn't know where she was headed. He kept quiet as promised, and the further South they journeyed from Waspachick's center, the more dilapidated the houses became, as the continuity of the fortified structures gradually warped like rotting pumpkins. At every block liquor stores appeared more frequently, the graffitied garbage cans overflowed with Styrofoam cups and fast-food wrappers, obsolete cars whizzed by, and Noble even noticed markings on a retaining wall which read in large, bold letters: "U.S.A. Skins."

Noble found the new environs more exciting than the stillness of the park. There was more to observe, as though the pot-holed roads and the cigarette advertisements lent a twisted pleasure, a new freedom from childhood into an arena of survival and danger. He nearly fell in love with it, like being dropped on another planet, and he peered at his mother beside him.

She stared straight ahead, her pace quickening. They arrived breathless at a crumbling house squeezed between a ninety-nine cent store and a kiosk. The door was open. They entered the place cautiously.

Empty bottles of whiskey lay above and below a coffee table. The motley furniture arrangement, if one could call it an arrangement, clashed with a faded green carpet. The place looked like a student's apartment, only messier. Noble spotted an aluminum dinner tray sticking with dried tomato paste and tossed into an empty corner. A set of stairs stood before them.

"Charlie? Charlie, are you there?" called Noble's mother.

"Yeah," came a drowsy response, "Come on up."

"Now Noble, you sit quietly in the living room, and don't make a sound," she whispered hotly. "Remember, you're a fly; act like it. Pretend a camera is watching you. Not a sound, or else I'll never take you anywhere again, you hear me? Not a sound. I'll be out in twenty minutes."

She disappeared upstairs, and Noble sat on one of the sofas, making sure not to move, not to think, not to breathe too loudly. But after a few moments of sitting in a complete silence, he heard noises from upstairs, a cacophony which turned rhythmic, squeaks and bangs with an established pattern. These sounds continued for ten minutes, and they grew louder and faster, a crescendo leading to some unknown end. Noble thought it would be a violent end, as when his mother and father fought late at night.

He had to stop it. He feared his mother was being beaten upstairs, but then he remembered her strict instructions, and for what seemed like hours he deliberated, confounded on all sides by indecisiveness. The noises became louder. He knew she was being harmed by a stranger. If it were his father, he would have sat in silence, but no stranger would dare abuse his mother and get away with it. The stranger must be stopped, and the heroic Noble would rescue her from the clutches of a killer.

He quickly ran upstairs, but tip-toed to the door through which these noises came. He heard squeaks, bangs, and their moans. She's being suffocated, he thought, or the stranger is forcing poison down her throat, or the stranger is stabbing her with a knife, just like the television show. The stranger must be stopped.

He banged on the door softly, and the noises continued, until he banged so hard that his fist swelled.

"Mom, are you okay? Mommy, are you okay in there? Is he hurting you?!"

The noises ended, and after a few moments, his mother stood at the doorway blocking Noble's view of the bedroom. Her hair was tangled and frayed, beads of sweat graced her upper lip. Her white blouse was untucked, and Noble noticed, to his surprise, that her pants were unbuttoned down to the end of the zipper. She panted, and then yelled at him:

"Noble McCloud! Go downstairs this instant! I can't take you anywhere!"

And then in the background a faint voice:

"Hey baby, the meter's running."

"Noble, downstairs right now!"

"But he was hurting you…"

She caught her breath and knelt before him.

"Oh, Noble," she said softly, "what am I to do with you? No one's hurting mommy, okay. Mommy wouldn't let anyone hurt her. She's a strong woman who can take care of herself."

"Daddy hurts you all the time," as tears welled in his eyes.

"Come here, Noble," and she embraced him.

"Now go downstairs, okay? Mommy will be right out, okay? Don't worry about me. I'm fine. Now sit on the couch, and Mommy will be down any minute."

The mind has the special quality of storing trauma, hidden like old clothes in the attic, only to be rediscovered at a garage sale. With trauma in the mind, a remembrance occurs which never delivers the exact experience, only a tamer version, a lingering impression. And when these old, soiled, moth-eaten, out-of-style clothes are gathered upon the lawn by its owners, a collection of lost memories arrives: the dress worn to the prom, the flimsy coat during that terrible winter storm, or the socks given by a deceased friend as a gift. The mind, burdened with memories, operates in a similar manner. It encounters a sign and attaches a special significance, a causality created by experiential recollection. Signs, however, are neither determined nor defined by sight alone. The senses work interdependently, some senses more powerful than others, and perhaps it's a gift when one particular sense overrides all others: the keen eye of an art collector, the taste of a food critic, the smell of a perfumer, the touch of a shirt-maker. Or maybe not.

Noble's mind only reacted to sounds: the bed creaking, the headboard banging, the moans escaping from his mother's lips, her scolding when interrupted, her comforting voice as he cried. His lopsided sense of sound freed these traumas diluted by time, released by his father's countless words, sustained by plaintive chords weeping through the night.

And it wasn't the case that he had any natural proclivity towards sound. Rather, it had been inculcated through experience, not the genes. A natural ability left unshaped and malnourished by inexperience results in a flag fully furled, a light-bulb without an electric current, a guitar without strings. And concrete experience without a natural talent engenders necessary skills which soon become talents. In other words, there is no such entity known as natural talent. It's a myth formulated by those who have little understanding of experience and its absolute, unwavering effect upon the individual. Neither do they understand natural talent to which they cling stubbornly, as though this tired explanation for the success of an individual in a certain discipline acts as some unknown variable, the margin of error in a poll, the invisible hand of God, or, only slightly compelling, the simple gene passed from one generation to the next. They will tell you that genes are the cause of it all, they will lure you by placing Wilt Chamberlain on a pedestal, they will seduce you by measuring the interior of your cranium with dried mustard seeds, they will examine your cognition by administering utterly useless tests, and then they will stuff you into a category, house you on the Southern side of Waspachick, separate you, degrade you, plunder you, rape you, accuse you, and offer the only explanation possible: 'That's the way things work. Sorry, chum, it looks like you'll be unemployed, broke, homeless, and a beggar in accordance with our genetic evaluation. Sorry, there is little hope for you. Here's the shot gun. Shall we pull the trigger , or could you do it for us?'

They will never mention the deaf Beethoven, the dark Satchel Page, or the imprisoned Malcolm Little. The will never fully explain how Helen Keller communicated or how Einstein developed theories from a poor foundation in Mathematics. Neither will they ascertain how people in wheelchairs, convinced they will one day walk again, win gold medals. And in return for their flawed advice and specious research, they will offer a total, all-encompassing lack of vision which inexperience provides. And then they will blame you as the contradictory element in their plans for a perfect world. Young Noble's sense of sound derived chiefly from the battles between his mother and father late at night. He heard thumps, bangs, clattering, clanks, yells, cries, screams, wails, slaps, and smacks.

After the unfortunate outing with his mother who explained the event in child-speak, or rather her euphemistic lies which satisfied his curiosity, they returned home to a drunk McCoy McCloud. The second he raised his voice, she ordered Noble to his room.

He lay in bed, twisting into all sorts of positions, the glow of the sunset casting intense light on his skin. And then he heard familiar sounds, plates crashing, the kitchen table scraping the linoleum, doors opening and closing, anger and heat exchanged like a ball in a game of catch. And from these repeated battles, Noble found a strong sense of sound, a strong sense due to his acquired ability to distinguish cacophony from euphony. Each night ended in a mystery. The sounds outside of his room ended in an eerie silence, and due to this silence Noble had trouble sleeping. He had grown accustomed to noise, and from it he made musical notes, melodies arranged from airwaves of junk.

The next morning, the young Noble awoke with his mother by his side. He had slept in his clothes. His mother had broken her fingernails, a red welt bulged below her left eye, and coagulated blood on her chin. She had put on heavy make-up to hide these facial anomalies, and Noble knew her face different, but did not assume things about her, one of Noble's many flaws. He never had the power to judge in a world overwhelmingly judgmental. He looked at his mother and assumed they had exercised, that their family was as wholesome as those on the glowing screen. Whatever intuition he had was crushed by his belief in things innocent and ideal. He rarely saw the reality of his mother's swollen face. This had all seemed normal to him. He connected the sounds of fighting on television and these similar sounds he had heard the night before, but he couldn't assume or generalize. No, the young Noble McCloud could only believe what his mother said, and he adhered to her explanations, no matter how ridiculous.

He believed her more than his own intuition. This may indeed be the result of an over-protective mother, the rearing of a beautiful loser unable to distinguish fact from fiction, truisms from all out lies. On that morning, a sunny one, Noble did not ask any questions. She answered them for him in the delicate way only a mother can.

"You look different," he said.

"How so? I just woke up, maybe that's why."

"You're face looks bigger."

"Well, you're face looks redder," she said with a grin.

And in this roundabout manner, his mother would pry him further from the truth, and at these times she became tender, understanding his curiosity, understanding his need to understand. She brushed his hair to the side before pulling a fresh set of clothes from the bureau. She made him bathe and brush his teeth. And when all was ready, they went to the supermarket in the used Oldsmobile McCoy had recently purchased.

Waspachick that morning was coated in beige: beige cars, beige polyester clothing, a beige lawn in the park, beige signs, and beige pedestrians underneath a beige sun. This beigeness added to a stickiness in the car, and they inched forward in silence to the supermarket a block away from the main strip. His mother said to stand by her as she rolled the shopping cart at a snail's pace through five aisles crammed with stuff Noble found unappealing. And suddenly in the middle of an aisle she stopped short, and they both spotted a rotund man in bell-bottoms and a crooked smile.

"C'mon Noble, we forgot something," she said.

They quickly moved to another aisle but found themselves confronted by this same man, his curly hair dripping with oil, and a gold medallion resting on his chest. He gave them the same smile and slid towards them. There was no avoiding him, and from that startled calm in which she ran from him, she told Noble to stand where he was in the middle of the aisle with the cart full of soup cans. She approached him carefully, and Noble followed her.

"Hey baby," he heard his mother saying.

"Aww, I really missed you," said the rotund man while feeling her arms and back.

"Listen, we should get together sometime, you and me, baby."

"Yeah, I really missed you last night."

And they embraced in the aisle as Noble gawked, still unassuming. Their voices were barely perceptible, almost a whisper but submerged within a baby-talk of which Noble was jealous.

"So when can I see you? Tonight? I've been waiting a long time for you. I got some nice stuff for you..." said the man.

"I'm a little busy right now, baby, but I'll see you later, okay? I'll call you later..."

The conversation ended there, and Noble had many questions: Who was he? How did his mother know him? Why was he feeling her up? But most of all, why did she talk in the language reserved only for him, that special child-speak, as though their conversation were some defective, pirated copy? She was very quiet and dispirited after the encounter, and Noble asked not a single question due to his mother's mood, as though she might be angry with him. But in the car she said suddenly:

"Noble, one day we'll leave Waspachick. If there's any place you'd go, where would it be?"

"I don't know," he said glumly.

"One day, Noble, we'll go far away from here. And every day I'm saving the money, and soon enough we'll have enough to leave Waspachick-what do you think about that? Just you and me..."

Chapter Three

He awoke the next morning with a start, the dream of his mother melting away, and his backside inflamed and throbbing. Exhausted, he remained in bed for some time in a silence which soon made him uncomfortable. The stereo stood at the foot of his bed. He reached for it and played the same tunes to which he fell asleep. The pain was so bad that he could hardly move, and he remained in one position for several hours falling in and out of a restless slumber.

His father had left for work without the slightest instruction. He came and went as he pleased, and Noble had little idea who he saw, where he went, or when he would return. He was grateful enough to have the house to himself, to enjoy a full recovery, and again he saw a large stage in the middle of an open field, the band playing, the young women swaying, the sun hot and heavy in a sky of azure, not a single cloud, only a deep endless blue, and the women in their shorts and tight tee shirts dancing with a brilliant clarity. Noble made a dangerous leap in vision from this point.

For the past several years this particular fantasy always placed him in the audience, and he was satisfied with his position as a consumer of the all-mighty guitar and the virtuosos who played it. But in this particular and pioneering vision he saw himself on the stage.

He fought this self-indulgence. He had always been a very modest and humble young man, whether in principle or in the avoidance of confrontation, he wasn't sure, but in this picture he held the delicate, weighty instrument and cradled it like a newborn. And the guitar sang in waves, screaming and moaning through the branches which shook and blossomed in the summer air into the ears of the women who hungered for another lick, any chord to transport them far away from bitter, harsh realities. And these women somehow heard his voice through the electric medium. The voice called for them, yearned for any woman to find him attractive, and the man without a woman transmogrifies, slowly but surely, into a beast fit for the climates of hell, the beast which attacks sheep in the dark and devours horse-flesh with blood-curdling exactitude, leaving not a single string of meat on the carcass.

The changing of man into beast doesn't come quickly or even gradually, rather it takes on a creeping, insidious character, the transformation beginning on the inside, an implosion of the immune system, a disease eating first the liver, the lungs, and then the heart, until it finally feeds on the skin, scathing it with a corrosion and disfigurement like an acid. And without a woman Noble had little idea how he would regain his sanity which oozed from him like a thick, gluey puss. Although he played a fast and precise guitar in this grandiose vision, he saw an acid burning through his skin, his hair aflame, his legs gangrenous, legions and cysts about his face, until there was nothing left but a skeleton with a fixed grin, covered by maggots burrowing through its marrow. He knew misery well! A man without a woman, he called it, and instead of being pinned to a vision which haunted him, he intimated having a woman, and the once-egregious scene shifted to a countryside of green hills and a brook which trickled by a fertile cherry tree, the melody soothing and everlasting, and a nude woman lying beside him, her blonde hair luxurious and her skin as smooth as Chinese silk. He fetches some water to quench their thirst, and he submerges the ceramic pitcher into the mellow stream. They share the pitcher, the woman sipping it slowly with a slight affectation, and Noble looking into her eyes and finding a meaning he couldn't define, only these shards of half-blues and greens like a deep painting. And he wants to know her, he wants to feel what she feels, he wants to become a part of her, to assess her needs while touring her clandestine vaults where she has stored the little girl collecting lilies taller than her crown, and he opens these vaults, these secrets which collect like old newspapers, and in them he finds the same eyes looking back at him, the eyes of a young maiden swinging below the cherry tree, her heart racing with delight, her white-laced dress lifting in a warm breeze, and himself below, ready to catch her should she fall.

Within a woman there is always the little girl, he thought, a girl who remains young and free like her hair which brushes against his lips, his chin finding a resting place between neck and shoulder. She's ticklish there, and he kisses her, penetrating years of hypersensitive armor, and she lets him in, a gate stretching over the moat, the bridge laden with mines, and he enters her carefully as she resists and whispers his name, but he enters without sword or shield. He is not there to conquer or steal, but to understand the girl to which the woman so stubbornly clings, to know her ultimate purpose, her phantasmal beauty.

He hears nursery rhymes and faint voices emanating through her walls. He sees paintings along this fleshy cavern, these stages of womanhood slowly deconstructing and devolving, and when he can go no further, when these child-like rhymes dulcify to simplest terms, he finds the young girl singing on the grass, her secrets released like a set of apparitions floating in mid-air. He reaches for her impetuously, but she vanishes. He is instantly returned to the wine and those perplexing eyes in which he first drowned. He then notices the tranquil scene from on high, the illusion fading. The skeleton plays the guitar. The puss oozes back into his boils. The boils fade. The burning acid smoothes his skin. The women dance and sway before him while he's on the stage. Finally, he finds himself in his bedroom again, the door shut tight, the tunes on the stereo, his rear-end throbbing.

He returned to consciousness as quickly as his fantasy began, and he thought more realistically about his woebegone woman situation. He recalled the summers in Waspachick. He entered headlong into that lonely area where he couldn't get women at all, as all of the Waspachick women had steady boyfriends with expensive cars. They had all the money, and Noble hardly a cent to his name, only an allowance saved up in a piggy-bank, and he used those funds to buy herb. He didn't feel sorry for himself, but rather found his situation impossible.

A lack of money was not the only reason for his inability to get women. With Shylock he talked like a true bachelor, eyeing women who strolled the strip and making some joke about them, but he would only talk of women when he was with Shylock. Alone, however, he would never even consider approaching a woman, and some of them did look at him with seductive eyes, but he would turn away in shyness. More than any one element, he feared most the rejection, the embarrassment and humiliation of being turned down and perhaps scoffed at by a woman he thought attractive. He also believed he had nothing in common with the opposite sex. He knew only that they had a zest for life, that they wanted amusement constantly, that they needed a strong, virile man saturated in his own testosterone, a man who brawled when another man looked at his woman the wrong way, the man who was controlling and obsessive like the father who surrounds her in a wall of stone, getting jealous, getting angry, ready to defeat anyone's ego more inflated than his own. He admitted that this was only one type of woman and one type of man, but these pairs would roam the strip of Waspachick in droves, particularly on the weekends when the housewives and their strollers finished their weekly shopping.

And what hurt most is that these women knew of their attractiveness. They all seemed to know that beauty, as defined by Noble's magazines, was the only foundation to their self-esteem. They actually enjoyed being the prize of the man's struggle. They liked being enclosed like a doll in a case of glass, a glass never broken, only a doll within it smiling, modeling, moving about with wily, cat-like manners.

It's not to say that these women of Waspachick hadn't their wits about them. Actually the opposite was true. When compared to these competitive, pugnacious males they possessed a wit and wisdom infinitely higher. They used the simple rationale of letting the man prove worthy of them. The men sought gifts on display at the corner jewelry store, or drove down the center of Waspachick with their radios booming, sending shock-waves through the coffee houses, the restaurants, and the new art gallery. Unfortunately, Noble admired the prize, never the woman standing right in front of him, only the woman he hadn't a chance in hell of getting. He knew that about himself. He didn't kid himself either. He liked the ones out of his league, and he hated himself for it. He hated having attended the local high school, watching young, pubescent teens driving expensive automobiles. He hated how 'like' people stuck with 'like' people, little cliquish groups already formed, cliques he couldn't enter on account of his wallet, on account of his total uninterest in school work. He didn't fit in anywhere, only roamed the outskirts, as he did to this day. He was unsure whether his marginalization was his own fault or everyone else's. And he wanted the woman who every single male would do anything for: the Waspachick woman, one type of woman for one peculiar village.

But why not at least try? He did the night before with the fair Alexandra, a woman he most likely would never see again. Why not abandon his childishness and take the leap of faith required of every man? After all, doesn't every man have to put on airs to attract women, even the men least desirable? And with rejection, with each leap that precedes a fumble into a dark abyss, doesn't each rejection thereafter become easier, until one is totally numb from these rejections that they come naturally, like a whip cracking over someone's back over and over again, or repeated lunges at the heart when only the first stab takes his life?

But approaching a woman took a confidence Noble lacked, a confidence which would lead to a fight with other males jockeying for the same position. And how would he look walking down Waspachick, he in his threadbare clothes, and the prize of a woman in an elegant evening dress- a mismatched mutt-like couple, a pair which lacked a convenient symmetry, and what pressure the woman of Waspachick would be under: her stalwart father who wants her to marry a man in a suit, the paranoia of constantly being judged by the entire town, curious eyes peeping through cracks in the walls, the eyes which follow them down the strip and glare at Noble the misfit and this woman who could have done better. The sensitive Noble would be subject to snide remarks by men who thought they could achieve that calculated symmetry, that stroll about town with a trophy in their arms.

And from this contemplation and criticism of these haughty mating practices, he escaped once again to the stage where he picked and poked at the strings, sending notes into the huge crowd which gathered before him. He was the expert, playing the instrument nonchalantly, a quiet poise, and once in a while smiling to the bassist next to him. He played such mean chords that he made it look easy, and his body while on the stage didn't move or run around to elicit any excitement. He stood there quietly, concentrating totally on the instrument, and letting it sing voices he couldn't articulate for himself.

The crowd on its feet, the women in the front row crying and screaming, and still he remains quiet, the front rows having little idea why he refused ostentation. They not only loved what he played, but also respected him. He became to them an icon, a representation of what it meant to play guitar, a representative of a generation from some extinguished era reincarnated upon the stage clouded in a venerable and austere light.

While in this reverie, he accepted the prestige but none of the money. He made playing the guitar an art form, and the heaving crowd knew this, but he did not. His world was confined to strings, bobbin, neck, and pick-up. He made sounds no one ever heard but somehow knew, for these sounds were not his own but everyone else's, moving like memories through their hearts. And this guitarist (which is Noble) had a back-story, something tragic and surreal which codifies his true artistry and his fans' undying loyalty. Perhaps he lost a woman in his early days at the height of his popularity, and then went underground, hiding from the flashes and microphones stuffed in his face. A frenetic media followed him, but he chose to hide from his adoring public due to his bereavement, and through the years of his solitude and grief, his fans' adoration never waned but grew exponentially, to such a degree that he was forced to appear on the stage for this rare performance, and within an instant he rose through the echelons of popularity only to arrive at this tremendous stadium, the faces becoming faceless as each one liquefies into one corporal element. But he rarely looks up from his guitar, like a New Englander's focus on his shoes, his solos lasting for hours, a long, trippy synthesis of mood distortion, an inability to follow one established path, but many of them at once, form and structure thrown to the dogs, the freedom which only comes from being heard and respected no matter what he played, because he had earned that right, surpassing the ordinary and latching onto the divine, controlled by the voice of some mysterious power flowing through him, a voice which kept him as humble as the Waspachick town bum, but adored by its women, his stardom working on another level, as though time and space were endless enough to discredit exploration and find within that crying fan in the first row a world all her own, and the guitar feeding her world, nurturing it, transforming her own values and beliefs, breaking them down into a simple box of happiness, the ecstasy which comes from guitar appreciation...

Noble dreamed in this way for several hours as he understood that a man without dreams makes his days intolerable, and he tolerated this dream of becoming a great guitarist, although he felt somewhat guilty in elevating his jobless, penniless status into something sublime and therefore unreachable. But he knew that this daydream was put before him for a purpose. It was a new fantasy, not new to others, but new for him. He had made that transition from consumer to producer, a stance in which he must actually do something, must actually work to achieve that which fulfilled this dream. Could this be his calling? To become a guitarist? To pick up a guitar and expose himself to the world?

Well, he needed a guitar first, a slight consideration he initially missed, but a guitar would certainly aid in his plans. He asked: 'why hadn't I thought of it sooner? Most of the great guitarists started early, in their early teens. Am I too old?' 'It's never too late,' he heard himself mumbling, but do people say that to defy old age? To give them an excuse, almost a permission to begin anew? He wasn't sure, but he knew this had to be his calling, and the excitement of this new purpose made him pace the room like a strategizing dictator fueled by this unknown element known as success and respect, perhaps fame.

And this fame would bring him what he desired most: a beautiful woman, not just one but tons of them. He would amble down the tired strip of Waspachick, and they would turn their heads: 'why isn't that Noble McCloud, the guitarist extraordinaire?' He would no longer be the man the saleswomen laughed out of their stores, he would no longer be associated with the riff-raff on disability, hanging out at the town park late at night, gulping Thunderbird, complaining about their monthly checks, nor would he ever be smiled at by the town bum with his red, bulbous nose and his red cheeks, as though he just arrived through a time portal. And finally, with the women and his guitar, he would leave Waspachick never to return, and follow that elusive path to the West, that shrine of heightened consciousness.

He couldn't play part-time. He couldn't do it only when he felt like playing. He had to do it all the time, working his days and nights on the guitar itself. Half-measures would be like flushing this dream into the sewer. No artist ever did it halfway, he thought. They played despite the pressures of money and the rats who scurried for it. For rich and for poor he must marry the instrument, the blessed union giving way to a new lifestyle: that of the infamous genius who, when his eyes wandered across the street, could always find someone who knew him well, even the most distant stranger. He could enter the bar and order a drink on the house, a picture of him and his guitar hanging by the whiskey bottles. After all, it didn't take much to make it in music these days. All you needed was a hackneyed beat, a bass for rhythm, lyrics which made little sense to anyone but the musician, and boom! Presto! You had a song. Yet Noble refused the easy route. He would avoid the most common pitfalls of penning these one-hit wonders. He would write operas and symphonies with his guitar, those thirty-minute songs which the record industry likened to death, but the kind people listened to. He wouldn't have a particular group of fans either. His guitar playing would be universal, effecting the town bum as well as the chairman who returned by train from a feud with his board of directors.

This could work. It will work. No longer would he sit in his room and dream of a distant happiness, the same distance between him and the unattainable woman. He had definition now, a clear purpose.

'Don't rush it,' he thought. He understood he had plenty to learn, yet instinctively he wanted it immediately. He even thought of music school, but knew that no great guitarist ever emerged from their ranks. He would stick to reality and swear off this surreal grandiosity, the unattainable pinnacle which ironically thrust him forward.

Good. He had a vision and suddenly a purpose, and his days beforehand had been spent listening to the great ones. All he needed now was the guitar. Electric or acoustic? He meditated on this for some time. An electric guitar offered greater sound versatility, but an acoustic seemed more venerable, almost monkish, as though an acoustic were an essential rite de passage for any budding guitarist. But he didn't want to become a folk-singer, or end up a camp counselor singing Bingo the Dog to a group of snot-nosed youngsters. Yes, playing guitar has its underbelly just like anything else: the night club with a handful of drunkards, the city block where hurried pedestrians dropped coins in his case, or a status so poor that he would have to hock the guitar for stale bread. He vaguely pondered these scenarios, but they were infinitely better than living at home with his father. In fact, anything was better, aside from having a job, of course. He would sleep with his guitar if he had to, he would sell his soul to demons, he would beat his own head against the wall until a new riff escaped from the strings, he would play until his mind bled through his ears, until his melodies seemed freakish and dark, until his fingertips blistered and callused. The women would love him for it, the whole world resting below his feet and at his command. He had it all planned out, not a stone unturned, except for the perplexing question: how to get a guitar without any money? But he fought against dipping into financial waters and instead envisioned the dark arena flickering with a thousand lighters during a slow song about life on the road, suped-up buses equipped with televisions and amplifiers, and the gang of groupies, women no doubt, engaged in a never-ending striptease. And if God filled him with this ultimate purpose, then undoubtedly he will aid in this pioneering voyage away from Waspachick, a guitar in hand, recording tracks at a luxurious studio in Monserrat.

He knew little about buying a guitar. There were no musical shops in Waspachick, maybe a piano shop, but nothing dealing with things guitar. His finances were already pressed. He had little for his next meal which he preferred to eat at the all-night convenience store where Waspachick ended and the ghetto began. He would have to cut these sandwiches from his budget. But then what about herb, yes, that precious brown Mexicali substance which he needed after a good spanking? Well, he would have to cut this as well; deep cuts all around. He would have to live off his father to a greater degree, but this was the plan, the vision. He would never go down like the soldier unknown, the hero unsung. And he hadn't a dime, nor did he have credit. 'Get a job,' he heard his father mumbling in the back of his mind, but a job would take the focus from his art, and what's the use of being oppressed and enslaved by the mighty greenback? The vision, the hero, the great guitarist in front of thousands, and a job would crush this. So he returned to deep cuts which would largely confine him to home, and his days would be free to strum the guitar.

In one of the rundown roadhouses where he stood upon the stage, a record producer in a metallic suit would spot him and sign him to a mega-million dollar deal. If there were any logic to the artist's rationale, the next step had to be a record deal, the big break which comes after years of playing clubs, drinking watered-down whiskey, and taking tokes from someone else's joint. Yes, the big-break. All he needed was this one chance, and ding-ding, he would win the prize from which would follow platinum records and interviews with the music mags, but no, he would throw it all back to them, because he wouldn't sell-out his fans, those true believers who followed him, the dirty gals who hung around after the show.

It was now a duty. He would play for better or for worse, a marriage with his instrument. Another step in the logical procession: first the marriage ceremony, or the purchase of the divine guitar. Then, of course, the big break. He saw it unfolding, but first, deep cuts, and he found himself lost in thought, almost a confusion, no longer at bliss from receiving the vision but a need to scrape every penny, to bleed it from his father who already provided a monthly allowance. Homo economus. And then the piggy-bank, not a pig actually but a container stashed underneath the fetid dampness. He opened the lid and found maybe seven dollars in bills and the rest pennies and lint. Seven dollars wouldn't get him to Manhattan and back. Shit. What to do?

He would save this money, put it in the bank and earn a penny every month, or maybe he could buy a penny stock, one share, in a fledgling company that would sky rocket and give him a return of two hundred percent, or approximately twenty-one dollars. Then we factor in the commission charges, the Exchange commission fee, capital gains taxes, and bam!, we are back down to the same seven dollars. Democracy and Capitalism at their finest. He actually contemplated this, but the vision, the calling, the sold-out arena. Fine, the stock market wasn't the best route. He needed more liquidity anyway.

He stood motionless in his room, the volume at a simmer, his rear-end no longer shooting through his back. He squeezed the bills in his hand, the rustling of faded green, the presidents wrinkled and dry and burnt like a suburban lawn in the summer. And the guitarist on the stereo filtered through the speakers. He heard the voices transferred from the guitar into his own head, such that the walls oozed with this guitarist and his talk, as though a tacit, unspeakable, unutterable communication took place, a spirit which came through the walls:

"Are you sure about this, Noble," came the sound, and he looked beside him, and there stood an hallucination? Could it be that this guitarist was the same man who was pictured on the CD jacket? Noble couldn't believe that a man could just emerge through the walls. He blamed his overactive imagination at first, but this spirit, the quasi-hallucination talked to him in mellowing tones, the same spirit he considered his idol, the greatest guitarist ever to grace the plucky instrument with mean tone and unquenchable rhythm. Yes, the spirit of the great one sitting on his own bed, understanding his predicament, as though Noble had crossed a river and this guitarist at the foot of his bed demanded payment in terms of psychic disturbance.

'Now I've been a guitarist a long, long time, and well, let's just say that you may never make it."

Noble played along with this conversation, real and unreal, something he couldn't prove or disprove, only this hero, this idol with burning eyes and his infamous, custom guitar.

'Are you real?' asked the unsure Noble.

'Are you real?' replied the guitarist/apparition.

'I dunno,' replied Noble, the conversation taking place in his own mind, his entire body immobilized, the apparition strumming the chord to his own tune. Maybe the weed was laced with lysergic acid.

'No, Noble, the weed wasn't laced,' he said, (or it said, Noble wasn't sure). He was dumbfounded, unable to differentiate his own subjectivity from this objective apparition in full concert gear. The apparition wasn't part of objective reality, he couldn't be, and yet he tried to disprove it with a simple declarative sentence:

'You are unreal…' and then to himself, "and I must be tired, very tired, and I must save some dough for a guitar just like his."

"Ah, yes," replied the apparition, "Dreams and visions of grandeur, ah, I remember I was like you…"

"I said you're not real, hear me, not real!"

"Then why are you talking to me?"

"Why aren't I talking to some out of work junkie, then, down South Waspachick way? Why does it have to be someone famous, why does it have to be you, a virtual legend, why can't it be Joe Shmoe from the gas station?"

Out of the blank wall came Joe Shmoe from the gas station, a tall, thin, middle-aged African-American in a mechanic's suit stained with grease. He must have held the carburetor for effect.

"Is this what you wanted," asked the African-American, sitting side-by-side with the infamous guitarist.

Noble thought this some unruly misperception, something baffling, as though his mind were slowly slipping into an ether-like tank drenched with a strong, inexorable hallucinogen, that or maybe a party-goer dropped a sugar cube into his drink, but how? These two figures before him smiled conspiratorially. Then he tried hard to disprove it. He looked at them once, twice, thrice. His imagination had always gotten him into trouble, and he had no one to blame but himself. He stood frozen. He didn't move, and his calf muscles cramped. He could not shake them.

Perhaps he was lonely, and loneliness had divided his mind into the imagination and objective reality, a chasm so extreme that all of his might could not bridge the gulf. The imagination acted on its own without precept. The tubular mass of gray matter between his ears led to his grandeur, and his imagination became this limitless entity, its baffling propensity blurring those boundaries between objective reality and subjective projection. Should he believe in these apparitions? Or should he discard them into the land of his wandering, nomadic, grandiose visions to which he had been so accustomed?

But they just sat there, and if he reached for them they may vanish and return to that dense gray matter, and all would be lost, the vision, the guitar, his intense desire to jam in the eyes of millions with this idol and the auto mechanic. He shut his eyes and shook his head. They sat there. He rushed to the bathroom and flushed his face, then returned. They sat there. He turned the volume up. He threw his canister filled with spoiling copper pennies into the adjacent wall. He did push-ups and sit-ups. He ran about in circles like a chicken after its feed. They sat there and smiled knowingly. And Noble: why had he been selected? He was a nothing, a nobody who was too absorbed in himself.

Delusions are cruelest to those who approach them with skepticism and an indefatigable will to disprove their existence. He tried to discredit the two men with all the reasoning he could muster, but he grew tired, and after a couple of hours he accepted them as fixtures which wouldn't go away.

"Are you done fighting it, Noble?" asked his guitar idol with a smile.

"Y'know it would make it a lot easier on yourself if you stopped fighting us," chimed the mechanic.

"I'm not fighting you personally, okay, it's just that, well, this is so very strange and new."

"Of course it is," said the idol. "You want to play the guitar, and we are here to help."

"You'll teach me how to play?"

"No, you have to do that on your own."

"Then why the hell are you here? Just to bother the shit outta me?"

"We're here to support you- a little moral support."

"This can't be happening," said Noble. "Now I know that I sometimes get carried away, but I never thought it would come to this. I must be going mad, and maybe I need some help."

"You can't afford help," said the mechanic.

"And besides, you could use our help."

"Well, I can't make you go away, so I guess I'll have to put up with you."

"Only…don't push us too far," said the guitarist with a solemnity which scared him for a moment.

"What's that supposed to mean?"

"Let's just say, that you have quite an imagination," said the mechanic, "and you shouldn't try to disprove us. We are a part of you. Just go with the flow."

"Exactly. I couldn't have said it better myself," said the guitarist.

"Shouldn't we establish visiting hours? You guys can't waltz in anytime you please. I mean, I have reality to deal with too, y'know."

"You can't cope with reality, Noble, but we will come at those times when you need us most."

"Can you throw in a woman maybe?"

"Goodbye, Noble, you'll be hearing from us."

And they left the room by floating through the walls.

He stood bewildered and amazed. He was now certain the guitar was his calling, a vision sent to him by God, his power manifested by these two eerie apparitions. What did it mean, 'don't push us too far?' And when would they return? He suddenly thought himself important in the universe, as though he were special enough to deserve these psychic visitations. Yes, he would be an important guitarist, but important even to the women clustered in gossipy groups walking down the Waspachick strip? And if he couldn't be important right away, then his imagination would somehow transport him to that place and time where he lived on the lips of mankind? His skepticism remained. His grandiosity, however, overshadowed his disbelief.

Dreams are not meant to dangle in the mind, he thought. They are not meant to be reduced to imaginings one merely hopes will come to life. It is a duty and obligation to follow the dream, and the more grandiose, the more self-indulgent, the more un-real, the greater the obligation. The individual who ignores and merely wishes and hopes for these dreams without taking action within the established parameters of society sentences himself to a purgatory where these dreams are expiated, as though the reality is correct and the dream somehow incorrect. In this purgatory the man who once dreamt is transformed to an inferior organism. His equal becomes the amoeba which oozes over a morsel, or a more contemporary example, the rat who feeds from the purgatorial cloaca. The common misconception does not ring true: this false belief that man and woman are above the amoeba or the rat by their ability to reason. No, it can't be, thought Noble. Rather the man differentiates himself from those lower creatures by his capacity to dream and his willingness to follow that dream until the darkness settles upon him.

He needed money, and the next alternative was Shylock. Money had always been a thorn in Noble's side, a constant irritation. He saw everyone but himself climbing the social ladder, only that the climb wasn't an orderly process where one person patiently followed the other, rung after rung, in a silent but assiduous climb. Rather the slow procession exhibited a chaotic mess of people climbing over each other in a mad race, hands crushed upon the rungs by soiled shoes, sore hands grabbing a coat-tail from the man directly above, a man from up high falling, and from this laden mess of men transformed into insects a certain structure is formed. And to believe women want to equate themselves with these specimens?

There are those who remain at the bottom, because one can't fight and claw forever, and they seem to stay at the bottom in this huddled mass, almost asleep but active enough to engage in the art of cannibalism, as they feed on their livers without the luxury of salt, marinade, or onions. Rarely do they move from their appointed area on the ladder, and rarer still does anyone fall to this level. Those above them have an interest and incentive to make them stay in their places, as they not only feed upon themselves but also on the waste products of those above, and since their feeding habits result in a total, oblivious lack of energy, they remain in a constant state of 'clinging,' meaning they hold onto the rungs by their fingernails as though the ladder were unstable, a large rotor spinning out of control but keeping them huddled by the sheer force of gravity. The ladder, however, holds its stability like a stone in wet sand. They neither have the energy nor the perspicacity to see above them. They are at the bottom, and they stay there. If there ever were so lowly a group damned by the divine, hopeless, and impoverished in mind and spirit, it would be those who cling to the rungs of the ladder by their fingernails.

Oddly enough, those above them occasionally identify with this helpless pack of cannibals, but only in a watered-down, lukewarm way. The level directly above has no idea what this lowly group experiences, but imagines that they do have an idea. Such a horrible vision keeps them climbing. They understand the predicament of the lower ones but spit upon them. This group does not cling but climbs at a painfully slow pace, as though haunted by what they see below and enamored of what they see above. Yet the destitution among this climbing group doesn't waiver. They climb with ferocity, but they seem to remain on the same set of rungs due to the deluding elasticity of the ladder itself which seems to ascend into infinity. They too feed from the waste of others, but they climb hard and live fast. Their muscles develop as they fight each other violently while despising with an incalculable hatred those above them and especially those clinging masses below. Anyone in their path is killed, especially those who fall to their level without the ability to manhandle, stab, and beat to a pulp those in their company. And they kill with a certain satisfaction which is derived chiefly from an advancement upon the rungs: the ability to kick, scratch, and bite those who choke their necks and hug their legs like iron cuffs. And so they climb slowly while killing those around them, but the killing doesn't improve their situation, paradoxically, because they are deluged by more and more men and women who sink to their level, as most of their prey falls from the higher rungs. They are merely insects with a goal to climb, as climbing consumes them. A twisted religion. They never reach their goal but believe they are doing so, and therefore live in the moment more than any other group on the ladder.

Above this group lives the worker who abides by a system of values which sustains their belief in work for work's sake, thus they climb as a result. But they do so at a snail's pace. At least for this group there is a progression. Clad in blue work pants and tough, steel-tipped work boots, they understand the benefits of a collective form of labor, and here Noble encountered the first signs of a group climb. They believe that whether the labor be intellectual or physical, it is the labor which counts, as labor in itself keeps them on a steady, uninterrupted climb similar to the violent mass below them. They do not resent those below and neither do they envy the misperceived corruption and bacchanalia of the higher-ups. Their labor is physical, but the mentality used to sustain their work is highly imaginative, even perplexing. Their concern is not with climbing, but in their defiance of the ladder construal itself, as though they are the enlightened ones with a kernel of truth in their lunch-pails high above the world on reinforced beams. They pride themselves on being the true creators, the ones who are called upon to forge visions into truth, heightening their own sense of importance and satisfaction and maintaining a sense of dignity and honor as the most collectivized of groups. They see below them and wish that they could work honestly. They look above, with a tinge of resentment, and wish they could work honestly as well. Anyone living at this level must understand the value of work, not the value of climbing. It's not the case that they accept their inability to climb, because they do indeed climb, it's more the issue of accepting their situation upon the rungs: to forever remain workers and to maintain their position. And their busy, muscle-inflaming climb offers a relief from the ladder. They believe if they work, nothing else will matter, and they will thus survive. They work in the hive, but never taste the honey.

The group above them is more vast and complicated than any other. They constitute the meat of the ladder, as they are in a position to observe with a greater degree those above and below them. They have the highest turnover rate of either climbing or falling, but their goal to be perched on top of the ladder is unequivocal, and when they fall, either by mistake or misfortune, they scurry more fluently, and what makes them scurry is this idea that the top of the ladder is a position and status worth achieving, and they work hard towards this goal. They exhibit the characteristics of those above and directly below, but they fear below and worship above, and as a result they are more atomized, their families more nuclear, their offspring jockeying for a higher position, a belief that they should do better than their parents, and more often than not, they usually do better, as they master the art of scurrying with speed but without grace, and their reward and sometimes their substitute for a higher status is the amassing of material items: the new set of duds, the automobile, the lobster from Maine. These materials in turn add to the delusion of success, as though their materials somehow symbolize their connection and pseudo-equality with the group above. Although the ladder as a whole is characterized by chaos, the middle group maintains a physical order but enacts a more subtle, institutionalized chaos. Their chaos is more technical and strategic, and the results more diverse. They lack a unity and culture of their own due to a rapid mobility (either up or down the ladder) which they view as their right. While they are suspicious of the insects above them, they still employ their services for the containment of and protection from the workers below, and especially the homicidal mass below the workers. They appreciate the finer things, but only collect them as objects, once again symbolizing a higher importance. But they climb just like any insect on the ladder, and they fall with a melodramatic thud, only to climb towards a ceiling above which they can climb no more. The infamous bourgeois, thought Noble; insects more passionate about their right to climb than any other. Yes, they come to a certain rung where their ovipositors are crushed. The ceiling. And then they tumble to a lower rung- only to rise to that same ceiling and tumble again.

The ceiling, above which they try in vain to permeate, is actually a swelling mass of sated, slow-crawling bugs. Although this particular group are insects at heart, they are able to hide their exoskeletons and insectaries by stylish fashions of the day and sturdy walls, respectively. They have little incentive to climb fast, since they seem to be bred with many layers of fat. These are bigger and fatter bugs, but they lack a physical strength. As a result, they employ the killers below who are in turn fed by the idea that they are approaching a higher status, when in reality they're merely climbing and killing at the same time. Since these slow crawlers have more time between rungs, they divert their attentions from the ladder construal and enlarge their insectaries. Any thin, scraggly looking bug is immediately squashed by the second level killers who feed from mighty amounts of dung. Falling is rare, but if the slow crawlers do fall, they engage in the art of clinging due to their utter and irreversible disillusionment, and then they are killed by those same murderers they had employed. Between rungs they sip wine and talk of Michelangelo. But their view of the top is eclipsed by bigger and juicier bugs *ad infinitum, ad nauseam.* They keep climbing with a simple philosophy: what goes up, must come down. Hence, they are driven by omnipotence and opulence. They believe in the ladder, although they are constantly distracted by the view of fatter bugs dropping waste products upon them. Their belief stems from their inability to imagine anything else, as their perceptions are restricted by searching for that next rung in their drive to be as perfect as the all mighty bug above. They ignore the clinging masses, they employ the killers, they exploit the worker, they tempt the confused middle, and during this entire charade they stretch their hairy arms towards that next rung, and the next, and the next...

Noble was frightened by this negative and somewhat extreme view of the people in and around Waspachick. He understood what they were becoming, how the small suburban village which used to be a simple road with hardware and convenience stores had become a township hardly anyone could afford: the apparel shop selling expensive knit shirts, only to be sharing the building with a bank whose fees were outrageous. And he saw himself becoming the bug upon the ladder- not the ones who blindly clung to the rungs, but the ones who killed. This frightened him for a moment, but then there must be some way out, there must be some escape from becoming the insect. And then it came to him. The guitar was that ticket admitting him to paradise, the paradise which is derived chiefly from the conscious ability to step away from the ladder, not merely to observe the chaos or to add a lubricant to those crispy exoskeletons or to judge the ladder only to facilitate its climb, but to change the ladder into an entity more meaningful. In other words, to convert each insect into a human being. We are born human beings but somehow become the insect, the rat, the shark. Noble realized that there is only one way to restore our humanity, and this must be through art. And the way to art is through the guitar, and the guitar must be played with the help of the imagination.

Noble had never before trusted his instincts, and for good reason. He never really had any instincts vis-a-vis the commonsensical insectary of the ladder. Experience only taught him to imitate and regurgitate, leaving him in the killing zone. His inability to infer or deduce from a simple set of clues led him towards the imagination- perhaps the only ingredient within the human psyche which keeps us human. Yet the imagination is usually framed by the overwhelming force of the ladder construal. We use the imagination to a limited degree: only to advance upon the rungs. And Noble saw this happening all around him. The teenagers emerged on the weekends wearing gold watches, a fashion show on the strip. And during the weekdays the housewives compared their children sleeping in strollers. These housewives typified the insect but resembled transparent shells of the human beings they once were. They tongued the insect language: 'Oh yes, little Seton's first words from out of the womb included the Latin declension of the verb 'to be,' isn't that just like him? And then the little devil, why he recited Caesar's *De Bello Gallico.*'

Prior to the vision of the guitar in his hands, Noble resented them, and part of that anger took its place within the swirl of immediate memory, but now he felt downright sorry for them. He aimed to restore their former selves to a point where the rusted perceptions were cleansed and that modicum of dignity replaced like a set of new batteries.

The guitar served a dual function: to transcend the ladder and to help these insects to whom he felt a distant connection. The guitar his medium, the imagination his symphony. But can the imagination be trusted? 'Only, don't push us too far,' he recalled the famous guitarist mentioning. The imagination, quite ironically, would produce everything but the guitar itself, and somehow he would bargain with insects only to arrive at a compromise: that reality is reality no matter how vast the imagination, only that reality does not necessarily have to change people into rats and rhinoceroses. Shylock was a rat slowly becoming an insect. He would somehow convince him for the money. His options afforded no other alternative.

After all of these confusing thoughts, he finally left the house and tread upon the snow-covered lane towards the coffee shop. The snow crunched beneath his shoes. The temperature had warmed, although his fingers numbed in his jacket pockets. The main thrust of his presentation rested on a solemn promise to pay Shylock his full allowance on the first of every month until he was fully reimbursed for the guitar. Noble disliked mixing money with friendship. The strongest bonds of friendship often break over money-matters, and he had kept his financial woes apart from Shylock who seemed to be doing well for himself. He asked for a few dollars on occasion but never for an all-out loan of this magnitude. Noble kept business and friendship separate. He had always kept them separate, as the former was rooted in self-interest and complication and the latter in altruism and purity. From childhood their friendship survived as a result of this separation. It's either money or a Waspachick woman which wrecks a friendship. Losing him over a woman would be quite another matter, but never over a loan. He rehearsed the presentation but forgot it when entering the coffee house.

"No business today, Shy?"

"Hey, well if it isn't Noble McCloud. Still recovering from last night?"

"In more ways than one," said Noble with a chuckle.

"C'mon, your father didn't get that pissed off, did he?"

"Nah, not really. I had a good time. Did you hook up by the way?"

Shylock flexed his biceps and kissed them.

"I dunno how you do it."

"It takes balls and a tongue of silver."

"The two things I lack," said Noble as he sat on the wrought-iron chair which he had always found uncomfortable, especially now that his rear-end hurt. Shylock poured two cups of house blend and sat across from him.

"I'm so hungover. We had quite a night. Did you get back all right?"

"Yeah. It was a good five miles in the cold, but at least one of us got laid."

"It'll happen, Noble. Sometimes, the wait is worth it."

Noble could never understand why men who craved sex usually got it, and women who complained of these men gave themselves freely anyway. This was not a misperception. It happened in Waspachick on a nightly basis; a conundrum as frustrating and haunting as his own shyness.

"I can't wait around forever," said Noble. "Women won't fall from the sky, that I know. Things don't happen. One has to make them happen. I'm not sure if that's good or bad."

"Then make it happen. You're a...somewhat handsome guy, in a way, all you have to do is get 'em. They'll never come to you, especially in this town."

"Listen, Shylock, I have something very important to ask of you."

"Fire when ready."

"All my life," he began, "I've been searching and searching for something to do, a principle to build my life on, and this morning I found it. I was in my room listening to these mellow grooves, and the riff just came out and bit me, and then there was this really long jam, not in the usual sense of a regular jam, but chords so sentimental that I had to get out of bed and think about how nice it would be to be a part of that music, not only listening to it, but making it with my own two hands, and right then, I swear it, these ghosts visited me, right into my room, and they sat on the bed, one of them a famous guitarist, the same guitarist on the stereo, the other an auto mechanic..."

"An auto mechanic?" asked Shylock.

"Yes. I couldn't believe it myself, and they were talking to me, Shy, telling me how I've got to become a guitarist, and I knew they were right. I felt it in my soul, and the earth seemed to move and rotate and gyrate, until suddenly I was at the center of the universe, I was the man up on the stage, jamming the guitar, but I wasn't pretentious about it, I was a revered but humble guitarist in a suit and tie, and I was jamming at the Hall of Fame with all these old-time rockers, and the fans undulated with each pick of the high note. It was incredible. If ecstasy has a road, then the road to ecstasy has to be the guitar, and what's so weird is that these spirits came through the walls right at that moment, the moment I made my decision to become a guitarist. You know as well as I do that I've never had any ambitions before, and this comes as some sort of weird message sanctioned by the divine, and Shy, my days are now committed to it. It was incredible, it is incredible, and now my goal is clear, as clear as a blue sky."

"Wow, man. I'm happy for you. Visions and everything, huh? You've been smoking too much pot."

"I'm serious. It's not the weed, man. It's something sent from the heavens, I swear it. I've never before felt so inspired in my life. I can make it as a guitarist, I know I can. I have a highly specialized ear, and music filled my days and nights up to this point, you know that more than anybody..."

"Excellent, Noble, excellent. I'm happy for you, only I don't know why you're trying to convince me. Maybe it's because you haven't gotten laid in a while."

"Please. This has nothing to do with getting laid. It's something pure and holy, as if I were meant to play the guitar, as if the spirits of the underworld and the heavens above are pushing me."

"That's pretty deep, but don't blow it out of proportion. Spiritual visitations are all fine, but relax a little. You're supposed to enjoy it too. It doesn't happen overnight."

"But don't you see," said Noble with possessed eyes, "this is what I was meant to do, this is what I'm supposed to do."

"You said that about checkers, Noble. Don't you remember? You never stopped talking about checkers, and how your life would revolve around checkers, day and night. Don't think I forgot."

"Shy, that was twenty years ago. I was young. Have I felt anything like this in my adult life? Well, have I?"

"No, not really," said Shylock.

"Listen. I'm going to make it somehow. The road will be steep and hard and long, and I'll starve, and I'll be out on the street, but I would do it all for the guitar."

"Noble, you're not a young kid anymore," said Shylock very seriously, attempting to ground him earthwards. "I'm not saying you can never be a guitarist. If you want to play the guitar, that's no problem. Play all you want. But you're twenty-seven years old, the big two-seven, and you haven't a dime, you don't have a job, you live with your father, it's not normal. Life, Noble, let me put this delicately, is about change and growth and progress. College obviously didn't do much. You barely got your degree from college-what was it in?"

"Business."

"Yes, business, and then you did nothing. You sat at home, smoked all that pot, and locked yourself in your room. Once in a while I gave you the financial papers to read, but you never found interest in it, and I even tried to teach you some economics, and you did nothing. You do nothing. Is that existence? Is that normal, majoring in dollars only to defy our society by toking it up? That's not the way."

"Well, mister collegiate-man," said Noble sharply, and he never had the wits to argue effectively, "I was holed up in Waspachick while you and your snobby friends got these degrees and jobs. And I stayed in this town the entire time, while you went away, because your parents could afford it..."

"Hey, man, I had to work for it. College wasn't a free ride. I might have left this town, but don't you dare say that I ever milked my family for the tuition. I was on aid, and I slaved in the cafeteria for all those rich little snots who never earned a dime in their lives. I'm not a trust-fund baby, Noble. Don't insult me by even insinuating that I was."

The heat of Shylock's words washed him with regret, but in the same vein Shylock had no right insulting him in the first place, and so Noble continued with alacrity.

"Bullshit, Shy. You've always had it good, but don't forget that you grew up on the South side. A classic example of a man forgetting his roots. You've forgotten. All these shops and fancy cars are playing with your head.

Take a good look at them. It's hilarious, that's what it is, and sometimes I laugh to keep from crying, but I'm gonna get out of here, Shy, and my guitar is the ticket, and once I go, I'm never coming back."

"Grow up, will you? Just for once in your life just develop along that line from crawling to walking."

"What do you think I'm doing? I'm coming up with an idea, and you just, just, just waste it?"

"I'm not spitting on your idea, Noble, I'm not doing that. When does it end? These fantasies, when does it end? What's wrong with an honest job, some hard work, living like the rest of us? What's so wrong with leaving that haunted room with the same music playing over and over, making the women stay away from you? You walk down the avenue, and they part like the Red Sea, only they do it to stay away from you, not because your God's gift to creation…"

"That's enough, Shy. It's obvious you have no idea what I'm destined to achieve," he said with a resonance which oddly made him more legendary in his own mind, as though this argument were all part of a musician's experiential repertoire.

"And what does it mean, to achieve absolutely nothing?" retorted Shylock angrily. "Let's look at the facts, Noble. You're an out-of-work fantasizing flunky, a zero. And you wonder why you can't get any women, you wonder why I'm always one better than you, no, twenty times better?"

"Oh yeah, sure. Much better," as he stood from his chair to leave the coffee shop, the miasmic cloud of anger and frustration hovering over them. "Sure," he continued, "only because you're able to sleep with every single woman you come into contact with? Don't be surprised if you come down with some disease. Herpes, Syphilis, AIDS, it's all out there. Don't feel so proud. Even I can bang a slut or a whore."

"I guess you really are the real-life example of a mother-fucker."

The full impact of his words didn't register at first. He expected Shylock to say something more, to run with the insults like a flurry of city pigeons. But when he said nothing, when a guilt-ridden silence festered in the empty coffee house, Noble solved the riddle of this remark. He had help. Shylock's expression paled with disbelief and shock, as though he had witnessed a poltergeist, and then Noble bolted from the coffee house into the cold and headed South in the consternation which comes at the time of injury.

"C'mon Noble!" he heard a voice from behind, growing fainter as his pace quickened.

And then he heard stomping feet approaching. Shylock chased him, his green apron flying in the chill. Noble took one look and ran from him along the deserted lane. He ran, his blood flowing with an hormonal surge, his bronchioles exhuming years of stubborn tar, his muscle fibers devouring gallons of inositol, his mind picking and scraping the flaky cell walls of consciousness in the futile escape of a fugitive, and suddenly a guitar rang through his ears which made him forget his physical weariness and fatigue, and placed an image of him on the stage, the instrument's neck and body hugged by his hands, and the strings picked between his fingers like berries between a beak. He glided over the snow, his soaked shoes losing importance, his mother calling him from behind, and ahead of him the stage soaked in kaleidoscopic light, the electroplated bobbin pendular and goading him with temptation and hypnosis. Beyond the bobbin lay a vast ocean undulating from the shore's breach and upon the wet sand a woman sunned herself, her body carved and chiseled into contoured maple, the sunshine strumming her limitless legs, and her voice calling for him, as though 'Noble' were the only name she knew, and she giggled and shuddered with an ecstatic delight, her rapture reaching for the sky, overtaken by the sway of the ocean and its infinite roar.

The footsteps behind him became weightier, and suddenly what was perceived as a beast behind him, huffing and wheezing with a similar fatigue, grabbed his shoulders and pinned him to the wet snow. Shylock was now on top of him, his body holding him down like a paperweight.

"Calm down, Noble, just calm down," said Shylock.

"Are you crazy, are you fucking crazy," yelled Noble, his arms and legs flailing.

"I'm sorry, all right, I'm sorry…"

Noble lay underneath him and acquiesced to this interesting method of apology. His strength slackened, and he caught his breath. His clothes were soaked with slush. He brushed off his pants, pulled back his blonde hair, and returned with him to the coffee shop, Shylock's arm around his neck, as though they were just released from a Vietnamese prison camp.

"I'm sorry, all right, I'm sorry," said Shylock once they were seated across from each other. Light, whimsical snowflakes fell like ballerinas beyond the window panes.

"I didn't mean what I said," he continued, "and if you want to be a guitarist, man, if you feel it in your heart and soul, then why should I stop you? It's just that, well Noble, you don't think realistically, you know what I mean? These days aren't easy, especially for the musician. You have to be really good in order to make it out there, because the large majority doesn't make it. Only the few make it, those who have a natural gift for it. I don't mean to douse your fire, but I think you'd be better served if you got a job, even a part-time job, to get you out of the house. Isolation tends to create these hallucinations, these dreams of becoming a famous and important man, but Noble, you have to think practically. I'm only looking out for you. You can be a guitarist, but not full-time. Why don't you play in your spare time?"

Noble considered this for a moment, but instead clung to the original vision. A musician simply can't do it part of the time. He has to do it full-time, a dedication to art surpassing and superceding these half-measures.

"Shy, this is my life. This is my duty."

"Where did you get this idea- that you somehow have to sacrifice your whole life? No one in their right mind does that. You'll fail, and then you'll feel worse."

"Nothing in my life has meaning," said Noble, slumping over his coffee. "I want something more than this town."

He knew Shylock would attempt to dissuade him, but a man who knows what he wants will do anything to get it, especially the man whose grip on his own existence and purpose was slowly weakening.

"First, you need a guitar anyway. You can't afford that, and therefore, you will need a job," said Shylock triumphantly.

"That's where you come in," said Noble.

"Me? I can't get you a job here. The manager can't afford another worker."

"But you can get me a guitar."

"What do you mean by that, Noble?"

Noble smiled like the child who did something mischievous.

"No way. Absolutely not," said Shylock finally.

"What? I haven't even asked you for anything. Not yet anyway."

"Hey man, I'm strapped as it is. I can barely afford to live in Waspachick myself. And I'm working my ass off."

"C'mon, Shy. It'll only be a loan, and I'll pay you back every month."

"With the money you're father gives you? Do I look like a fool? Do you think money just grows on trees, and good ol' Shylock just picks the money like goddamned apples off the orchard? I'd love to help you out, man, but I'm strapped financially, man. I can't help you."

Noble sat in thought for several moments; he had to come up with something quickly.

"Shylock," and Noble rarely used his full first name save for the gravest of circumstances, "I know you're reluctant to lend me the money. But remember when I helped you out? When you wanted that BMX bike? Remember that?"

"That was ten years ago, no, twelve years ago."

"And who gave you the money to buy it?"

"These are different times. You're still living on the same allowance..."

"And who helped you out then, when the bike was the only thing in the world you ever wanted?"

"Let's get real. You only lent me a quarter of what the bike cost."

"That's not the point here. The point is that I believed in you. You wanted a bike, and I helped you out. Now it's your turn to help me out."

"Is that the best you can do? Go back twelve years? Not good enough, man."

"Listen, Shy, this is my dream," he said more forcefully. "This is my future, and you will make it possible for me to pursue the only thing I've ever found courage to pursue. I've never asked for money before, and it's not easy to ask for it now, but damn it, Shy, I really need this. I've always supported you. When you needed someone, I was always there. Now it's your turn. I need the money to buy a guitar, and believe me, I'll pay you back, you know I will. I promise I will."

"And what if you don't?"

"I promise. I'll give you my full allowance every month."

"Can't you save it all up and then buy the guitar?"

"I need the guitar as soon as possible. I don't have much time."

"Well, how much will it cost?"

And here Noble nabbed him. He preyed on his guilt, and the proposal tested the boundaries of their friendship, as though they both had passed a threshold, a simple childhood friendship cruising through the murky adult world, a line Noble never wanted to cross. But squeezing Shylock was the means to the necessary end: the vision of himself upon the stage, and he was prepared to blame Shylock should he refuse the request.

"Noble, I'm taking a huge risk here," said Shylock. "I mean you're putting me in a terrible position. Guitars are expensive, and what happens when you don't pay me back?"

"I promise. You will have my full allowance, I swear it."

By the looks of him, Shylock traveled in and out of deep thought, as though in a trance. He must have hated the entire concept, but Noble captured him like a frightened moth. There is nothing more enervating and irritating than a friend who promises to pay you back but never does, especially when such a loan places you under rigorous financial constraints so tight that the friend becomes the object of all your anger and wrath as you listen time and again to his empty promises and intricate plans for what must take place before he can repay you. 'Well, first, he owes me money, and she owes me some money, and once that money comes in, I can give the money to you right away, but right now I just don't have it, but I promise I'll get it to you, I know you need it,' et cetera. When Noble lent Shylock the money for the dirt bike, he had to press him every other week, and without this constant prodding Shylock would have never repaid him. Their friendship had been tested then, but their deals were covered by the fog of childhood, where time exists in generous supply, and the need for prompt payment loses its edge and immediacy. But now the circumstances were much different. Shylock had auto loan payments, credit card bills, the rent. Noble sensed his inner turmoil, and normally he would have relieved him of the burden, but chose not to, not for the pursuit of his fantasy.

"Shy, you shouldn't worry so much…"

"I'm just thinking about how I'll find the money. I'll probably have to put it on my credit card."

"Bless you. May God in heaven bless you."

"Shut up, Noble," he said bitterly, "You better pay me back, and if you want to be a guitarist, you better practice every day. Don't give it up. Stick with it. This is not a dream, it's reality. Get used to it. I'm investing in your future, and I want a return on my investment. Now let's go and get something to drink."

They sped towards the same bar beyond the Waspachick town line. The place was nearly empty, and Shylock downed several shots of tequila while buying Noble beers. For someone who was strapped for cash, Shylock seemed a rich man compared to the impoverished Noble who enjoyed the air of celebration despite his suspicions over Shylock's finances. A band was noticeably absent, but a disc jockey in a tiny booth near the stage played industrial music: a stream of harsh, mechanical distortions accompanied by an off-center beat which seemed hazy and myopic. 'Those who listen to it must wear black,' thought Noble, gulping his beers. The bartender was amazed at their stamina. Shylock, after gulping down shot after shot, paused for a moment in between his alcoholic decadence and toasted Noble who was somewhat embarrassed.

"This one goes to me deeerest budddy, Nowble McClowd, Nowble if you don't pay me back, I'll sware by golly I'll kill you. Cheers."

And he made toasts in this manner for the entire night, thoroughly irritating the bartender. The industrial tunes were bearable for a spell, but soon it piqued Noble's nerves, and since the bar was empty, no women in sight, since his lips were numbing and his head swam in a semi-toxic bitterness, he made a motion to leave.

"Nownsense, Nowble. You bess lisssen to this musak. It'll make you play bettah, and you bettah be good," before another shot. And then: "Lisssen Nowble, I'm so vewy sowwy about, you know, saying that about youwe mama. I didn't mean it. I'm sowwy. You know I didn't mean it. If I evewe say that again, you have the wight to clock me wight in the face, you hear me Nowble, Nowble McClowwd."

Noble simply patted him on the back and whispered into his ear: "Shy, you won't regret it. I'll play the best guitar you've ever heard, and you'll be reimbursed, man. Hey, I'm not about to lose a friend over money…"

And their conversation for the next hour dwelled upon their friendship and mutual admiration until the bartender couldn't stand the sight of these sentimental young adults slobbering over each other. They could have married instead. Noble sensed the bartender's impatience, as last call had been sounded some time ago. Shylock just wouldn't get the hint. Noble hoisted him from the barstool and carried him to the exit. Shylock staggered spewing out sentence fragments and meandering from one idea to the next connected by vague associations, some of them outlandish. In short, Shylock was plowed, and Noble was plowed to a lesser degree.

They stumbled into the parking lot and found that one of them had to drive home, and it wouldn't be Shylock who could hardly stand straight. Noble was the better candidate, only that Noble hadn't driven for several years. He didn't have a license. He didn't have a choice.

He placed Shylock in the passenger's seat. The trick was to follow the speed limit to perfection and stay on a straight path like a militia marching to meet the enemy. Not too fast, not to slow, keeping in between the double yellow lines and filling himself with a confidence while driving, a similar confidence that the sober driver took for granted. When he slid into the driver's seat, Noble heard snoring, the snoring of Shylock who had passed out next to him. Calm snowflakes hit the windshield which fogged at the turn of the ignition. He blasted the defogger, but even the best of defoggers never work at these crucial times, and so while driving towards Waspachick, he crouched his neck to the spot of windshield which didn't fog.

Each car at the intersections could have very easily been the police, but he kept driving, making sure to stay in the middle of the road with a fierce, intense precision. He was convinced all the cars on the road at this late hour were the police, waiting silently like swaying snakes before the bite. Another car soon followed him, and Noble was driving so slowly, or the speed limit, that the car tailgated him for a couple of miles until it turned onto a side street. This gave Noble a quick relief as he wiped the windshield with his fingers and continued for what seemed like the longest drive of his life. A green rectangular sign read: "Entering the Village of Waspachick," and he had more reason to celebrate. Soon he was coasting along the main strip, the snowflakes dissolving on the windshield. He turned off the empty strip and headed North. Slowly the houses grew more stately and the roads more treacherous, but it was only a short drive to an apartment building sitting on a hilly terrace which overlooked the strip. He parked the car. At first Shylock wouldn't budge, and soon Noble pat his cheeks until he moved unagreeably. He carried Shylock to the front door.

"Nowble, if you never pay me bahk, why I'll put a curse on you. You'll never get laid in this town again," he whispered.

In his small one bedroom, he removed his shoes and covered him with a blanket like a coroner. Noble then stood on the balcony and observed the quiet street below. Not a single car dashed by, and the silence unsettled a deep gratitude for his friend Shylock and the instrument he would soon purchase for him. He saw himself upon the stage for a short time, but then jumped upon his own, pressing despair. A woman would not be waiting for him at home. He wasn't exactly the most handsome creature, and his clothes reflected this fact, but ah he had a mind, but a mind which couldn't fathom living alone. Alone. The town bum who searches for crushed cigarettes along a sidewalk, the twitching mouse who loses its way through a living room, the single note which holds and cries itself to sleep. If he must remain alone for the rest of his days, he would accept it, but his own needs would never find a suitable resting place.

He then wandered the Waspachick strip in the darkness, the cold chilling his innards, his mind deluded by the vision of a woman, and his heart breaking piecemeal in the pursuit of this singular delusion. The streets were silent and empty, the liquor losing its blissful effect. Any place but home was better. Any place where he could touch the lips of a woman. Where were they all hiding? It was fucking incredible. Where did they all go? Certainly not to the night club, but if not there, then where?

He considered a personal advertisement in the local paper, but money was tight, and besides, only the weak placed ads like that, and Noble was somehow above this method. 'Guitar player seeks attractive single white female to serenade in the darkest pit of night. Please contact him immediately or he may go mad with prolonged loneliness and isolation. He may be found lying prone on the frozen pavement.'

He was the only person on the streets of Waspachick that night. And within these periods of emptiness and hallucination, as though he were the only soul left on the planet, he heard a voice calling for him from the far reaches of his memory, loose stones which wiggled free and disentangled his mother.

Chapter Four

Late in the afternoon, a younger Noble lay in bed, taking a short nap after school. A shaft of bright sunlight stretched across his body, and he slept in is perspiration uneasily, his subterranean dreams at the tip of waking. He felt several nudges on the arm, and in response he simply rolled to his side and resumed his slumber. But the nudges wouldn't leave him, and he awoke with his mother by his side, her gaze suggesting a deep frustration.

"Where's your report card?" she asked while nudging him.

"Lemme sleep," said Noble.

"Where is it? You're hiding it from me."

"It's in the knapsack."

She rummaged through it to find a yellow slip of paper buried beneath graded homework assignments. She fished it out and dangled it above him.

"So let's go down the list of subjects one by one, shall we?" she said, Noble knowing full well that his poor grades would only upset her. "Okay, English. C-. Mathematics. D. Spanish. D. Science. D-. Gym. Incomplete. Home economics. C. And band- my Noble with all that music you listen to, why am I not surprised? An incomplete in band. I've had about enough of this. Are you listening?" as she nudged him again. "I'm sick and tired of your grades, and don't think for a second that I'm signing this. I want a meeting with your advisor right away. Get up. Get up," with more nudges, and Noble stumbled to the bathroom and washed his face, while his mother called the school in search of Mrs. Cuthbert, his advisor for what seemed like centuries of his inability to learn, his grades in the same substrata since elementary school.

Add to this his total apathy towards school work. He audited these classes like a lost spirit drifting from room to room, staring at a branch which shook in the breeze, daydreaming about achieving a status of manhood unachievable, and thus settling for a status he could achieve by default: the daydreamer, looking at the girl at the desk by the door and asking her to the movies, his arm wrapped around her during a suspenseful scene.

His teachers never flunked him, nor did they pay much attention to him. He was no more than a clump of matter like the green tile of the classroom, traces of algebra on the blackboard, the heavy oak desk where the teacher sat, and his immaculate attendance record which provided them with the inkling that he was at least trying.

The subjects failed to interest him, but the concept and functioning of the school itself kept him occupied through the boredom of mandatory classes, as though these classes were thrown into the mix as events of secondary importance, the priority being the co-mingling of guys and girls during noisy study halls, lunch breaks, and after school programs, and perhaps the passing of notes beneath obscene desk-tops. He never gossiped much with his few friends but concerned himself with the gossip of others, as though he were some distant observer collecting information never to be used, only stored within vaults like looted relics. It's one thing to specialize in observation, but it's quite another thing to observe mindlessly without the acumen of judgment or the unpopular conscience of a referee. He was an observer by nature but did so to avoid interaction. He didn't remain within any one social circle. Instead he kept to himself while belonging, in his mind, to each one of them. He was liked by all, but known by none, with the exception of Shylock Winston who at that time played football.

Their childhood friendship survived the diaspora of higher learning. During football season Noble rarely saw Shylock, as he was clearing the hallways with his fellow teammates, a right tackle and a defensive end, and maybe once in a while offering a brief check-up to see how Noble faired without him. It was in this autumn of loneliness that his mother confronted him with this report card.

"Is there something going on at school I should know about?" she continued, "or better yet, what the hell is not going on? Well, that's obvious. It's obvious that you don't give a damn about your future, and I can't see my son, my only son, throwing his future away. It would be one thing to try and then fail, but not to try at all..."

He responded to his mother's questions by not answering them. He waited for the end of her soliloquy and then promised to do better. Her threats of visiting Mrs. Cuthbert were usually mollified by his promises to do better. She would always leave him with an ultimatum, only to be forgotten until the next report card.

It was during this time that Noble drifted apart from anyone with a pulse or fondness for him. His mother's exhortations became empty words after a while, only to be repeated in similar verse later. But there must have been a reason for this drift, as though he had developed normally but gradually broke from everyone around him. Perhaps his own pattern of reasoning dumped him into a growing isolation: the ability to break two into one plus one, but the inability to understand how one plus one could equal two. On a more tangible level, his father's beatings didn't help matters. McCoy McCloud would beat Noble every once in a while for leaving a dinner plate unwashed, but his wife almost every night for reasons unknown. Noble's dominant reaction was to wait in his room until the noises had stopped and then emerge in the darkness of the household, his mother weeping silently on the couch, her cheek with yet another welt served like a dinner special.

Most people would react fiercely to these occurrences, but Noble buried them like the nurse who treats the wounded soldier. He crushed ice into paper towels and applied it to the swelling. Most people would fight, but Noble was ambivalent, and as a result knew himself a coward. His soft walk in the school building never carried a big stick, and he noticed how the women in the hallways suspected him of this cowardice. Shyness can sometimes be perceived as arrogance, but the women saw little evidence of arrogance. After all, he dressed poorly, almost awkwardly, and the climate of social interaction was such that the women sensed his weaknesses more than the men, who attributed this shyness to a worthy innocence.

He won many acquaintances, especially from Shylock Winston, who, although the same age, knew him affectionately as a younger brother. But it was the idea of cowardice which accounted for this drift, and at certain points he contemplated military service, not as a brief thought, but as a long, drawn-out fantasy. The fantasy survived long and far enough to rest ultimately upon basic training: a maddening physical exertion where a boy is dismantled and rebuilt into a man who sleeps with his rifle, and as soon as he saw grueling work involved, he abandoned these intimations but not the awareness of his cowardice. It goaded him to the point of visiting a recruitment facility in Hackensack just to see what military service was all about. He believed the service could cure him, and it was this cowardice which the lieutenant noticed immediately.

"The Air Force is not for everyone," said the lieutenant in a monotonous hum. "It's six weeks of basic training, and I understand your fears about Boot Camp. We all had them, and soon each officer got over it. The military life, however, is not to be matched. Not only would you be serving your country- actually it's the most patriotic maneuver you can ever make- but Air Force will teach you more about yourself than what the rest of society teaches. We help our own. We give you the tools to conquer these deep fears inside you. Basic training is just the beginning of a career in the state-of-the-art technology for our war planes. If you've got fears, then we help you deal with them, there's no question about it. Our soldiers come in boys and go out men. That's the bottom line. Courage is our creed."

He left the cramped office with a promise to call the lieutenant later, but he never called. He was locked into indecision until the matter evaporated, and in the days to come while walking along the Waspachick strip, he asked himself: "What the hell was I thinking?" and abandoned any more of his so-called crazy ideas. And every once in a while he would return to this terrible awareness, as though cowardice was the worst insult to his manhood, and knowing it the fatal injury. And thus the coward takes the rashest route, but not until he has exhausted every avenue of assimilation with the men he sees at the morning train station, dressed in two-piece suits and reading the newspapers. The coward knows everyone around him has achieved a plateau of bravery, whether in deed or thought, which he cannot himself obtain, and thus to each man who possesses any assertiveness whatsoever he obsequiously bows and offers his servitude, his cowardice providing its own form of slavery, (the only escape a terrible yet blissful isolation away from men of achievement and command, which meant everyone), and if he were to estimate where these men of command and achievement gathered, he believed them to be found in the military. Noble thought it a crazy idea, but one which popped into his mind every so often.

His grades told an horrendous tale. Noble could not muster more than a D average, and in that autumn morning his mother called him on the bet that he would continue to do poorly in school. She arranged a meeting with Mrs. Cuthbert. Noble was surprised by the move but thought it nothing but a token gesture. After it was over, they would all forget the meeting and resume the dalliance of their lives. Or so he thought.

They sat in Mrs. Cuthbert's office on a rainy afternoon. They were silent before she darted in with a manila folder under her arm, hurriedness sitting on her thin smile.

"Hi, I'm sorry, if I'm a little late, Mrs. McClellon."

"But we're the McCloud's," said his mother pointedly.

"The McCloud's?"

"Yes, we have an appointment for this afternoon."

"Oh, yes, and you are here, I see, of course, and your son is in the eleventh grade?"

"Tenth grade."

"Oh, okay, let me look in my desk, here, and maybe I will find...yes, here we are, Noble McCloud, yes, tenth grade. What can I do for you?"

"I'm concerned about Noble's grades."

"I see," as she studied the file.

Noble had seen Mrs. Cuthbert once before, at the beginning of his ninth grade year. He was invited to a get-together of her advisees, but he never went, and so this Mrs. Cuthbert, he realized, knew nothing about him. He was a stranger who happened to be in her group of advisees. Noble knew he would get away with a slap on the wrist, nothing more. They were aliens familiarizing themselves with each other.

"Well, Mrs. McCloud, these files don't paint a very good picture. His test scores are below average, and his grades, well, they speak for themselves, but his attendance record is strong, and he has no history of any disciplinary action. He may not graduate tenth grade with his grades so low. He may have to repeat, but that mandate comes through the academic dean. I can only recommend..."

"Wait a second," said Noble's mother, "my son is no flunky. He's been working really hard, and we cannot have him repeat the tenth grade."

"I understand that, Mrs. McCloud, but that's not my decision to make."

"Well, I want to see someone in charge. What about the principal?"

"I understand your concern, but the principal doesn't address individual parents' concerns. You would have to petition the academic dean who would then decide if a meeting with the principal is warranted."

"It's obvious. No one in this school knows a damn thing about my son."

"Please, Mrs. McCloud. Let's try to discuss this constructively. He may not have to repeat if he does well in our summer session."

The two words threw Noble into shock. He hated the idea, as any student would. He was about to say something, but his mind grew so heated with the heinous thought that the conduit between the brain and the vocal chords short-fused. His mother, however, took a more reasonable stance. Summer school didn't sound too terrible. Anything to keep Noble busy.

"I'm open to that," said his mother. "Maybe it'll be the best thing for him."

"My only concern," said Mrs. Cuthbert, "is that the academic dean will refuse this request, because even a summer session wouldn't repair this damage. She may think he needs to repeat."

"No, my son won't repeat. He's going to summer school."

"Mrs. McCloud, I don't understand why you have such an aversion to your son's repeating of the tenth grade."

"Because my son will graduate with his peers like every normal student ever to pass through this stuck-up high school. It only works for the rich, doesn't it? The donation to the alumni fund, isn't that what it's all about?"

"Mrs. McCloud, I understand you're upset, but please, your objection to his repeating the tenth grade is noted, and we will see about summer school, but what we really need to see is some dramatic improvement on Noble's part, and we can't really go further unless and until Noble improves. There are a number of after school tutorial programs, but these programs do cost a little more…"

"Money? You actually want more money from us? Unbelievable!"

"Mom, I think you're overreacting…" piped Noble.

"Quiet," she snapped.

"Mrs. McCloud, I understand. Your son is not doing well, and you would like him to do better. That's obvious, and we are here to help him, but your son needs to be more committed to his school work. I will note in the file that he would like to attend summer school, but the process is there for a purpose…"

"Bureaucracy," she said.

"Call it what you like, but really, the effort needs to come from your son."

The meeting ended there, and they wandered from the collegiate school building west towards the center of town. The sunshine split through thick clouds. The rain had cleared, and all through the town Noble heard agreeable waters trickling through aluminum funnels, dripping from leaves, gushing between the sidewalk and the road, spitting from tires, and he knew his mother was angry, but he kept quiet.

"Noble, do you want to be left back?" she asked.

"Well, if it's for the best, then I guess…"

"No son of mine will be left back. You're every bit as good as those other kids. You're intelligent, smart, and talented. I know what they do in that school, because I went through the same thing. You have potential just like every other kid. We may not have the money to buy our way through the school, but I bet we'll get by. Firmness, a little toughness, that's all it takes. You're not lazy. I want to see improvement, hear me, and then you'll go to a college and become a doctor. That's my plan for you."

"Mom, I think..."

"That's the problem. Don't think. You've had plenty of time to think. Do!"

As the sun came out, the Waspachick strip thrived with pedestrians. Old and young jammed the sidewalks from some unknown location, and Noble hid his embarrassment while seeing the other women from the high school wander by. He seemed like the only young man walking with his mother. His feet moved faster, but his mother kept a slow pace. Ah, the women of Waspachick, women he would never communicate with, but women all the same. All he needed, he thought suddenly, was one of these Waspachick women from the North end, their tender legs inherited from good stock, flowing and intermingling with his own blood. The product: a creature far superior than his own kind, a creature perhaps who wouldn't understand what it means to be a coward in a town of clean-cut athletes, a product who would interact rather than shy away from conflict. Yet Noble viewed himself through the eyes of these women, and he envisioned a young man who had little conception of what he'd do if he were privileged enough to capture one.

And the Waspachick woman must be captured. There was little alternative. The conscience was a maudlin sign of weakness, gentleness a defect of character. With his mother by his side, telling him to slow down, he envisioned himself even more foolish; a young man who couldn't take a leak without his mother holding him, a little boy so lost and indecisive that choosing a place to eat puzzled him. And Noble encountered that cloudy area beyond desperation, his mother trailing behind him, his heart on its knees and begging, and perhaps for one moment he would finally find that high school woman from the elite sect who would break the all-too ridiculous boundaries erected by self-important gentility, a woman who cared enough about herself to see the benefits of a young man like Noble McCloud, his joints with the wounds of hormones on the verge of imbalance, his chest pounding, and all the while his inability to mutter a single word, only watching these women pass. Some of them plain, most of them proper. He was unable to cross boundaries, and they were unable to fathom a connection with a self-absorbed and dysfunctional student.

"Noble, will you slow down," she cried from the rear.

But he wouldn't slow down. His breath grew hot. His pace quickened, the trot into a canter, the canter into a gallop. He passed the town park where groups of kids assembled on the stone steps, mocking him, defaming him, until he concluded the entire town derided him in concert, his body on parade through the center of town, the shop-keepers hired thugs, brandishing crow bars, maces, and horse-whips. He sprints down the strip.

"Where the hell are you going? Slow down," cried his mother.

The crowd closes in on him, his body paralyzed and prepared to accept blows, and then he felt a hand on his shoulder. He was about to yell into the sky, a primordial scream to the dark creator who illuminated the strip with a phony light, and then he returned to the same young Noble McCloud, his forehead wet, his heartbeat slowing, his sense of order restored, his breath resuming its normal pattern, his mother worried.

"Noble, where are you going? Are you all right?"

"I'm fine," he said after a long pause.

"Are you sure? What got into you?"

"The sunshine took me by surprise, I guess."

"But it's not that sunny out."

"Yes, I guess there are too many people out today."

"C'mon, let's go home," she said tenderly.

And home was the last place he wanted to go. He wanted to be alone, as he felt more comfortable there, away from his mother, left to his own devices along the turgid strip, resuming his role as the quiet observer. And then his mother said knowingly:

"Noble, I do have some errands to run. Why don't we meet at dinner time? You've had your share for today. Why not go to the library? Really, you should be studying hard with your grades and all," her sweet voice like a lullaby, "and, Noble, I want you to do better in math especially," as she brushed his blonde hair back, "because one day you will be a great man. You will be an important man, a doctor most likely, and I'm putting enough money together so that when you graduate from high school, you will go right into medicine, to medical school, and you'll have patients to care for. See, Noble, whether or not you know it, your mother has faith in you. I know school is hard. For us McClouds it has always been hard. We've never had it easy, and maybe that's a blessing in itself, otherwise we wouldn't know what to do with ourselves. But you must succeed Noble, you must. High School isn't easy, especially with all these teachers on the take, especially with kids wearing all those nice clothes, but you'll make it, I know you will, and once you do, you'll have tons of friends, and we'll leave the South side and house ourselves on the North side for a change…"

They parted ways. Her soliloquy surpassed his expectations, and he spent the rest of the afternoon on the strip, saying hello to several male acquaintances, but ignoring the females. They were too dangerous to touch, much too dangerous.

Chapter Five

On the night that Shylock and Noble drank, the same night that Noble, by himself, wandered the strip of Waspachick in the dark, evading the silent sentry of police cars by walking quickly in some direction, perhaps weaving from the edge of the sidewalk to the shop fronts, with images of his mother erased by the stale coldness which usually haunts the traveler while drunk, as though he were treading a walk of shame, he retreated South, away from the ghostly emptiness of the strip.

The town always shut down at the precise moment Noble wished it open. He wished it stirred with pub-crawling women. But Waspachick at night offered no such luxury. The walk of shame brought him to the household.

He expected his father asleep, but a light showed from the front-door windows. His father was a fierce, loyal conservationist of electricity, and immediately Noble sensed trouble. He would have crawled through his window, but he kept it locked. In the shape he was in, he dreaded seeing his father, a drunkenness which required sleep but provided instead an intense throbbing at the temples. He could tiptoe, but the door squeaked. The door always squeaked, and the noise would wake the entire street. He mustered what little courage he had, since the liquor lent him more than usual, and he entered the house nonchalantly, routinely, as though he had just gone out for milk. McCoy McCloud was slumped on the couch, a bottle of whiskey half-empty and a glass half-full on the side table. Noble shuffled as quickly as he could to his room, but he was caught by a slow voice.

"Noble, come here boy, I want to tell you something," through the slurring of intoxication. The deep baritone sounded fatherly. He had rarely heard this voice before.

Noble approached him cautiously, wanting to share his whiskey, but his father never shared much with him, especially his private stock. He did recall a time when he shared a few extra dollars aside from his allowance, but this was years ago, and in the shadowy light he stood over the slumped figure. His father never waited up for him before.

"Twenty-nine years. Twenty-nine years," mumbled McCoy McCloud.

Noble was fearful of extracting any information. His father would have barked, so he let him sit there, words dribbling from a dyke, his flesh rotting.

"The shaft. That's what they call it, and the shaft hit me hard today...Twenty-eight years, and they cut you like a whimp from the football team, whimps, all of them cowards and brats, it's damn unpatriotic. I'm the best fucking collector in this state, and then they say: 'you don't collect enough, hit the fucking road.' No one, and I mean no one presses these delinquents more than me. There's no one in this state who does the job better..."

Noble was surprised. Over the slow dribble of words, almost a mumble, he understood that things were about to change, but he couldn't penetrate his father's rationale. It was leading up to something, but he couldn't determine what it was. His father actually spoke like a human being, exposing his weaknesses, and Noble, who was still quite drunk, thought of twisting the knife within his open wounds. He had never done so before, and naturally he was frightened of doing so. He wasn't at all curious how his father had lost the job. He heard pain in his voice and wanted it to continue, exacting blow for blow. But this revenge existed within the mind, where all of his aggressions were stored. The movement from thought to action to deed never extended beyond his mind. And his father continued, most likely relieved to be heard.

"...nothing but a bunch of whimps. Back when I headed the place I hired the best bug-up-your-ass men in the state, and now they want soft and nice and correct. Well, McCoy McCloud ain't done yet. That whole place is going to hell anyway. Without me they don't know what it takes to survive. Bunch of sissies. No, I'm not done yet..."

Noble did his best to contain himself. He could have cried the urge to laugh was so great, but he knew his father could react quickly and impose some sort of penalty, physical or financial. He kept calm. He again buried this dubious but delicious pleasure. It was wrong to laugh in his time of greatest need, but a hideous chuckle echoed from ear to ear. He stood in front of McCoy McCloud like a rock, not certain how to react.

"Now, I'm out of work, and that means cutting back, and you're included in these cut-backs. You waste the electricity, the water, the food. Maybe you'll learn how to be a man like your old man who started out with the shirt on his back and a dollar bill in his pocket. I started with nothing..."

'And you still have nothing,' thought Noble.

"…and I had that whore of a wife, and now it's you. I want you out of the house in forty-eight hours…"

"Dad, don't you think you're…"

"Damn it, I want you out," he seethed, anger resuscitating him. "Find a job like every decent law-abiding citizen. Save your money, shack up with a woman, and survive damn it. I've been babying you for too long, so long that you'll probably turn out a pinko-Commie sissy. And don't expect a dime from me. Go on, get lost."

Noble shut the door and turned on the stereo. He put on something mellow and smooth, and he clawed under his mattress for the cellophane bag. He toked on a joint until his head grew light, the guitar chanting in a wistful undulation. Things were indeed changing for Noble, but finally he had been given the order to leave, a permission slip, and this newfound liberation blunted the excitement of his father's failure. He reflected in that time, which elapsed very slowly, that leaving the home had been inevitable, that it was better to leave than to be beaten whenever orders weren't followed. He wouldn't have to live in fear any longer, wondering if his father were asleep or awake, home or out drinking at the fabled bar on the North side. And no longer would he have to accept his threats.

Perhaps this is exactly what he needed, to be out of the house, alive and free, with his music, his laundry, and his thin coat. Yet a fear encroached upon his reflections. As we already know, Noble had but seven or eight dollars, and in forty-eight hours he would be without a place to live. He needed money for a hotel, but there were no hotels in Waspachick or its surrounding townships. And this fear multiplied with each chord. His fragile skull was soon to be cracked by dirty looks, snobbery, and the aggression of the outside world. But this was far better than living with his father. A sense of doom, however, came with the next association: getting a job.

Money. He needed money quickly, but he wasn't about to throw away his fantasy of becoming a guitarist. This was the goal: to become a guitarist, and Shylock's vow had assured this, but getting a job meant forsaking music. His all or none approach had a certain merit. It was brave. He had reasons for avoiding a job. He observed its effects on people, especially in Waspachick. It blocked empathy, compassion, and conscience in favor of an insect pathology. But he couldn't handle a job even if he wanted one. He attributed this to hypersensitivity, an opposing pathology. Any sensitivity at all ruins the man. He had expected the beatings from his father, but the cruelty of others he could not bear, as though he sought acceptance unconditionally from the strangers wandering the strip. Such is the nature of the terribly abused, both men and women alike. They look for acceptance in the eyes of those who cannot possibly accept them. A job was simply out of the question. It would threaten his guitar-playing and his own thin shell. He could go on welfare, but with the latest round of reforms the paychecks would be small and a job certain. But then there was Shylock Winston, and suddenly all seemed calm.

Noble would simply live with Shylock for a while, maybe a couple of months until his guitar playing proved lucrative, and until then he would practice daily, and he would leave Shylock's place when he came home in the evenings, just to give him breathing room. He had forty-eight hours. It was Shylock's place or a homeless shelter; Shylock, as we have mentioned, had an one-bedroom on the West side of Waspachick, next to a real estate agency, as the town was full of them. Even one person cramped the apartment, but they could manage. They would have to manage, and after learning the guitar he could play the Manhattan night clubs and earn enough for his own place, and a record executive sitting in the crowd of dancing maidens would sign him to a modest record deal, providing a sizable advance, and he would move through the music world like an express train, if only Shylock would agree to it. In return Shylock would receive all the benefits of Noble's success. Yes, the plan had to work, and Noble was prepared to go the distance. He vowed to himself and the Gods above that he would never stop, and gainful employment only obstructed his success. He would make it like every big name in the business.

Despite his disbelief in natural talents, he estimated two months before playing the night club circuit. He would start small, at the bar from last night, and then he would branch to the city beyond the tranquil Hudson, to a tired night club where the beer ran free and the women danced until sunrise. And then to the stage, a modest but popular auditorium, and finally to a stadium where thousands jived below a raised platform. He had one stadium in mind, but as the guitar jam on the stereo quickened, he knew this vision outlandish, even for his own overactive imagination. The main goal was the record deal. He needed this to pay the bills; the essentials of food and drink and lodgings. But first he had to find the right words to break Shylock.

He pulled from memory all the things he had done for him. Unfortunately Noble could only recall giving him half a sandwich in middle school and the BMX bike. Sad but true, but what Noble would promise him was unbelievable. Why, he would hand him wealth, women, wine, and of course, a song. Why, he'd dedicate an entire album to him. Yes, this was the plan, and the universe bent to his dreams, dreams which need to be acted upon. And if one does not act, then the negation degrades the man to the common insect. Dreams and their fulfillment were the only principles he knew of, so long as the dream had some sort of positive social benefit.

There are those dreams which exclude the benefit of others, and Noble sensed that these negative dreams never come true. But dreams in which others may benefit, even to a fractional degree, must have the sanction of higher powers operating in the universe. Human beings, individual or collectivized, were not as powerful as these universal elements which bend towards the positive dream. Noble saw the woman in the front row, her golden locks afire, and her body shaking in celebration, her ecstasy easing the pains of everyday existence. And once the dream is delivered, then he could rest.

The night soon ended, and he lay in an embryonic position on his small bed, half asleep, half awake. He was awoken at daybreak by McCoy McCloud who ordered him to take out the trash and sweep the hallway from bedroom to bedroom. Noble listened patiently and fought the urge to say 'Do it yourself,' but a bit of hope surfaced when stodgy, stocky McCoy McCloud failed to remind him of his eviction. Maybe his father had forgotten. They were both very drunk.

Noble closed his door slowly and paced his room like a worrisome school boy awaiting punishment. But sure enough, McCoy McCloud reminded Noble, first to get up from his "lazy ass" and clean the place, and second to vacate the house within forty-eight hours. McCoy's voice resonated upon this order, and Noble got packing. He stopped midway, though. He needed clean clothes.

He did his laundry at the local Laundromat. He felt silly carrying his entire wardrobe in a heavy sack along the busy strip. The Laundromat itself was too unsightly to be a part of the strip. Instead it was tucked away on a side street towards the eastern end of town. Carrying the sack in the biting cold was a nuisance, but he endured. He forced both loads into one machine. He hadn't the money for detergent.

Many of the townsfolk avoided the Laundromat. It was an eyesore in an otherwise pristine town. In fact, the town council at one time revoked the owner's zoning license, but the owner slapped the town with a lawsuit and was allowed to open the business. Noble seemed like the only person in Waspachick who benefited from the litigation. He sat on the metal bench, the washer spinning. Rarely did anyone enter the place, but once in a while people from the South side used the machines. Strangely enough he looked down upon these wayward stragglers just as he looked down upon himself.

But the Laundromat was unpeopled at this early hour, an electric hum of industrial washers and dryers forming its own harmonies. He strategized for a bit, wondering how in the world Shylock would take him in and pay for a guitar and amplifier in the same breath. His boredom deepened as the washer commenced its final cycle, the imbalance of the double load banging and thumping. The place was at least warmed by these machines.

He transferred clothes to the dryer, and then it happened. The universe bent towards him. A woman entered with a light load of clothes. It was she. Her features were unmistakably North end. He wasn't dreaming. The fair and lofty Alexandra Van Deusen placed her dainty load on one of the tables. Blue jeans hugged her curves. His eyes were fixed upon her with a pleasant shock bordering on a manic and mystical belief that this coincidence was a sign from the heavens, the universe bending, the stars hearing and thus responding to his wishes. He had heard of socializing in Laundromats, but this was all-too ridiculous. What would a woman of this caliber be doing in a joint shunned by the entire town? He really didn't care. He could have fainted, but he acted as though nothing happened.

He piled the wet laundry into the dryer. He wished he had a book or newspaper to hide his preoccupation, but he simply sat on the uncomfortable bench while the fair Alexandra worked quickly towards washing and then vanishing. Being caught in the Laundromat would be social suicide. She must have known this, because her dumping of clothes into the washer proved frantic.

He looked at her from a short distance. Her beauty frightened him. He sat like a rock. She paid him no attention, and Noble reciprocated; a quiet retaliation. But the silence proved too much. He searched for an opening line, all of them hackneyed clichés. Ah, the shyness! That horrendous rejection without even trying, the self-defeat. A curse, he thought. The universe no longer bent towards him but cursed him once again. He was the thirsty man who cupped the water only to let it slip through his fingers. She dumped her clothes and left. Noble was partially thankful. It gave him time to devise an opening line: 'Would you have any fabric softener by any chance?' Yes, those flimsy, waxy tissues which did nothing for one's laundry. He would ask her for it.

Inevitably she would return. And in that space of time he imagined her smiling and flirting with him. They dine at the pasta and steak house near the railway station, drink a jug of wine, and they kiss passionately- while then men along the Strip during mating season gawk in jealousy. Noble is piqued by their overtures, and he gets into a fight, the pure measure of manhood, and the fair Alexandra comes between them. She's a one-man woman, and Noble is her choice. Although she insists fighting solves nothing, she finds Noble all the more attractive for defending her against the muscular hunk who tries to steal her away, and again they kiss and drink another jug of wine.

During this reverie Alexandra Van Deusen returned, alone and hurried. Noble had been monitoring her machine, and it was on the last spin cycle. She didn't look at him at all. She waited at the machine, most probably eyeing the glow of the indicator light, her back turned, and what a back it was, as shapely as a backside could be. To think she was without a boyfriend was a lapse of all mental faculties. Yet she was alone, and Noble had to say something, anything.

"Excuse me," said Noble finally, his heart racing, "would you by chance have any fabric softener?"

"No," she replied," but I think you're laundry's done."

"Wow! Didn't notice that, but I've seen you some place before. Where was it, I can't really say…"

"I don't think so."

"That's where it was. I saw you at the bar outside Waspachick. I remember you."

"I go there quite a bit, as a matter of fact."

"So do I. Great place, huh?"

"Yeah."

"I saw a great band there the other night."

"Listen, I don't mean to cut you off or anything, but I'm in a real hurry."

"Of course. I didn't mean to hold you up," said Noble quietly.

The deepest blow came when he noticed the indicator light was still on. He retreated to the dryer where he unloaded his wardrobe and stuffed it hastily in his cotton sack. He left the Laundromat thereafter, the universe shrinking him with every slab of sidewalk. The universe had offered meaningful signs, but then betrayed him. He had no one to blame but the cloudy sky, its comatose silence the only possible object of his anger. The man who blames himself blames more the universe which created him, the skies torpid and bleak. He should have known better than to approach a beautiful woman. Any other man would have easily recovered.

He returned to the house, his father gone luckily. He shut himself in his room. He commiserated with dark guitar jams and more herb. He was about out. This isolation sparked thoughts of grandeur once again, standing upon the stage, women everywhere but nowhere.

Later that afternoon Noble composed his presentation for Shylock on his way to the coffee shop. He at least did his laundry. He wore a clean shirt and trousers and walked in the cold towards the main avenue. Sure enough, Shylock was in the coffee shop sweeping, and he approached him carefully, forgetting the intricate proposal and its hypothetical delivery.

"Why, isn't it our rock n' roll star," called Shylock.

"Not too busy, eh?" said Noble.

"Man, this shop is never busy when you come around. Maybe it's a curse."

"I wouldn't be surprised."

"C'mon, I'm buying you the damn guitar, remember?"

"Yeah, Shy. I appreciate all your efforts."

"All I know is that you better pay me back, and soon. I've got a week's salary invested in you. We'll go to the music shop tonight, and you better practice every day and night."

They sat in their usual places overlooking the Strip. No more than a handful of people meandered the windswept Waspachick streets.

"Let's go tonight, the House of Music by the highway," said Shylock, "and what's the matter? You seem so down all the time. Why don't you smile? You're not as hung-over as I am."

"Shy, you're my friend, right?"

"That depends," said Shylock suspiciously.

"Why don't women like me, Shy? You know, I hear all those songs about taking the guy with the lonely eyes, and yet, they turn away. I can't understand it. Is it something about me they don't like? I mean, maybe I am cursed like you said."

"Aww, quit it. I'm sick of hearing about your women problems."

"No, I'm being serious. I tried to pick up a woman in the Laundromat, and she blew me off. It's a horrible feeling."

"So? You get up from that self-pity, and you try again like every adult in the human race, but there's something else that's bothering you, isn't there?"

"What makes you think so?"

"Don't shit me, Noble. There's something wrong when you ask a friend if he's really your friend, and besides, you're not that hung-over. C'mon, out with it."

He paused for a moment and gulped at his coffee.

"Shylock, I'm in trouble," said Noble.

"What kind of trouble?"

"Well, it's hard to say. Where do I begin?"

"No, Noble, not again."

"Shy, I'm in big trouble. After we went out last night, my father, well, basically, he, well, he sort of...kicked me out."

"He what?!"

"He kicked me out. I've got forty-eight hours to find a place, and the clock's ticking, and I don't know what to do."

"Oh Noble," said Shylock while patting his shoulder, "you'll figure something out. You always do. Time to get real. Time to get a job."

"Actually, I was thinking about another way..."

"...I mean, you and your father have always had a rough relationship from the get-go, and maybe it's better that he kicked you out. Now you're able to see the reality, approach things more realistically, and now at least you don't have to worry about your father breathing down your neck all the time..."

"I was thinking about one particular way..."

"...and besides, now you can move into the world like the rest of us, get a job somewhere in Waspachick. There are tons of jobs listed in the classifieds, and pretty soon you'll be able to afford an apartment. Believe me, things are much better this way, Noble, better for you, better for me..."

"This particular idea which has been in my mind ever since he kicked me out..."

"...better for everyone concerned. I mean now you'll be an adult about things, establish yourself, get a job, a paycheck, maybe even a good dental plan, you know, put that degree to work, and soon, you'll be able to put down a down-payment for a car, or even take the bus to work..."

"...and I think this idea has some merit, and it involves..."

"...there are a lot of hot women on the bus, Noble, and if you can't take the bus, you can walk. Hell, I walk to work everyday, and I find the morning air invigorating, and I wake up with a cup of house blend and a newspaper. Yes, the newspaper is so terribly important..."

"...some real delicate negotiations with my friends in the area, and since I'll be moving out soon, I know that my friends..."

"...and it's a good and vital source of information..."

"...will help me, and I know I could count on you, Shylock."

"Ah, bullshit, Noble! Bullshit! Don't you dare ask me. The answer is absolutely not, no, zip, zilch, absolutely, positively no. Do you hear me? No, Noble McCloud, no. I have to draw the line somewhere."

"But I haven't even asked you anything. Yet."

"The answer is no," said Shylock angrily.

"If you would just hear me out. Let me just present to you a plan that will work for the both of us..."

"Whaddaya mean 'us?' It's not 'us,' Noble, it's 'you,' it's 'you,' not 'us,' not 'we,' not 'ours,' it's all 'you,' and only 'you.' Get that through your thick skull, okay? You get a job, and you become a part of what everyday society forces you to become."

"Shy, I'll pay you. I'll pay you so much money."

"Oh yeah? Fine, where's the money?"

"I have it all planned out, see, once I get the advance money..."

"Wait a minute," chuckled Shylock, "wait a second. Advance money? You mean from, like, a record contract?"

"Exactly. A record deal when I land one, and every cent will go to you, I promise."

"This is unbelievable!" as Shylock pounded the table, "this is unbelievable. You mean that you will pay me once you get a record deal?"

"Exactly, and once I get it, you will be the beneficiary. I will pay you right when I get the check."

"Oh yeah? You mean to tell me that you, first off," as he counted his fingers, "don't even know how to play the guitar, and second, you don't even have a guitar to begin with, and third, you'll get some sort of record deal without any clue how to play the guitar, and without even owning a guitar? Tell me, Noble, have I lost my mind, or have you completely gone bezerk? I mean, tell me, am I the foolish one here? And of course, you'll blame it on me, oh yes, I'm not the victim, you are..."

"It's all so perfect, just let me tell you what my plans are before making a decision. First, I'll earn lots of money from the deal, and I'm optimistic that someone will discover me. I have faith. I'm the perfect candidate. Second, I've been seeing the signs everywhere. Really, the forces are with me on this one."

"Noble, you cannot stay at my place," said Shylock, articulating every word.

Noble finished what remained of his coffee. Shylock's words, despite their lucidity, drifted over his head.

"It'd just be for a few weeks," he tried, "and once I learn how to play, I'll go out on the club circuit, and all that money will go for the rent."

"See, Noble. Now you're the victim, and I'm the one victimizing you. You pull this shit on me every time I see you. When does it end? Why can't you get a job? What's so wrong with having a good, honest job? So what if the boss yells at you? So what if you got fired from your first job?"

"I can't get a job. It would compromise my artistic values, and besides, I couldn't handle it."

"Artistic values? You don't even have the fucking guitar yet! The answer is 'no,' Noble, and you should seriously think about a job."

And after a prolonged silence, Shylock asked:

"What happens next?"

"I guess I go to the homeless shelter."

"Okay. You've got to do what you have to do, don't you?"

"Yes. Well, first I'll have to, well, find some sort of telephone number to the shelter, and I suppose I'll have to throw away the things that I don't need, like my record collection, and my CD's, and maybe my stereo, yes, I'll have to throw that away..."

"Damn you, Noble. You are not the victim here. I am. Every time I wipe your nose clean when you get in trouble."

"Shylock, it would only be for a few weeks."

"I need a definite deadline here. I mean who do you think I am? What do you think this is?"

"Please, Shy, don't get upset over this. Just take me in until I can get a few gigs, and once the advance comes, you'll be paid for every day I spend at your place."

"My place is tiny. How would we both fit? It'll be terrible, and what about the food? Who's gonna do the grocery shopping? Noble, can't you get a job? I mean these are the realities. You need to support yourself. Nothing in this world comes for free. It will take you months before you learn the guitar. Months, and I can't keep you for months, only a few days until you get a job and settle on your own. Y'know I do have a life apart from you."

"If you do this for me, I'll be forever in your debt."

They both fell silent again. Noble stared out the window. He understood the gravity of the request, but thought it part of the necessary progression of the guitarist. He also needed reconfirmation of Shylock's promise to buy him the guitar. But for some reason he didn't feel any guilt for imposing. Shylock was always there for him, and this he took for granted. His confidence in his guitar-playing abilities, however, soared. He was certain thinks would work out, that a record deal floated on the horizon. Getting kicked out of the house, being blown off by Alexandra Van Deusen, encountering Shylock's resistance and skepticism were all subtle signs of his ability and potential. If one were to make a case study of all the great guitarists of his time, Noble would somehow fit into the profile, or at least that's what he tried to show Shylock who sat in utter disbelief.

"I mean who cares if I'm out on the street," said Noble, "I mean why would it affect you of all people. You don't care, right, if your best friend is homeless."

"That's not the point."

"Oh, really? Then what is the point? That I have a shot at something, and all I need is a place to stay to keep me afloat? That's okay, because I don't need any help from you or anybody."

"Oh, yes, like I'm problem, I'm the one who gets in the way of your dreams, like I'm the one who caused the world of shit you find yourself in. See, you turn the tables to make me look like the bad guy."

"That's how I see it. You are the one who could help me out, and to think all those times I helped you out. No gratitude at all."

Shylock banged the counter in disgust, and the two fell frigidly silent.

"All right, Noble, all right," said Shylock finally, "you can stay at my place for a little while."

"And the guitar? You'll buy me the guitar?"

"You're really testing our friendship. It's not a one-way street."

"I promise, Shy, I'll pay you back."

"Yes, Noble, in your heart you'd pay me back."

A smile surfaced on Noble's lips. He patted Shylock's hand as though giving comfort to a bereaved relative.

"You won't be sorry," he said.

"I can't believe I'm doing this. Noble, by the way, are you retarded? I mean are you playing with a full deck? Are all you're marbles accounted for? Has a horse left the corral? Or maybe it's me, I'm the retarded one, for letting an idiot like yourself, and you are an idiot, wait, no, I'm the idiot..."

And Shylock rambled in this manner for quite some time. Noble, on the other hand simply looked out the window. He was relieved in all senses of the word. He could keep his record collection, his tapes, his CD's, and his stereo, and soon all of this would be complemented by a guitar and an amplifier. Soon he would be practicing late at night, then the night club, the small auditorium, the arena, and the stadium. It was all planned and preordained.

They headed East on the dark, slushy strip. The sun went down as early as expected. They passed the retail shops and the real estate agencies. They passed the East Waspachick bar where they had gone the night before. The larger residences shrunk into smaller properties. More cars populated the avenue. Shylock played music Noble abhorred, but he would have to endure his terrible tastes and domestic idiosyncrasies. It was his apartment, and he was the master of his domain. Noble had to expect this. At least he realized it. Once again he had avoided employment, his psychic drift nearly complete, his days on the planet filled with purpose. And there was no turning back, he thought. Despite his reliance upon Shylock, he was finally taking action towards a desire which touched his inner core.

"It'd be nice to have some company," said Shylock through the blare of distortion on the radio.

"We'll have a fine time."

The trafficky avenue led to a highway girdled by all sorts of shops and restaurants, the cars on a slow crawl towards oblivion. Noble had rarely escaped the gravitational pull of Waspachick. He regarded the journey away from town as something delightfully new. The highway was filled with more businesses since he last beheld it. Every empty space was accounted for: the carpet dealers, the automobile malls, the office supply stores, and the fast food joints, the culture of retail and a long highway. He wouldn't have minded if Shylock headed south along this stretch of road until the Jersey border melted away. But the House of Music was simply across an overpass; more a department store than the shack he imagined.

When they first entered, they faced three rows of new electric guitars, their bodies refracting the track lights above. Their hues ranged from bone white to shiny black, and Noble particularly liked a maroon model, a six string which called out to him. But Shylock noticed the prices of these first display models and directed him towards an area to the side guarded by a glass door.

They walked into a room arranged solely for guitars. The guitars hung above the floor on pinched holders just where the nuts met the peg-heads. They were all electric, as the acoustics stood in their own special area, and they were also too expensive. Nevertheless Noble was taken aback by so many guitars in one area, like a vault filled with treasure. He could have wandered in this one room for hours while eyeing the same guitars the greats had at one time used. The room trembled with their spirit, and of all the new and glossy bodies, he noticed a shy, classic guitar in the middle of the row.

He looked at it for some twenty minutes, admiring the long neck, the offset double cutaways, the sensitive pick-ups, the tremolo bar, the volume and tone controls, and the tail-piece. This had to be the perfect guitar for him, and he was about to ask Shylock for it, but Shylock had disappeared. Noble took the liberty of pulling it from the rack. He held the laminated body close to him, strumming the steel strings. In this short time alone with the instrument, his knee supporting the body, his hand pressing the frets, he was taken from the cold hollowness of highway beyond the glass room and into the same night club where Alexandra Van Deusen waits at the bar. In keeping with the fashion of the night, she wears a black dress highlighting her every curve, as though the dress needn't be on her at all. Noble, his blonde hair gelled back, walks up to her and begins a quiet conversation, only that she isn't interested in his overtures. As in the small Laundromat she pays him little attention despite Noble's black leather jacket and black suede boots. And suddenly the band starts to play, only that there is a space missing where the guitarist should be. He looks into her deeply as the bassist calls him to the stage. Noble fills the empty space and begins a long jam which surprises her. Little did she know. And after the long set Noble returns to the bar, only that he is surrounded by other women, the fair Alexandra looking on in an unfortunate envy.

Yes, this had to be the guitar for him, and he would accept nothing less than this classic model. It felt cool and weightless, like those hot women surrounding him, and it suddenly made sense. He hungered for it, and then through the walls of the guitar room came two familiar voices. He broke from this fantasy only to stumble into another one. The two apparitions, the rock n' roll idol and the auto-mechanic, standing beside him. He blinked twice, rolled his neck, rubbed his eyes, but they were still with him, no matter the obvious attempts to shake them.

"Thinking about the women, aren't you?" said the idol.

"It's a shame," said the African-American auto mechanic while cleaning a carburetor.

"Are you really sure about this? Don't you think you're getting carried away?" asked the idol.

"This is not real. This is all part of my imagination," said Noble.

"Maybe yes, maybe no," said the idol, holding a double-neck guitar.

"You should reexamine your priorities," said the auto mechanic.

"This is no game, Noble McCloud. This is your life, and maybe you should, oh how shall I put it?, come back to earth, and think about what you're doing," said the idol.

"I know what I'm doing, now both of you get out of my way!"

"Tut, tut, Noble, you can't get away from us that easily. We're here to help you after all."

"You may need us more than you think," chimed the auto mechanic.

"Fine," said Noble, "say what you need to say."

"Heh, heh," laughed the idol, "there's so much you need to learn about the object of your obsession, because that's what it has turned into. You think learning this instrument will bring you that pot of gold at the end of the rainbow, don't you?"

"This is my calling," said Noble defiantly.

"Oh yes," continued the idol, "your calling is tied up with something so, how shall we put it, so important and..."

"Self indulgent," said the auto mechanic.

"...and of course you are unable to take your place in this world, because you find it so animalistic, so beneath you."

"I respect what others do," fired Noble.

"Oh, hogwash," said the auto mechanic.

"You don't care about anyone but yourself. You're just as bad as the rest of them. And you think playing the guitar will fill your need for fame and everything else which follows."

"Fame and fortune, McCloud, fame and fortune. Ain't never done any man any good," said the mechanic.

"The only reason why you're even thinking about this instrument is for the materialistic value it will produce."

"That's not true!" Noble yelled, "and you're not real. Get away from me. You're second album sucked anyway, and you, I have no idea why you're even here. Don't you have a transmission to fix?"

"Think about it," said the idol," you're a twenty-seven piece of white trash, and all of a sudden you want stardom? Let's examine this stardom for just a moment."

"Let's not."

"This is what you want: a luxury hotel room with cold ones in the fridge, women of all sorts, you're so called music to the hilt, and then it's cocaine on the mirrored glass, an all-out orgy on the floor, and then what? A meaningless hedonism is all you want. You don't care about the guitar, you only want the money which will get you nothing but the golden calf."

"Then you'll cry for respect," said the auto mechanic.

"Precisely. You just want to be someone you're not."

The antagonism of these two apparitions continued in this manner for some time until Noble returned the guitar to its original place. Suddenly they vanished, their images and voices leaving a damaging residue, and for a few moments Noble stared at the place from which they disappeared, the blank wall between the rack of guitars and a back room.

Perhaps they were right, he thought. Perhaps the guitar was a means to an end, a symbol of hedonistic longings, and perhaps he wasn't worthy of such an instrument, that he undertook the playing of it just to attract the opposite sex or to inflate a buried ego, playing the guitar for all the wrong reasons, and this startled him, because now he was no different than those mindless insects crawling up the ladder, because insects also have a sense of who's important and who's not, who deserves respect, and who does not; insects had their own particular culture and behaviors, and perhaps he was no different than the lowly insect vying for importance with the rest. But the vision. Yes, the ideal of having a purpose in life, his calling, these strange coincidences and signs which pointed in the direction of this one guitar, and he would play as an artist paints or sculpts or performs. Never mind their antagonism. He would continue with or without them, for he had no other purpose than to play the instrument, and he would do so with a dedication and discipline which would rid him of these apparitions.

Shylock appeared with the salesman who looked like a tame folk-singer, round spectacles perched upon the bridge of his nose and long, curly locks connoting mountainous regions, either the Appalachians or the Rockies.

"I found a guitar," said Noble, and pointed to it.

"We found a guitar," said Shylock.

"From what I understand, you're a beginner, and your price range is limited," said the salesman.

They pulled him away from his first choice and took him to the back room occupied by cardboard boxes and metal shelves. The salesman opened one the boxes and removed an oblong box.

"This has everything you need: the guitar, picks, a strap, strings, and a ten watt amplifier. All-in-one."

"What about the other one? I really like the other one."

"This is basically the same design," said the salesman, "only its body is made of two parts rather than one long part where the neck and body are one single piece. It's the same style, and the difference in cost is quite dramatic. It's perfect for a beginner."

Noble had his heart set on the first guitar but remembered that Shylock was footing the bill, and so without much argument he accepted the all-in-one guitar kit, priced at three hundred dollars, a fraction of what the first guitar cost. A cheap imitation. Nevertheless he was content with buying this lesser model, a tricycle compared to a ten-speed.

Noble then had a look around the shop while Shylock paid with a credit card. Drums and percussion instruments were stationed on an island in the middle of the store, and a salesman with a shaved head pounced on bongos. Further back the keyboards on auto-pilot played bluesy melodies. A long-haired guitarist facing a wall of giant amplifiers jammed into a multiple effects processor. The shop suddenly came to life in this manner, another sign that Noble was treading the right course. He even encountered a bassist who plucked heavy steel strings with dexterous speed and a timbre which dominated the other strangely harmonious instruments. There couldn't have been a better send-off, a triumphant return to Waspachick, the all-in-one guitar kit stored safely in the trunk of Shylock's car.

"Hey, how about a drink? We'll celebrate!" said Shylock while driving back.

"I don't think so. I've got to get home."

"Noble, you don't have a home anymore. You're home is with me."

"Oh, I almost forgot," as the flood of recent memory washed over him.

"A drink won't hurt," said Shylock.

"Okay. I guess I'm living with you now."

They parked behind the East Waspachick bar. The place was empty, and the same bartender eyed them suspiciously. They ordered beers and shots, and they celebrated amidst the lazy silence. Noble's expectations for the celebration were a bit high at first, but when no one entered the place, he found himself bored. A lack of eye-candy, he thought, but they sat there for what seemed like several hours, getting so blitzed that he could hardly lift himself from the bar stool, weaving once in a while to the bathroom. He had put on weight in recent months. He was in horrible shape. His pants didn't fit him anymore, but he had the guitar in the trunk of Shylock's car. Yes, that one instrument which would remove his fears and worries, and this indeed was a celebration, a distinguished moment from the string of dull, drunken episodes which left him alone at the night's end.

Before long more people entered the place, and by this time Noble could hardly move. Yet Shylock bought him drink after drink, shot after shot. He could have passed out right on the bar, but Shylock nudged him a few times upon sight of beautiful women. They seemed to enter all at once.

Noble waited for Alexandra Van Deusen. He was certain she would show, but as the minutes elapsed into dreamy hours, the hopes of her arrival were dashed. Shylock enjoyed himself though. He talked with the women effortlessly, and Noble by comparison became the mute filled with a desperate longing, an internal yearning which could not be expressed through simple conversation. His composure was a rock. Outwardly he displayed not the slightest interest in the company of others. He turned his back while the socializing behind him commenced like a swarm of fleas, but on the inside he wished for a woman to initiate a conversation, that one woman who would know him inside and out upon a quick look into his blue eyes, as women sensed these things, and perhaps they kept their distance from him, because they knew how lonely he had become.

Yes, they sensed his despair, and if only one broke from the pack, he would shower her with his affection and care for her completely and unconditionally. Instead the women caged him within the category of a man who slowly deteriorated while the world around him grew stronger and more complicated. Perhaps they knew him better than he thought, and as a result, kept a polite distance. Was this the way it had to be, he asked himself. Alone for the rest of his days? But within this tired acquiescence he remembered his guitar, and suddenly a spotlight bathing him, and a woman in the audience who listened and shared his despair, the same woman who blew him off at the Laundromat. But this sudden recurrence of a hackneyed fantasy failed to inspire him. It grew old like the countless shots served by the bartender.

Shylock had taken off some place, probably using his charm on an unsuspecting woman, but soon enough he returned to an embittered Noble.

"C'mon, let's get outta here," said Shylock.

"What's the point in that?"

"Don't you want to play your new guitar?"

"Yes, right after we bought it."

"Let's go then."

"Who's gonna drive?"

"You are."

"Me?" asked Noble in surprise. "Why me?"

"I'm drunker than you are."

"Maybe we should walk."

"Nah, it's just five minutes away."

"All the more reason," said Noble.

"No, because then I have to come all the way back here to get my car. Let's just go home," as he handed him the keys.

Now Noble recalled the few simple rules for the drunk driver on his way home. First, observe the speed limit. Second, don't swerve. Third, keep silent and concentrate on the road. Shylock turned on the radio when they pulled out of the parking lot.

"Shy, would you turn it off?'

"No."

"Whaddaya mean 'no.' I've got to concentrate."

"Keep your eyes on the road."

"Then turn it off!"

They bickered like this along the main avenue which eventually led into the Waspachick strip, and Noble counted the miles before the town line. He was almost there, but then Shylock turned the volume up a notch. Noble became so incensed that he concentrated instead on the radio itself, lowering the volume, fighting with an irascible passenger who turned it back up in defiance, both of them drunk, the car swerving onto the other side of the road and accelerating in the darkness.

"Would you cut that out!" yelled Noble.

"Leave it on!"

And Noble swerved to the right so hard that the car hit the curb and almost ran through a mailbox, one mile before the Waspachick town line. He regained his senses and gave the car a hard left, missing the mailbox and continuing along the winding avenue, one mile, a half-mile, then a quarter of a mile to the strip, his brow sweating, the radio blaring. He could have punched Shylock, but he continued, as though the town line would immunize them from accidents or run-ins with the law.

He sped through the remaining East Waspachick avenue, his vision blurring, the car swerving and gaining speed, until he observed in the rearview mirror a car with blinking headlights, the roof spinning red and blue casting a wide aura along the otherwise dark and silent avenue. This was it, as Noble's insides tweaked with fear and dread. They were caught right on the line where East Waspachick and Central Waspachick met.

He pulled over and waited, the lights sending a shivering message to the few, cozy drivers who passed.

"Oh, shit," muttered Noble.

He rolled down his window, a flashlight beaming in his face.

"Hello, officer. Can I help you?" asked Noble calmly. "Was I speeding or something?"

"License, registration, and insurance," said Comstock, the same officer who had caught him pelting a street sign.

"Is there something wrong, officer?"

"License, registration, and insurance," he repeated.

Noble provided his gum-ball identification, the insurance card, and the registration from the glove compartment. Comstock retreated to his vehicle. Noble wished he would turn off those ostentatious lights.

"Oh man, Shy, we're in trouble."

"Busted by a nigger cop," said Shylock suddenly.

If Noble weren't filled with fear for his present situation, he would have belted Shylock for the racial epithet, if not for his refusal to turn off the radio. He had never known Shylock to be a racist. Noble assumed that he himself was no racist, yet the simple egregious epithet swam with the booze on his breath, and he hated everything about the word, he hated hearing it. He hated understanding the dark, mutilated history behind it. He had always abhorred racists, but lately around Waspachick he had seen this young, wealthy African-American sporting two stylish dogs, walking towards the coffee house. This young man must have been his same age, and he seemed no different than the average Waspachick male, with the exception of his skin color. African-Americans were quite rare around Waspachick, but when Noble spotted him with these two dogs, the word "nigger" came to his mind for the first time like a shot through an otherwise innocent, healthy, and worthy mind. At the time he couldn't fathom how such a word could enter his head, and he fought against it by calling himself terrible names, but this was a poor substitute.

Lately, however, it had been happening all over the place. Unruly epithets entered his mind when he saw anyone who somehow deviated from the appearance of the wealthy, athletic Waspachick Caucasian and their blonde girlfriends. It disgusted him, but somehow he couldn't help it, as these were involuntary thoughts which popped into his head without warning. He couldn't understand them, as though a darker being or entity sprang from his innocence like weeds in a garden.

When he saw an African-American, he tried with all of his might to squelch these epithets, but they usually entered his mind so quickly that he couldn't avoid them, like a reflex action. And then he would criticize himself as a retaliatory measure. He called himself a 'honky' and 'poor white trash.' But soon enough, a necessary psychic wall developed between his correct self and his incorrect self. The reflex action, however, remained intact. He would berate himself and complement African-Americans as a people afterwards, usually by recalling Dr. King or Frederick Douglas.

His mind, then, was bitterly divided into four distinct parts: the incorrect self, the correct self, the imagination, and the overriding conscience. The overriding conscience sought to suppress the incorrect self, prevent the correct self from becoming too generous and ethical for its own good, and instill the imagination with a sense of welfare for all people, regardless of race. Yet the damned reflex action: that terrible instinct from the incorrect part of him which provided negative signifiers for those few non-whites who lived on the South side but mysteriously journeyed to the center of town. He suspected his conscience for being too weak, and the reflex action too primordial, perhaps atavistic. Shylock used the epithet in a drunken stupor, and Noble condemned it. He knew it was plain wrong but had to wonder if his strong internal condemnation of Shylock was sanctimonious. Again the reflex action, a part of him he kept distant from the law-abiding, generous, self-sacrificing Samaritan, and correct self of purity and justice. And here must be the problem: that racism went against moral principles only, not against these reflex actions which were hauntingly natural and involuntary, like the heartbeat or breathing, and if he could arrest such mental functions he would do so. The alcohol helped him drown these reflex actions. The herb soothed their haunting character to the point where he could reflect upon them with the aid of music, and soon his new guitar in the trunk. And in these moments of reflection he tried to find an escape from these involuntary thoughts or reflex actions. In a town which prided itself on natural abilities, these reflex actions fit right in. The government can't legislate morals (although it does well at parenting). There is little way to prevent the reflex action from recurring. It could be a defect of character, a moral weakness, but there is little incentive to be moral, and everyone has a different level, some embracing the reflex action as an essential part of the human animal, some casting it aside as a societal malady. He could have trusted reflex actions as instincts, but again the conscience squelched them, as it should. Besides he would never live with himself if he let the reflex action determine his days, and yet it happened again and again. He thanked the heavens for alcohol, marijuana, and music. It quelled the reflex action, or better yet, buried it until he was sober by morning, and with a clear head he isolated these instincts like black sheep, a box of racist, violent, deviant, incorrect thoughts swept to the corner by the broom of conscience.

Racism pointed to a failure of conscience, the failure which comes when a reflex action overrides the correct self. But it went much further. In Waspachick there was also a growing Indian population. In a kiosk off the strip, he overheard an African-American calling an Indian shop-owner a 'swammy.' A real surprise. The racial problem, then, was not confined to white men alone. Every culture was somehow involved with these suspicions of difference. How could it be that African-Americans also shared these same reflex actions? Perhaps we're all racists to some degree, he thought, and higher moral laws accounted for our few correct behaviors. Human nature, then, accounted for these dreadful reflex actions or involuntary thoughts. Yet there must be an underlying reason.

Noble offered the explanation of economic insecurity and competition which drove one person of color to dislike the other. He knew without a doubt, though, that the decision of same colors sticking with same colors was made by an underhanded, imperceptible force at work. The underhanded force involved a societal system which groomed and supported the incorrect self instead of the correct self and the conscience, a cruel system which relied on the laws of survival rather than moral laws. These moral laws were not necessarily fostered by religion. Secularism at least dealt effectively with religious chauvinism, but at the same time never cultivated enough morality buried within the human animal. Even the shards of morality were too tenuous to be taken seriously. What then accounted for this racism, if not human nature?

Perhaps racism among all people had been fostered by limited knowledge and a limited time frame in which one may acquire a higher knowledge. If we had enough time within our busy work week, we would realize that the African-American exhibits much more complexity than the mere color of his skin. Same with the Indian shop owner. Perhaps we don't know enough, and the limited information, the color of one's skin, for example, is the only knowledge we can ever know. And without sufficient information we are left to judge the man, not by his character, but by the color of his skin, as judgments of character take too long. And the immediate brokers of knowledge and information are these newspapers and magazines which he perused at the family pharmacy.

Supposedly, the writers and the photographers spend enough time collecting information yet are totally unoriginal and incapable in their pursuit. After all, they need to sell, and what a better money-maker than what traditionally works, collections of unoriginal scribbles before a deadline, a snap-shot of the same anorexic model until the viewer has no choice but to accept her beauty. And so the powerful brokers of information decide what's good and bad under the auspices of objectivity; what's beautiful under the guise of a uniform taste which everyone copies. No wonder African-Americans are excluded. They do not fit within the paradigm of beauty, and they try meekly to be accepted on a similar level of beauty and intelligence as the white male depicted in the newspapers, films, and television sit-coms. When the African-American sees the Indian shop-owner, or vice-versa, they both see an ugliness. They have been programmed to accept the white conception of beauty instead of their own.

Noble's perspicacity only penetrated the racial question this far, but he also knew that he himself had been programmed in such a way. He could not see the beauty of an African-American or an Indian. He could not find beauty within the limited knowledge of their color. Despite his sandy hair and blue eyes, he could not see himself as beautiful either. He hated to generalize, but if African-Americans were thought of as beautiful, there wouldn't be a racial problem. Blacks would freely mingle with whites, and vice-versa. Instead he saw the African-American as a man of poverty housed on the South side, imprisoned within brown-bricked projects. Rarely did he see a black investment banker, neurosurgeon, or congressman. He saw gang-related rappers with incipient drug addictions. A case of the incorrect over the correct. The dark skin color, wide noses, and thick lips proving no match for the bombardment of slim and pubescent blondes. White correct; black incorrect. The only escape from racism involved the denial of so-called traditional, uniform tastes and an acceptance of the so-called ugliness most of us possess. Ugliness included Comstock and fat women with pimples and cheap clothes, the ghettoes further South, the tenements and destructive hoodlums.

In the side mirror he saw the tall, shadowy figure of Comstock approaching.

"You nearly took out a mailbox," said Comstock, "and this car smells of alcohol. Please step out of the car."

Noble failed all three tests. First, missing his nose with extended arms. Second, losing his balance while walking a straight line. Third, slurring his speech at L-M-N-O-P. He agreed to take a breathalyzer test at the station house. A tow truck was ordered for the car, as Shylock was too drunk to drive the single mile to his apartment. Noble's hands were cuffed, and he was sent to the back seat of the familiar flashing cruiser. He faintly heard Shylock who yelled that he would bail him out somehow. And then the sterility of the police cruiser. He was caged behind wire-mesh.

"I'm afraid," said Noble through his tears.

"Don't be," said Comstock, "but you're in a shit-load of trouble. You could have killed somebody. And you're driving without a license."

His head rolled along the blue, vinyl seat as the cruiser made a couple of sharp turns. He wished himself dead. The world could have died that night.

They arrived at the police station, a place he vaguely remembered, housed within a building of court chambers, borough clerk and district attorney's offices, and an assortment of other legal rooms any man in their right mind would labor to avoid. He sat in a separate area of the precinct. He blew into the breathalyzer, a tube which fed into a box with digital readouts, all of this a blur.

Then he heard Comstock saying gravely, "You're twice over the legal limit," and he read him his Miranda rights. Noble was led to a jail cell beside the cluttered desks, and the clunky gate was shut. He lay on a metal platform which hung by a chain in the wall. He longed for the guitar in Shylock's trunk. And then he longed for something unattainable, the visage of his mother, as she was the only one in the world who could save him from this terrible mistake. The only thing that made sense at the time. In his momentary hallucination, inspired by those endless shots and flat beers and presently his jail cell, she came to him. He wasn't sure if he had passed out or simply died with the world around him.

Chapter Six

In the household during a thunder storm the power went out. It was a sudden twitch which eclipsed the house in an excited darkness. Everything was dead- the tuner, the CD player, the refrigerator, and the fan which kept his room bearably cool. One of the hottest summers on record, and the thunder battered the sky like fighting rams. He didn't move. He only sucked up the silence, a lifeless world without the guitar bellowing through the speakers. He wasn't about to leave his room either. The darkness and the silence actually brought a quaint relief, as though his listening habits had recently become a twisted obligation, he knew not why. In the darkness he lay there, hearing footsteps beyond his door, and then a quick knock. His shadowy mother appeared, a figure of blackness against the dark. The lightening struck suddenly, and he caught a glimpse of her in a red satin robe. She returned to blackness, as though a void stood in lieu of her body.

"Are you alright?" asked Noble.

"Fine, but I'm expecting company soon, and now there's a blackout. Do you have any matches? I've got a candle or two."

Noble was reluctant to venture beyond the sanctum of his room. He had grown comfortable in it, almost like a clubhouse away from his parents at the other end of the hall. He should have been doing his homework, and yes, he did repeat his tenth grade year. He was now towards the end of his twelfth, on his way towards a two-year college in the Southern stretches of Jersey. His mother had saved up for his education and originally wanted him to pursue medicine. But the money was tight, and together they settled on a career in business.

Noble loved the image of dressing in banker's gray with a leather attaché, doing deals over cocktails. Under the Reagan presidency it seemed that business or anything money-related would ensure prosperity, and in keeping with the herd of young people flocking towards the financial sector, business seemed like the best route. And Noble was determined to work hard for his mother. One day he would repay her every penny, and they would live together on the North side of town. It was unclear whether or not his father was included in this plan. Simply put, the man was never around, and when he did happen to stumble in after his stint at the North side bar, he either collapsed in the bedroom or fought with his wife. Noble never included his father in his plans, but some moral impulse, or perhaps it was the image of a strong family, placed him in the grand scheme.

Noble had little power to change the ways of his father, and if he had the chance he would avoid it for his own safety and welfare. He had always been afraid of the staunch McCoy McCloud, as though he were a living legend in the household, breezing in once in a while with a stern look, and then out again, leaving terrible traces of frustration. His mother remained his only link to McCoy, not a liaison but as an indirect form of communication—the noises beyond his room transmitting a rage and misanthropic disgust. Noble didn't know how his father felt about his career path. He didn't know how his father felt about anything, and his rare appearances in the doorway after a long day only meant that Noble should retreat, shut the door, and listen to music. This became common practice.

In the darkness, the brief flashes of light exposed her thin satin robe, and he followed her into the kitchen, the rain and wind pelting the home which could have easily blown over if the fierce weather willed it.

They set up candles in the living room which was merely a continuation of the long hallway between the two bedrooms. It was clear to Noble that his mother had something serious on her mind.

"A girlfriend at your age is essential," said his mother by the flickering light, her smile hinting a certain girl-like embarrassment.

"Aww, Mom," said Noble.

"Oh don't 'aww Mom' me," as she touched his knee. "A boy your age needs a girlfriend. You're a strong, handsome kid, on his way up the ladder of success. A girl should be with you."

"Do we have to talk about this?" he complained.

"It's important. Soon you'll be on your own."

"Don't act like you'll never see me again."

"Noble, it's time for a woman. I can never be there like a good girlfriend can. It's a Saturday night, and all you're doing is isolating in your room. Shouldn't you be out with Shylock somewhere, chasing all these girls?"

"I don't hang around Shylock on Saturdays."

"Well, he hangs around you."

"He hangs around his football buddies."

"Noble, I want you out of this house on Saturday nights. I know a thunderstorm never stopped me."

He always had a vague sense of what his mother did for a living- how she earned all of that dough for his education. But remember, Noble never assumed things. In order for him to believe what other maladjusted classmates mentioned in passing, he would have to see it in the raw, the actual deed, the hard evidence. He had never seen his mother doing the things his classmates spoke of. As a matter of fact, one classmate said that he had been seeing his mother on a regular basis, that he wasn't the only one, that there were many others in the school who were active clients. He never believed them, and yet the hearsay glared at him almost every night. He was naïve by choice, the incorrect thought squelched by the correct image of the upstanding disciplinarian. But in the candlelight he asked her:

"Mom? How did you get the money for college?"

Her girlish smile turned solemn.

"I worked for it," she said.

"And what's the work that you do? I know we've never discussed it, but people at school tell me terrible things, and I want to know straight from you. What is it that you do?"

"You have no right to question me," she said.

"If you'd just be honest about how you got the money. I know Dad doesn't help out. All the money's coming from you. I just want to know how that money was earned."

"Noble McCloud, you don't have the right to question you're mother. Do you actually believe what all those boys say?"

"Mom, I think you're..."

"No, I'm not. I'm not overreacting at all. You believe those damn kids more than you're own mother..."

"But you haven't answered me yet."

"And I won't answer you. To think that my only son believes the words of those idiots, and doesn't trust his own mother, the same mother who made you what you are today- a business man ready for success, a young college man just like the rest of those rich bastards..."

"Please Mom, don't be angry with me."

"Why shouldn't I be? To be questioned by your only son?"

"I need to know," said Noble quietly, "I need to know who you are, and whatever you tell me, I'll believe you, and I will never ask you again, I swear it."

She stood, and her red satin robe fell loose about her body, exposing a thin line from neck to midriff.

"If you must know," she said, "I'm a therapist."

"Oh."

"Yes, I'm a therapist, and I see my clients either here or at their homes."

"See, mom, that wasn't so difficult," he said in relief.

"Let me put it to you straight. You are never, never allowed to question me again. No son of mine has the right to question his own mother. You will never again question me the way you just did."

"Okay. I'm sorry, mom."

"Sorry isn't enough. Never again are you to ever ask me. Is that clear, Noble McCloud?"

"Yes, mother."

He wished for his room, but the house was still dark from the blackout. He had no haven to relieve himself of his mother. An awkward silence followed, and he hoped his mother was still on his side. He yearned for normalcy, the candlelight exposing her moist eyes. The correct part of him believed her, not the underhanded ramblings of malicious kids. His mother, he thought, had told him the truth, and he would never ask again.

"So back to our original topic," said his mother, the disciplinarian waning, the tender mother waxing. "What about a girl for you? A nice Waspachick girl. Have you tried asking one out?"

"Like on a date?"

"Of course on a date, silly," a flush filling her cheeks.

"I have my eye on a one girl, but she's out of my league. They're all out of my league."

"A man can't stand alone his entire life. He needs a mate. That's natural law."

"I'm the exception to the rule, especially around Waspachick High School."

"Start asking. They won't fall from the sky, and you're a very handsome gentleman, college-bound."

He dare not say that most of his peers would be attending four-year colleges. Such an admission would swing her mood the other way, and he wasn't about to wound her again. He answered her delicately, trying to change the subject.

"First, the money," he said.

"Yes, these Waspachick girls are no match for my son," she said while tugging his chin, "and one of these days, my son will be a great man, and they'll fall all over you."

This idea of becoming 'great' perplexed him. He saw no evidence at all which pointed to this. No one ever approached him and said: 'Noble you will one day be a great man.' He knew a firm belief in the self was a necessary prerequisite. He lacked this prerequisite. He also knew that great men had high intelligence quotients. He lacked a high intelligence quotient and scored miserably on the standardized tests administered by the high school and the testing service. He had heard many things about great businessmen, especially Carnegie whom historians say may have possessed an additional cerebral lobe. Noble lacked this addition. And what of brute chance, luck, or divine intervention? Possibly. And yet the metaphysical world couldn't cut him a break, especially with the opposite sex. From what he had learned, greatness was an impossibility. He could have acted like a great man, and thus delude himself into believing that he was a business wizard, junk bonds and greenmail, along with an exceptional acumen for cost-cutting and competitiveness. He could have played the part, as image and suggestion proved more powerful than the genuine article. But it's a lonely world when one becomes a legend in his own mind, mainly due to his reluctance to exit that mind and test difficult realities where one is a number, a statistic, and eventually an insect. Better to be an insect than a man striving for a greatness he will never achieve, and yet his mother mentioned greatness repeatedly. Absolutely no evidence, but he hung on to her soft, balletic words. They were ingrained within his mould. He couldn't shake them, and thus began Noble's phantasmal quest towards greatness- a Carnegie, a Getty, a Buffet, even a Rockefeller. He would become great, because his mother ordained it. And from his enterprise, most likely a brokerage firm, he would amass wealth and move with his mother to the North side of town.

Greatness would not end there. Why, he would parlay into the construction business and erect powerful buildings and phallic monuments, purchase most of Waspachick, and wander about the town on a warm summer's evening, pass the same women on the strip who refused him in High School, as they wonder in awe at the kid they once knew who penetrated aristocracy. His name would live on the lips of women, and a respect would show on the faces of the men who beg the Gods to become him. And when placed in the ordinary world, the paraffin slipping into a well of hot liquid, a greatness would be achieved. She was the only woman ever to believe in him. Yes, he would take Wall Street by the horns, and the ordinary world would turn magical, making him the center of attention and activity. Was this, then, his idea of greatness? To be loved and respected by the passerby on the strip who outcasted him? Or to control events like the ruthless dictator rife with paranoia, hanging a picture of the sun in the window to feign daylight in the dark? Noble would never be satisfied with the uniform dealt him.

"I'll get us to the North end," said Noble.

"I expect nothing less. We McClouds have to work extra hard, so hard that our skin raws and our muscles bleed. Your father came here with nothing, and the son must always better the father."

It was close to midnight, and his mother ordered him to his room while she prepared for a client. Noble didn't think it odd that she received a client so late at night. He had his suspicions, but the correct self prevailed. He could only think good things of his mother. He was never a fighting man. He would recoil from and withstand the vituperations of his peers.

He lay awake that night, the music gentle. He wanted to skip school in the morning, his acceptance into the two-year college semi-secure. He did have to graduate, and another day of truancy would imperil his chances. He couldn't handle another day with women who avoided him. Even Shylock avoided him. Mating season, he supposed.

He heard the whack of the screen door, and then the locking of his mother's bedroom. Then a few bumps, maybe a high-pitched moan. Moments later another whack of the screen door. Silence. A knock at the other end of the hall. Louder knocks. A gruff, inebriated voice. A soft, panting voice. A gruff voice hollering, two men wrestling by the kitchen stove. A struggle, then a whack of the screen door, and fast footsteps outside. More hollering, Noble couldn't distinguish the words. Then a scream- his mother's scream.

He should do something. He couldn't sit there and take it anymore, the anxiety within him twitching like a crushed mosquito. He pressed his ear to the flimsy wooden door. More yelling, more smacking, more crying. Now he must do something, anything. He should confront the conflict or remain in his room. Another normal night in the household, but the anxiety, the twitching of bugs beneath his skin. He must stop it. He will protect her and then steal away with her in the night, take her to college, set up a business, move to the North side. Both of them could handle McCoy McCloud at once.

He slid to the floor, powerless, his sensitive ears registering every sound like a reel-to-reel, his future atop a university tower gunning down innocent students, a pedophile chicken-hawking on lonely street corners, the cannibal slurping fresh liver, chewing, chewing, gulping flesh in a dark basement, the incorrect self exploding in his brain, mushroom clouds sucking dust, bloody crow bars, crushed skulls, all of it exploding, and himself leaning against the door, poker-faced and still, the screaming becoming another measure in his symphony, the hollering a mere character in his opera.

Later that night he tiptoed to the living room. His mother slept quietly on the sofa, a romance novel on the floor beside her. The power was back on. He bent down on one knee and in the light from his room, he brushed her hair to the side. Both cheeks were heavily bruised and swollen. He made a decision that night to take his mother away with him. They would live near the college. She could continue her therapist-work, and he could obtain his business degree. He would open a small shop in the college town, and there they would stay free from McCoy McCloud. A new life would eliminate all the cacophony cluttering his mind, a deep disturbing trauma which hid beneath his fingertips. It had to be done. He would ask her in the morning. Finally, he would leave Waspachick and head to the unexplored frontier of another Jersey town. His mother wheezed in her sleep.

Chapter Seven

A policeman's nightstick banged the iron bars and jolted him to consciousness. Drool puddled between his cheek and the metal platform. He had blacked-out. A tidy prison cell. He was alone. Apparently he was the only criminal awaiting release. The initial shock stung but subsided, and he implored Comstock to relate everything about the careless night.

Comstock described the scene and said it was a routine drunk driving arrest. He then tossed him a ham and cheese sandwich through the space in the cell door. Noble devoured the sandwich like a half-starving wolf, but immediately threw it up in the corner toilet bowl. He had never felt so ill before. He swam in nausea. He curled up in a ball on the heavy platform. Ironically he didn't want to leave, as though the precinct was a safe-house. Nothing but time to recover and return to his same, gentle, contemplative self. But his bowels turned and ground. He then sat motionless on the same toilet bowl for what seemed like hours, hoping that the sickness of the booze would evacuate from his otherwise healthy system.

The notion that amazing accomplishments were born from stints in prison, even greater ones sitting on toilet bowls, didn't ring true. He never before acknowledged what an animal he had become. Comstock and another police officer sat at paper-covered desks beyond the bars, typing reports. He discovered a silly but striking similarity between his setting and their's. Whether the bars were near or distant, prison still existed for every individual. Sure, there are degrees of imprisonment, but a prison is still a prison whether in jail or in Waspachick or within the borders of a nation. Whether the bars are of iron or gold, they are still bars. No matter where one traveled, one was always stuck with oneself. The encasement of flesh and blood incarcerated him more than any jail cell could, the same incarceration which coerces the moon to spin around the earth or the flag to cover a casket. He didn't, however, accept the extreme view that an escape was impossible. As we know already, his escape took the forms of fierce, verisimiltudinous daydreams. After all, the moon glowed, and the flag furled, but all within acceptable limitations of their purpose. And Noble's one purpose was to play the guitar, or so he thought. He would have given anything to have the guitar in his jail cell, but its absence degraded him to the animal or the man unable to fulfill his chosen purpose.

Purpose lends meaning to existence, he thought. It separates the man from the insect. Even more important was the choice to determine that purpose and to accept the consequences of that choice. But in a prison cell with a terrible hangover, consequences were costly. But the greater purpose is derived from the imagination, not from necessity and circumstance. Necessity and circumstance flirt with coercion, while the untrammeled imagination develops the seed of greater purpose.

Damned is the man who has an imagination. His trials begin the day he follows it. Damned more is the man who has an imagination like Noble's. It interferes with every aspect of his being. Necessity and circumstance wither away. The moon no longer pulls tides. The flag no longer hides a dead soldier. The moon becomes a pockmarked face, the flag a rat's tail. The imagination complicates things which are simple. It deceives and betrays, and yet one may never attain freedom without it. Essential to purpose and consequentially costly, the imagination targets the man who is most alone. Companionship keeps it frozen. Loneliness sets it afire. How awful it is that the same instrument of escape, the same medium which distinguishes the man from insect, drives one into a prison, not of flesh and blood, but of mind? Without limits the imagination can destroy, and within limits it serves a transparent purpose as a slave to necessity and circumstance; the difference between an outlandish visage of the moon and the methods devised to land on its surface. The mortal becomes a God in his mind, and any element encroaching upon his divinity is murdered. The imagination, then, must be limited by the force of conscience, that firm belt-buckle which spanks the imagination down to size.

Noble was getting lost in thought. His buttocks grew numb while contemplating these inanities, this pseudo-psycho muck into which he was sinking. He concluded that the benefit of others must be the goal of any wild imagination. He would play the guitar for others, not for himself. He would bring happiness and serenity to his audience. And if he had the guitar in his cell, he would dazzle Comstock. It was all according to plan, all preordained by the sky above the precinct. Besides, great musicians always landed in prison at some point.

"You're free to go," said Comstock some hours later.

"That's it?" said Noble in a daze.

"What were you expecting?"

"Something more. What I did was terrible."

"Terrible as it was, East Waspachick doesn't have a law amputating your steering hands," he smiled, "not yet anyway."

Noble actually expected a beating, but for now he faced probation, which didn't matter, and a hefty fine, which mattered more than life itself.

"The judge will decide all that," said Comstock.

"What if I can't pay the fine?"

"The judge will decide that too."

Noble left the precinct in the mid-afternoon, still suffering from the hang-over. He recalled a montage of last night's events, but nothing so seamless as to recreate the entire night. At least it didn't snow on him while walking towards Waspachick, the sky another dull, lugubrious blanket over everything living. The cars passed slowly. He headed towards Shylock's apartment on the other side of the railroad tracks. He would have eaten to allay the nausea, but he hadn't a dime. He arrived at Shylock's by evening.

"Oh shit, Noble," said Shylock rubbing his eyes at the door.

He was half-naked in a pair of plaid boxer shorts.

"Come in before I catch pneumonia."

Shylock had been asleep on the sofa, the only part of his apartment saved from the crumpled clothes strewn all about. Noble wished he had his old room back, but his fate to live with this hairy, pouchy drunk was somehow sealed, and he accepted it. He was angry with him for dragging him out in the first place, but why make matters worse. Shylock returned to the sofa, and Noble found a spot on the floor. He could think only of the new guitar in Shylock's trunk.

"Did you get your car back?"

"Not yet."

"Let's get it then."

"Not now."

"Not now? Why not?"

"Because I can't even fucking move."

"You were supposed to pick me up at the police station."

"I know."

"I'm in a shit-load of trouble," as Noble waved the summons in the air.

"I know."

"The court date is in thirty days. I'm wondering if I should get a lawyer."

"With what money?"

"You've got a point. I guess I'll represent myself."

"Well, you know the saying: 'A man who represents himself has a fool for his client.'"

"Thanks for the encouragement."

"Noble, I know you don't want to hear this," said the fatigued Shylock, "but I'm shelling out lots of dough for the car. There's towing costs and a big fat ticket, plus a whole mess of other costs. It's a nightmare. The government really shoves it to you when they impound your car..."

"What are you telling me, Shy?"

"I can't afford to get my car back..."

"Don't you dare..."

"Noble, these are realities, okay, the real rough and tumble world of money and prison and cars towed away by an unforgiving police nation. And I have a better handle on it than you do. You'll have to trust me."

"No way. Absolutely not."

"I haven't even said anything yet," said Shylock.

"Don't fuck around," said Noble bitterly.

"Yes, we have to return the guitar. I'm sorry."

"You can't!"

"How am I gonna get my car back? I don't have money, man."

"You have the money, I know you do. Ask your parents for the money if you have to."

"My parents won't give me a dime."

"Yes they will."

"I mean, who do you think I am man? You think money just falls from the sky?"

"You're the one who wanted to go out, remember? You're the one who wanted me to drive home, and like an idiot, I listened to you. We never should have driven in the first place."

"What's passed is past, alright? Let's focus on the present. I've got a car in the pound which I need for my livelihood, and I have no money to pay for it. Ergo, we have to return the guitar and get my car. It's either your guitar or my car."

"Leave your car in the pound then."

"Each day I leave it there, they tack on a storage charge."

"Shylock, we had a deal."

"Circumstances have radically altered."

"We're turning into barbarians," fought Noble. "This whole world. A world where money counts for more than art. It's all going down hill, and soon we'll be killing each other over competing interests for glue in Thailand, and the only tune you'll ever hear is the sound of clinking coins, not the violin, not the flute, or the trumpet, and not the sound of my fucking guitar, because you, Shylock, you!, turned my guitar in for money. It's blood money…"

"Thai people make glue?"

"Blood money! You're choosing blood money over art. You are contributing to the decline of the Western world, and soon we won't be walking down these fields with flying orchids…"

"Flying orchids?"

"Quiet! Yes, flying orchids, and instead we'll be back to square one, some modernist nightmare, a Mondrianic nightmare, where everything's geometrical and electronic and automated and inhuman, and the music we hear will be violently digital, and short, so very short, damn shorty-short lyrics controlled by one giant monopolizing conglomerate administering blood tests, lie detector tests, breathalyzers, entrance exams, all of the Western World taken over by realists like you who choose blood money over artistic expression, and then we'll blame some dictator in the desert for all our problems, or even worse, we'll blame ourselves and usher in the Second Civil War, not because of our government, not because of a spike in some demographer's chart, no, because you, Shylock, put money before art. It'll be so bad that anyone with the faintest vision will be put in prison, and you'll be the one slamming the door…"

"Calm down, okay?"

"I will not calm down."

"I get the point, okay?"

"Then you'll save art? You'll save the music so the little kids can play in the green grass?"

"Damn you, Noble McCloud. You always fuck with things."

"Tell me you'll spare my guitar. It's the only thing I've got."

It was his finest performance. Thoughts which gathered piecemeal in his mind somehow synthesized into one gigantic turd upon the bewildered Shylock who was too fatigued for debate. A gust of pride swept through him, the pride which comes with winning an argument over a childhood friend who had always dominated.

"I'll be dipping into my savings," said Shylock after a long period.

"You'll spare the guitar?"

"Yeah, yeah, I'll spare the rotten thing. I don't want to be known for the demise of the Western world and kids with flying orchids in their hair."

Noble couldn't contain his exceptional happiness. He jumped upon Shylock and hugged him with joy.

"Get off me, you idiot!"

Yet he hugged him tighter, and Shylock had to accept. Their friendship had somehow survived the guillotine of adulthood, and whenever a frienship passes this high hurdle, both members mysteriously touch the divine. Friendships in maturity usually begin with a series of trades, tit-for-tat, and slowly a relationship develops which never transcends mutual suspicions. Never does one acquaintance fully trust the other. There is always some barrier, as though both acquaintances have mastered the art of self-interest, and if one friend feels cheated, the relationship is severed and the two go their separate ways. As one grows older, the ability to trust dissolves. This may seem like common knowledge, but it's used here only to highlight the special relationship the two knew they possessed, a friendship the world couldn't break. At least not yet.

They retrieved the car from the pound the next day. They waited on a long line, and after Shylock had withdrawn the money from a cash machine in town, he handed over the crisp stack of bills to the clerk behind the thick plexi-glass.

"It's like throwing money in the garbage," remarked Shylock.

Afterwards, Shylock drove to work, while Noble remained at the apartment where he eyed the box containing the new guitar. It stood in the corner. He was afraid of opening it, as though the item represented an obligatory madness. He had yearned for this moment. He had spent many days and nights dreaming of the guitar in his hands, but suddenly he found a madness without even opening the box. Thus was his introduction to the creative process.

He paced the room. He wrenched his hands. He ate the ice cream in the freezer. He did everything but open the guitar. His desire to play was strong while his will to learn from scratch what others had already known remained weak and deformed.

He sat on the sofa for a few hours wondering how to approach the instrument. He even tried talking to the box: "You and me, see, we have a special connection," and other such palaver. But for some reason he couldn't open the box. He would have rather thrown it from the balcony. He tried listening to music. He utilized Shylock's stereo, which was a much better system than his own. He played his CD's loudly despite the thin walls. The box wouldn't open by itself. Perhaps this was all just one big mistake. Once again he must have been betrayed. No, it can't be a mistake. What about the signs, the sychronous events which led him to this one moment with his most prized and frustrating possession? Yes, it was his calling to play the guitar for the rest of his days, a life sanctioned by the Lord, and he couldn't bring himself to open the damned box. Such a simple action left him spent and fatigued, as though he were fighting the instrument like a gladiator fighting a lion. And his impatience led him to the kitchen.

He knew where Shylock kept the whiskey bottles: underneath the sink towards the back. He poured himself a full glass, and the initial gulp burned a hole through his stomach, Nevertheless, it did blunt the edge of his frustration. Soon enough he was drunk and confronted on all sides by insecurities. Who was he kidding? Twenty-seven years old without a job, a girlfriend, money, a place to live? By all accounts he was a miserable failure. He was treading the road less traveled without a decent pair of shoes. Add to this his drunk driving arrest and a court date thirty days away. And then this guitar which he supposed would answer all of his problems. Everyone succeeded but Noble McCloud. Everything he looked upon turned to stone. He was drowning, and soon he would fulfill the legacy of the Waspachick town bum who looked marooned and starved from any connection with the productive, working world. If there were any man alive who would replace this weathered, disheveled, salty bum of the town, it had to be Noble, the perfect candidate. And he would wander up and down the strip in search of dimes in pay-phone receptacles. He would push a shopping cart loaded with cans, recyclable plastics, and a guitar never opened. He would delve into trashcans in search of half-eaten sandwiches. It was all so lucidly lurid and probable. Perhaps while fumbling with the half-eaten sandwhich he would run into Alexandra Van Deusen pushing a stroller.

"Hi," says Noble, only to be ignored. He follows her along the strip wanting a single word with her.

"I don't know if you remember me from the Laundromat," he says.

"If you don't stop following me around, I'll call the police," she replies.

He doesn't know if she's playing hard to get. Perhaps he should persist and develop a conversation, the same conversation he had imagined having thousands of times.

"I collect cans now," he says, "and I have a nice collection of interesting cans. I mean the can has really evolved since the days of our youth. Take the can of diet cola. At first the can was manufactured as part of a set, the six pack, but over the few years after its inception…"

"I said I'll call the cops if you don't cool it," she yells.

And from out of the Italian trattoria come two men in slick suits.

"Is there a problem?" asks one of them.

Noble and Alexandra look at each other.

"No problem," says Alexandra, a tacit observance of her own powers to have Noble beaten if she so desired.

And Noble ambles down the strip, and Alexandra continues bouncing from shop to shop, two people born from the same place, and yet two individuals who could never hold a decent conversation. This was the nightmare. All of these Waspachick women stuck in their mansions and old colonial homes never to associate with the man who collected cans.

He must open the box, just rip it open and force the strings to sing of his pain. In his sour inebriation he untucked the cardboard edges and pulled out the guitar by its neck. The gloss of the laminated body reflected his haggard face. He held the guitar delicately like a new pair of sneakers, not wishing to scuff it. He brought it to the sofa and carefully tested every chord. He drank more of the whiskey and experimented with the instrument for several hours. He plugged it into the amplifier and tested the tremolo bar and the variable pick-up switch. He flirted with the tone settings. He pressed his fingers to one of the frets and strummed softly. He didn't sing along with the chord. Doggerel would have resulted, and singing was never his intention anyway. Only the guitar occupied his narrow sights.

No longer would he collect cans and bother women. His self-pity exited with his strumming, and the tremolo bar and the pick-up switch added a versatility to his monotonous strums. But the beginner can only go so far in his first attempts at manufacturing melodies. If he were to succeed, he must master the fundamentals. A thin beginner's manual came with the guitar kit. He thumbed through it and was overwhelmed by the sheer amount of material. He drank more of the warm whiskey.

The sounds he produced were repetitive. He was moving in circles. He had pushed his cold beginnings to the limit and knew he had to study the manual and release the guitar's spectacular capabilities. But he was too drunk. After beholding the mountain, he passed out on the sofa while judging its height.

After returning from the coffee shop, Shylock woke him. Noble slept with the guitar in his lap, the whiskey bottle half-drained beside him. Shylock brought home Chinese food, and they ate heartily. The days before the trial were filled with Noble's cautious and curious study. He wanted to learn everything by the book, and while Shylock worked during the day, Noble learned the guitar with the aid of whiskey and an assortment of other spirits. He learned step-by-step how to tune the guitar, to read standard notation and guitar tablature, including note values. He practiced string exercises with time signatures, from the thickest string to the thinnest. Then came the combination of two or more notes, or chord exercises, three string chords, rests, anacrusis, the tempos of andante, moderato, and allegro, bass chords, the dynamics of piano, forte, mezzo-forte, and fortissimo. From natural notes he tackled whole steps, half-steps, sharps, and flats. Then he maneuvered through ascending and descending scales, enharmonics, arpeggio chords, and transpositions, and soon enough he played a basic melody by Bach, a bluesy tune he had heard countless times before, and major scales. He repeated these exercises until he heard them in his sleep.

His learning did not arrive magically. Sure, he prayed for some unique, dexterous ability, but his fundamental skills didn't come overnight. Learning took a severe emotional toll on him. He sat within the four walls of Shylock's living room, alone with his instrument. On some days he grew so tired that the scales blurred on the page. He had been drinking heavily to blunt the frustration of learning, and his intoxication led him towards awkward improvisations akin to lunacy. Nevertheless he began each day with a shot of whiskey (which Shylock replenished every few days) and then a repetition of the entire manual several times over, each chord exact and each major scale played with an ingrained precision. And all the while Shylock grew alarmed at his roommate's failing mental and physical capacities.

Noble made it a point of ending his practice sessions when Shylock arrived with dinner. At night he would perform for him. Shylock was not as impressed as he was alarmed. Noble hadn't showered or shaved. He grew thin and sickly. Shylock determined that he was eating only one meal per day and substituting whiskey for other meals. Shylock appreciated his dedication, but on one windy night, he intervened.

He walked in with dinner, and Noble was finishing the familiar bluesy melody, a new bottle of whiskey opened and drained a quarter of the way.

"Hey, Noble," said Shylock.

"Hi," said Noble, clearly preoccupied.

"Practicing, eh?"

"Yeah."

"When did you get up?"

"After you left," as he looked at the manual and strummed.

"Listen, Noble, can we talk for a bit?"

"Lemme finish this scale."

"No, Noble, I mean now."

"Just wait a few minutes."

"No," as Shylock clutched the neck.

"Hey man, let go!"

"Noble, we have to talk. Put away the guitar."

"I'm almost done, now lay off!"

Shylock pulled the guitar from him.

"Whaddya think you're doing?"

"What am I doing? What am I doing? What the hell are you doing? I come home every night to find you drunk, malnourished, and ill, man. You've been drinking so much booze you can't even play straight. You're going too far, man, and I'm getting worried."

"There's no reason for worry."

"Oh no? Noble, you're going through a bottle of whiskey every two days, man. You're sippin' the shit like water. What's gotten into you? You've learned the basics, now it's time to rest a little while. Can't you see what you're doing to yourself?"

"I know exactly what I'm doing."

"I don't think you do. You're pushing it too far. You're not improving, man, you're burning out."

"Ah bullshit. I've mastered these chords," as he lunged for the reverberating guitar.

"Relax, Noble. Relax, okay? Calm down. You're exhausted and spent."

"Give me the guitar, Shy. Don't fuck with me. Not tonight."

"I'm worried, man. You're sick. You need a doctor."

"I don't need anything but that guitar."

"What's the rush, huh?"

"First of all," yelled Noble, "I have to learn this instrument in a short time. I need to be good enough to make money from it, okay, and until that day comes, I will work my fingers to the bone, you hear me? To the bone. I'm learning the fundamentals, alright, and I must perfect them. You're the one who wanted me out soon. Can't you see that I'm working for you too? I'm playing until I can play the night clubs."

"Not this way," said Shylock, "I never intended this. You're hooked on the booze."

"The booze is nothing, man, it's nothing. It only relaxes me."

"Then do it without the liquor, okay? That much you'll have to compromise," as he grabbed the whiskey bottle with his other hand. "I want you to see a doctor tomorrow. It's my day off."

"Forget it. I need the practice time."

"Fine. If you don't see the doctor with me, I'm kicking you out. Let me put it plainly."

"Listen, I don't need a doctor. I'll stop drinking, if it'll make you happy. I won't drink."

"I'm worried, Noble. Really worried."

"There's no reason for it. I've been working hard. Maybe I need a break. My court hearing's coming up soon. I'll use it as a break."

Shylock returned the whiskey bottle to its spot under the sink, and they ate dinner in silence. Noble was thoroughly irritated without the whiskey bottle by his side. He strategized. He had to adjust his practice schedule in order to include the whiskey. He could neither play nor function without it. What began as a fleeting experiment with practicing under the influence turned into an obsession. He was running from that image of collecting cans along the Waspachick streets. He knew the guitar was his only ticket, and at the same time he craved the drink. His plan called for a readjustment of practice schedule. He would end his sessions a half-an-hour before Shylock came home. But then how would he replenish the whiskey? Shylock wouldn't bring home the precious goods anymore, and Noble hadn't the money. He could take the money from him in his sleep, but Shylock would kick him out. Well, first things first, he reasoned. He would lay off the booze until Shylock fell asleep a few hours after dinner. Noble needed sleep as well, and the booze usually put him to sleep quickly. Yes, he would drink a glass after Shylock fell asleep. He would wake up long after Shylock went to work, drink what was left of the last bottle, and practice the fifth string exercises some more. When the whiskey ran dry, he would get used to the scotch, then the Jaggermeister, until all of his stock were drained. Then he would steal the money from Shylock's wallet in the middle of the night to buy the same brand of whiskey. Shylock would be visibly upset, but by the time he figured things out, the court date would arrive. This was the target date: the trial, the day when he looked for gigs at night clubs around Waspachick, a magical date which meant an end to stealing from Shylock and drinking whiskey.

So far his plan worked. Over the next few nights he succeeded in drinking all of Shylock's liquor. Shylock hardly noticed. He too would come home drunk from long nights at the East Wapachick bar. Whether he drove back was unclear. Shylock stopped worrying about Noble's irregular sleeping hours, his diligent guitar playing, and the vomiting in the early morning. Noble routinely stole money from Shylock's wallet on the nights he went out. Shylock assumed he spent it at the bar. It was all working perfectly. Noble could play while drinking, and that's all he cared about. In Noble's mind, the guitar playing steadily improved. He worked on improvisation with the aid of the tremolo bar and the pick-up switch. Chords gelled into broken licks and the occasional sustained note which hung like a whining buffalo. Noble's speed and dexterity increased. In his mind, he had mastered the fundamentals, and he needed to prove to Shylock that he was ready for the night club circuit.

Just days after the intervention, he hardly spoke with Shylock. Noble feigned sleeping when he wandered in from work. He deliberately arranged his schedule to avoid him. He kept the whiskey bottles in a special place- the guitar box.

The night before Noble's trial, they ran into each other. He hadn't seen Shylock in over a week, and their reunion was a festive occasion, but sadly so. By this time they had both become drunkards, Noble in particular. Without his dose of booze he could neither practice nor sleep. Shylock faired better, although he was hubristically returning from the East Waspachick bar by car. He learned little from Noble's predicament.

"Noble, Noble McCloud," sang Shylock happily as he shut the door.

"Where have you been all my life?" asked Noble.

"Working, drinking, working again. You haven't been drinking too much, have you?"

Noble resented his parental tone. He sat with the guitar in his lap.

"Good," said Shylock. "Anyway I have a surprise for you. Tonight we celebrate. You're trial's tomorrow, and we'll order some pizza."

Noble had taken all of Shylock's kindness for granted. He longed for Shylock to present him with a bottle, a big send-off before the trial. Instead a large pizza was ordered. Noble ate a few bites, not more. Shylock munched across from him. Without alcohol the festive occasion turned boring and frustrating. It was now Noble's job to push Shylock into getting more liquor.

In their small-talk he dropped hints, but Shylock didn't pick up on them, and all the while he grew more irritated with his benefactor. His irritability intensified by the last slice, and he knew the night was over when Shylock yawned and made a motion for his bedroom. He wasn't too sure whether he had come home tipsy or not, for he did retire on the early side. But his priority remained as clear as the empty bottles in the guitar box: to obtain more liquor at any price, so that he could get through the long night.

He waited for Shylock to fall asleep. The apartment was small enough to hear the low rumble of Shylock's snores. It took a few hours, however, and in that time Noble perambulated the living room, pulling at his blonde locks, long and oily. He had little patience, and checked on Shylock every few minutes. The guitar leaned on the wall next to the sofa, and he could have smashed it to bits, if not for the snoring. He tip-toed into Shylock's room and felt the night table for his wallet. No luck. He checked the top drawer of his bureau. Still no luck. In the weak light from the living room, he spotted the wallet in the back of Shylock's trousers. He could have easily picked it, but there was one problem: Shylock slept with his pants on. Regardless of this small glitch he was prepared to do anything for his art. Normally he would have given up, but he must continue practicing. Carefully he pulled the wallet from his back pocket. When the wallet was safely in his hands, Shylock rolled over and faced him. His snoring halted briefly. Noble thought himself caught. But the low rumble resumed as before.

He fled to the living room and marveled at how much money Shylock was holding. He carried at least a hundred dollars. Noble pulled two twenties, slipped his shoes on, and hurried to the liquor store near Shylock's coffee shop. He purchased two pint-sized bottles and returned to the apartment building. Even the cold Waspachick winter couldn't keep him from burning up. He wiped the febrile sweat from his face before entering. The lights were out, so he assumed Shylock was sleeping. He entered quietly, the apartment darker than the night behind. He felt for the light switch. The apartment then illumined with the swiftness of a head-on collision. Shylock spoke from the sofa.

"What do you think you're doing?" he asked.

"Shylock, Hi, I thought you were asleep."

"Where did you go?"

"Just to get a few groceries."

"Don't lie to me, Noble, not if you want a place to live."

Noble dropped the bag, and Shylock waved his wallet in the air.

"How much did you take?"

"Listen, Shy, I'm sorry, but I didn't want to wake you."

"Bullshit. You wanted a drink all night. Don't think I didn't notice. You were sweating and trembling for Chrissakes."

"I can't work without it. I can't work at all."

"You call that work? You don't even have a job. You lie around here all day and night. You use my apartment, you use my shampoo. I've given you so much, and now you're stealing from me? To buy liquor of all things? What's gotten into you?"

"I needed a drink. That's all."

"I think you have a drinking problem."

"It's not that at all. It's not the drink. It's the trial tomorrow. I just needed something to relax and sleep. I can't play the guitar without it."

"I've been calm and patient with you. Now I want the truth. How many times have you stolen from me."

"Oh, just this once," said Noble as his irritability shot through the ceiling.

"Once? Are you lying to me?"

"No. Just this once, man. Now if you don't mind, I bought this whiskey from the store, and I even bought a bottle for you."

"How considerate."

As he set the bottle down he became more conscious of his profuse sweating and his shaking. Shylock was right. His body reacted irregularly. He hadn't eaten for days aside from a nibble of the pizza, but as soon as he downed a couple of whiskey shots the sweating and the shaking stopped almost immediately. He became less irritated and suddenly congenial. He poured Shylock a drink as well, and he accepted it. They stayed up through the early hours of the morning, listening to tunes, trading apologies, admiring each other. It may be difficult to imagine how Shylock admired Noble, but within the swill of drink anything's possible. Shylock heard him practicing on occasion, but not enough to judge his ability. He asked him to play a few chords, but Noble refused. Noble guarded his playing as a fierce and solitary endeavor. He would play for Shylock when he was good enough and not before. Shylock soon went to bed, and Noble stayed awake through the night. He practiced until the sun dawned over Waspachick.

An hour before trial, Noble drained another bottle. He stashed a full bottle behind the sofa. He felt calm and sedated. The living room was a disaster area. Noble hadn't unpacked, and his fetid laundry resembled a small mountain with cliffs and precipices and lips made from underwear and socks. He put all of his belongings in a vacant corner. He left the small apartment only to return a few minutes later. He wanted one more shot before the magical trial which would end his drinking. A graduation from the creative process. He wasn't scared of what the alcohol did to his mind and body. He was more afraid of the mind and body without alcohol. How would he practice with the same level of abandon and assiduity? He retrieved the full bottle from behind the sofa. If he had a flask he would have filled it, but a couple gulps sufficed. Although he had been drinking heavily, he still disliked the taste.

He descended the slope from the apartment driveway and turned onto the main avenue separated by the ubiquitous railroad tracks. He knew the date and the time of day, but not the day. It could have been Saturday or Sunday until he was reminded of the municipal court hours. It wouldn't be open on a weekend. He walked through the graffitied underpass to the continuation of the avenue. The streets told a weekday tale. The snow slowly melted. The sun had cast a delicious warmth over his jubilant intoxication. The shoppers meandered from store to store, the early signs of spring apparent in the few suburban birds which flew between power lines. He was hot under his thin jacket. He walked some five or six miles to the East Waspachick municipal building.

He knew he was guilty but didn't think about the trial. His thoughts were with his guitar. He merely touched the surface of its potential. He was slowly developing a style of his own, and yet he knew somehow that he would fail eventually, that multitudes of amateurs and professionals alike are beguiled by similar visions of success. Success somehow had common addens of fame, fortune, and women leading to some strange sum of widespread respect and adoration. In the attempt to arrive at this sum, he may have forgotten about the life taking place outside of this mythical equation. He was numb to simple pleasures. He gained an insatiable desire for his own grandiosity and vanity. He missed the meaning of the earth. Instead the temporary stars seduced him. Call it human nature, he thought. He had choices. When confronted with failure he could do two things: first, try something else which offered a greater opportunity. Second, hold on with both hands and pray that you don't wind up in the gutter. Noble followed the latter route. He would use the guitar as a means to an end. By this admission he had violated the sanctity of his instrument. He played for all the wrong reasons, as though his foundation were corrupted by these vainglorious ideas: the arena, the stage, the wailing fans, the record deals, the impromptu snap-shots, and a bronzed bust in the shrine of eternal guitar heroes. Making music was never the point. He was no different from the insect. Even with his surge of devotion he arrived at another rung and crawled with the rest of them. There must be a way out, he thought. He must somehow learn to appreciate the process, not the end result. This is how the artist avoided failure. And by the time he ruminated on these particulars, he found himself at the municipal building, a place which attracted insects of all kinds.

How could it be that everyone in the building was an insect but he? Derelicts, drunks, and criminals lined the walls of a small antechamber. A loud speaker called names every ten minutes. His intoxication brought him to the strange realization that he was merely one among many, a single gnat trapped among complicated cobwebs. He was no more deserving of his outrageous dreams than the rest of these misfits. The room stank of urine over mothballs, a perverse and pleasurable smell. He was one among many, and if every life had an intrinsic value and meaning, how on earth could one man thrive while these others could not? The question of meaning, or lack of meaning, bubbled in his intoxicated brain. The old man wiping his nose across from him, for instance. He didn't mean to belabor the idea, but he had never seen a wretch so up-close. His days had meaning, and yet the man was so incredibly lowly that his entitlement to a particle of meaning had been forsaken by something cruel and sinister. If the old man got there by his own doing, then how could he have been built with such gaping imperfections, so imperfect that he coughed up his own lungs? He appeared alone and troubled. Understandably this was not a perfect world. But do the imperfections have to be so glaring and obvious?

The old man coughing into the fast-food napkin didn't matter to anyone but himself. No one cared about him. He had no station in life. He possessed nothing but the clothes on his back and the phlegm which collected in the napkin. How utterly maddening to observe an absolutely meaningless old man on his last legs. Everyone has a story, sure. He must have had his day in the sun. But the deeper problem involved the meaninglessness of the man in relation to Noble McCloud.

A few chairs over sat an African-Anerican woman with an infant asleep on her lap. While this woman offered a greater meaning, she was still so terribly alone in her own world, the world of her son and a traffic violation. If she looked at Noble, what would she see but another misfit having no consequence in her life? Noble saw himself through her and found another misfit, just like his perspective of the old man. The woman had a greater importance, because she had a child to look after, but her meaning was no greater than the insect, the animal taking care of her offspring. He pondered the same old question: what distinguished the human being from the insect?

If he were to place value on certain persons and not others, then the persons who fell below par are meaningless, or insects. Noble theorized that the only way to become a complete human being was to place an intrinsic value on every single human being. The greater obstacle involved degrees of meaning. If the woman with the sleeping child proved more meaningful than the old man coughing up a lung, then the old man held less of a meaning. But this doesn't make sense, because both ought to be valued. One plus a half does not equal two. They were two separate entities. Hence, the only way to elevate both insects to human stature involved a flat, basic equality of meaning for each of them. Call it parcels of equality assigned to each.

This satisfied him for a spell. He usually thought of such inanities while drunk. If only he could express such thoughts through his guitar. What type of tune would it be? A tune which lacked a form and structure, something original but not so morose, a tune which would bring meaning to these three individuals sitting next to him. He saw finally where everything was heading-the ultimate collapse of the American infrastructure, all because men and women placed more meaning in themselves than an equal meaning in others. It couldn't be as terrible as that. Somehow the earth keeps spinning despite the prophets of gloom and doom who carry signboards on street corners and yell to all the passersby 'The End is Near,' while ringing a bell. He thought it silly that one man in traffic court could predict such an outcome, yet this scenario is easily feasible when the human being is atomized and placed into an arena with countless others, not breaking bread, but fighting over it. Every man for himself; the weak and the unfit ripped apart for the price of their hides, their skins somehow worth their weight in coin.

When his name was called, he entered into a modest walnut courtroom which was empty, save for the usual court staff of clerk, prosecutor, and black-robed judge, his build thin and wiry, an older gentleman who seemed bored and sullen, more of a law professor who weighed the issues than a judge who punished law-breakers. He didn't smile or welcome him, only looked him over like a disgruntled husband window shopping with an extravagant wife. The clerk tinkered with files at a desk off to the side. The prosecutor, an attractive woman in her mid-twenties perused copies of the police reports and other miscellaneous documents which added a bureaucratic aura to the proceedings. Noble crossed the railing and stood at a podium across from the prosecutor.

He marveled how she fingered tons of paper, the clerk many files, and himself a sack of flesh and blood loaded with the terrible liquor. The judge raised his chin as though scanning the expanse of the court room.

"Mr. McCloud?"

"Yes, your highness," said Noble.

" 'Your honor' will be fine. Where's your lawyer?"

"I don't have a lawyer."

"I would highly recommend you get one."

"I can't afford a lawyer, your honor. I'm representing myself, and I'm throwing myself at the mercy of this court. I am but a humble man with humble beginnings. I'm a spiritual man, your honor. A man who must abide by the laws of this great nation, a place where justice must be served by the blind weight of opposing viewpoints, where the prosecution must prove beyond a reasonable doubt..."

"Mr. McCloud, you are not Atticus Finch. This is a municipal court. Spare us the grandiloquence."

"Yes, your honor," said Noble meekly.

"How do you plead?"

"I guess I'm guilty, your honor. I have no excuse but to rely on your esteemed judgment in this matter."

"Yes, your honor," said the prosecutor, "this young man blew twice the legal limit. The arresting officer found probable cause on the defendant's swerving on the road late at night. He was clearly drunk and at the wheel. He has no license. The police record shows that all the proper procedures were met by the arresting officer."

"Fine," said the judge. "Mr. McCloud, do you have anything to say in your defense?"

"Your honor, if justice is to be administered properly we must take into account that this is my first offense; I can't believe what happened. Yes, it was foolish of me, downright foolish, but in all honesty, your honor, I find more foolish the undue burden this society places on young drunk drivers like myself. Yes, I was drunk and at the wheel, but it is not mentioned in those police reports that I had only one mile to go, one stinking mile before the car would be parked on the side of the road. I was definitely impaired, but can't this esteemed court see what is happening here? The big picture? Before long, any type of stimulant in the chemistry of the driver will violate the law: cough syrup, nicotine, cellular phones, and the need to go to the bathroom. And soon elderly drivers will be thrown into jail for moving too slow, and the laws will grow so rigid and thick and complex that this entire society as we know it will break down, or if we view things positively, society will evolve into robotic precision, where everything must be done correctly and perfectly, that a single mistake, a single violation of a law will ruin a man, and what we know as humankind will transform into a mechanized world of slave labor and robotics. Yes, any man who doesn't break the law becomes the robot, your honor, and simple men who make mistakes will be crushed under their clanky feet.

"The prosecutor is correct- I violated the law, but I violated it only because I am a human being. I could have killed somebody, and the world could have exploded, but I didn't hurt anyone, and the world didn't explode. It will come to the point where a person who doesn't look right will be prosecuted to the fullest extent of the law. The death penalty will be used for those who park in a tow-away zone, and ultimately the law will prosecute those who cherish that one ounce of freedom which allows a man or a woman to progress in a society saddled by laws governing the style of hair, language, music, speech, religion, and those other freedoms which everyone boasts over and glamorizes. If the law can sentence one man for drunk driving, then it can easily sentence another for thinking. There are laws for everything, there are precedents for everything. There has not been one original thought for two-hundred and fifty years since this nation's inception. And yet the law will prosecute that man or woman who thinks with originality. You may not agree with me. No one agrees with me. I am but one man in this courtroom, and soon you will forget my case. I am a minority of one. The drunk driving charge will be hard on me, but before you sentence me, think about how your decision may impact this entire society, not its present but its future."

Noble was totally out of breath. The prosecutor and the clerk smiled in mockery, as though this small inconsequential municipal court had been visited regularly by crazies, freaks, drunks, druggies, outlaws, wierdos, buffoons, and morons all representing themselves. They had heard these dystopic rants many times over, these streams of ideology and vast, vague generalizations with little or no proof or example to buttress them. And Noble once again entered that whimsical area where an overactive imagination melded with the treacherous reality. It put him at the center of all things. He spoke, not as a suitable defense for his crime, but more as a last statement before an execution, that last inhalation of noxious but satisfying smoke before bullets riddled the body. This must be the problem with having a negative or positive vision- one must always confront a horrendous stream of ideology to describe what one sees, as there is no proof, no contemporary example, nothing but the vision itself, and the individual's attempt to express it. And everyday speech did not do his vague vision justice. Music had to be that medium which not only predicted the end of all things but also described the human resiliency to overcome such staggering odds. Only his guitar would allow the human being to triumph over the insect, the difference between living and surviving. He craved his guitar. If only the judge could hear what he had learned.

Words, after a time, become pointless as carriers of experience and vision. They cannot and never will uncover the hidden valor of the man at the mercy of a court or his surge of elation when he is set free without punishment. Words are twisted, misused, confused, and misunderstood. But a solitary man with a guitar avoids the ideology and generalizations which accompany his vision, that he may learn to play with acute honesty and truth, and most importantly, specificity, not superfluity. If only he had the guitar in the courtroom. If only the judge could hear his diligent advancement towards the bends, trills, accents, and slides. The guitar would be his best defense, as words had always failed him.

The stillness of the courtroom after his rant provided a brief psychic window where he was again visited by the two persistent apparitions. From the corners of his eyes, he saw them sitting in the chairs behind him. What could have triggered their uninvited presence? The proceedings stopped for a split second, just enough time for the intoxicated and bewildered Noble to have a conversation with them. They waved while he spoke, but he had continued despite the distraction. And in the silence, the guitar idol said:

"Think you have all the answers, don't you?"

"Yeah, you've got it all figured out," added the mechanic.

Their antagonistic tone hadn't changed since their last visit.

"I'm in the middle of something here," snapped Noble.

"Yes, you're drunk at your own hearing. Mighty smart, mighty smart," said the idol.

"You point the finger," said the mechanic, "when you can't find any solutions."

"I agree with my partner," said the idol.

"Would you leave me alone? What more do you want from me? I'm practicing all the time. I'm working so hard, and now I'm defending myself."

"The guitar has all the answers, huh?, when all you've got is criticism, huh?" said the idol.

"I'm doing exactly what you did. I'm an artist. It's the only way. I'm not an insect. I am a human being, persecuted by a malicious system. It's been that way ever since Christ was crucified."

"So now you're a theologian?" mocked the mechanic.

"Please, I'm on trial here."

"You make it sound like all humanity is on trial, because you were drunk driving. Always playing the victim," said the idol.

"I'm not a victim."

"Oh yeah, I forgot- you have visions of doom and destruction, suddenly it dawns on you that the whole world will end, nothing grows, nothing continues, everything is destroyed, and you can't do a damn thing about it. Well, join the rest of us."

Noble wasn't sure what the idol meant by this. He didn't know what the apparitions meant about anything.

"Look at us," said the idol, "look and see what you're making us."

"I am not making anything. I am not creating you. You are disturbing me- let's make that very clear."

"In your whiskey-saturated mind, I represent the human being, while my friend here, who happens not to play the instrument in question is but an insect. That's right. By your narrow-minded, destroy-all beliefs, this very able auto mechanic of twenty-two years on the job is but- an insect."

"Ain't that the truth," said the mechanic.

"That's not true at all," countered Noble. "You're totally misinterpreting what I'm, well, what I'm thinking or imagining or whatever. Would you get thee gone, man?"

"See," began the idol while strumming his vintage guitar, "in your mind everyone who doesn't play the guitar is an insect, and then you go blaming the entire system because everyone somehow forced you to be so internal, so individualized that they don't value one another. The hypocrisy of your philosophy, however confused it may be, is plainly obvious: you call everyone but yourself an insect climbing some weird ladder, and then you cry over how no one values one another when you yourself have already defined them as insects. To make it short man, you don't value anyone but yourself, and then you condemn the world for making insects when you have defined them as insects in the first place."

"I'm thoroughly confused."

"Of course you are, and that's why you will never, ever become even an adequate guitarist until you start seeing individuals as human beings, when you stop predicting the end of the world, when you offer something positive, or, and this is really the point, when you assign a meaning to every human being you see. That is the key to art; to make meaning out of your dismal nothingness."

"You might as well quit now," said the mechanic," and don't insult me. What I do has meaning, get me?"

"Mr. McCloud? Are you intoxicated in my courtroom? Mr. McCloud?" called the judge.

"Obviously he's drunk," said the prosecutor.

The apparitions disappeared when he turned around. The judge's gruff voice hit him like a mallet, the prosecutor's underhanded remark like a kick to the ribs. He had never been so confused, as though his brain liquefied in a blender. The judge sentenced him to probation for six months, fined him two-thousand dollars, and perhaps the most tiresome of penalties, ordered him to Alcoholics Anonymous for a period of ninety days. He had never felt before like such a non-entity.

"I can afford the fine, your honor. I'm dead broke and homeless."

"The court clerk will arrange a suitable payment plan. Call in the next defendant…"

"Judge, your honor, I'm in a lot of trouble here. I don't have anything, I have nothing but, well, I have nothing."

"Let's go. I'm on a tight schedule."

He agreed to pay the fine over a period of three years. Where he would be in three years he wasn't sure, only that the fine had to be paid or else the court would issue a warrant for his arrest. And then the horrible AA meetings. He wasn't sure what to expect, only a misshapen cluelessness which comes after being stripped and gutted by the courts.

He returned to the antechamber and sat next to the coughing man and the mother with her child. He hung his head in his hands. The darkness behind his eyelids transported him to a beach somewhere in California, chiseled women playing a game of volleyball, and of course, the ocean.

He did not surrender to the waves, he only saw a limitless horizon where the water mingled with a sky at twilight. His immediate urge was to swim those waters and never return. The ocean offered this possibility: to leave and to be swallowed by its serenity and infinite wisdom, a graveyard of old ships and barnacled treasure chests, and home to mermaids who rescue him. Although he knew mermaids as mythical, he had little choice but to rely on a myth, to drown in a fantasy, and to be relieved of a cruelty which sand, soil, buildings, and above all, human beings had inflicted upon him. And maybe, just maybe, he would dive into the current and find his mother among a group of gentle mermaids? And then he remembered that horrible memory which hit him in the municipal building, an indelible stain on his heart, the catalyst, the impetus which returned him to his mother, as though all thoughts eventually converged into one glaring image, her image. He fought against it, tooth and nail, but like the current of the ocean he was immediately tugged to a pool he wished he could forget.

Chapter Eight

Noble spent most of the afternoon packing for college. He even cleaned his room as his mother had ordered. He didn't have many clothes. He had a cycle of wearing the same jeans for a week at a time, and his shirts once every three days. He stuffed what he could in a large green duffle bag his mother had bought from an Army-Navy store. She had gone off somewhere to run her usual errands and to meet with her clients. Noble was alone in the household in a joyous mood. Even the slightest hint of leaving Waspachick excited him in the past, and finally he was leaving for a period of two years for an associate's degree in business. Wonderful. But the joy could not be complete without his mother joining him. He had prepared a proposal for his mother, a plan which would involve leaving old McCoy McCloud and living with him near the small campus.

While surveying his room for anything he may have forgotten, he ruminated on the proposal. He must convince her, and he had a reasonable certainty that the plan would work. For the rest of the afternoon he remained in his room and cranked up a familiar tune. He had never been so excited, an excitement bordering on glee. He and his mother would find a small apartment, and the two would live without, without- even here Noble couldn't put his finger on the problem, only these terrible noises from the other room, the rumors around town which somehow got back to him, the entire ordeal which required an immediate and unfettered flight from Waspachick. It would work. It had to work. He hated the idea of leaving her behind, leaving her to the terrible noises. For the first time he would be helping her. He would refund the comfort and the shelter she had given him. This was the general idea, and the main thrust of his proposal involved the concept of security, that she would no longer have to endure the absence and the drunken behaviors of her husband. If only he could put it in such a way that would convince her.

She had always been obdurate, the kind of stubbornness which only hurt herself and the emotions of those close to her. Noble had to insist with the same stubbornness. He must use her own logic to make his proposal salient. He paced his room and inspired himself. He would approach her with an indefatigable energy, so incredibly stubborn that she would have to concede.

He heard the door slam. He would not shy away as before. He would stand up, and if that failed, he would try again until her own determined will was shattered and instantly mended by Noble's glorious vision. Yes, the vision was glorious, good, and true. Never in his life had he such a positive vision, a vision pure, overflowing with optimism. To fly from Waspachick, to row a battered boat on a deep blue ocean never to return. How glorious this vision, both of them on the campus. She would cook for him and find another line of work in the town, while he attended night classes. It was all so incredibly perfect as visions ought to be.

He knocked on her door, not once, but several times. She didn't answer. He knocked harder. She opened the door, and yet another welt bulged under her eye.

"What happened?" he sighed.

"That's not your concern," she said.

"Damn it, what happened?" his glorious vision replaced by a boiling anger.

"Don't worry about it, Noble. Just pack your bags. You're off to college tomorrow," her tone self-sacrificing.

"Don't worry about it? Are you nuts?"

"Don't raise your voice, young man."

"I'm not raising my voice, okay, I'm not raising my voice. Listen, I don't care where you got that swelling, but we have to talk. It's very important."

"Yes, my dear, successful son is going to college," as she moved in closer for a kiss.

"Don't touch me," he said. "Get into the living room and sit down. I have something very important to say."

He was followed into the living room. She sat in her bathrobe on the sofa.

"Would you like some tea?" he asked.

"Listen, I'm really tired, okay. I just want some sleep."

"Okay," and then he began the speech which would convince her: "Mom, I'm leaving for college tomorrow, and it's all because of you," how marvelously he pontificated, "and in return I will take the business world by storm. I'll be the next Andrew Carnegie, you'll see, and one day we'll have fried chicken every night, but there is one thing that we must do."

"I know you will. You were made for success," she said.

"Mom, this is not the life for you. It's not the life for us. I hear what goes on. I stay up all night hearing those terrible fights you and Dad have, and it hurts me to see you like this. You can't stand it either, I know."

"Your Dad and I have fights like any other married couple."

"But it's not good for us. You've worked so hard, and I want to repay you, if you'll only let me. I have a plan for all this, and this is not something for you to accept or reject. It's something that we both must do in order to lead decent lives, happy lives away from Dad. I've already arranged all this. I have rented an apartment close to the campus..."

"With what money?"

"I've saved up."

"Don't lie to me, Noble."

"All right, I haven't rented an apartment, but the next step for us is renting an apartment near the campus, a two bedroom with a small kitchen, probably a split-level, and for you and me to live together near the campus. You'll find work in the town, and I'll go to classes every night..."

"Wait, Noble. I'm not going with you. That's your own time to learn. And what would I do? Hang out with your fraternity buddies?"

"You're coming with me, and we are leaving this horrendous house and your horrendous husband."

"He's your father," she said sternly.

"I don't care who he is. We're leaving this place tomorrow. I won't stand for this anymore. You and I are going, and from now on I'll take care of you. We leave tomorrow. Dad won't be home anyway. Let's go, get your stuff together. We'll leave Waspachick poor, but we'll return with a mansion on the North side. This is all according to my plan."

"I'm not going anywhere. You have to take care of yourself. It's you I'm worried about. Don't waste your time worrying about me. I can take care of myself."

"Oh really? Like that swelling under your eye? You'll need reconstructive surgery pretty soon."

"Don't get wise with me, young man. This is your mother you're talking to."

"Yes, you're my mother, and that's exactly why we're leaving first thing in the morning. Get your stuff together."

"Noble, I'm not going anywhere. Let's get that straight. I've got my job, and my place is with my husband."

"You call him a husband?"

"Don't raise your voice in this house."

"A husband? He gets drunk every night at Greely's Tavern, and you call him a husband? He's never here, and when he is here, he does nothing but, but, but beat you up."

She stood and brought a finger to his nose.

"You are never again to talk to me the way you just did. Now get to your room before I get really mad."

He would have acquiesced at this point, but the plan and the vision overrode the obedient child within him. He knocked away her hand.

"No, you get your stuff together before I get really mad."

"You expect me to leave my husband and my work just to live with my son who has the benefit of leaving this God-forsaken place? What do you think I've been working so hard for? To live with my son? To spend the earnings I've raked up for your education?"

"What work?" he seethed. "Let's not kid each other. Even I know you're the town prostitute with a husband who beats you because of it."

She slapped him. She had never done so before. Hot tears flooded his eyes, the tears of an angry child. He pushed her to the floor.

"Now you listen to me," he whispered hotly, "you're coming with me, and that's final," and he dragged her with both arms towards her bedroom. He never knew defiance could be so easy.

His mother struggled while being dragged, and she tore away from him, got to her feet, and slapped him a second time. A red anger burned within him. He closed his fists and prepared to strike, until he heard the whimpers, not tears, but whimpers, as though her tear ducts had been dried by so many conflicts.

"Go ahead," she said in the silence. "Go ahead. Do it. You're just like your father. You'll always be like your no-good father. What are you waiting for? Do it, damn it."

He wanted to. All those lies. All that discipline, for what? And then he said calmly:

"And you'll always be a whore, nothing but a common everyday whore."

She stood in the shadows. He bolted to his room and slammed the door. The horror of it came not with the deed, but in its satisfaction, like hitting a baseball with the meat of the bat, the thump which sends it to the bleacher seats, his grand plan, however, ruined.

He stayed in his room for several hours. He didn't want to leave on such terrible terms, yet the satisfaction of what he did meant that he was finally growing up, moving away from his mother's protection. The comment of becoming like his father hurt him. He would kill his father, if he ever touched her again. His music, however, settled his rage and homicidal intimations. His bags were packed. All was set for the journey. Perhaps the best remedy for a conflict lies in its avoidance.

He soon fell asleep and awoke in the uneasy hours of the morning. He opened the door to the bathroom. He flicked on the light. His mother lay in the bathtub, in a dark pool of blood.

Book Two:

Light

Chapter One

"Hey, are you alright, mister?" said the woman next to him, the infant prodding her lap.

He longed for the darkness of his own internal world, as though he drew pleasure from its tragic consequences. His inebriation hung with him, and he was lucky enough to be released on his own instead of thrown into jail for contempt.

"It's not that bad," she said, "and it isn't the end of the world."

Noble wasn't sure if that was good or bad. He rubbed his eyes and acclimated to the crowded antechamber, a loud speaker belching numbers and the climate unbearably muggy. The winter ended abruptly. Even though his disliked the cold, the warmth signaled new lows.

Things couldn't have been worse. Sweat wandered down his temples, and his irritability erupted into agitation and unease. He had to get out of there, away from the dregs of society and onto the familiar turf of upper-crust Waspachick villagers. The beige linoleum, the mildewy walls, the pea-green disposable chairs, the mother with her child, and the old coughing man were less symbols of his predicament and more examples of an ugliness from which he needed immediate flight.

The unseasonable sunshine followed him the five miles into Waspachick's center. All about people were celebrating spring's arrival. Women in spandex and college sweatshirts jogged passed him. Bicycles whizzed with the flow of afternoon traffic. All around him the flush of melting snow, an indoctrination of the new season. The breeze brought relief from the municipal building, and yet his irritability bit like unruly stable flies. What would happen if he just turned around, dropped everything, and made his way Westward? What was so special about Waspachick that he had to remain there like a dog tethered to a parking meter? He could hitchhike down Route 17 and over to 80 West. Once on the interstate he could flag down tired truck drivers and make it to the Coast in time for high tide and those delectable beach-women who would never refuse him. What a risk. From quiet, assiduous guitar player to fugitive-at-large, running from a Mid-Atlantic probation officer to the shrines of the Pacific, meeting others who shared his dreary visions, the world exploding, the only remedy these flirtatious nymphs and the righteous breath of ocean...

He stopped on the sidewalk and looked into a wide road which led to Route 17. He could have dropped everything and followed this road. In his projections, however, he didn't get far.

He arrived at Shylock's apartment in the late afternoon. Luckily Shylock was at the coffee house. He searched behind the sofa and found a whiskey bottle. He poured himself a full grass and watered it down with ice cubes. His guitar leaned against the wall. As he drank, a joyous gaiety supplanted his irritability, but he viewed his guitar as menacing. He was afraid it may not yield its previous efficacy. He always encountered this difficulty before playing, a prediction of total failure when trying to recapture that high note. The longer he evaded the task of playing, the harder it became to play. He had been separated from his instrument for only a few hours, but it seemed like days, weeks, years, since he strummed the strings. What was the big deal? he asked. Just pick it up and begin another session. The booze was with him, the apartment empty. What was so difficult? Perhaps it dealt with his notion of achievement, that every practice session needed to approach a level of greatness or perfection.

If the guitar didn't obey his slightest command, then the session would be useless. The guitar must bend to his will, like dissidents on a dictator's work camp. His initial gaiety caved in to this unbelievable frustration, the dense wall which separated him from his instrument. He could have smashed it to bits; he could have thrown it off the balcony, or dunked it into a tub of scalding water, anything for it to stop calling his name, needing him to liberate its hidden sound. Maybe he put too much pressure on himself. He was also inhibited by the great many guitarists who came before him, these same idols who pushed the instrument beyond its limitations. He had little idea how to encapsulate his every waking experience through this one shining instrument. And then loomed this idea that the total of his practice sessions were worthless, that he would somehow fail in his glorious attempts, that he would never be great, only a lesser known player who never had the potential of a greater artistry. He felt a deep hollowness at the one particle of an idea that his efforts, his toil and struggle, would never bring him the same satisfaction as living his most precious dreams, that he would be buried as a man unsung, a statistic in a dusty encyclopedia, as though his soul couldn't thrive without proper recognition from those housewives who scurried by. Perhaps this was the root of the problem: his determination to become a great guitarist without the toil of practice. He could skip the rudimentary phase and latch onto an image of greatness and notoriety, living his dream without having to play. The convenience of image over substance.

He squatted next to the instrument and sipped his whiskey. If only he could practice through proximity. If only his fingers could release a greater magic, or unearth a tune which had never been played before. He clutched the instrument by its neck and jerked it from slumber. He practiced between gulps of whiskey, going over the tabulations, the string exercises, the tremolo deviations, touching every string with deference and caution, as though the session may collapse and fail at any moment, the misguided fear that failure hid behind a flat chord or a severed continuity or a jam which faltered before epiphany.

He pushed hard, the pick grinding every string, his hand inching closer to the high-pitched end of the neck, and suddenly he stopped. The internal critic censored his playing.

If only his play would make sense, follow some established form and structure, never decline into the muck of careless improvisation. Was he mad in thinking a record executive would fall for this? Again the internal critic with its cold rationale and knowledge of market forces and demographics. This stuff will never pass for music, he thought; the second one breaks from logical melody, the moment when a guitarist shows his infinite personality through his playing, the internal critic puts an end to the slightest musings of utopia in favor of a more patient, earthy sound.

He gulped at his whiskey and tried again, a slow strum which hurried into loud, huffing bellows, and then a break into the intricacies of a high E note, sliding from fret to fret, inching his way towards a similar high-pitched wail, and suddenly sliding down towards the nut in keeping with a pattern, no longer the self-indulgent improvisations, and in this manner he appeased the critic by establishing a structure through which he could still maintain his originality, a prison where license plates were manufactured and rocks were chiseled.

He followed the same pattern until he was too drunk to practice. He collapsed on Shylock's sofa, the warm inebriation humming in his brain. He had played for ten minutes, and already he showed fatigue and discomfort.

He wished he could rush the process of learning, to arrive at a level which flirted with mastery, and then begin from the stance of notoriety and expertise, as though the guitar-playing world would follow him no matter what he played. He dreamt lavishly, with women who wanted him for what he represented. Not a thing had changed since high school; those sun-drenched beaches, the award shows, the clubs. No, this is not the way, he thought, as he accepted an award for best all-time guitarist. And when the image became clear and utterly preposterous, he crawled from the sofa and drowned in more whiskey, squelching these fantasies. There must be an attempt to cure image with substance, and he would be the first artist in a long time to do so. The other great artists of generations passed had sold themselves out, and Noble remained the last pioneer. He would accept no money, no glory from his expertise...gulp...and he would donate all of his money to charity...another gulp...and the world would be indelibly marked by his style of play which would move mountains...another gulp...and cause a joining of hands and minds...until he finished the bottle. Amazing what Noble endured to be a person other than himself. He too had been captured by what others had- an image. He must now cast aside the image and work from the very bottom, those same creatures at the municipal building who the apparitions insisted were more than insects but living spirits within flesh and blood.

He strummed slowly. He recreated the three of them in the municipal building, their vacuous stares suggesting poverty, sickness, and above all oppression. These people were not insects, they were not numbers on an actuary's list. They lived and breathed, and for that isolated moment they were connected through their various infractions. And only through a gentle strum can their voices be heard, the voices of those millions calling plaintively for mercy, an alleviation from penalty through an empathic strum getting thicker and more complicated as their stories were. And it is art through which these voices are carried, from one section of the ladder to the next, this thing called art which transformed climbing into a flowering spiritual quest. They were people just like him. He couldn't comprehend how alike they were.

He searched for more whiskey. He searched the entire apartment. He knew he had stashed several bottles throughout the household. He checked behind the sofa, under the sofa, the cabinet beneath the sink, the closet in Shylock's bedroom, the guitar box, and the utility closet. Instead he found a ten dollar bill in Shylock's bedside drawer.

He headed into town and went to a second, more obscure liquor store further south, not the one next to the coffee house, as Shylock could have easily spotted him. He purchased another whiskey bottle and cruised home with his gaiety recharged. He played his guitar with an abandon until Shylock returned.

Noble explained the events of the day and told him about Alcoholics Anonymous.

"It may be good for you," said Shylock.

"I'm no alcoholic, but if I don't do it, they'll put me in jail for sure."

"It's getting late. Shouldn't you be getting to a meeting?"

"I can go tomorrow, and besides, how would I get there?"

Shylock picked up the phone and made a toll-free call despite Noble's protestations.

It turned out there was a meeting in Waspachick, at a sprawling stone church near the supermarket.

"I don't want to go. I have a lot to do."

"Like what? Sit here all day and night drinking and stealing money from me?"

"Shy, I'm not stealing from you."

"If you don't go, I want you out, is that clear? No more nice-Shylock. You obviously can't handle liquor."

"I'll go, all right, I'll go."

"I'm only telling you, because I've seen what's happened in the last few weeks. Ever since you bought the guitar, it's gone all down hill. Are you, like, drinking so much because other musicians drink a lot?"

"It has nothing to do with that," snapped Noble.

"All right. I didn't mean to upset you."

"This is very hard work," as he gulped at the bottle. "I guess I'm going out with a bang."

"I mean it, Noble. No more of this. You're a guest here, okay? Let's make that clear. Don't abuse my friendship further."

"This is the last whiskey bottle you'll ever see around me," as he finished it.

"Prove it then. Prove it by not drinking. Prove me wrong."

In the evening, Noble was driven to the church which occupied one full block of a lesser-known avenue parallel to the strip. The entrance to this heavy, gothic structure was well-lit, and on the steps gathered people of all sorts smoking cigarettes, some sitting on the long stone slabs which tumbled from the doorway. Some stood and conversed. Noble gawked at them through the car window and shook his head.

"This will never work, Shy."

"How do you know? Besides, if you don't go, you'll be tossed in jail. The probation officer will be after your ass."

"I'm not an alcoholic."

"Prove me wrong, then. Give it a try. I'll meet you home later."

"Where are you going?" he asked in alarm.

"I have a date at the bar in East Waspachick. No offense."

"None taken."

"Hey, here's a breath mint," as he dropped one in Noble's palm, "don't want you getting into any trouble. You're pretty drunk in my estimation."

He crushed the mint between his molars. He hoped it would prevent anyone from suspecting him. He would act totally clean and straight in their company. He was there only for the DWI slip. These slips, with the seal of New Jersey on them, would be given to the probation officer as proof of his attendance. He would not talk to anyone; he would march in, sit for the full hour, grab the slip, leave, and ultimately return to his guitar and the whiskey.

He darted through the pack of smoking alcoholics and entered the church. Its external architecture deceived the lay onlooker. Inside the floors were made of blonde wood, and the walls of white plaster. In the congregation room, the lights were turned low and candles on the tables illumined the expanse. He also detected a stage at the head of the room. Apparently it wasn't being used. He heard the din of conversation rolling from one end of the hallway to the other. He avoided this area and quickly took a seat.

The darkness soothed his initial anxieties. His shadow loomed sinister on the walls. After reaffirming his intentions not to utter a word, the AA-goers trickled into the room through a side door. The meeting commenced with a vague preamble.

The people sitting next to him smiled. He smiled back. 'Remember, keep silent, get the slip, and get out of here,' he thought. He didn't own a watch, so had little clue when the required hour would end. He sat quietly and hoped the format excluded him. A medium-sized elderly gentleman talked of DWI cards. He wore a blue polyester suit. His speech was hard and methodical. Noble earmarked him for after the meeting.

After a long preamble the leader of the meeting, a tall, heavy-set woman of middle age, a face as demure as a sheet of ice, went around the room starting with the person next to her. She mentioned a topic-'powerlessness.' Noble again paid little attention. He grew nervous, as he sat only two chairs away. He would have to participate.

When his turn came he 'passed' without mentioning his name or the 'I am an alcoholic' disclaimer. He wanted to participate only in his buzz. He didn't listen at all to what they said. Their contributions were cryptic and esoteric, as though they belonged to an occult. The Branch Davidians came to mind. He did notice how they looked in the mellow candlelight. Their ages ranged from teeny-bopper to old and toothless. They were unattractive or far below the Waspachick standard. He saw this as a significant drawback, but he sat in a drunken daze, waiting for the coveted DWI slip and boom! Walk out into the clear evening and gulp the whiskey at home.

The bits and pieces of talk only intensified his longing for the drink. The discussions focused on alcohol exclusively, and as each drunk shared, he could taste the bitter elixir running down his gullet. Thank God he wasn't like these people, he thought. Imagine not drinking for the rest of their lives? What would they do without liquor? There would be little joy, little escape from the rest of the world. It would be so incredibly boring, so tremendously empty and vacuous. There would be little reward for a hard day's work, little enjoyment, and few women.

The attractive women hung around the bars, especially the one in East Waspachick. There were no beautiful women here, only ugliness; old maids, widows and widowers, corpulent and grotesque, agitated and irate. They would never again experience the beauty of alcohol, its power to relieve the pains of existence if only for a few moments. No great man of any society had ever emerged from these meetings, certainly not a guitarist, and they would go through their lives dismissing the only substance which provided an escape. This was Noble's reasoning. These alcoholics were ugly, weak whiners who stuck together for an hour or so, living boring and difficult lives. He had no place with them, as they had no place within the calculus of his artistic ambitions. They were losers who admitted they had lost everything through their inability to hold their liquor. Alcoholics were bums on the street without a nickel to their names. They ended up sodomized in prison or in the psychiatric wards walking like robots, or in the gutter. He had little connection with these nuts, these crazies, these outlaws who hid in these churches and complained of their misfortunes. How absurd.

He heard from a stray voice that the only requirement for membership was a desire to stop drinking. Since Noble didn't fulfill this requirement, he didn't belong. But he stayed, because he was forced to stay. He had grown anxious and irritable. His thoughts screamed for a drink, anything for the bliss of a drink to drown these miserable misfits, to eradicate them from memory. He heard words like 'Higher Power,' 'God,' and 'Spirituality,' and he instantly rebelled. Overpowering evidence suggested there was no such thing as a God, and if a God existed he had created evil from everything holy and pure. As far as he was concerned, God didn't exist. The concept remained a psychological opiate for the weak, sick, and hopeless. Only people who had frontal lobe damage prayed. Only the depressed, lascivious, and suicidal prayed for this manna from heaven.

He fought the urge to scream, to shout, to vomit upon these candles and mouths moving at the surge of syncopation towards the tail end of the discussion. He needed a drink immediately. He couldn't handle it. He wanted to shout, kick, and yell, but as usual with Noble, his composure was dead enough to pass a polygraph. He didn't move an inch. He didn't even shift positions in his chair. His buttocks numbed. He sat like a congealed bowl of oatmeal, his brain melting into porridge. A tingle spread from the tips of his fingers into his hands, then his arms. The temperature of the room turned cold while his body grew warm and feverish. A cold sweat, and then the inclination to shit in his pants. Finally, he shivered in his seat. He tried desperately to control it, and when he focused on the task, the shivering stopped. He was relieved at the power of his mind to overcome this embarrassment.

The meeting soon ended with a group prayer. Noble prayed for his guitar, his whiskey bottle, and his instruction book. All he needed were these three objects operating in his life, nothing else, certainly not AA. Alas, he needed a DWI slip from the man in the blue polyester suit. The lights were turned on, and the candles blown. He rushed to the man in blue polyester, his pale eyes reminding him of a retired school teacher, an ex-cop, or a man who hated big government.

"Listen, man, I need a DWI slip," said Noble quickly. "I heard you're the man."

"What's your name, son?" asked the man.

"Noble. My name is Noble."

"First time here?" he said with a derisive grin.

"Yes, my first time. Listen, man, I'm really in a big rush. Can you give me the slip or the ticket or whatever?"

"What's your rush?"

"I've got some people to see, business and all."

"You're not fooling anybody," he said solemnly.

"What? What on earth do you mean?"

"You heard what I said."

"Listen, man, I need that slip or else my probation officer will throw me in jail."

"It's called a 'card,' a DWI 'card,'" his articulation slow, precise, and enervating.

"Well, whatever it is, I need the 'card.'"

"You come to this meeting tomorrow, sober, and I'll give you the card, okay?"

"Let me make this clear. I don't know who you are or what power trip your on, but I need that card, and I need it now. This is not the time to fuck around with someone's life, okay, now give me the card so I don't have to raise my voice."

"I said, come here sober tomorrow, and I'll give you both cards- one for tonight, and one for tomorrow. Satisfied?"

"No, I'm not satisfied," snapped Noble. "I've been here at this meeting for an hour straight listening to this bullshit, and I want the card immediately, now, pronto, in haste, got me?"

"Is this the way you want to live, a young guy like yourself? Sweating and shaking for another snort?"

"Spare me the lecture, man. Give me the card," he whispered hotly.

"That's my offer. Come tomorrow sober, and you'll get your card. Until then, I don't want to see you."

Noble flew from the church and rushed for Shylock's apartment. He could have punched the man in the ear. He could have pulled apart his limbs like the centipede he was. The nerve of such an imbecilic weasel, this decaying K-mart shopper with his shit-brown tie and his slate blue suit which mimicked his eyes, those albinic insect eyes which didn't move when he spoke. He could have been blind, that worthless two-bit lush, his black zipper boots from some oriental import shop, his mind bought from a gum-ball machine, his body like a warped wooden plank. The nerve of this lonely, dismal man avenging himself for years without the sauce, so vindictive that he took out all of that pent-up frustration on him.

Noble needed a drink before his body went into convulsions, before his brain liquefied into a soupy, drippy ooze. He hated that old windbag, that geriatric, diaper-wearing, cryptofascist failure. They were all as ugly as insects, failures by default, and Noble would drink just to spite them.

He almost ran up the slope to the apartment driveway. He searched frantically for the keys, searched again for his keys, searched a third time. Shit, he forgot his keys. He could have banged the door down, but then a window of calm encouraged him to think.

On the narrow balcony he peered through the window. The apartment was dark, and he couldn't see a thing but his own harried reflection. He tried the window. His fingernails chewed the crevice where the window frame met the sill. He succeeded in getting it open and crawled through it, banging his knee in the process. He switched on the light and spotted the warm whiskey bottle by the sofa. It was half-full. He chugged it from the bottle, the amber dripping from his chin.

After polishing off the entire bottle, he felt normal again. The shivering stopped. The cold perspiration dried. The anxiety left. His anger towards this one man drained into the sewer of distant, unimportant memories. He was whole and complete again.

He thought things over in a rational manner but discovered that the whiskey bottle was drained and needed replenishment before the practice session. He still had change from the last purchase. He journeyed to the liquor store next to Shylock's coffee house. A town should always have two liquor stores, thought Noble. That way, the counter people don't ask questions or get too suspicious.

He walked to the first liquor store, but it was closed. He got nervous again. He couldn't see the night through without another bottle. He moved further South towards the other liquor store. He walked briskly, the climate getting colder, his temperature steadily rising. Shady characters appeared more frequently. He thought they looked him over without provocation, as though it were odd to see his type on the southern streets at night, a spectacle, a young man out of place. He cruised by them and to his delight found the liquor store open, even empty.

The South side liquor store was unlike the one in the center of town. The counterperson sat behind thick, bullet-proof plexiglass. The whiskey bottles were stacked in a fuzzy blur behind the plastic. He panted within a cramped space, one-on-one with the salesperson and the drawer which he pushed open. Noble dropped every last dollar and dime he had.

"Whiskey," said Noble, "your cheapest and largest bottle."

The counter-person flashed a variety of sizes. Naturally, Noble chose the biggest bottle, regardless of the brand. It could have been mouthwash for all he cared. Before leaving, he downed a mouthful, his mood elevating. On his way towards Central Waspachick he was unencumbered by the patrolman on vigilant watch, as the Southern areas were still kept under the town's jurisdiction like a prodigal son. A short man with a wide-brimmed chapeau offered him "coke, reefer, coke, reefer," which he would have purchased had he the money. Instead he swigged from the paper bag. By the time he climbed the slope to Shylock's apartment, the whiskey bottle was half-drained. Nevertheless he was content with his purchase and saved some for the long hours ahead. His guitar waited for him, and the sessions would be easier.

Before picking it up, however, he again encountered this fear. He couldn't understand this fear before playing, this haunting conniption which rendered him impotent. He looked at the instrument in horror, as though the booze weren't enough. It went beyond a lack of inspiration. Even the fear of failure wasn't acceptable anymore. He had to surpass these ghosts, these guitarists who revolutionized the sounds of each steel chord. He put himself under pressure again, but there was more to it- the stubborn problem of the creative process- the movement from amateurish day dreams to realist professionalism, the attempt to create a product for public consumption.

He reasoned that the creative process within his practice sessions concerned the mind and its attempt to inspire itself into a form of work, as though it were a muscle which needed conditioning. The bottom line involved the work. Not inspiration. Noble could have easily been inspired by the mosquito slipping through the window screen, or the noise of the jet airplane. Inspiration, then, was not the problem. It was the idea of work, the suicide sprints after practice, or the long dirt road in front of the out-of-shape jogger. In order for the creative process to ensue, the guitar player must first find a conducive environment.

So he cleaned Shylock's apartment. He threw away the beer cans, folded the sheet on the sofa, dusted the cobwebs from the corners, arranged the CD's, even sprayed air freshener which stung his eyes as it misted to earth. Between each of these tasks, he chugged the whiskey and mistakenly drained the entire bottle.

He didn't get a drunken high from the intoxicant. Again, it brought him to a level of normalcy which avoided the anxiousness, the irritability, and above all else the shaking. He reasoned that if he left for more whiskey and then returned, the new environment would freshen or cleanse his spate for work, like setting fire to a palace.

There was no time to waste. He ran to the South side liquor store, purchased what more he could from the change in his trousers, and returned with a half-pint of whiskey.

The apartment was as clean as could be, a remarkable difference from the combat zone he had traveled through. And once again, the fear- the idea that he must sweat, toil, and bleed with each string, a chore, a bureaucratic entanglement.

He took out the trash and strategically left the bottle next to the guitar. It must be the fear of work, thought Noble.

His mind projected into the session, visualizing the uncomfortability when a riff didn't sound right or a chord played off tune, or the struggle when the internal music externalized into something pathetic. The guitar was the nucleus around which everything revolved, and he avoided the nucleus, as though the main drama floated around it. Perhaps he was burning out. Maybe he was a terrible player, but the dream, the vision, an inundated arena and himself on the stage, plucking the strings. Somehow the vision seemed unimportant and the goal of working a high priority.

He found it harder to stick within the bar lines. If there were no such impediment he could have explored the complexity of his instrument. Someone had to listen, and if the tune entered the irrational or the nonsensical, if it flew beyond traditional limits, the tune would fail. His audience became the cheers and jeers of his own brain. To please the censor, to shout within a three-minute format, to have that shout make sense, and for the audience to interpret this sound in the correct manner became the equivalent of hearing Noble's own voice through cluttered technicalities. This leads to the idea that one's own private play, one's private world becomes easier to construct than its movement beyond it.

If he were to strum for himself, if he had an internal audience which accepted anything he played, what would he play but music completely irrational and at heart rebellious, a loud distorted thunder, a primordial shout within darkness, a bathtub full of blood? In no way could he be so indulgent, and yet that's what he wanted, not the rigid framework provided, not the commonsensical definition of what music should be, but what it ought to be.

He tried this new approach, playing recklessly without tablature or notes or bar lines. He didn't see it as work but something which brought pleasure for the first time since purchasing the instrument. His chords didn't make sense. They were never meant for public consumption, only fulfilled a private desire to express what he saw, what had happened, what was to become, almost like stuttering, until the internal audience took over and coerced him to make sense and walk the line and articulate positive sounds.

Become too original or outspoken and the public will reject him. Stay trapped within traditional boundaries and the public will ignore him. These were extremities, but all guitarists walk a centrist line of play, the precise optimal point where tradition and innovation meet, and by innovation he meant doing better what some old-time guitarist did before him, taking the instrument one step further, but no, he thought, there is little pleasure gained from reaching this optimal point. His guitar must be the dose which alters perceptions, so that listeners may grasp the implicit message and at the same time elevate their consciousness as a result of that message. A tall order, but the guitarist who fails to be true to his own vision, whether negative or positive, self-indulgent or altruistic, becomes the statistic which collects dust in a CD vault. When the artist follows his vision, he accepts himself. Betray the vision, and one goes along the well-worn route of the status quo.

Ultimately it was his choice. To follow the primordial scream or ensconce himself with the tired bar lines of tradition.

Another matter apart from this bothered him more. He had noticed that most music, especially popular music, had a singular theme which ruled over others. He put it simply in one miraculous word: women.

If playing the guitar requires experience, and only experience (in accordance with his own theories), then the lack of a woman diminished his capabilities. Before, his womanlessness was inconsequential, but now the lack of a woman fueled his fantasies to the point where they never connected with reality, and at the same time, created a label of reality which was destructive, nihilistic, iconoclastic. This negative view would preclude a relationship with the opposite sex. For a moment, he believed that the primordial scream was inappropriate. His daydreams too self-indulgent (how he hated that term). The woman provides a relief from the scream and the impetus for the fantastic. And is not vision truly an acceptance by a beautiful woman, his instrumentals a reflection of this longing?

He was on the cusp of either finding a woman or damning them as an alien species. The only woman he had ever known well resulted in this primordial scream, which was pleasurable but wholly unconstructive. Aye, but the conscience- an equal rights amendment, an end to sexual harassment, the goals of a woman's empowerment. Yet a guitarist who could easily hate the opposite sex lingered like his inebriation. Certainly he aimed for women out of his league, but such was his imperfection. Too much television, too many Waspachick women who copied what they saw. He hated dwelling on past particulars, but a woman must be part of the creative process, not the reward at the end of it. He will find her in the East Waspachick bar, twirling an umbrella in her drink, all alone, sitting in the hollow emptiness, and he walks up to her, and by the simple look into her soft eyes, he knows her. The crust of glaciers melt into the heat which lies beneath, the instant where words exchanged are absolutely pointless.

But she insists on conversation, as though this may unite them in an ethereal bond. Naturally, he tries to impress her with his worldly knowledge, the mythical places he's traveled, the money in his nonexistent bank account. He puts on airs as though flexing muscles on a beach and calmly takes all of this in and sorts through the web of disinformation. She flashes a price tag above her head. He passes her initial test. He peels the layer to yet another barrier. He must first qualify as a good provider, he must pay the price in terms of dollars.

The next layer soon appears: are they compatible? Do they have anything in common? They discuss living in Waspachick. She on the North end, Noble farther South. He isn't much of a conversationalist, but he plays along, his smile on the verge of twitching, a phony laughter. He believes she's transmitting signals, speaking in the cabala of batting eyelashes, the waving of slender hands, the girlish giggle suggesting that he has broken another barrier only to encounter another one.

Quick sex is not her style. She definitely has a boyfriend, a serious boyfriend. She tells him that they are flying to Cancun, and she's afraid the vacation may be too overwhelming. She has never taken a trip with a man before, yes, that greasy, slimy excuse for a guitarist. Is she really that attached? If she is, then why on earth are they talking? Why is she sending signals as overt as glowing pistils? If he doesn't play his cards right, if he reveals his infatuation, the house of cards will collapse. There is no such thing as honesty, as it is always too brutal. He carries the conversation to its limit. There is a barrier he can't penetrate, and they revolve in similar pleasantries until the forced conversation avoids uncomfortable silences. He can be honest and say that she treads on his dreams, he can lay his cards down, as she is a better player, but he holds and waits for one last card.

Friendship follows a kiss and never before; the kiss which unlocks this torrent of desire. Platonic friendship is too unmanly for him and never enough for a woman. She must be swept by his bravado. She reveals herself only after undressing in her apartment, the two of them nude and connected by tender energy. She invites, and he explores her nature, not so complex as he initially sensed, not so secretive as he had heard, nothing so hidden and other worldly as old-time guitarists had claimed, but another person shaped by experience, the gender difference only an excuse. After all, is not part of him woman as well? Isn't she part man? But experience hath made him man, and her woman, equal with complexity and simplicity, the only barrier their gender, and once this is removed as he enters her, there is the sex which breaks them apart and causes a slow, meiotic fission. She returns to her own world, and he to his, and never again shall they meet except within their drifting memories, those moments when they first touched, to the moment they fell apart in exhaustion and cold awareness.

This was the extent of his session, turning the primordial scream into a soft, but limited ballad. He would never land a record deal with this crap. He must experience a woman again. It had been dreadfully long, and he had one woman in mind. If only the bar didn't sound last call so early. He would have walked to East Waspachick only to find her talking with that greasy, long-haired nobody.

He could play better. He could win her with his superior talent. Yes, even artists compete. He hesitated on this point. He was so tired and inebriated that he couldn't rightly probe the result of two artists competing or what happens to music when its thrown into a maze of rats chasing the same cheese. It bothered him, but beyond this he fell asleep, guitar in one hand, the whiskey in the other.

Shylock never made it home. Noble awoke in the late afternoon. Although the apartment was clean, a great deal of laundry had piled up. He had no intention of washing it. It was getting close to meeting time, and he couldn't show up drunk or else his DWI card would be denied. He needed a drink badly. He vomited in the bathroom. He shook all over. A nausea returned, and he vomited a second time, a fit of dry-heaving, and still he shook. The shaking followed him to the church.

He tried conquering the shakes by squeezing his hands. This technique settled them, but not the rest of his body which quaked in defiance. A paranoia accompanied his trembling. Everyone around him stared in some fanatical delight, deriding him, taunting him. He had never felt so humiliated before. He ran through the crowd gathered on the church steps, and took a seat in the empty congregation room. His eyes watered and streaked the candle-light.

He couldn't sit still. He would stay only for the DWI card, and then sprint to the liquor store. He regretted not stocking up on a case of whiskey beforehand. He would have traded his guitar for one tiny, harmless shot of amber liquid. Steady, stay steady, fold the arms, cross the legs, don't shake, don't sweat, only an hour and fifteen minutes, and then he could get to the liquor store, and this entire miserable and nauseating experience would fade into the blackness like intermittent shadows on the walls, those damned walls with those idiotic signs posted between the casements: 'Think,' 'Easy does it,' 'One day at a time,' and here was a laugh: 'But for the Grace of God,' Well, God sucked. God had never been kind to him. God alone contributed to this horror. Stop shaking, for one minute will you stop shaking? His heart pounding, the room freezing cold but his body moist and febrile, his legs numb and dead but alive with nervousness and agitation. Look at these people, so ugly and boring. Look how they hide within the dark shadows. Creeps, everyone of them. They will never know a pain such as this. And there's the man in a gray polyester suit, not blue anymore, that old, miserable cockroach, a little insect he could have squashed. Damn it, stop shaking, hurry up, not more than an hour left, get the meeting started. Stop sweating, stop shaking.

The meeting focused on him. He couldn't understand a word of it. 'Keeping it green,' he heard several times. And then he felt a tap on his shoulder. It was the man in the polyester suit. Yes, the same man with the DWI cards. Perhaps they saved an extra bottle for emergencies. Noble followed him to the kitchen where these sanctimonious pricks hung out before the meeting. Noble shook all over.

"I want you to remember how you're feeling right now," said the polyester man.

"Don't screw with me, old man," said Noble, "I know you have some booze stashed around here someplace."

"Just remember exactly how you're feeling right now. C'mon, let's go."

He followed the polyester man to his car. He assumed the old man was taking him to a bar. He got in and hugged himself, the shaking uncontrollable and violent.

"Quickly, old man, quickly- let's go to the bar, I could really use a drink."

The polyester man stayed calm, as though he possessed a greater wisdom. They drove in the darkness. A hint of rain stained the windshield. They came upon an area flooded with light- the Emergency Room of Waspachick General Hospital.

"If you want to get better, you'll follow me."

"There's no way I'm going in there. Take me to East Waspachick. I know a good place. You're an alcoholic, aren't you? Don't you need a drink once in a while? I mean, an Emergency Room? I can't afford medical care, old man. Let's go, I'll buy you a drink. Don't you crave a drink once in a while, you tired old curmudgeon?"

"Get out of the car," he said sternly.

Noble followed him into the emergency room. The area stank of noxious antiseptic, the linoleum white, the walls white, the nurses clad in white like larvae. His body ached in exhaustion, the muscles shooting spurts of pain. His brow swam in sweat, and his shaking continued.

On the contrary the emergency room was silent and calm. The smell of band aids, gauze, sterile needles, rubbing alcohol, syringes, prosthesis, suction tubing, latex gloves, and scrub brushes suggested sanguinary incisions, ice-cold scalpels, scissors, steel spreaders, and cadavers.

"Just settle down, okay," said the polyester man.

"I need a drink, man, okay? I need a drink. No medicine can do the job as a well as a drink, man. What kind of place is this? Isn't there a nurse around here?" he shouted, and then continued: "I can't stop shaking, it's so hot in here, and then when it's hot, it's too cold, damn it, help me. Give me a shot, pour me a drink, but help me."

The polyester man pulled aside the nurse and conversed with her. Noble neither heard nor cared what they said. The old man returned, his voice a mellow baritone:

"Listen, these people will help you for the next couple of days. I can't tell you how important it is that you remember this moment. I'll come and get you when you're discharged."

"You're a bastard, old man, y'know that?"

The polyester man left through the sliding doors. He grew highly suspicious of people who helped him for free. At least the nurse who rushed to his side was on the payroll. She withdrew blood from the bend of his arm. She led him into a smaller room and gave him a large tumbler of watery, black liquid. He assumed it was a medicine containing alcohol, like methadone for heroin.

"Swallow all of it," she instructed. "Just in case, there's a bathroom behind you."

He had trouble bringing the tumbler to his lips. He cupped the tumbler with both hands and forced the black liquid down. He stopped midway, his tongue dry and chalky, his stomach rejecting the liquid. He ran to the bathroom and upchucked what he swallowed. He shouted: "What the hell is this stuff?" He was touched by rage. This was definitely not alcohol, but some other sludge.

The nurse returned.

"It's activated charcoal," she said, her demeanor tough and annoyingly persistent. "Drink all of it."

He drank slowly and achieved the same result, a vile vomiting in the toilet. He never knew a mouth could be so elastic. He finished it off and was too exhausted to move. The nurse gave him a blue gown. He lay on the gurney with a saline solution dripping into his arm. The shaking abated to manageable levels. He felt more exhausted than anything else, and he drifted in and out of sleep until a tall doctor in a lab coat handed him two thin pills.

"What is this?" he asked in a daze.

"Ativan. It will help you sleep."

He awoke several hours later in a dark hospital room. The hallway beyond the threshold was brightly lit. There was no human noise, only a buzzing of the lights. The saline solution had been removed from his arm. He walked barefoot on the cold linoleum. In the hallway an old man sat at a wooden table, reading a newspaper. Noble had no idea of the time, since the windows in his hospital room faced a boiler. It could have been high noon or midnight, and the quietude suggested the wee hours of the morning. He was right. A clock with an iron facemask read five-fifteen. AM or PM? He had to ask an old man, sitting there like a stump.

"Where am I?" asked Noble.

The old man smiled.

"You're on the psychiatric ward of Waspachick General Hospital, or we like to call it: West Four."

"You can't be serious."

"Take a look around you. This is a hospital, wouldn't you agree?"

"I dunno," said Noble. "I've never been to a hospital. What time is it?"

"It's about five-fifteen in the morning. Breakfast is served at seven."

"Listen, man, I don't mean to break anyone's plans, but I've gotta get out of here. I'm not a psychiatric patient. I was put here only for a visit, not an overnight stay."

"What's your rush, friend?"

He had also been suspicious of that 'friend' word.

"I'm not in a rush, it's just that, well, I have no reason to be here. Now if you'd just give me my belongings, I think I'll be going. Sorry to disappoint you."

"Why don't you have a seat?"

"What am I doing here?"

"Remember those questions the doctors asked you?"

"Questions? I have no recollection of any questions."

"Well, the results got you here. You were in pretty bad shape. Alcohol will do that to a person."

"Yes, I did have quite a lot." And then: "What am I supposed to do now?"

"Try and get some more sleep," said the old man. "I'll wake you before breakfast."

He tried to sleep, but his mind wandered in many directions, encountering questions like: 'who put me here,' and most perplexing: 'when can I leave?' He feared he may have a psychiatric disorder, but not even the most gifted psychiatrist could have diagnosed him in such a short time.

He lay in bed, twisting into every position imaginable. Sleep never came. Instead he paced the hallways in his hospital gown, avoiding the old man who smiled each time he passed. Noble wanted to see the man in charge, but that was several hours away according to the porcelain activities board scribbled with bright markings. He passed the rooms on the unit and overheard snoring, wheezing, and restlessness. The minutes slipped into slow hours, nothing to do but pace the hallway.

A couple of hours later a kitchen crew rolled in a warming cart holding all the food. Slowly the patients lumbered from their rooms and waited on line. They all wore hospital gowns. Noble likened them to corpses, their hair tangled, their faces puffy, their gait painfully slow. Men in their forties or fifties, he guessed. He had to escape the ward somehow. He could easily wind up like one of them, locked away for years, the blood siphoned from their veins, their dermis dead and leprous. The sight appalled him. He was by far the youngest person on the ward, until the far end of the hallway revealed a woman younger than he, yawning, throwing her arms above her head, only that she was the skinniest, most emaciated creature he had ever beheld.

The gown covered most of her, but oh those attenuated, stringy arms and sunken face, as though her flesh had been sucked through a powerful vacuum. She was hideous, but in a strange way, pretty. Perhaps at one time she had been beautiful, before a fascination and obsession over her looks set in. If the slightest hint of wind were to sneak through the windows it could have easily carried her off like a lost balloon. A pat on the shoulder could have broken every bone.

He joined her on line, her arms dangling from her sockets, as though she sanctioned wide-scale genocide on her body, an assault on every living cell, until the hungry mitochondria starved and gasped for body fat. Noble encountered an emotion he had never felt before, not exactly anger, not exactly pity. It was close to compassion, he decided, a compassion for this waif, a woman damned, not by any eternal ailment but damned by herself. Ghastly. A small nick on her skin could have ended her life, a bread crumb the equivalent of a Thanksgiving meal. Was there a God? How could a woman do this to herself?

He had a vague idea. The conception of beauty these days was narrower than her wrists. Perhaps she had a fear of obesity, or did she place all of her eggs in the basket of beauty, as though this beauty meant survival, and obesity a decline, a loneliness, an ugliness which meant instant banishment from the kingdom of the living? Or did a false trigger in her mind set off a complete and total assault on cellulite, as though an inch more, and then another inch just to make sure the first inch did the job, and during this obsession she slowly lost her appetite, until food became the enemy, and attenuation her only defense? Or maybe she had been alone, without a boyfriend, for the first time in her life, and thought that weight reduction remained the only way to land a man. Could she not for one moment accept herself as beautiful? Or did she have a keen eye for what was ugly and avoided it until her very life hung in the balance? Maybe she was teased as a young girl. Yes, her schoolmates called her names. Ever since those insults she defended herself by striving for super-beauty, above and beyond all expectations, each stare by strange men a point in the win column, every man judging her, every molecule of food adding more weight, more ugliness, more cellulite. Add this psychophysiological condition to the wealth of pretty faces shaking their perfections at cameras, the high standards she had come to accept, the cruelty of stray insults, and the sum was this ghost of a girl standing on line, her eyes peeled to the hospital-issued slippers, her body leaking like bleeding meat.

Noble followed her into a common area. He sat next to her. Another gentleman sat with them. Noble uncovered the tray and found a box of cereal, a hard-boiled egg, two fatty bacon strips, a package of orange juice, a cantaloupe quarter, and a soft roll with packets of butter and jelly. He looked to her tray: a small salad.

She ate the lettuce carefully with a plastic spork, leaf by leaf. She chewed gently, a band aid grazed her hand where a nurse had drawn blood, her spork picking at carrot shreds, each bite a weighty decision. She concentrated solely on her salad. It didn't matter who sat near her. Noble could have been a stuffed animal or a ghost or a spider, it wouldn't have mattered, only her painstaking poking of the lettuce and how each leaf fell from the spork on the verge of being chewed.

"Hey, do you want my roll?" asked Noble.

She didn't look at him. She simply picked up her tray and moved to another table.

"She's like that," said the gentleman across from him.

The day began with a community meeting. Doctors, nurses, orderlies, group facilitators, and the patients, even those who had slept through breakfast, all converged into the same room. Noble wanted nothing more but immediate discharge. Instead the floor was open to discussion about life on the ward. The meeting ran smoothly until a corpulent woman with stray wisps of hair stormed in. She yelled and pointed:

"There's something you're not telling us. Obviously the CIA has it in for us, and all of you are involved. It says so in the book of Revelations, yes, you are all liars and thieves, every one of you."

No one seemed phased by the outburst. The orderlies forced her from the room. Noble could not help but catch scars on her wrists, her brown teeth jagged and twisted like a bombed high-rise. Despite the brief interruption, Noble figured the quickest route to discharge involved cooperation and compliance with these psychiatrists, to follow the schedule, to participate, to ask intelligent questions instead of foaming at the mouth in lunatic frenzy. He would not make the same mistake. Aside from this, however, he focused most of his attentions on this one woman who left his table at breakfast.

He wasn't attracted to her. He didn't hold any romantic feelings towards her, only that her slow disintegration needed pause, and he would do a good deed by befriending her. After all, they were of the same age, give or take a year. The rest of the patients were much older. She sat across from him, her ankles gaunt below her gown, her skin a pale white. She didn't say a word during the meeting. She rocked in her chair, her arms hugging her upper torso, her eyes on her slippers, her hair in a bun.

Huge clumps of time followed every activity. Noble wandered the hallway, tried to sleep, then wandered the hallway, tried to sleep, then wandered the hallway again. Some of the patients watched a morning talk-show on the television. Terrible reception. Others had pre-arranged appointments. He had roamed the hallway for some time, bored out of his mind. The girl must have been in her room, but as the hours elapsed she also paced the hallway. It was wide enough for the two of them. They traded positions from one end to the other, and Noble grew so perturbed by this ignoring of him that he intervened.

"Listen, I'm sorry about what I said at breakfast," blurted Noble, when their paths crossed.

"Sorry? Why are you sorry?"

Hark, she speaks. As with her body, her voice lacked nutrition.

"Let's say that, well, since we're here in this hospital, we could speed up the time by talking to each other."

"Talking never got anyone anywhere," she said, her cheekbones sliding against translucent skin.

"But it may kill time."

"Time was never meant to be 'killed,' only 'filled.'"

"Okay. Let's 'fill' some time. Are you from Waspachick?"

"Yes. I live on the Northern end."

"West side myself, for now at least."

They walked together and exchanged basic information. She had gone to the local high school and then to college in Rhode Island for a year, only to drop out."

"You must be pretty smart," said Noble. "What did you major in?"

"Biology."

"Fascinating stuff. I have a degree in business. But I'm learning the guitar, and I guess that's what I'm doing. I'm a musician. Are you going back to Rhode Island?"

"I can't go back."

"I'm sorry to hear that."

They walked back and forth. Noble thought himself affable, and it appeared she valued his company. They stood near the room where breakfast had been held. She called it 'the Meeting Room.' She asked excitedly:

"You wanna draw a picture with me?"

"I'm terrible at drawing," said Noble.

"Give it a try. It'll be fun, all in the name of filling time."

They sat at the round table. She took a long piece of construction paper from the shelf and spread it before him. She also pulled a box of crayons. She first made a design on the page, and then Noble made a design. They took turns. Noble initially thought she would draw a house or a flower, something concrete and less chimerical. But she instead doodled, and he did the same. While drawing she let out onomatopoetic sounds, a scribble here, a murmur there, a crash in between. Noble found artistry in her simple doodles, and they alternated until odd designs filled the page. Could it be that Noble was actually having fun? And of course he ruined it by getting awfully serious.

"Can I ask you a personal question?" asked Noble.

"Only if I can ask you one."

"Why aren't you eating?"

A dark silence sliced clear through their amusement. A record skipping.

"For the same reason you drink," she said finally. "Now can I ask you a personal question?"

Noble nodded, although he was confused.

"Do you drink because a lot of the great musicians drink, and you feel that you have to drink in order to be great like them?"

He remembered Shylock asking the same question. Perhaps it began that way- the notion that creative people suffered from alcohol or drug addiction or were mentally ill and declared themselves insane. At first alcoholism seemed a rite of passage for any budding musician, much like heroin to budding fashion photographers. It began as unique. He followed to every detail the lives of the musicians who preceded him, as though music and substance abuse where forever intertwined, a rebellion of what the straight, status quo had to offer. The musicians who died early of drug-related illness were instantly hailed as geniuses, while the artists who followed the rules produced trite, meaningless sound. Sobriety was anathema to any artistic endeavor. And Noble had always craved the unreachable status of musical genius. This is how it began, but once within the throes of substance abuse the reasons behind drinking changed. He abused alcohol only to facilitate his sessions. It loosened his fingers. It placed him on original turf. Add to this his grandiosity, the appearance on the stage, the audience filled with women, and suddenly the drink becomes his escape, his one defense against creative paralysis and deterioration.

The creative mind, if left undisciplined, devours all experiential phenomena through the senses. Despite the body's limitations, the creative mind never ceases until the body expires. Drugs and alcohol provide the fodder: the obscure perspective, the vague vision, a drug-induced psychosis, anything to occupy its sharp claws and rancid breath, until it kills all which is light and imposes an abysmal darkness on the soul. Luckily Comstock pulled him over.

"I dunno," said Noble after thinking these things. "It all got out of hand, and I wound up here of all places. But I still don't understand why you stopped eating."

She smiled.

"I don't know either. I guess I got carried away. I've always thought of myself as ugly, like an ugly bug, a fly, or a locust."

Noble was alarmed by this admission. Where were those damned apparitions when he needed them?

"I don't think you're ugly," he said.

"Look at me. Have you ever seen anything more ugly? C'mon?"

"I'm being honest," said Noble, "you're not an ugly woman, and with a few more pounds on ya, you'd look like a super model."

"I'm ugly, okay? Let's drop it."

"But you're not ugly," he exclaimed. "Look at these drawings. They're beautiful, and you're face is beautiful, if only you'd stop starving yourself, if only you'd accept the way you are and stop torturing yourself."

"Listen, you don't know anything about me."

"I know you're beautiful. Isn't that enough?"

"I'm ugly, all right? And nothing will ever change that! And you're an alcoholic. Nothing will change that either."

She trotted down the corridor and disappeared into her room. Her angry voice besmirched the artwork they made. What was once sublime was now putrid.

After a brief session with a psychiatrist, Noble was told he was soon to be discharged. A glee spiked his heart. He lacked health insurance, and so the doctors were ordered by the cost-cutters to discharge him. He never knew poverty could be such an asset. The psychiatrist told him repeatedly behind closed doors that he was an alcoholic, and if he drank again, the consequences would be severe- liver damage, wet brain, pancreatitis, polyneuropathy. They determined this from his questionnaire, all the same questions worded differently. Noble insisted that he could moderate his drinking, and that the creative process demanded getting drunk. Not so, said the psychiatrist, his sallow, lanky body suggesting full erudition of this disease, and that creativity had nothing to do with alcohol, only an irony that creative people drank. 'We never hear the healthy stories,' he mentioned. This struck a disagreeable chord, but since discharge was imminent, he let the psychiatrist ramble in this fashion. His thoughts, however, were with the gaunt girl and how she would fair without anyone pushing her forward. Hard to believe Noble had feelings for her.

He left the brief appointment in search of her. She was in art therapy. Several of the other patients were also there, and he gazed upon her in wonderment. She seemed totally concentrated on the task. If only she could help herself outside of these therapeutic walls, if only she would think herself, well, beautiful.

"Tsk, tsk, isn't it Noble?" he heard from behind.

The apparitions again. They were dressed in standard-issue gowns, the idol carrying a guitar, the mechanic fiddling with the carburetor.

"Thanks for ruining my one moment, the only moment of, how do you call it? Of serenity," said Noble wistfully.

"Whoa, Mr. McCloud has feelings for someone other than himself, eh?" said the idol.

"I think we're finally getting through," said the auto mechanic. "See, I told you we weren't wasting our time. He needs a lot more work, though. A lot more. We're not done with you yet."

"Can't you two have a conversation by yourselves somewhere, away from me?"

"It's a long way to the top of you wanna rock 'n roll," said the idol.

"Yes, he loves his alcohol," said the auto mechanic. "Can't play the guitar without it."

"I won't make the same mistake twice," said Noble. "I won't drink so much next time."

"Really?" said the idol. "So it's not about the guitar, is it? It's all an image with you, isn't it, yeah, being cool, drinking booze. All of those famous people are in rehab, aren't they? And you'll join their ranks by doing what you do best right? The poor rebel, drinking the whiskey, living on the edge every day, and then choking on his own vomit, just like the great ones."

"It has nothing to do with that," he fired back.

"Oh no? What is it then?"

"I can't play the guitar when I'm sober. The practice is too frustrating, and I need more access to other modes of thinking, other experiences which make playing easier on me."

"Nicely put," said the mechanic, "but by following that line of reasoning, I guess I can't clean this here carburetor without alcohol in my veins. Ain't it a shame?"

"Admit it, Noble," said the idol, "you're not interested in playing the guitar. You're more interested in the fame, the glamour, the image."

"Maybe I do need a psychiatrist. You just don't understand."

"Oh, but I do," said the idol. "Tell me, young Noble, when does it stop? How much is enough? How many complexities of your character does the world need to see? You're self-centeredness runs so deep that you can't live without the entire world adoring you. Don't think we don't know about your daydreams. Don't overleap your vaulting ambitions. Even greatness has its price. It's obvious to us that you don't love playing the guitar."

"I don't love anything," he yelled.

"Hey, are you all right?" as the girl snapped her fingers before him. The third snap magnified the meeting room, as his vision was out of focus. In a trance.

"Umm, yeah, I guess," said the subdued Noble.

She seemed thinner than before, her front teeth prodigious.

"Listen," he continued, "I'm sorry about what happened before. I should have known better than to get in your business and all."

"Forget about it," she smiled.

"Also, I'm leaving soon, probably tomorrow morning."

"At least one of us is leaving."

"Yeah, it's been interesting. An interesting experience. I only hope that you get better, and have…a decent life. No one needs this, this place, this ward. I hope to see you in Waspachick one of these days."

"Probably not."

She did, however, extend her hand, not for a handshake, but to give him something. She gave him a piece of chocolate. It was the last he saw of her.

Chapter Two

Noble awoke early the next morning. He took a long shower and dressed in the same outfit. He signed a few forms at the nurse's station. He expected a clean getaway, a return to his old habits. He knew only that he should drink in moderation, perhaps a beer or two to loosen the fingers. He didn't view his hospitalization as an event which ruined his drinking. After all, he was still an artist. Two days apart from the instrument, however, seemed caustic to his artistic progress. He would bolt to Shylock's and attack the instrument. He would practice until his fingers blistered. Experience made him smarter and more prepared. Nothing would get in the way. Just sign this last form, collect the money they confiscated, and- wait. He was almost out the door when the polyester man barricaded the exit. He wore a three-piece lime suit, polyester, in keeping with his style. Noble had been half-asleep, but this suit electrified the dull brown of the psychiatric ward. He wore a kelly tie and a gold tie pin, an insignia of the Knights of Columbus. His hair was meticulously combed. Noble figured he was the type who got a shave at the barber's, his features carved with wrinkles from every kind of disgruntled facial expression. He didn't smile. He didn't offer a handshake. He stood like a drill sergeant on the cusp of berating his one cadet. He did, however, offer Noble a ride into Waspachick. Noble accepted, and once in the car, he remembered that nothing comes for free.

"I'm taking you to a meeting," said the polyester man.

"No thanks."

"Do you want to end up where you just were? That's insanity."

"Thanks for taking me to the hospital. I'm in a great deal of debt to you, but I really don't want to attend a meeting right now. Y'know, I have responsibilities."

"Like what?" he asked with a drawl.

"My job. I have work today."

"Bullshit. Never bullshit a bullshiter. He can easily detect it."

"Seriously. I have my job to consider."

"Wrong. You have your life to consider. One more drink will put you right where you started. Your job can wait. You need a meeting. You said you were indebted to me. Well, now is payback time. You will go to this meeting, and afterwards if you don't feel that AA is right for you, then you can leave with my blessings, and we'll call it even."

"I don't even know who you are. You can't force me to go."

"DWI cards? Not from me."

"Okay. I'll go," said Noble, "but we have a deal. If I don't like it, then you give me DWI cards for the rest of the month, and I don't come to any more meetings, deal?"

"No deal. I can't give out the cards if you miss the meetings."

"Then what's the point in going to this one?"

The polyester man pulled to the curb. Then rammed the gear into park.

"This is your life," he said angrily, "and I don't make deals when it comes to someone's life. You came to that meeting needing help. You were shaking all over the place, poisoned with liquor. How quickly you forget. Now we're going to this meeting, you and I, and if you don't like it, tough. Don't shit me. You may end up saving your own life. Now take the cotton out of your ears and stick it in your mouth. Sit there for an hour is all you have to do. And another thing- Don't piss me off."

They arrived at the sprawling church which appeared august in the morning light. The sunshine lent a different character to this strong structure, its dark, misshapen rocks collecting grime from the cars darting along the avenue. The church anchored an otherwise flimsy section of Waspachick. It offered a touch of the bucolic in an otherwise dense suburbia. The supermarket across the street with its shopping carts strewn about its parking lot confused an otherwise tranquil setting. On the stone steps familiar faces puffed on cigarettes and drank coffee. Noble figured nicotine and caffeine to an alcoholic must have been the next best thing.

A few of them said 'hello' to 'Harry.' So that's his name. To Noble they smiled. He wanted nothing to do with these people. They had done irreparable damage to themselves. Noble had only made a mistake, a slight miscalculation, which landed him detox. He intended to drink moderately, never again to go overboard in his pursuit of artistic excellence. A life without alcohol blunted one's creative impulses, as though sobriety were inimical to artistry. Nothing novel would ever supplant the hum-drum, contemporary, even hackneyed view of experience supplied by these alcoholics. Nothing would ever result, and these men and women would never affect the human race as would Noble McCloud and his guitar. It was as cut and dry as the supermarket and the church building.

He followed Harry into the church. They sat together in the illuminated congregation room. A few members were already seated. They too drank coffee and looked depressed. It took a will of iron to get up this early, especially for a meeting. It must have been seven in the morning by Noble's calculation. Harry sat with him in silence, waiting for some divine transformation. A life devoid of alcohol was somehow stale, dull, ordinary, lifeless, as dead as this room. He certainly couldn't play without it.

The room filled with thirty people, and an overweight man in his thirties read the preamble. He said his name was Milo. The name fit him well, his bowl haircut boyish and his tone mellow and calm, hiding anger. Noble couldn't put his finger on it, but this Milo character wasn't who he seemed. If pushed in the wrong places, that serene, even gentle demeanor could erupt into a tantrum, a cudgel splitting the thick skulls of everyone in the room, because the man could never swig a drink for the rest of his life. Imagine that? Not drinking for the rest of his life? Never tasting a cold beer on a hot, muggy afternoon, or celebrating with a sip of whiskey when he finally gets a promotion? Abstinence was not only ridiculous but unfeasible. The people around him were God freaks engaged in the occult. Soon they would abstain from nicotine, caffeine, gambling, fatty foods, and masturbation, and by doing so, abstain from the ethos which gives society its amusement, its fundamental joy, and above all, its necessary escape. Then the proliferation of abstemious programs for every single vice known to human kind. Why, Alcoholics Anonymous could be conceived as a danger to society, seditious, or the equivalent of high treason. Does the Department of Defense know about these people? Do they recognize the threat to our great nation?

Noble measured the dimensions of the congregation room. Light streamed through the casements which offered a view of a courtyard. Noble concluded that all of these people were brainwashed by an extreme pseudo-spiritual condition. They could be aliens living in an underground city, only to emerge at these meetings. The head alien was Harry who indoctrinated the innocent into their cult-like clan, and soon they would capture Noble and drug him. They would then drag him through a trap door in the floor. Once they arrived in their labyrinthine city, they would conduct odd experiments, and eventually drain him of blood, because they fed from human blood, not alcohol. That's what they were, freakish vampires waiting for a spacecraft. They needed Noble's blood to get to their home planet, the blood a form of rocket fuel, alcohol a virulent poison…

Milo asked if there were anyone new or 'coming back' to the meeting. Noble, still lost in phantasmagoria, felt a nudge on his arm. He regained his senses and discovered that the entire room awaited a response. It was Milo who hung onto this pervasive silence. Noble had to respond, and he said simply: "Hi, my name is Noble, this is my first time to this, uh, whatever it is, actually my second time, coming back, I suppose."

"Welcome back," said a few scattered voices.

He clung to the false hope that many of these drunks wouldn't remember him from two nights ago, shaking violently and pleading for mercy. Luckily, however, the format of the meeting was speaker/discussion, and so Noble had the luxury of non-participation. Once he introduced himself, he relaxed as though taking in a film. The group was arranged in a circle, and across from Milo sat a middle-aged man with a long, prominent scar wandering down his brow and into the inner corner of his eye. He must have strayed into the meeting surreptitiously, because Noble would have immediately caught this aberration. Nevertheless, the scar interested him, and so he listened to this man's story.

"Hi, my name is Cliff, and I'm an alcoholic."

"Hi, Cliff," said the group.

"Thank you for inviting me to speak tonight, I'll try to keep it as brief as possible, and hopefully through my story I could tell you what it was like, what had happened, and what it's like now.

"I took my first drink when I was thirteen years old. My father stashed a few bottles of bourbon and rum and wine in a small liquor cabinet in the living room, and one night when my parents were out, I tried some of the bourbon. It was the worst thing I ever tasted, really, it tasted so bitter; but I heard people get high off the stuff, and naturally I had to drink some more. I drank half the bottle and felt such an incredible high. While my parents were out of town, I'd invite people over, y'know, a few friends from high school, and we used to have parties. That was my first experience with the booze. I also took the occasional beer from the fridge, but these parties happened more frequently. Nothing too drastic happened, but soon I was partying every day with my friends, and my grades slipped. My parents wondered why, but they never found out. I even went to school drunk, and my friends also go hold of some marijuana.

"Marijuana is combination with the liquor was the perfect high. I was getting drunk and high before school and after school, and the whole time, my grades were sinking, and my parents never found out until I was caught by one of the teachers. She noticed I had been drinking, I think she smelled it on my breath, and I was reported to the principal's office. They called my parents, and now they were thrown into the mix. So as you can probably tell, my drinking habits formed when I was fairly young. My parents, though, didn't do much about it. They sat me down, gave me a long talk and a slap on the wrist. They also locked up the liquor cabinet. But my drinking was far from over.

"I continued drinking in high school. Never went to college. I got a job landscaping and worked my tail off for a few measly bucks a month. After work, we'd all go out for beers, and I was the life of the party. I'd hit on the girls, dance on the bar, get into fights. One night while driving home after being very drunk, I was stopped by the police. I had been drinking vodka all night, because vodka is hard to smell on the breath. I thought I was clear, but the cops suspected something, and next thing I knew I was hauled into the station. They gave me a breathalyzer, and I was jailed for DWI. Arrested. They took away my license, everything.

"After the DWI, I settled down, although still active. I just made sure not to drive. I met my wife in the Southern Waspachick area. We got married, and I insisted on using both drugs and alcohol on a regular basis. My wife never touched the stuff, but I kept on using. One night I was at a bar over on the North Side, and I had a few too many. I thought I could make it home by car, and I got on the road, and I was stopped again by the same police officer who arrested me the first time. Some police officer. He knew I was coming from Greely's on the North end, and once again I was taken in for my second DWI. See, I couldn't stop drinking. I always wanted more. This is a disease of "more." One beer, one hit, was never enough. I drank to get drunk and obliterated. In fact, I remember one night I was at the bar, and one of my old drinking buddies told me to slow down. "The night is young," he said. "Try and enjoy the buzz." So I tried, and it turns out I didn't even like the buzz alcohol gave me. I kept pounding beers along with my favorite drink, which was bourbon.

"In the meantime, my relationship with my family deteriorated, simply because I hardly ever saw them. When I did see my wife, I was usually very drunk. I would drink right after work, and sometimes I wouldn't come home until two or three in the morning reeking of alcohol. We'd have fights, even though the children slept down the hall. I remember fighting almost every night, and it was always over the drinking.

"One night our fighting turned physical. I woke up the next morning, and my wife had a black eye. I blacked-out, so I had no clue as to what happened. And then she told me how I hit her and how the kids came down the hall and begged me to stop. Of course, I didn't stop drinking. I knew I had to come home by supper time, and I would make it to supper drunk from happy hour at the bar. My kids saw me drunk, and the fights between my wife and me happened openly at the table. I would stay home for a little while, and then I'd go out again. Everything aside from the booze was unimportant. My wife and kids didn't matter to me anymore. Instead of my life surrounding them, it surrounded my drinking. I loved getting drunk, but the more I drank, the more my family suffered, and they paid a heavy price.

"The landscaping continued for a couple of years, but my drinking had gotten worse. Instead of drinking at happy hour, I was now drinking at both lunch time and happy hour. Me and a couple guys from work went out and basically got drunk, or it wasn't them who got drunk, it was me. They could stop after a couple, but I kept on going until I returned to the job drunk. Everything turned into a daze. Most of the time I was confused, and after two or three years on the job, I was fired for botching up a lawn job. Incompetence, they call it. For a couple years more, I collected welfare, and at times I couldn't put food on the table.

"My wife and kids left me a few months after I had lost the job. I remember the morning clearly. My wife simply told me in the bedroom that she was leaving with the kids, because I failed to take care of them. They went off to my in-laws, and I was in the house alone. It was amazing, because now I could drink the way I wanted to drink. No more hassles. Instead of going out for drinks, I bought the liquor home. I would wake up in the morning, have a shot while looking in the classifieds. I would drink in the afternoon, and then go to the bar at night. I was drinking around the clock. The bills weren't being paid, the mortgage especially. I basically ignored all the bills and drank most of my savings away.

"It wasn't until the winter, and I recall it was an exceptionally cold winter, that the bank foreclosed on my house. I was also in trouble with the IRS. I was homeless for a little while. I stayed with my mom and dad. They soon kicked me out and wanted nothing more to do with me. I had threatened them over money, and they rightly figured once was too many. These were hard times. I was now broke and an alcoholic, only that I didn't realize it. I then stayed with friends, but soon they kicked me out for similar reasons. I would grub and steal money from them to support my habit. The social worker at the welfare office told me I had an alcohol problem, but I never believed it. Meanwhile, I was drinking every day and night. I hung out with drunks and drug addicts, although I stayed away from the harder drugs. Besides an occasional joint, drugs were beneath me, I thought, and meanwhile I was drinking bourbon like water, hanging around with the dregs of society, the maladjusted, the unemployed, basically all the addicts. I rarely saw my wife. I usually saw her for money. She'd give me all she could, before my in-laws told me to get lost. I put my wife through hell, and even my kids through hell. I was a lost soul. Alcohol took away my family, my house, I had to sell my car, but more than anything it took away my dignity and self-respect.

"One night the crew I was hanging with knew a small bodega which didn't have good security. I was so broke at the time that I thought it was a golden opportunity. At the last minute though, I ducked out of the plan. I was too scared of going to jail. I was lucky enough not to go through with it. Last time I heard, those same guys who robbed the store are now serving fifteen years in Rahway State Prison. I could have been one of them. It must have been my Higher Power operating in my life. Otherwise, I would have gone to jail.

"But still I was broke. My love for liquor never left. I was looking for liquor everywhere, and usually I found some. But when I had no money for another bottle, I got so uptight that I stole mouthwash from the pharmacy and drank that instead. The mouthwash burned a whole through my stomach, but it was an average substitute for the booze. I got my money from selling drugs on the streets, but luckily I was never caught. I had the feeling that I had somehow been damned by the universe, damned by God. I was never angry with my wife for leaving me. Nor was I angry with my family for turning me away. I was never angry with the dealers, drinkers, or drug addicts in my life. I was, however, angry with God for bringing me into this world. I thought God had forsaken me somehow, that he allowed these problems to occur. I would sometimes curse his name, but I still prayed to him during my most frightening moments. The relationship with my Higher Power back then was pretty rough. Little did I know through all of my problems my Higher Power really never left me. He was with me the entire time, making me learn from my insanity. Yes, I made the same mistake morning, afternoon, and night by drinking, and insanity is making the same mistake over and over again. I had no control over what I did, who I saw, what was happening. It wasn't until a warm summer night that I finally woke up from my darkness and embraced the light.

"One night I was in a homeless shelter. I had been living there for some time, and I knew many drunks who lived there too. That's not to say that everyone who lived there drank, but there were a few there who drank like I did, meaning that they drank round the clock, and so I found instant companionship with those who had no life except for alcohol. Near the shelter was a high retaining wall, and some of the people at the shelter hung out at the knoll next to it. I was constantly drunk by this time. I woke up in the morning and vomited mouthwash, and I hung out with these guys who always had a bottle, either of mouthwash or the real thing.

"Well, on this particular night they had the real stuff. They had told me so when the shelter had its lock-out period. I hung around them the entire day, and then at night near the retaining wall. Drunk and out of control, I fell from the retaining wall, about fifteen feet. Next thing I knew I was in the hospital. I had been in a coma, and when I came to, the doctor told me I had fallen and was left by myself in a pool of blood. My skull had been severely fractured, and I had been in a coma for four days. They handed me a mirror, and I observed for the first time, this long undesirable gash running down my forehead. It took four hundred and ninety stitches, and they had to replace a part of my lip. I knew then that my drinking had to stop, only that I didn't know how.

"In the hospital an AA meeting was held almost every night. The doctors told me these meetings would help me stop drinking. I went to a discussion meeting, and I kept going until I found a sponsor. At first I thought these meetings were terrible. I thought about what my life would be like without alcohol. I couldn't imagine it, yet I knew I had to make drastic changes. In my hospital room I read the big book, and that gave me a lot of comfort, because I identified with the stories and its message. And all the time I was going to these meetings, and I found people who understood me, a strong fellowship with those who were in my shoes, who had similar experiences. I went to these meetings, because I knew I had to change, or else I would die. Somehow death was not the problem inasmuch life was the problem. I found within the Big Book a blueprint for sobriety and a new life beyond alcohol. At first I latched onto the slogans: 'One day at a Time,' 'First Things First,' and 'Think.' The one that helped me the most was 'One Day at a Time.' It didn't mean that I had to go the rest of my life without a drink. Only one day without a drink. Everyone in this room, regardless of the sober time we put together, has but one day. And in that day, I don't have to drink or drug. In that one day I can go on with my life without picking up a drink. It's the present which is eternal, not yesterday, not tomorrow, but this moment in time. I learned that the present or today is where all the joy is, that yesterday is history, and tomorrow a mystery.

"I left the hospital knowing that if I were to return to the booze, it could mean jails, institutions, such as the hospital, and ultimately death. With the help of the program, it was now time to put my life back together again. In the hospital I found a great sponsor. I must have been on the phone with him twice, sometimes three times a day. A good sponsor is one of the essentials of this program. I would have picked up a drink without his support. And so I wanted my life back. I found a job with the hospital, an administrative position. I earned enough money to find an apartment in Southern Waspachick. I contacted my family and made amends with my wife and two children who are now on their way to high school. My wife divorced me during my drinking days, but now we're hammering out a plan which may unite us a second time. Picking up the pieces wasn't so easy. Every day out of the hospital I had urges, and at those times, I called my sponsor. I also networked with people in the rooms who I consider good friends.

"Today, I have a life. It's not like the absence of alcohol took away my joy and excitement. The opposite is true. Sobriety has given me a new lease on life. The scar down my forehead, which is now my most distinguishable feature, is a constant reminder of what my Higher Power did for me. My scar is my message, or better yet, it was His message to me. I almost died at the hands of alcohol, and without these meetings, I would have certainly drank again, only that I would have never returned. I would have died drunk and impoverished.

"I've noticed there are a few newcomers here tonight. When I first entered these rooms, I didn't believe this program could work. The idea of going to a park, or having a cook-out, or going to the beach without alcohol seemed ridiculous. And the first few weeks in the program were certainly my roughest. But in time, after forcing myself to these meetings, I eventually liked and soon loved coming. I find in these rooms a strength and an energy to continue but for one more day. Today I have my family back, my friends, all of those things which my alcoholism took away. To those newcomers-stick around. You may just have the time of your life."

The audience furnished a warm applause, and the man with the scar smiled as though touched by a divine hand.

"Well, we've come to the discussion part of the meeting," said Milo. "Did anyone have a problem with their sobriety today or wish to share on a specific topic?"

They all seemed to stare at Noble whose hand reached toward the ceiling.

"Hi, my name is Noble, and I was discharged from detox this afternoon. I'm not sure if I'm an alcoholic."

"Hi, Noble!" said the members. And random shouts of "Welcome."

"Okay," resumed Milo in a gentle voice, "let's talk about 'powerlessness' and what it felt like when we first got sober."

A hand was raised.

"Hi, my name is Ivan, and I'm an alcoholic."

"Hi, Ivan!"

Ivan looked about Noble's age. He was thin. His crew cut animated his prodigious ears. His cheeks were pockmarked with acne. He wore a loose blue tee-shirt, and he looked into the table while speaking.

"Thanks for your story, Cliff. I have close to six months now, and I remember what it was like when I first came into these rooms. I had been drinking so much that the doctor said I would die if I kept drinking. I also drank under medications which can give you brain damage. But now I'm coming up on six months, and I have this good chunk of sobriety. I have to admit I'm powerless over the alcohol. One slip, and I'll be back in the institution. It's either jails, institutions, or death, that's all that's waiting for me out there. I can't go back to that way of life. My mind is still clearing up after six months. I remember when I first came in, after a two-day bender, and I needed these rooms as I do now. Sober is better. It's simply a better way of life, and I'm grateful for the things sobriety has given me. It's also important to keep my mind green. Before I came in, my mind was gone due to alcohol. I only cared about alcohol and nothing else. I'm grateful for being sober another day. Thanks for letting me share."

"Thanks Ivan!"

Another hand raised.

"Hi, I'm Eddie, and I'm an alcoholic."

"Hi, Eddie!"

"What can I say? All right, I know. I was riding down the highway the other day with a new worker in the truck, and it's obvious to me the guy's been drinking, so he asks me if I want a beer. I tell him 'no, I don't want a beer," but he keeps askin' and askin,' and he won't stop asking. So I pull over by the road and tell him straight: 'No, I don't want a beer, and if you keep on bugging me about it, I'll tell the boss.' The next thing, you know, he's breakin' out another beer. And I'm drivin' down the road to another site, and he keeps on askin' me to drink with him, and he's goin' on and on about how his wife left him, and how his marriage fell apart, and now he's respecting me, because I'm sober, and he's drunk. I mean why drink in the first place? Right? So anyway- hmmm, I just lost where I was- oh yeah, so we're drivin' down the road, and he starts crying about his wife, and I couldn't believe it, I should have left him on the side of the road, but then he again offers me a beer after all that cryin'. And I get home after a long day's work, and my sister yells at me about a raffle ticket. I didn't wanna buy one, but she keeps forcing it on me, and we got into a huge fight about it. I said 'I'm not gonna buy one of those tickets, because I don't wanna. I have more important things to spend my money on,' ya know? So I guess I'll keep coming."

Noble didn't know what to make of this good-humored litany. The man was older and shorter, a laborer, probably a landscaper or a surveyor, something to do with soil or dust. He laughed at his own predicaments and strayed far enough from the topic to warrant another alcoholic sharing with a point and purpose in mind, like steering straight a vessel which had drifted off course.

"Hi, I'm Phinaeus, and I'm an alcoholic."

"Hi, Phinaeus!"

Phinaeus resembled a giant octopus, his head completely bald, and his cranium immense and irregular. He wore square plastic eyeglasses which could have easily been confused as goggles. He sucked on a stubby corncob pipe. He might have been an alien from a planet far removed or a squid with its tentacles squeezing normalcy from the meeting's atmosphere. There was little chance he would guide this sinking ship.

"I've got to remember where drinking got me," he shared with celerity, "I mean, I've been out of the hospital for three weeks, and I was in the hospital for three years, eleven months, fourteen days, and six hours. I mean I don't understand why I have this obsession for drink, it's horrible, it really is. I had a beer just the other night, I can't control it. I had a beer at my mother's place, I mean it just gets worse and worse. I was at my mother's, and she's committing adultery all the time, and I know what it says in the Bible about adultery: 'Thou shall not covet thy neighbor's wife,' and all she's been doing is committing adultery, which puts me into the oddest position, because my father died a long time ago, and all he did was drink, so I don't know where I get this obsession, but ever since I got out of the hospital, I've done nothing but think about drinking. I don't want to go back there, my God, I've been in there for the longest time, and one drink will put me back there, and I can't stop focusing on the drink. My mother used to drink a lot too, and ever since my father died, she's been committing adultery. I tell her to stop, but she never listens. It's really a tough situation. She never lets up, and I talk to her about drinking, but she never listens to me or to anyone for that matter. It says so right in the Bible, but whenever I bring this to the attention of my mother, she basically tells me to get lost, and I think that drinking will make things better, as my mother commits adultery and- it's all a question of adultery. She's sleeping with this old…"

"Phinaeus," interrupted Milo, "I'm cutting you off, okay. Time is very precious in these rooms, okay? We have to give others a chance to share, okay?"

Phinaeus seemed more confused than humiliated by the interruption. A hand was raised towards the back end of the congregation room. A tall, athletic, good-looking young man shared next. He wore a silk suit, his tie hanging loosely from his collar signifying a decent-paying job, a car, an apartment in Waspachick, and indicating that he was now off-duty like a sign in a store window which reads 'closed.'

"Hi, I'm Willy, and I'm an alcoholic."

"Hi, Willy!"

"Yeah, powerlessness is a great topic, and I guess the best way to describe powerlessness is by remembering what got me here. As a kid I was timid and unsocial. I was a loner and had very few friends. I wasn't exactly the violent type, but if someone looked for trouble with me, I lost control easily. I wouldn't stop. I almost choked a guy to death over nothing. This was a few years ago. By the time I was twenty-three I was drinking every single day without fail. I tried on my own to stop, but white-knuckling it got me nowhere. I continued to drink until I vomited blood, that's how sick I was. Luckily someone in the hospital was kind enough to take me to an AA meeting. I was totally powerless against the alcohol, and it took me a while to admit powerlessness, but I had to in order to surrender to this insidious disease both cunning and baffling. Today I know that I have the disease known as alcoholism. I dug a deep enough hole for myself. I lost everything, my job included. But admitting powerlessness was the best thing for me. It allowed me to surrender to this disease. Without admitting defeat to my alcoholism, I would have been out there, and possibly I would have wasted my life as a drunk and died early.

"I still get urges, but I know I'm just one drink away from having all that misery refunded. One more drink will leave me right off where I started, this endless progression. I'm very thankful for these rooms, because without them, I would have been dead and buried by now. It's hard to admit defeat to anything, especially to a simple beer or a shot, but for me admitting that I was powerless over alcohol certainly humbled me and in turn saved my life. And to the newcomers out there, my life is so much better without alcohol. I have a life today, all of that insanity is gone, and at times I'm even serene, a feeling where I don't have a worry in the world. It's life on life's terms, and when I

Noble McCloud

confront situations which used to baffle me, I do it with a clear head. I make better decisions. I do the next right thing. No one said getting sober was easy. When I first came around, it was one of the hardest things I ever did. But there are benefits to sobriety, I kid you not, so I'll keep coming."

"Thanks Willy!"

Milo picked the woman directly beside Willy. She had been crying the entire meeting. Willy dexterously massaged he back as she spoke. Noble noticed her slight, subtle beauty.

"Hi, I'm Missy, and I'm an alcoholic."

"Hi, Missy!" and the room fell gravely silent.

"I'm living with an active alcoholic," she cried. "I should have taken the suggestion, never have a relationship within the first year of sobriety. I'm living with an active alcoholic, and all he does is drink around me. I don't know how long I can go on living like this. I just don't know…"

Smilin' Willy messaged her shoulders as she wept. He took pleasure from it. They were part of the same clique it seemed. He noticed the young women near her understanding her pain, and yet Noble found a twisted and macabre delight in her unapologetic emoting in front of people she barely knew. It added a new dimension to the meeting. Noble could not identify with her but saw another facet to AA, as Willy rubbed her shoulders. AA was also a fellowship beyond the rooms. It could have been a huge social club with cliques resembling high school. Noble assumed cliques ended at some point, but now that women were thrown into the bouillabaisse, these cliquish activities flourished. Noble believed he would never become a part of them. He must remain aloof, not allowing anyone too close. He was there to stop drinking and nothing else. Another woman shared directly afterwards.

"Hi, my name is Meredith. I'm an alcoholic."

"Hi, Meredith!"

Another slightly good-looking woman with long, frizzy locks plunging to her shoulders. Her features told a sorrowful tale of the social butterfly she had become, or this may have been Noble's misperception. They sat in the same area, near Smilin' Willy who kept stroking the fair woman who wept.

"I know the situation she's talking about. Relationships within the first year is a definite no-no. I have learned this from many people in the rooms. We have to place principles before personalities. I am here for one reason, and that's to stop drinking. AA isn't social services. It's a place where we come together for one purpose, and that is to fight our disease. I know that if people, places, or things cause me to pick up, or even cause me to think about picking up, I need to reexamine my priorities. I am powerless over alcohol, but I am not so powerless over people, places, and things. I no longer hang out with old friends who do nothing but drink. If they were true friends, they would have helped me, they would have been happy for me, but old drinking buddies, it turned out, were not healthy relationships and were not my friends at all. Our only commonality was the alcohol, and when I stopped drinking, they no longer wanted my friendship. If I wanted to stop drinking, I had to cut off all my ties to the drinking world, that meant no more going to bars and having a soda while others around me got drunk. It means that I can't hang out with anyone who drinks, because it may adversely affect my sobriety. I will go to any length to stay sober, and this means no relationships in the first year. It means calling my sponsor, and coming to meetings, because meeting-makers make it. It means using the phone, establishing some connections with people in the rooms. I don't want to go through the horror of getting sober all over again. There is a life for me in these rooms, and also outside of these rooms. To the newcomer, I would say stick with the winners, come to meetings, come with the body, and the mind will follow. Also know that it's a spiritual program. When I first heard this I thought I would be brainwashed into worshipping God, but one of these days, I will understand that Thy will be done, not mine. Things have gotten so much better for me, and at this point I can feel myself growing along spiritual lines. Thanks for letting me share."

"Thanks Meredith!"

Milo called on a middle-aged woman.

"Hi, I'm Dianne, and I'm an alcoholic."

"Hi, Dianne."

"First of all, thanks for your story. I really got a lot out of it, that sense of hopelessness and despair, and the personal suffering we have to go through before we find the program. It's my belief that we all find these rooms at the right time, not a moment too late, not a moment too soon. It's God's way, in God's time. At first I also thought of AA as a brainwashing program. I guess back then I was proud to be an active alcoholic, I have no idea why. I thought I was fortunate to have the freedom to drink. I always felt sorry for people in AA. They seemed to be missing out on the life around them, and they took abstinence from alcohol so seriously. I was happy I wasn't one of 'them.' But then after a DWI and other drinking catastrophes, I had to come to AA.

"The law forced me to come. I hated it initially. All of my friends drank freely, and when I first came around, I too drank almost daily. I thought the whole thing was a hoax, but during this period, I was so depressed, I never got close to anyone, I was on a self-destruct mission, I lived on the edge. I didn't care if I lived or not. My nights were a blur, because I blacked-out and found myself in another place by morning. Everything was so unpredictable. For quite some time I'd put together a few days sober, just to prove that I wasn't an alcoholic, and then I'd go back out. I was driving myself insane. I was out of control. Then I bottomed. They say that you've reached your bottom when you stop digging. Well, I reached bottom, and I knew I had to give AA an honest try. Notice the word 'honest' here. I was constitutionally incapable of being honest with anyone, especially with myself. I finally did get honest. I knew I was powerless over alcohol, that my life had become unmanageable, but I also couldn't imagine what life would be like without alcohol. But I really worked the program. I changed the old drinking buddies, the bars, and the liquor store, the things that triggered my alcoholism. The teaching was simple: don't drink and go to meetings, and I did this for several months. I then relapsed, because sobriety and my Higher Power weren't priorities. Slip is an acronym for sobriety lost its priority. I returned to AA in worse shape than before, but I made sure to do what was suggested, and I haven't had a drink in three years and six months. I live my life in accordance with the twelve steps. It guides me along. As our speaker shared, AA didn't take away my life. It gave me one. And for this I'm forever grateful, grateful enough to live one more day sober. Thanks."

"Thanks Dianne."

A few more alcoholics shared, but Noble no longer concentrated. The lingo became a freakish example of how deeply ensconsed these alcoholics were within program ideology. They easily gave their lives over to a force which severed their connection to the outer world, as though they lived in a protective bubble apart from society's gears. They gave all of themselves and found, what was the word, God? This can't be, thought Noble. God had abandoned him, and to return to this Higher Power as all of these zombies had returned to Him? Who were these people anyway? They seemed transformed from raving lunatics with alcohol to raving lunatics without alcohol.

He gave it a try. He was thankful that Harry had brought him to the emergency room, but this meeting bordered on the ridiculous. Noble was about as spiritual as a neutron bomb, and yet there was something about the young people. They were zombies, somnambulists in a trance, and yet this so-called simple program brought them together and ultimately changed their lives. Perhaps he wasn't so powerless over the sauce. Maybe he could control it this time. And what of the guitar? Yes, he needed the instrument in his hands immediately. The guitar first, sobriety and this crackpot program second.

The notion of admitting defeat over the booze didn't agree with him, like sour milk. Yet, he couldn't, in good conscience and in deference to this kind, polyester man, return to alcohol as before. His cravings were visceral. He could not comprehend living a day at a time when the world lived in both the past and in the future, the present a mere millisecond, a nanosecond, the speed of light.

This middle-aged woman with silvery hair talked of a bottom. Noble figured he hadn't hit his bottom yet anyway, so maybe another night out would do it. What would he do about Shylock? Shylock drank like a fish, the lucky bastard. And then these little groups, these cliques. Who would be his alcoholic friends, not that he had any friends to begin with, aside from Shylock, but to make new friends amongst such a pitiful group, these degenerates and misanthropes, these lackluster dogmatists who found pleasure in things too boring to contemplate? What does one do when one is sober? Where does one go for entertainment? But the most perplexing issue once again involved the creative process- how would he learn to play? What would his fans think of a sober guitarist? His life should imitate art, and he was all poised to become the quintessential rock 'n roll guitarist, rife with addictions of every sort. Maybe the gaunt woman in the hospital was correct in suggesting that Noble wanted not only his guitar to sing but also his own life to become some phantasmal cloth stitched with misery and pain, embroidered with tortured darkness, only to be torn by these grateful zealots preaching the word of God as subtext to this morass of sobriety-speak.

After similar babble, the meeting ended, and the group made a circle and said the Serenity Prayer: "God, grant me the serenity to accept the things I cannot change, the courage to change the things I can, and the wisdom to know the difference." Noble was surprised by the alcoholics on both sides of him squeezing his hands and saying: "It works, if you work it, so work it, you're worth it." And with this final remark, the group broke. Some went to the kitchen. Some returned to the sunshine on the church steps. Noble was left alone with Harry who asked him to sit. Harry crossed his legs and pulled out a filterless cigarette.

"What's your schedule today?" asked Harry, lighting up.

"Why should my schedule concern you?"

"If you want to stay sober, you'll tell me."

"What if I don't want to stay sober?"

"You'll end up in the emergency room, but this time I won't be there. Is that what you want? The emergency room with all the psychos and the crazies, because if that's what you want, you won't stop until you get there.

It's a very wise man who not only learns from his own mistakes, but also from the mistakes of others. Remember how you felt?"

"Listen, man, not to slight you, but I think this AA thing is too big a leap for me. I can't go without drinking. Everyone I know drinks."

"It's a simple program. Just don't drink and come to meetings."

"I'm not ready yet."

"When will you be ready? At you're own funeral? Because it's your life. Your life," he said while pointing into his chest. "If you can't make it one day without a drink, would that prove you're not an alcoholic?"

"One day?"

"Yes, for one day can you go without drinking?"

"Easily."

"Okay, then let's do it this way. For one day, just one day, you're not to drink. And if there are any problems or questions, you'll call me, and I mean call me at any time. Attend this afternoon's meeting if things get rough. At this church there are three meetings- one at seven, one at noon, and one at seven-thirty in the evening. So you have both my number and all these meetings. Also, take some literature home…"

"I don't have enough."

"Money?"

"Yes, I'm broke right now."

"It's our price, your terms."

"And what's that supposed to mean?" asked Noble, still encountering the language barrier.

"The price is set, but you can pay for it over time, all the time you need."

"I won't need it. It's just one day, right?"

"That's right, one day. We have a deal?"

"And you won't bother me anymore?"

"No, you'll hear no more from me."

"Okay, it's a deal," and they shook on it.

"Don't forget your DWI card," said Harry.

Noble walked in the resplendent sunshine. He knew he could easily make it without a drink, as though he suckered this old-timer. It would be easy. Drink in moderation. But then he considered- what of the DWI cards? Damn. Noble had been fooled. He needed those cards. In the middle of his journey, he turned around and returned to the church. Harry was long since gone. No one was there, and the church doors were locked. He walked again under the auspices of the sun and noticed how the women wore less clothing.

Such a sight would drive any man to drink, and thank the heavens for hops, barley, yeast, malt, wheat, and the power of liquid sustenance. The beautiful women also drank, he reasoned. Everyone drank but himself on this day. Drinkers knew happiness. Isn't it better for the cardiovascular system to drink once in a while? Doesn't drinking lubricate the personality while talking with the opposite sex (not that this concerned him)?

He arrived at the apartment. Shylock was at work, as planned. Everything was a plan. He had four long hours until the noon meeting. He sure as hell wasn't about to call Harry. He'd only feed him more sobriety-speak, and his creativity would be ruined, yes, his guitar. His world surrounded the guitar. The rest of the world didn't matter, and if he must drink in order to play, then so be it. But he remembered the deal: just don't drink for one day, twenty-four long, baleful, horrific hours, before he could play yet again with that adroitness and intense skill. The guitar leaned against the wall, the ten-watt amplifier still on, only that he couldn't play. How could he play sober? Weren't sober people part of the mainstream, the establishment, the same progression of chords, the tired riffs which contributed and defined popular music, nothing meaningful or revolutionary in sound, but melodies which were rehashed, the same dish served: hardened ham, only to be replaced by the same ham cooked differently: ham soup, a salad with ham, a ham sandwich, a three-layered ham cake for desert, ham pudding, and a drink of ham oil? Noble must revolutionize sound like the great guitarists of days long passed. He must make a place for himself between the snug spaces of platinum albums. Surely no one successful ever played sober; their fangs were deep into the lotus, or they died in plane crashes. They died early, they choked on their own vomit, they entered rehabilitation programs until their livers ballooned and their hearts exploded.

He paced in front of the guitar as though he lacked, not the will, but the ability. Nothing loosened his fingers.

After a good hour of imagining himself letting loose, he finally grasped the instrument by the neck, sat on the sofa, and strummed gently, acquainting himself with a piece of his mottled history, as though the guitar were more a haunting presence than a healing one, an artifact when sober, but something fiery, electric, and alive when drunk.

He couldn't play to his liking, and for an hour he merely sat motionless, the instrument in his lap. He would have eaten the instrument whole, chomped on the wood and wire, if he thought he could play with the same vitality and skill, but he could only hold it like an infant with an incurable disease, dying slowly in his arms, and once he lost the hope of playing, he fought the urge, not to drink, but to smash the guitar into bits, and what a unique sound it would be, a good smashing with the amplifier on.

He then went searching through the apartment for his friendly whiskey bottle. He found only empties, as Shylock must have hid the full ones. He could have easily run to the liquor store, if he wished to preserve what little artistry remained. He did take himself too seriously, and he couldn't play while stuck in his own solemnity.

Have fun with the instrument. This was his next assault against the silence. Merely pluck the strings, there, a simple chord, a slide, a tight hold against the fret, another slide, his fingers accenting each chord, bending a chord, fingering a chord, slowly becoming demented by each sober chord as though each note specified an exercise, a drill, which pained his arms, the burning tendons and ligaments adding to his general disdain, until he could only envision re-smashing the guitar, or attacking the tailpiece with a fork and knife.

'It builds character,' he thought. But then he concluded that character didn't count when the guitar couldn't sing. Character was a secondary, if not a wholly unimportant attribute. The silence of the room killed him slowly. He had a strong urge for whiskey. He had an hour and a half before the meeting. He called Harry.

"It's Noble," he said in resignation.

"It's not that easy, is it?" as though Harry knew the results ahead of time.

"Listen, I think this whole sobriety thing is wrong for me."

"What's wrong with not drinking?"

"I can't seem to function. I can't operate without whiskey."

"Go on."

"Well, see, I'm a guitarist, and the guitar is my job, and without whiskey, I can't play. I've been sitting here for a couple of hours now, and I can't play at all. What does one do but drink, and I think I'm on the verge of a drink here."

"So that's what you do," he exclaimed, "you're a guitarist like Woody Guthrie or Bill Haley?"

"Not quite."

"Well what's troubling you? That you're too sober to know what you're playing?"

"You wouldn't understand."

"Try me."

"I've never played sober. It's so lifeless, so dull. The strings won't cooperate."

"If you're looking for easy miracles, sobriety won't help you much."

"Then what's the point? What's the point of staying sober if I can't work or function?"

"See, the things around you don't necessarily get better, but there's one thing I know for certain: *you* get better."

Noble thought: 'what a load of...'

"You are able to handle situations better," he continued. "You can learn how to practice your rock 'n roll, but at the same time live a good, fulfilling life."

"My life's not worth anything if I can't play."

"You expect one day sober will miraculously give you some fantastic ability? It doesn't work that way. Sobriety works one day at a time. You can't become a virtuoso in one day. It takes time. Time takes time. We are all here for one day, and in that one day we learn how to live, and we enjoy our lives."

"I don't want to enjoy my life, okay? I want this guitar to cooperate with me."

"Lemme ask you something: do you enjoy playing the guitar?"

"It's not a question of my enjoyment. I was put here on this earth to play this instrument. I, in essence, don't matter. How I play this instrument does matter."

"An 'all or none' approach. But what happens if you do drink? Are you prepared to lose your guitar?"

"What are you talking about?" said Noble angrily. "I will never, ever lose my guitar."

"With alcoholics, it's usually the same old story: anything we place in front of our own sobriety, we end up losing. What I'm trying to suggest here is that you won't become a great guitarist unless you're a sober guitarist. Sure, it will take time, it will take many long hours, and they won't be easy hours either. But soon enough you'll learn how to play sober. Misery, pain, and frustration don't last forever. These things pass. You have to give sobriety a chance, and maybe this time around, you'll actually hear what you're playing."

"I've never been so frustrated, that's all. When I was drunk, I could really let loose, but now, I can't play a simple tune."

"That will come in time. It's always tough in the beginning. We all went through it. But if you're urging, the best thing is to make a meeting. Make the noon meeting."

"Listen, man, I don't think this is right."

"That's because this your first day sober. Go to the noon meeting, and I'll meet you there, all right?"

"Fine, okay, fine. But I'm saying that I can't play, and that's the most important thing."

"Believe me," said Harry, "by the time you get sober, and it does take time, you'll be a much better guitarist than in all your days drunk."

"Is that a guarantee?"

"Son, that's a guarantee."

Noble needed a drink, and he needed one badly. He was suspicious of Harry's guarantee, like this Harry knew the pressures of creation, of turning thin air into a melody, as though this Harry had been privy to an exceptional knowledge which is derived chiefly from boredom. How could this one geriatric degenerate who had ruined his life over alcohol know the anxiety Noble McCloud faced, the type of anxiety which comes attached to an absurd universe, the hidden anxiety which approaches a young man who knows his work may amount to nothing, that the world wouldn't stop when he left, that when he walked through Waspachick the women turned their heads, and the men laughed. This is a special anxiety only Noble faced, or so he thought; the idea that his death would end tragically (and who's death doesn't end tragically?). But the world could somehow go on without him, that his days and nights were meaningless unless the guitar cooperated, that he served little purpose unless he played deftly, and alcohol loosened anxiety's grip; it eased tension like a talk with a beautiful woman over pasta, her milky fingers massaging the stem of a wine glass, her eyes a sedative removing the idea of nothingness, removing the thought that he may end up a beggar in rags, holding a tattered coffee cup, shooed by the cops as a menacing eyesore, and yet he couldn't break from that haunting image of journeying farther south into the ethnic mix, the liquor store open at all hours serving mouthwash under the counter. A fleeting thought, but a thought which had resonance, since he was close enough. Yes, he needed to compose music and compose it quickly; time but another pressure adding to this senseless anxiety like habitual tardiness in morning traffic. It all had to happen immediately. *A priori* success with his instrument, a perfect, flawless composition, professionally done to warrant a record deal. And he looked about the apartment. Laundry sat in the corner, empty whiskey bottles strewn about the place, and of course the guitar which would miraculously deliver his most unruly fantasies. Was this the sum of his existence? Mastering this wooden, metal, oblong contraption in a single stroke? Yes, he demanded a drink from himself but remembered Harry's solemn guarantee, that an alcohol-free Noble would play better.

He quit the apartment and walked through town. An ordinary late-morning. Cars passing and a woman smoking a cigarette by Shylock's coffee shop. Shylock, by the way, was the last person he wanted to see. He could never explain polyester Harry's proposal. Without incident, he arrived at the church and sat on the steps. It could have been a daydream. He appears on stage as an old man, his hair white and his body overweight. He begins a song with a popular band, a cameo appearance so to speak by this master-guitarist who, of course, is himself. The guitar solo would put any weathered professional to the test, and yet he plays it with ease. He plays with ease to the popular tune, the guitar solo exact, which shows his incomparable versatility, but he doesn't flaunt his mastery. Noble upon this stage is modest and humble, a guitar-Buddha.

A simple sunny day devoid of pleasure. His ambition blocked the unseasonable warmth. His grandiosity prolonged this one day. He could have tumbled from the steps, sprawled on the ground for the church minister to discover.

Before he resorted to such a display of suffering, however, he was met by Milo, the group leader, who arrived on the early side. Milo wore a black parka and black jeans. His bowl haircut exuded gentleness, and Noble knew that such a man could never survive Waspachick's wrath without government assistance. He looked poor but well cared for. Milo smiled and extended his hand.

"Here for the meeting?" he asked, his mouth full of too many teeth.

Noble nodded and smiled.

"There's coffee in the kitchen."

"Thanks," he said but didn't follow Milo inside. Instead he waited for others, perhaps the women who would also attend, he hoped. And then an idea struck- what if he could get laid through this preposterous program? It would then be worth his while, but when elderly men approached, Noble knew he would find no sex here. The old-timers filed passed him, and in the distance, in a bright yellow suit came Harry. The suit must have been from his spring collection.

"You made it," said Harry.

"Yep, I certainly did."

"Urges?"

"Yep indeedy, I've been having urges ever since I got home. We still have a deal, right?"

"I don't make deals when it comes to someone's sobriety, but I will tell you this- you'll play the guitar better than ever."

"Oh yes, you're no-nonsense guarantee. How could I forget."

"One day. Only one day."

"How could I forget? Never mind that I'm going out of my mind."

"What do ya mean?" asked Harry with a grin.

"I'm losing my mind, that's what I mean."

"Or maybe you're gaining what you once had."

"I've never had a stable mind. Even I know that."

"Who says?"

"My whole life says."

"But you haven't lived you're whole life yet. How do you know?"

"Okay, I won't argue with the wisdom of a sober wizard like yourself."

"Remember, it's only one day."

The congregation room was well-lit, and the few who gathered for this noon-time meeting showed little vitality. Milo read the preamble, but in the middle of it, a young man Noble's age stormed in. It was the young man with the prodigious ears and lanky frame, a real whacked-out freakish young man who energized the room with his innocence, as though the old-timers were suddenly resuscitated. One of the old women even smiled. During the preamble, this young man made more noises than the entire group put together. He shifted in his chair. He couldn't sit still, and despite his restlessness Milo continued as if nothing distracted him.

"Okay, with that, we've now come to the discussion part of our meeting. Did anyone have a problem with drinking today or have a problem affecting their sobriety?"

Noble caught Harry looking at him.

"Hi, I'm Noble, and for one day I'm an alcoholic."

"Hi, Noble!" rang the group.

He didn't expect the ring to surge like it did, but the old-timers were startled out of dormancy. Their eyes came alive, and they focused on him suddenly. They hung on his every word.

"For one day, I'm an alcoholic, I guess, and for this one day, and only one day," with a side glance at Harry, "I will not pick up a drink. So far the day has been horrendous. This must be the longest day of my life. I can't concentrate, I can't function, I can't do anything, and the whole time I've been thinking how easy it would be for my healthy, yes, healthy body to wander to that liquor store. But, no, I agreed, and for one day I'll go along with this insanity, because it's my genuine feeling that you are all insane. Yes, everyone of you. You are insane for thinking that a man can go his whole life without drinking. Insane, every one of you, because these meetings will never be a good enough substitute for what we all crave at this very moment. Yes, I made the mistake of landing in detox, and due to the kindheartedness of this elderly gentleman, I am here sober. I have no idea why he's helping me, I have no idea who you people are or why you're wasting your valuable time listening to me, but if you get a kick out of it, fine. I am here for one day, and after this, you will never see me again."

The meeting hung in abeyance. He was not saluted with the normal thank-yous but a contemplation by the few members present; a pause, until Milo broke the silence.

"Okay," said Milo, "why don't we talk about 'powerlessness.' I know when I first came into the program, I couldn't stop drinking, and it was only until I admitted powerlessness over alcohol did my recovery begin. It's that first drink which leads us to either jails, institutions, or death. That's what's waiting for me out there if I do pick up a drink. The only requirement for membership is a desire to stop drinking, and I don't think anyone in here would argue that the first step is the most important: 'We admitted we were powerless over alcohol and that our lives had become unmanageable.' I had to accept my disease in order to recover. Stick around," he said to Noble, "and get some phone numbers. It's important to get connected, get phone numbers, and find a sponsor. Anyway the topic is 'powerlessness,' and let's go around the room. We'll start on my right with Marcia."

"Hi, I'm Marcia, and I am a grateful alcoholic."

"Hi, Marcia!"

"I say I'm grateful, because I too was once insane like this young gentleman. I couldn't control my drinking. I wasted twenty years of my life drinking until I was taken by my husband to rehab. It was only until I was sober that I realized the irreparable damage done to my family. It took me many years to get all of my marbles back, many hours on the phone with my sponsor and people in the program. The first drink will put me right back where I started. We are all just one drink away, and no matter how much time we have, we all have today. So keep coming. This is a program of attraction, not promotion, and I have to come to these meetings everyday. Without them, I'd be out there, and I can't tell you how much my life has changed since then; but meeting-makers make it. You've got to stick around until the miracle happens. Thanks."

Noble paid close attention to these old-timers. He did not find anything remarkable about them, although they all tried to help. It wasn't until Harry shared that things became more pragmatic and lucid.

"When I first came around to these rooms there was a guy named Jimmy McNamara; he's dead now so I can use his name. I came to meetings just to spite him. One day I go up to him, and I tell him 'Y'know, Jimmy, this one day at a time stuff is a load of garbage, you mean don't drink for the rest of your life.' He looks at me and says: 'No, you big dummy. Don't drink one day at a time. If you want a drink, have it tomorrow,'" with emphasis on the word 'tomorrow' and a hand gesture arching from one period of time to the next.

"I have two suggestions for the beginner. First, get a home group, so you have a place to belong. Second, attend speaker/discussion meetings where you can, not compare, but identify with what's being said. Go insane if you have to, but don't drink just one day at a time.

"I remember a fella who came around these rooms, a man named Joe Colt. He had twenty-five years sober. One night he says to me: 'Harry, I don't think I'm an alcoholic.' 'What do ya mean you're not an alcoholic?' I asked him. I thought he flipped out. And then he says to me: 'I may not be an alcoholic, but I know- sober is better,'" with an emphasis on 'sober is better,' wide eyes, a smile suggesting illumination, and an extended finger which drove home the point.

In an odd, surreptitious manner, the meeting was actually making sense, as though there were some hidden logic to this entire program. So this is why Harry wanted him on the wagon for a day. The undercurrent of logic was barely noticeable. He could not venture any deeper, only that he must stay sober for one day and retrieve a DWI card at the end of the meeting. He grew tired quickly.

The meeting soon became a tribute to boredom, and every five minutes Noble glanced about for the time. The old-timers shared some more. Once again he encountered the language barrier, but soon enough the meeting turned to the freakish young man who couldn't sit still. What was his name again?

"Hi, my name is Ivan, and I'm an alcoholic."

"Hi, Ivan!"

"I have close to six months sober, even though I've been hanging around the worst characters in the town. I've really been working on my spirituality. I often pray to my Higher Power that he takes away the obsession with alcohol, and sometimes I am obsessed with drinking, and I pray to my Higher Power, and it certainly helps. I remember that this is a spiritual program, and Harry's right, sober is better. I know that now, and no longer do I have to pick up a drink just because the day is sunny. My Higher Power will get me through it, I know He will, I have to have faith. Sobriety is the most important thing in my life today, and anything I put in front of my sobriety I will lose. Prayer is key to my sobriety. Without praying on a daily basis I can't relieve myself of this obsession. So I'll keep coming."

"Thanks Ivan!"

This was exactly the kind of talk which made Noble nervous- the idea of spirituality. The old-timers mentioned self-will versus the will of a Higher Power. Noble's will versus that of God.

God had always been an easy target. Whenever anything went wrong Noble could curse God and get away with it. After all, God rarely responded. Perhaps blaming God for all of his defects was linked to his cowardice. Noble dealt with conflict by avoiding it, and in his careful avoidance he could always blame God for what went wrong, never another human being, as though people could do more damage than an invisible Higher Power. His relationship with God was like a boxer who fights without an opponent. The boxer fights hard, jabs and uppercuts, dancing with himself only to be beaten, not by anyone, but by his own fatigue. Spirituality sounded too dubious. The idea of God was invented by a damaged psychology, as though Noble McCloud could run the whole show by himself and accept the consequences when the production didn't work his way. This sounded very nice in theory, but in reality Noble couldn't accept the consequences. He blamed God for them. Why then should he return to God after the loss of his mother, his pathological shyness, his inability to play his instrument, his complete and utter failure to make anything valuable of his life? The thought of God seemed preposterous, as his relationship with Him had always been adversarial. He looked over these people suspiciously, and after the group prayer at the meeting's end, he asked Harry about 'God.'

"It's how you understand him," said Harry. "To me, God means 'Group Of Drunks.' The group is my Higher Power, but you shouldn't worry about it at this stage of the game. You keep track of today, not yesterday, not tomorrow, but today. How did you like the meeting? Did it help?"

"I still don't think this is right for me."

"Of course you don't. You're used to drinking and carrying on like a drunk. It takes a while. All you need is to focus on today and not picking up, just for today."

"I'm not sure I can do it. It's so difficult. I can't play my guitar."

"It's not difficult. It's simple. Don't drink, and come to meetings. Don't worry about all this God-hogwash."

Harry then roped Ivan and Milo into the discussion.

"Why don't you guys go to the diner this afternoon?" asked Harry.

The three of them looked at each other in bewilderment.

"Sure," laughed Harry, "you guys don't have anything else planned, do you?"

"Umm, I've got to practice this afternoon," said Noble.

"Practice? Hell, Woody Guthrie never practiced so much. C'mon guys, get you're act together. A lot of women at the diner this time of day. Young men like yourself? Hell, why not give it a try?" and he adjourned to the kitchen.

The three of them gawked at each other in the congregation room.

"I don't have a car," said Milo.

"I don't either," said Noble happily.

"You guys can ride with me," said Ivan, almost asking.

Noble studied them closely. They were obviously misfits and had little dealings with the fairer sex. Both were losers by Waspachick standards. They must have seen Noble in the same light.

"How does East Waspachick sound?" asked Milo.

"Let's go," said Ivan.

They hopped into Ivan's car, an old-model Japanese sports coupe bought second-hand. Its black body was dented in a number of places. The car hadn't been washed. Bird droppings covered the roof, and rust ate away the corners. Even though Noble never had a car in his life, he would have gone without if this were his only option. Milo rode shotgun, since he couldn't fit into the back seat. Fast food wrappers and empty soda cans layered the back floor, and a small radio rested on a little space of seat.

"Can you play the tape?" asked Ivan as they rode through town.

It was classical piano.

"Who is this?" asked Noble.

"Rachmaninoff."

"Who?"

"Rachmaninoff," yelled Ivan over the wind. "How do you like it?"

"It's interesting. Never really listened to classical music before. I'm a rock 'n roller myself."

"Me too," said Milo.

Ivan lit up a cigarette as they drove.

"Do you guys live in Waspachick?" asked Noble.

"We're both South-enders," said Milo, "but I grew up West of here."

"I grew up East of here," said Ivan, "I guess we both ended up in Waspachick."

"I lived on the South side, but now I'm living on the West side with a friend of mine."

"Does he drink?" asked Milo, the concerto unbearably loud.

"Yes, he drinks," said Noble.

They pulled into the diner and took their seats in the smoking section.

"I have a one-eighty-five spatial IQ, which is genius level, and my passion is to play chess," smiled Ivan.

"And I don't have a big IQ, and my passion is to attend meetings," laughed Milo.

"How many years sober you guys have?"

"Close to a six months," said Ivan.

"Four years," said Milo.

"I only have one day so far."

"Give yourself a pat on the back," said Milo. "Early sobriety is usually tough, but you'll get through it. They say in the rooms that we all have one day, no matter how much time we have."

"How'd you guys do it?"

"I did what was suggested," said Milo.

If only he could have a drink, just one miraculous drink to ease the tension, to take away the misery of these two misfits, to escape for merely a day, he would have given anything. But one drink, he intimated, would never end at just one drink. It would continue; it would lead to more than one, and would never end until he played his guitar in front of large audiences and dined afterwards at an exclusive club made for icons of his ilk.

He dresses in a black tuxedo and rests his arm against the bar. The women eye him from all sides, as he is the greatest known guitarist ever to tread this ordinary earth, a living legend, a man who could easily take home one of these model-turned-actresses, because at the heart of Noble McCloud spawned this belief that he would be known to everyone living, that people in Waspachick would look when they saw him prancing by. 'Is this the sum of my dream?' he asked himself. And then a pall of shame for thinking so highly of himself. He was a man burdened by unrealistic expectations. It would never end with kissing a comely actress. Rather he needed more, from guitarist to a representative in Congress, from Congress to the Presidency.

Noble realized that the key to a happy life involved being satisfied with what he already had, although he had nothing except for this one day of clarity and truth, this one day of reality. The world had somehow concerned itself with the rich, the powerful, the beautiful, and the successful, not the man who struggles over a drink. He could taste the alcohol when he encountered the ultimate extremity- it was either a beautiful woman waiting in a fashionable club, or it was nothing at all, a vast wasteland of nothing, a hell built for one, a constant binge of suffering, because he could never be more than himself, he could never be more than nothing. Strange how tempting the imaginary world becomes. It makes something out of nothing. It begs for trust and companionship. It leads young Noble towards visions of grandeur, and as the imagination possesses the mind and blinds him from clarity and truth, it propitiously plunges its dagger, it sinks its hooks deeply and never let's go. It never relinquishes its hold until the man not only trusts it but also believes in its visions. It places him at the center of his universe, as though his own existence were a work of art, filling him with a misguided importance and false prescience that one day he may mingle and hobnob with those more fortunate. Instead he found Milo oinkishly eating a cheese omelet and Ivan sipping coffee over a cigarette. Ivan had been smoking every five minutes, even as Milo ate.

"Do you believe in God?" asked Ivan.

"Wait," interrupted Milo, "keep it simple. Don't drink and go to meetings. It's recommended that you do ninety meetings in ninety days. Don't worry about God."

"I'm sorry," said Ivan. "God-talk would drive away anyone, but prayer certainly helps."

"This is true," admitted Milo. "If you're urging for a drink, and you can't get to your sponsor or anyone else in the program, then it's important to read the literature, and if all else fails, try prayer."

Noble wasn't paying attention. They talked like this for what seemed like hours, as he wrestled with his own imagination and the thought of visiting the South side liquor store.

"I really want a drink right now," he said finally.

"Think the drink through," advised Milo. "I know that every time I drank, I ended up in the hospital, on a psych ward, or in jail. Next time I could be dead. Think about where the drink got you, and if it didn't get you this time, it will get you the next time around. It's a trap when we think: 'well, I never got into a car wreck, or I never landed in jail.' The 'I-nevers' are a serious trap, because the next time you do pick up a drink, you could end up in the places you've never been before. Sure, drinking may work for a little while, but over time, we can't control it. It wrecks our lives.

"Lemme tell you a story about a fella I knew. He was a classic black-out drinker. He had eight years of good sobriety, and suddenly he went out and picked up a drink. As I said, he was a black-out drinker, and after a night out on the town, he woke up in a jail cell, not knowing why he was locked up. He then came-to and asked the officer why he was in jail. The officer said: 'You don't remember? You ran over a little girl last night, only four years old.'

"I don't mean to scare you, but this is what happens to alcoholics. We may kill another person, which in my book, is worse than killing oneself. When alcohol is in our system it acts as an allergy to our minds. We are, in essence, allergic to alcohol, because we lose control when we're intoxicated. It may have never happened to you, but from what I've heard in the rooms, the 'I-nevers' will eventually happen if you keep drinking. Try thinking the drink through, and what may happen if you do drink."

"We don't mean to preach," said Ivan, "but my life was miserable while I was drinking. I couldn't think straight. I was borderline psychotic the whole time."

"Just remember," said Milo, "it's jails, institutions, or death. This disease is cunning, baffling, and powerful. It's insidious, and there is no known cure..."

"I did hear LSD could work..."

"Cut it out, Ivan. Really, this is a very serious illness, and if you landed in detox the first time, there's no question you might end up someplace worse the next time."

"I can't see my life without drinking. It's embedded in our culture. I see it happen all the time. Even my roommate drinks like a fish."

"I had to change people, places, and things. I couldn't see my old drinking buddies, I couldn't go to the same bar I always went to, and I couldn't repeat behaviors which got me to pick up in the first place."

"That didn't take one day," said Noble.

"It took a long time," said Milo. "I had to drop a friend I hung out with for five years. He was my best friend, but I had to drop him."

"And how are you feeling nowadays?"

"Good. I know what serenity is, and I practice and work at it every day."

"But drinking never meant the end of your job or your livelihood," exclaimed Noble. "I can't play the guitar without drinking."

"You may never have a shot at a livelihood, if you continue at the rate you were going. You'll learn to play sober. It just takes time."

"Yeah," said Ivan. "For the first few months I couldn't play chess. I couldn't think straight sober, and I was used to playing drunk. I got drunk all the time, before tournaments, after tournaments, even during tournaments. I was drinking all the time, and I was even causing brain damage, wet-brain they call it. It took a lot of time. Time takes time. Now my playing is better." He smiled and said: "You and I are a lot alike. I can see your ambition. We want to achieve great things, but we can't do it when we're drunk."

Milo nodded along.

"It's not a question of 'if' I succeed," continued Ivan, "the question is 'when' I succeed. My goal is to become a champion chess player, and sobriety works for me. Who wants to be drunk all the time anyway? Who says that in order to be successful at something, I have to drink?"

"I don't think you guys understand," said Noble. "All the guitar players before me, all the great ones, anyway, abused drugs and alcohol. It enhanced their style of play. How much of a dent can a sober guitarist make? I can't even strum my damn guitar without making these heinous sounds. The guitar is my life, okay? And all I know is that drinking furthered it. Without the booze I can't even practice."

"Yeah, you are like me," said Ivan.

"Me too," said Milo.

"I can understand him, but you?" asked Noble of Milo.

"For a long time I was a lead singer in a heavy metal band."

"You're kidding," said Noble. He would have never pinned him as a lead singer. He looked so tame.

"Yeah, I played with a heavy metal band here in East Waspachick."

"Wow, I never would have guessed."

"But I can't sing anymore. It jeopardizes my sobriety. I couldn't find a group of sober people to jam with. I do understand what you're going through. There's a guy in the rooms I know. He's a musician. He even has his own CD out. It's a tough road. It's not easy being a musician these days."

"It's not easy being a chess player either."

They ordered more coffee, and Ivan lit up another smoke.

"I'm an instrumentalist," said Noble. "I go it alone. Right now I'm learning."

"Big dreams?" asked Milo.

Noble hesitated. Any statement regarding his visions was much too personal. He believed, that should anyone know of his true grandiosity, the dream would somehow never come true, almost like revealing the wish before blowing out the candle. He also sensed that anything divulged would be negated by their sobriety-loaded palaver and rationale. They too had wild dreams at one point; Ivan a world chess champion, and Milo head-banging in front of big-haired women. They represented, not a salute to sobriety, but the result of deferred dreams. They settled for nothingness instead of their pursuit of 'all.'

He wasn't prepared to live with nothingness on his conscience, and yet he knew he couldn't drink either. He could strive for 'all,' and arrive at nothing. This was better than abandoning the pursuit. He could go to his grave as a man who failed at everything but tried with all his heart. This seemed like the trend of his existence. The Higher Power took away his mother, and his home. The Higher Power left him with spare change and Shylock who drank every night. But what was it that the Higher Power couldn't take away? His determination? His pride? And suddenly on this one excruciating day, his sobriety? If the imagination is deceptive and reality ironclad, then Noble's journey means nothing except to the worms and maggots who gnaw at his corpse. If, however, reality were as strange and elusive as his own imagination, then he is left with knowledge at the journey's end, as though, after death, he could reexamine his existence and determine whether or not he acted virtuously. This was the word he searched for: virtue, that the virtuous man conscientiously follows his dreams, no matter the obstacle. But there is one small caveat: that the virtuous man follows with his conscience as well. The dream without conscience is a nightmare. Noble aimed to help and not to hinder. His dreams were self-centered, but once delivered, he could then contribute to the welfare of others. The virtuous man pursues his dream. Anything less than his total effort and commitment was 'evil?' Evil?

As Milo and Ivan preached, he could not escape this one word. It shot like a bullet through his brain. This implicated both Ivan and Milo as evil. Strange, because they could not be evil. They were good, honorable young men, sober and helpful notwithstanding. Sure, they had failed, but then what was failure? He was getting too caught up in his own inanities. He had encountered these issues before.

"You can say that," responded Noble.

"Want to change the world with one stroke of the guitar, eh?"

"As I want to change the world through chess," smiled Ivan.

"Well," said Milo, "we all want to change the world, don't we? We all want to change the entire world, when, honestly, we can't even change ourselves."

A thunderous point.

"Classic alcoholism," said Milo with a laugh.

"But we must take the risk," said Noble.

"Absolutely," said Ivan.

"Hey, if you want to be a guitarist, fine, but you've got to get your priorities straight," said Milo. "Drinkin' and druggin' doesn't work. If anything, you'll lose your guitar."

"That will never happen," said Noble.

"Anything you put before your sobriety, you'll end up losing. So goes the wisdom of AA."

"Okay, Milo, let's not preach anymore," said Ivan.

"Fine, but seriously, you don't have to go through what we have already gone through. It's just one day, as Harry said."

"How many years does he have sober?" asked Noble.

"Twenty-three years."

"Jesus. How he stays sober I have no idea."

"One day at a time," said Milo.

"This is the longest day of my life."

Then a couple of young women walked in. They definitely met the Waspachick standard, and therefore Noble's standard.

"Hey, by the way, how do we meet women when we're sober? The bar seems like the only place."

"They say no relationships in the first year. It takes the focus off yourself, and it could lead to picking up a drink."

"But not everyone follows that rule," said Ivan, grinning.

"No, not everyone does. The ol' thirteenth step."

"What's the thirteenth step?"

"It's the ultimate step," said Ivan, still smiling.

"Well, people who chase after women in the program," said Milo, "they're called thirteenth steppers."

In his crisis Noble found an opportunity. He may actually get laid. At last, a motivation, the sonority of a woman whispering in his ear after the exhaustion of love-making, after the boredom of an AA meeting. This could work.

"But don't expect to get laid in the rooms," said Milo. "Everyone, especially the women, want to do the next right thing."

"It certainly isn't easy, and there are so many cliques," said Ivan, "which makes it next to impossible."

"But people do get laid, right?"

"Yeah, some people do," admitted Milo, "but you have to be rich and an asshole. Two traits I lack."

"Interesting," said Noble.

"Or you could practice the three 'M's,'" said Ivan, still smiling psychotically, as though the humor he found in his original statement never left.

"The what?"

"The three M's," announced Milo, "Meetings, Meditation, Masturbation."

"The pillars of early sobriety," smiled Ivan.

"It's that bad."

"Yeah," said Milo, "but hey, if you hook up in the rooms, more power to you. But listen, you shouldn't be concentrating on that. Just don't drink, and go to meetings."

"And practice the Three M's," chimed Ivan.

Noble, as a newcomer, thought he had a chance. These meetings could be a prelude to a gigantic orgy, and if this kept him sober from day-to-day, then he wouldn't mind attending these meetings. The reward for maintaining sobriety would be the woman of his choice. Yes indeed, this was the plan, to get a woman, an opportunity the East Waspachick bar couldn't offer. He searched through the faces of last night's meeting.

"Who was the girl who was crying last night?"

Ivan and Milo looked at each other and smiled.

"You mean Missy?" asked Ivan.

"Yeah, Missy."

"She's in a tough spot," said Milo, grinning. "She met someone in the rooms and decided to move in with him. The guy then decided to pick up, and now she's living with an active alcoholic."

The two of them smiled wickedly, indicating a mutual disdain for her.

"I take it you guys don't care for Missy?"

"I wouldn't say that," said Milo.

"I would," laughed Ivan, "she's such a little socialite. She doesn't give either of us the time of day. I went up to her the other night and asked her out for coffee, and she blew me off. She's got such an attitude, we're talking first-class snob, but she's beautiful, and I have fantasies about her, total debauchery."

"When she shared, I felt a little sadistic myself," said Milo. "I suppose we find pleasure in other people's misfortunes."

"She deserves it," said Ivan, "and of course Smilin' Willy's giving her a rubdown. He should have brought baby oil to the meeting. It's so frustrating."

"Yeah, right?"

"We used to be friends too, Missy and I. Every now and then I'd show her a love poem I wrote, and she smiles, but as far as any action is concerned, well, that's out of the question. I'm sure Willy's had her."

"Yeah, Willy's the playboy-in-residence."

"He carries a cell phone wherever he goes," continued Ivan. "He must get laid. That's why he's smiling all the time. He gets laid all the time, I'm sure. He's definitely a thirteenth stepper. Any new woman who comes walking through that church, Willy's on her. You saw the way he was rubbing her shoulders, and Missy is crying her eyes out. That's quintessential thirteenth stepping, and of course Meredith's sitting with them. Meredith and Missy are best friends, by the way. Meredith also gets laid, probably a three-way with Willy," Ivan laughed.

"I don't care too much for Meredith either," said Milo. "That's one item we have yet to warn you about. There are certain people who are part of the 'in-crowd.' The ones who socialize in the program. It's just like high school all over again. But those who really survive sober are those who place principles before personalities."

"Like us," said Ivan sarcastically.

"Who's that other guy? I think his name is Phinaeus?" asked Noble.

"Oh, Jeez," said Milo, "he's a real piece of work."

"You cut him off last night," said Ivan.

"Well, the guy keeps going on. He doesn't stop. He doesn't care about sobriety. He just comes to the meetings and rambles on. He's been locked up in that nut-house for three years, and he keeps going week after week. He's a threat to my sobriety, and I get pissed off when he takes up valuable time..."

"He's a real character," said Ivan. "He looks so funny."

"But I mean the guy goes out every week, and he takes up space and time with his nonsense about the Bible and adultery. One of these days I'm gonna kick him out." And then after a pause: "Just kidding. The only requirement for membership is a desire to stop drinking."

"And do you know why he was committed?" asked Ivan, leading.

"Oh man," said Milo, "he got caught masturbating in front of a ten year old boy."

"You're kidding?" said Noble, shocked.

"That doesn't go anywhere. Just between us. But that's how he ended up in the nut-house. Be careful around him. There are some very sick people in the rooms. I mean we're not exactly good examples, but there are a lot of sick people."

"Everyone's insane," said Ivan. "That's the first rule of thumb. You were right."

"What about that guy Eddie?"

"He's been sober about three years. The last time he picked up he landed in prison, after forty-eight hours. Imagine that? Two days, and suddenly he ended up in prison. That's what drinking does to us. It's a progressive disease. He's generally a good guy though. He's taken his sobriety pretty seriously since then. He does tend to wander a bit."

"That's his medication," said Ivan. "He has seizures, so he takes meds which confuse his thoughts. He'll be talking about something unimportant, nothing to do with sobriety, and then he'll get lost, and continue on a totally different topic. He laughs like a hyena, and he smokes cheap cigars."

"But really," said Milo, "you'll meet a lot of people in the next few days. Everyone is here to stay sober. We try to put principles ahead of personalities, because resentments lead us towards another drink. A lot of people don't make it because of resentments in the program."

"I've never resented anyone," said Noble.

"Oh, you will," said Ivan, "if not now, then later. The best advice: strap yourself in for the ride of your life. It's a roller coaster."

He didn't know what to make of these two. They seemed mismatched, like two left shoes, and yet their judgments about others in the program were prurient enough to warrant further investigation. He did, however, grasp one pertinent characteristic of the program, that it could never exist without the gossip and rumor it generated. He was curious to know what others thought of these two. If his perspicacity served him well, both Ivan and Milo operated on the periphery of AA's social center. Ivan drooled into his coffee, and Milo ate a three-egg omelet despite his corpulence. They were sober but unable to climb the proverbial ladder. They hung by their fingernails. At least Ivan had ambition, but Milo, in his thirties, discarded his ambitions for this unknown concept called 'serenity.' From further conversation, Noble discovered both were on disability and both were unemployed. These meetings provided their only activity, and he soon identified with their poverty and frustrations over women in the program. "It's all about money after you're nineteen," said Milo. Ivan was also at the age when poverty slowly forces one into advanced bachelorhood. Noble, on this one afternoon of clarity, shared an uneasy bond with these two who seemed marginalized by natural selection. Milo exuded a maturity and an earthiness, while Alex, still determined to become a Grand Master chess champion, aligned himself cleanly with Noble's own preposterous daydreams. How they would make it together rested with divine providence, or at least Harry's providence.

They did mention a sober party held a couple of weeks ago. Ivan didn't attend, but Milo did. The idea of a party without alcohol was like a beach without the ocean, a dry, parched desert with the figment of ice-cold ale on tap, so cold and crisp that the carbonation burns the tongue as the bitter, satisfying liquid cascades through the body, hydrating the broken soil with an ethereal dizziness, the foam tickling his upper lip and a sigh of fulfillment as that one refreshing, begging, pleading, unmerciful pint sweats with foamy residue, slipping from the lip of the glass to its heavy bottom. But this one lapse wouldn't be the last. He needs a woman too. He finds her sitting at a roundtable during a fundraising dinner for the preservation and procurement of rare paintings and curios. The museum has invited Noble as an honored guest. And the woman, naturally, is a fan of his music. Noble is asked to perform at this gathering but declines. He simply moves among black-tied strangers with a replenished pint, and then another and another until his mind swims with the swill of booze, and the gathering inflames into a parade of the absurd. He then patronizes these highbrow insects and this urbane woman-insect who sips her wine. Among the affluent and cultured his is too holy, and among these two impoverished, unemployed alcoholics, too talented.

"I think we lost, Noble," said Milo. "Yoo-hoo," while snapping his fingers, "Earth to Noble, come in Noble…"

"Sorry," as Noble acclimated to the diner.

"As I was saying," continued Milo, "there were plenty of women at the party."

"Did you hook up?" asked Ivan excitedly.

"Me? Nah. I've got to work on my social skills. I did get a few pecks on the cheek, but that's about it. I'm tellin' you- tons of women playing volleyball, the food was really good, two full platters of shrimp."

"Did Missy go?" asked Ivan.

"She was there. She actually sat next to me."

"Beyond desperation," laughed Ivan, "The three M's, live it and learn it."

Ivan gave Noble a ride into Waspachick. They exchanged phone numbers. The transition from winter to spring revitalized the strip. The townsfolk darted from one store to the next, browsing but never buying. The shops stayed in business from expensive, periodic purchases by Waspachick's elite. The bus for Manhattan huffed towards its red clapboard shelter where mostly African-Americans and Hispanics waited on line. A police cruiser sat at the intersection adjacent to Shylock's coffee shop. The upscale liquor store looked tempting, but Noble had no money. For one day he would suffer. For a single moment in time he could observe the slightly ironic but predictable reality, as though under the surface lurked something dying to escape, a riot perhaps, or a lynching, or a shooting spree from the Methodist church tower. Although it lay only a half- hour from the vibrant city, Waspachick spun its own cocoon. The bus and the train served as the only links to progress and liberation, twice a day and usually late. He could have been on that bus with his guitar case, entering the metropolis, playing in the smoky clubs where the great ones got their start, but arriving at Port Authority at gloaming would dash the utopia he expects, for he must now live sober. The beach without the ocean. The sky line without lights, a guitar player without fingers, et cetera. Without alcohol the painting lost its color, and the outcome lost its wonderment in the name of predictability, stability, responsibility, even normalcy. Sobriety would compromise his grandiosity for something real. If, however, the dream of becoming a great guitarist is, let's say, delivered in this reality, then the dream itself loses its value. If he arrived at what he truly wanted, then what is the point of arriving, since it will have been reached? How far could it go? Again, images of the dictator shouting rhetoric, or the other extreme, the inertia of dreaming but never doing. Either-or, a dream delivered is also a dream abandoned. Noble didn't wish to belabor the point, but obtaining the woman of his dreams, let's say, would end dreaming of a woman, and if humankind lost its capacity to dream, what else would there be?

He never thought the simple bus could inspire these weird thoughts, but at least he was beginning to see how things really were, that the town of Waspachick was not so bad, that the inhabitants were not as haughty and condescending, that the system didn't change humans into insects as he initially believed, and that maybe one day he could play the guitar for the pleasure of playing, not for ambitious gain bordering on greed, but carelessly playing for his own ears, as though the concoction which tends to comfort us most is actually the tune created by the masses who sing it privately and separately to themselves.

His optimism, however, came to an abrupt halt when he entered Shylock's apartment. The guitar sat in the corner, menacing as always. He encountered the same fears, as his ambition far outweighed the pleasure of practice. He could easily think himself a guitarist, but without the struggle inherent in the creative process, there is no result. Even the oyster must grind before creating a pearl, and he paced the room. With each step his fingers faded into translucence, his body an apparition, and his mind longed for the simple paradise of dexterous ability. 'Do one thing, and do it well,' came to mind, but what happens exactly when one sells the farm for one object and can't for the life of him toot or tickle the damn thing? Alcohol would help, but he remembered the 'one day' challenge. He could then resume his drinking to further his art.

He picked up the guitar. Without booze he was coerced into experiential waters, refining personal experience into product. Yet his prevailing experiences, past tense and limited, were deep lacerations. The sounds were not euphonious but noise distortions, mood swings, frustrations, tremolo cries, piercing notes which fluttered into surgical bombings, wildfires and floods, self-immolation, and periodic upheavals, thus birthing a symphony of distaste, yet worthwhile in its execution, if only to relate the gist of his experiences. He created what was the equivalent of free-verse but with an undercurrent of pain, as though pain itself was the bond nearly everyone shared, whether spoiled or victimized as a child. But just as pain cannot last forever, his play then segued into a mellow, empathic dirge intensifying and soon erupting, not in disaster, but into a flurry of doves allaying hawkish tendencies. The denouement suggested pain again but with enough cathartic gentleness to stress hope instead of destruction. A less than perfect closure for this amateur completing a long-winded tune and remarking how simple it was to start.

For most of the afternoon he practiced more traditionally as though compensating for this decadence. He used his introductory guitar book. He progressed into muffled stringing, glissandos, and pinches, attacking each string with a trill. It wasn't so easy. He was thoroughly exhausted as the apartment darkened into twilight.

The practice session, however, didn't go as well as planned. Staying within strict boundaries made him urge for a drink and especially a hit off a joint. The need for cannabis-relief pressed his patience. He returned to free-style for a while, anything to keep his mind from marijuana and the booze which would surely follow. The frustrations grew so intense that he gave up playing and paced the room again. He eventually stood out on the balcony which offered a view of the flagpole and the rooftops of Waspachick businesses.

The air had grown cold, as though winter heaved one last time. He could have easily called Harry, but he didn't think it would help. Fighting urges was more an individual's battle, one he must face alone, as no one would ever understand his urges, the type which refuses sound advice and relies chiefly on time as the best remedy. But the lag before the evening meeting made things worse. He had allocated the afternoon for diligent practice, and yet he couldn't play, and this inability provoked his urging, his mind hungry for one hit of chubby verdant clusters dripping with resin, and the lungs which bleed from sucking it down to the hilt until a coughing fit expels a cavalcade of dense smoke, and the blood vessels deliver its message into the CPU which malfunctions from information-overload, as though every nook and cranny of the tarred rooftops held a profound significance. The church steeple and the waving flag, the beeps of cars and grumbling motorcycles syncopate in hidden tones for him alone, a self-referential concert breaking subconscious sluices and drowning real-world frustrations, elevating him above the town into a flight across the heartland and into an enclave. A dirt trail fans out and leads to a plush meadow where women, baked by the sunshine, dance in mirthful oblivion, and all prior frustrations are passwords to loosening an ecstasy which subverts road-rage on Route 17, haughty shopkeepers and restaurateurs along the strip, and beefy police officers arresting disorderlies.

A tight straight jacket binds the town-folk to brute survival, and yet in other surrounding towns the streets are tougher and meaner still. One needs a rude, booming voice to order a hot dog 'all the way' at the convenience store dotted with cigarette butts, microwave wrappers, and teenage vampires. The straight jacket is at first loose, but as the ideals narrow, the straight jacket squeezes whatever visions may persist, until nothing remains but paychecks, taxes, credit card bills, auto insurance, and the ceiling which collapses from water damage. And the anger becomes reinforced by others with a similar anger until they carry submachine guns to work at the local garbage depot owned and operated by the Mob. The anger builds and terrorizes fragile temperaments, and suddenly Noble is scared of these people, a terror directed solely at him, the women whispering 'loser' under their breath, and hard men looking for a fight, their straight jackets so tight that they fill their original purpose. All of this from one colossal but imaginary hit.

He returned to the guitar. He loosened one of the pegs until the string fell slack and then tightened it until the same string tweaked. He did the same with each peg. The guitar could be tuned to his specifications, like how geometry may deviate from Euclidean assumptions. But there was little point to this. It satisfied a child-like deviance the instruction book did not sanction; an odd arrangement of sour cadence which didn't follow the tablature or notation. Boredom set in. He headed for the meeting.

He headed straight for the congregation room, not stopping for those loitering on the front steps. The crowd was as large as last night. Lots of socializing, a party without alcohol, members shaking hands, smoking cigarettes, laughing, grooming themselves for the post-meeting orgy to which Noble wasn't invited. In any event, he was not there to socialize. Those who conversed on the steps would never stay sober. They were not serious enough. They cared only about getting laid, and this distaste stemmed from his inability to be part of the action. Instead he sat alone in the stark room until the members, crowned with sober gaiety, took their chairs.

Harry walked in after everyone was seated. He wore a khaki suit instead of his usual loud polyester. It must have been a special occasion to which Noble wasn't privy, because Harry looked better, something about his hair- a new haircut? Maybe he took a shower for the first time in a week, whatever it was, he looked concerned about something, some issue which needed venting. He looked prosperous in the candlelight, as though the polyester routine concealed his immense fortune. He could have been a CEO or a partner in a law firm, or the owner of a vast estate. There was something peculiar about him which Noble couldn't determine. Harry didn't smile. He didn't exchange greetings with those next to him.

Ivan and Milo made it. The same woman from last night chaired the meeting, but Harry exuded this intense peculiarity, a vibe which distinguished him from the other members. And why wouldn't he seem peculiar? Harry was staring right at Noble for some reason. Noble looked away, feigning his attentions to the preamble and the reading of the twelve steps. Noble looked at Harry again. Harry still stared at him. He looked around the room, to the women, to the 'in-crowd' of Smilin' Willy and his harem, but then again he encountered Harry staring at him, those pale eyes fixed right on him, not necessarily in anger or joy, but a deep concentration as though he was relaying a message, his stare suggesting a communication or a particular interest which Noble couldn't satisfy. How strange, this Harry. One day he's a savior, and the next day he's peculiar, as though nothing else mattered but those pale eyes offering what exactly? Why was Harry conspiciously staring at him as the meeting commenced?

The members shared one by one, and Noble felt those icy eyes burn through him, a constant presence which distracted him. Noble had always been the shy, quiet type, so he didn't confront him by raising his eyebrows or whispering across the table. For some twenty minutes Harry didn't take his eyes off him. He merely rested his head on his elbow, his eyes unblinking and burning through him like hot lazers.

During this Noble asked himself a good question. But it wasn't a question which began as an internal thought. It was a tonal question, a question which he asked verbally in his mind, as though speaking to Harry with the intention of letting him know how peculiar he was behaving. Noble asked: 'Jesus, Harry, why are you staring at me like that?,' as though speaking to him through the mind, a communiqué on the non-verbal level. But this was totally preposterous and absurd.

The meeting was in full swing, and an interruption would call attention to himself. Harry continued looking at him, and then tonally, Noble asked: 'Harry, fuckin'-A, why are you staring at me like that?' The question sat at the front of his brain. At the exact moment Noble asked this, Harry turned his eyes away, the first time he had done so during the course of the meeting.

Noble was relieved by this and labeled the incident pure coincidence, but as soon as he looked away, Harry's eyes were right back on him, those hot lazers dead-center into Noble's head.

Strange. He had spoken in his mind to Harry, and then coincidentally Harry looks away for one brief second, and then this game starts all over again, back to square one, Harry and his fierce stare, not a fierce facial expression, but his eyes, those pale, knowing eyes. Again, Noble spoke through his mind without uttering a word: 'Harry, would you stop looking at me like that!' And at the exact moment Noble thought this, Harry looked away for a brief moment and rubbed his nose, an ersatz itch, and returned to his staring.

Pure coincidence, thought Noble, but two coincidences in a row? How could this be? Maybe he really did need a drink, or perhaps it had been a very long day, since his practice session didn't go so well, and all of this sobriety-speak, three meetings in a single day, with new acquaintances like Milo and Ivan, and this escapism, and Phinaeus masturbating in front of a ten year old, and the women getting all touchy-feely with the 'in-crowd,' and this meeting so unbelievably boring and irrelevant, the drink ready and waiting for him once the meeting ended, and how could he forget, simply forget about this stimulation and return to the guitar with a whiskey bottle in one hand sliding down the neck, and his pick in the another, creating sounds no one in their right mind would pay money to hear.

It can't be. This is not happening. Pure coincidence, the conscious mind recognizing patterns in the unconscious mind. That's all. Nothing else. He would go home and drink, and Milo and Ivan and Harry would be strange memories. Nothing more than that. He had given his best for one day, and he could now go home, drink whiskey, and play guitar in keeping with his ultimate calling.

He avoided Harry by looking around the room. An old-timer was sharing routinely, and all eyes were on him. The women were looking good, especially Missy who wore a spandex top which defined her shapely breasts. She sat near Smiling Willy who also listened, probably with alterior motives. Phinaeus was absent, and Dianne held a stack of inspirational cards. Milo sat serenely, and Ivan fidgeted in his seat. The meeting seemed normal enough. Everyone listened and concentrated, except Harry. He was still staring at him, but this time with a smirk.

'Harry, would you please cut it out, I'm trying to listen, and stop staring and making all these signs. Why are you looking at me?' demanded Noble in tonal thought.

Then he heard suddenly, in Harry's voice:

'If you want a drink, have it tomorrow,' and once this was dispatched, Harry rubbed his nose in an overt, artificial manner, painfully obvious that something had taken place, only Noble couldn't believe it, and suddenly Harry stopped staring and resumed listening to the meeting, as though nothing had happened.

Noble, on the other hand, was so perplexed that he almost ran from the room. Harry's supernatural, paranormal behaviors frightened him. He thought he was seriously losing his marbles, but he remained composed in his mental frenzy. He acted as though he were listening, but actually he was ready to call it quits. Yet he may have been imagining this in keeping with his grandiosity. There was ample evidence to doubt what just took place, and he searched for ways to disprove it.

'Harry, what the hell is going on here? What just happened? Is it all in my mind, or did we just talk to each other without uttering a single word, or was it coincidence, I mean what happened here? Harry? Harry can you hear me? Shit, Harry, can you hear me, or am I losing my mind, damn you?'

No response from Harry. Not a word. Not even a glance.

"Hard to believe, ain't it," remarked a deep voice from behind.

The apparitions. The auto mechanic fiddling with the carburetor and the idol fingering the strings of his guitar. Their sarcastic, smug all-knowingness hadn't changed one bit. A mocking pair, and Noble fought the temptation to yell at them outright.

"Where the hell have you guys been? What the hell is going on? Now you show up? In the middle of what may be the greatest development known in the history of all humandom?"

"The man's still missing the point," said the auto mechanic, his overalls stained with grease.

"He may never get the point," said the idol.

"Well then stop dickin' me around. If there's a point, then lay it on me."

"The point has been the same ever since you found us," said the idol strumming, "you're still so self-interested, so selfish. You don't care about others…"

"Damn straight," said the auto mechanic.

"Listen, I'm working really hard here. I don't need a couple of, well, whatever you are, insulting me. I'm a guitarist, and I'm becoming damn good at it."

"Are you sure about that?" asked the idol. "What I see is an egomaniac who doesn't really care about anyone but himself."

"-And you're a racist to boot."

"That's nonsense," said Noble, "absolutely nonsense. I like people. I want what's best for them."

"Bullshit," fired the idol, "oh yeah, like Big Time Noble McCloud, the guitarist, up on the stage with his whiskey and his women, wants what's best for the world…"

"Can't handle that much bullshit in one day," said the mechanic.

"Gimme a break," continued the idol. "We all know you want money and fortune, recognition and prestige. If you really believed that what happened, happened, then you'll probably use it for your own gain. You would find a way to profit from it, until the entire world knew your name. You don't care about music, do you? We're not stupid."

"And what about you?" attacked Noble. "All you two do is harass me, because I'm human, I'm a human being, and the only thing in my life I ever wanted was to play the guitar for people, but no, instead I'm in this room, and I have to stay sober, and I'm hit with this new phenomenon, and there's nothing I can do. Yes, I'm guilty, guilty as charged for acting exactly like a human being should, so don't sit there telling me that I'm selfish, self-centered, narcissistic, whatever, because I'm working hard, okay, towards the realization of a dream."

The idol and the auto mechanic looked at each other as they clearly didn't expect so much vitriol.

"Yes, but your dreams are selfish dreams," said the idol finally, and both of them disappeared.

Noble caught Harry staring at him again. Harry rubbed his nose and looked away.

Noble was stunned. He didn't know whether or not to believe it. He couldn't concentrate on the meeting any longer. He rushed into the church kitchen instead. Ivan was speaking with an elderly gentleman. Noble had never smoked before, but he needed a cigarette badly. He and Ivan shook hands, and he bummed a cigarette from him. Not wishing to talk with anyone, Noble retreated into a quiet corner and smoked languidly. The kitchen was large enough to hide in, and his thoughts were racing. The cigarette calmed him down.

Okay, think. What just happened? Was it his own mind, his wild imagination, or was it real, a phenomenon he never learned of in high school or college. But if it were real, then why doesn't anyone ever talk about it, why has he never heard of it before, this mental communication business? And why should he, of all people, stumble onto something so bizarre, because at heart it was downright bizarre, and most importantly who was behind it? Why was he selected over all the downtrodden souls ever to walk within the AA doorway, or perhaps everyone else possessed this ability, and he did not, making all of these AA people space aliens waiting to drug him through his coffee. Perhaps Ivan knew and gave him a poisonous cigarette, and once he were drugged, they would carry him off to a spaceship and conduct torturous experiments and release him without a brain in his skull.

Besides these outrageous imaginings, bordering on the paranoid, he had many questions, not necessarily for Harry, but for himself. Was it real or was it imagined? This, he determined, was the first and foremost question. He knew of sychronicity, the idea of meaningful coincidences, and on occasion he did have run-ins with them. He never tried to figure them out. He assumed that synchronous events happened, and everyone shared these happenings. But for synchronicity to move towards an all-out form of communication between two people was something altogether different. Two people as solid as a tree or a brick wall, two people of flesh and blood exchanging a simple conversation without words? Only a spatial difference- Harry across the table staring and transferring signs? Three coincidences in a row at the exact moment when he spoke through the mind? Those pale eyes asking him, begging him to think just one word in response? Why, this is absolutely ridiculous, and if Noble experienced this, then perhaps everyone in the nation had already known this from the beginning, as though this phenomena was nothing new, and behind this was, of course, the CIA. Yes, he was actively being recruited by the CIA to help protect national security, and Harry belonged to this organization, and they were looking for people going absolutely nowhere in life, these disenfranchised alcoholic individuals who thought they were superior artists, overworking their brains to create one meticulous riff which would capture blonde women, when suddenly his perceptions are cleansed with a plumber's snake, and the world emerges from the rubble into new territory involving the complexity of human relations, the idea that two individuals from totally different backgrounds could relate to each other, mind to mind.

The power had been tilted to Harry and his long experience, his old age, his wisdom, as though only these factors were the overriding forces in the universe, as though Harry had all the answers.

"Relax," he said to himself a number of times. There must be a perfectly reasonable explanation for this. It was merely a series of coincidences, and he must exercise caution when investigating these coincidences, especially with his mind so fragile. But then again: who was this Harry anyway? He seemed so rational, so normal, and somehow Harry saw the apparitions too, because he rubbed his nose, as though he knew Noble completely, even his own grandiosity and egotism.

Suddenly Harry became the focus of this phenomenon, at least for the time being, and Noble must figure out this greater mystery which may benefit human kind, and he would do so altruistically. He now had the power to help others. He would show those apparitions what he could do; he could work towards helping others, world peace, a utopia right on our own planet so that no one would have to suffer the way he alone has suffered, and from the window in Shylock's apartment he could look below to Harry, Ivan, and Milo, and a street full of women and men colliding into dance, a huge celebration held simply for this idea known as life, this puzzle which most people dismiss as unsolvable, this conception which thrilled him and at the same time locked his feet onto the linoleum of the kitchen, the florescent lights pulling him into rationality, logic, reality, as though reality was the pain each of us had to endure, and that his imagination, his drifting thoughts, were only a way of keeping him happy during this singular day of trouble.

He laughed in the corner of the kitchen, as though this had all gone way too far, that his imagination was untrustworthy and should be used with caution. He was once again an unemployed drunk who wanted to play the guitar so badly that it ached in his gut, and if he could codify rational experience within one of his instrumentals, then he would do so without his imagination.

The imagination was a dangerous trap which continually led him astray. The sky, fixed with resolute stars, demanded truth, not the imaginary. The stars were rock-hard and cold and determined. They demanded reason and selfishness and freedom of choice and a hell built for one in a ship on a sea-sickening ocean, into the oblivion of the same old pattern of thought, the same ancient paradigm of reason and rationality developing into the soft ripple which keeps the concentric circle staid, lifeless, and limited, as the irritated center blames irrationality and emotion for all of its problems.

His feet were locked onto the linoleum, the cigarette sizzling into its filter, his mind fighting these tides of imagination, and finding himself in the corner as other AA-goers filed in and lit up cigarettes and poured more coffee.

He immediately searched for Harry above the smoking heads. Harry's entrance appeared regal. Noble approached him immediately.

"Why'd you walk out so soon?" asked Harry, lighting up a filterless butt.

"It got too heavy in there."

"How so?" he smiled.

Noble should spill it, tell him the direct truth of what happened, this mind-to-mind communication, but he believed if Harry negated it, it would shatter the illusion of a world beyond those fixed stars.

"Well, it just felt weird, you know what I mean?"

"Not really, but you stayed sober today. You shouldn't be concerned about what others say. It's just one day," as he held up a finger. "Now all you need to do is sleep tonight, eat, and get ready for tomorrow. I want you to call me as soon as you get up, okay?"

"You mean, you didn't feel weird in that meeting?"

"Remember, we only have one day," and he winked.

Both Ivan and Milo approached them. They shook hands with Harry. Wonderful. A conspiracy.

"You guys should go to the diner tonight," suggested Harry.

Noble definitely needed the diner. He wanted to go, but until they sat in those cozy booths he would keep his mouth shut and merely suggest the phenomenon occurred.

They piled into Ivan's car. Ivan turned up the Rachmaninoff. He also lit up a smoke. His plan was to investigate.

When they arrived, Milo asked him:

"So what did you think of the meeting?"

"It was interesting," said Noble smiling suspiciously.

"What?" asked Ivan. "There's something you're not telling us."

"Let's just say that it was a very interesting meeting," said Noble.

"Yeah, did you see Missy? She was looking good," said Ivan.

"At least Phinaeus didn't show up," said Milo.

"She was looking really good," continued Ivan, "but she didn't respond too well to my latest poem about her. I should tell her I adore her, simply adore her in every possible way."

"That's a good way to land in jail," said Milo.

"C'mon, I should tell her."

"She'll sue you for sexual harassment."

"All these frivolous lawsuits. Check out this story I'm writing. There's this guy who gets into a car accident, and he decides to sue the other driver, just for the money, and he wins. He then goes to a coffee house, and the chair breaks, so he sues the coffee shop. By this time the guy has a reputation in the town. He's suing people left and right. So he then takes a construction job digging ditches. He's working with two other construction guys. And he really hurts himself this time, right in the ditch. But instead of helping him out of the ditch, the construction guys shovel dirt on him until he's buried alive. Great story, huh?"

Noble and Milo looked at each other in bewilderment, and Ivan laughed as though thoroughly impressed with this idea. He wiped away the string of drool hanging from his mouth.

"Keep comin' Ivan," said Milo patting him on the back, sending the drool onto the table.

"What's going on with you?" asked Milo, clearly the most mature of the bunch.

"Didn't you guys think that was an interesting meeting?" asked Noble again.

"Then why did you leave?" asked Ivan.

"It's hard to explain. Maybe it was too, how do you put it, stimulating?"

"Yeah, I get that sometimes," said Milo. "Too many people, too many women and men interacting. It happens sometimes."

"But it was something more than that. Did you guys find anything interesting about the meeting?"

"Yeah, Willy's hands over Missy. She must have done him. I know she did."

"Why? What did you hear?" asked Milo.

"I'm a good keeper of secrets," said Ivan. "They used to call me the 'tombs,' because I kept secrets so well."

"Well, then spill it."

"I just heard Missy and Willy were seeing each other, that's all, from a very reliable source."

"And you're not the one she's sleeping with," laughed Milo.

Even Noble cracked a smile and said:

"Seriously, guys, did you notice anything odd or peculiar about the meeting, something barely noticeable?"

"Not really. Why?"

"I noticed something strange about Harry," admitted Noble.

"Harry?" they both asked.

"Yes. First of all, he didn't dress in his polyester suit."

"Hey, yeah," said Ivan, "maybe he wore a new suit tonight."

"Exactly," continued Noble, "he wore a khaki suit, almost brand new, and he didn't share once. Don't you think it strange?"

"Come to think of it," said Milo, "he usually does share."

"The same thing over and over again," said Ivan. " 'If you want a drink, have it tomorrow,'" with an arch of the hand.

"Doesn't that seem odd that he didn't share at all? I mean, I'm not an expert, since it's only my first day and all, but from what I've learned from you guys, he does share at every meeting, doesn't he?"

Ivan lit up a smoke.

"Usually," said Milo, "but maybe tonight he was just listening. He does that once in a while."

"But didn't it strike you guys as odd," insisted Noble, "I mean if he has a proven track record of sharing, wouldn't it be odd for this one particular night that he didn't share? Isn't it funny that he came into the meeting wearing cotton instead of polyester, and then somehow didn't share at the same time, like there was something unusual, strange, odd about him, like he was hiding something from us?"

"What are you getting at?" asked Ivan.

"I don't know, I just think it's strange."

"You're awfully serious about it," said Milo.

"I don't mean to be, but that entire meeting was so peculiar. You guys didn't think it strange at all?"

They both shook their heads. Noble was on the brink of confession, but he held his speech. His phony laughter was an attempt to resume the usual flow of discourse, but he had already planted the seed of his own oddity to these two who obviously felt nothing. And then he questioned his own thoughts, that maybe he was overreacting as everyone else overreacted. That maybe his mind wasn't so unique or special, that once again his imagination tricked him into believing something greater than himself, as though he were a false prophet or a messenger. The reality, however, was obvious. He was flesh and blood, a struggling guitarist who relied too much on his own capacities to dream, a sickening selfishness placing him at the center of things. He did what he could to drop this conniption altogether, as though nothing happened, as though he ought to have faith more in this reality than something so lofty and absurd as telepathy.

Chapter Three

Noble returned to the apartment and found Shylock on the couch with a beer bottle in his hand.

"Why, it's Noble, Noble McCloud," sung Shylock. "Where have you been all my life?"

"Hullo, Shy."

"So where have you been, man, I've been waiting for you," as he gulped at his beer, his speech on the verge of slurring.

"I've been out."

"Well, whatever; tonight we're going to East Waspachick."

"No thanks, Shy. I'm kind of tired tonight."

"Tired?" he teased, "Noble McCloud is tired?"

"Not tonight," said Noble.

"I'm not taking 'no' for an answer."

"You just need someone to drive."

"That's not it at all. You might even have some fun."

"I can't tonight. All right?"

"Noble McCloud can't go out tonight? How ridiculous is that?"

"You should know by now. I'm trying to stay sober."

"Noble, I've thought about it. You're not an alcoholic. You're just not. If anything, I'm an alcoholic. They probably have you hypnotized already. You're so naïve."

"Listen, man, I'm tired. It's been a hard day. If you want to go to East Waspachick, that's fine, but I'm sleeping tonight. I'm a little cranky. Can you get off the couch, please?"

Noble could almost taste the cold beer fizzle on his tongue, numbing his tightly-wound mood.

"Oh, well, massuh, after all, this is your house, ain't it? Sure, go ahead. Kick me off the couch. Maybe I should get another apartment."

"Shylock," sighed Noble, "I'm not in the mood, okay?"

"Noble McCloud not in the mood?" taunted Shylock. "Oh sure, he sleeps here every night, steals from me, plays the guitar which I bought him, drinking all of my booze..."

"Shy, I really don't want to get into this right now. You're drunk."

"Relax, okay? A beer or two won't hurt. It's better than being cranky. I don't know what they tell you, but I heard from a customer today that it's all mind control. They're controlling your mind."

"What do you mean by 'mind control?'" asked Noble seriously, in light of the earlier coincidences.

"That's what they do, man. They feed you with all this horseshit until you become hypnotized. This customer told me, and she was in AA for like two years. They take away you're mind. They brainwash you. Already I'm seeing the change. I haven't seen you for days. You don't even stop by the coffee shop anymore."

"You're the asshole who got me into this, remember? You thought it would be good for me."

"No, Noble, you got yourself into it."

"It's been a very long day, sober no less. There's nothing wrong with me."

"Right. Nothing wrong. Why don't you get a job," before swallowing more of the golden elixir.

The best way to deal with him was to smile and nod along, and hopefully, he would leave for the bar, and perhaps Noble could get a few, solid hours of sleep before calling Harry in the morning.

"You do nothing all day, and you come here in a shitty mood, and I have to suffer," said Shylock.

"You're starting to piss me off, Shy," as he sat on the floor.

"Whatever. The rent's due pretty soon, and of course you have no money. As usual, someone has to pay for your sorry ass. And where would you go? You have no place to go. You can't go back to your father's. For once I'm seeing what he sees: a freeloader."

Let it go. Let him hurl these insults, and they did hurt. In wine there is truth, but negative truths unearthed from the places we store them. He was a freeloader. By common definition, he was going nowhere as quickly as a bullet-train, but Noble wasn't about to argue with him. It would only encourage greater insult. Shylock stumbled out the door without saying anything else and headed for the East Waspachick bar. Gloom remained in the stuffy air, this single idea which meant that life was meaningless without accomplishment, without a reward at the end of the day, and his one day sober should have a reward, like a shiny star under his name in a kindergarten class. But for this amateur on his first day sober, the future was not necessarily bleak but predictable, a vast space of nothingness, loads of neutral time without progress, without reward, only some fuzzy belief that he was getting better, his fingers more limber, his sound more palatable. But no one else would ever confirm this belief, simply due to his reluctance to let anyone hear him, as though another ear would kill him slowly with its judgment, criticism, and complaint.

He figured existence was merely a flurry of rejections, not necessarily for his music, but for his character as well. Perhaps he was born to fail, unable to fill this vacuous space with anything worthy, his hard work as desolate as a bum harvest. But again it wasn't this bleak outlook which frustrated him. He didn't really expect a swaying audience below the stage, or attractive women hanging on each arm, or the lucrative record deal. Not anymore. The frustration came with the knowledge that hard work, no matter the walk of life, rarely has a reward. The hardest working people rarely get their day in the sun. Rarely do they reap what they sow. A paycheck becomes another slip of paper used to pay off other slips of paper. Less work is championed over more work. The guitarist who plays something with ease is preferred to the amateur who winces and sweats trying to capture the same note.

Similarly, the beautiful woman is preferred to the woman who tries to look beautiful. Apples and oranges, but this is how Noble's mind worked. He chuckled. Was it really that bad? Did the elite few reap the reward, while the rest labored for no reason whatsoever? The only reward left for him was a slow glass of whiskey, any liquor at all; yes, he needed a drink. Shylock was right. He had lost the ability to have fun, to find pleasure. He was a freeloader, a grub. Even though insanity would result from drunkenness, perhaps insanity served a greater purpose, making existence less boring and predictable in favor of crisis than its alternative: honest hard work. Aside from this, the 'mind control' issue bothered him. Was Harry's communication real? Did Shylock's customer know about this? Did she escape AA before it controlled her? Was the paramilitary wing of AA still chasing her?

He crawled onto the sofa and pulled the white sheet over him. He was too exhausted to practice. His mind, however, wandered and wandered, so much that he couldn't sleep. He asked himself where it was all going, if the destination had a point. He wanted to accomplish great things, not necessarily for himself but for others as well. He wished to affect his listeners the same way the great guitarists affected him. Without a gig, without a demo tape or studio time, there was not much he could do but sit at home and practice. The next step was definitely a gig.

He could ask Shylock about a coffee house performance. Surely Shylock could pull a few strings (no pun intended). This was a possibility, although he hated imposing. Despite his pride, he would ask him in the morning. He had practiced long enough, and it was time to put a few instrumentals together, perhaps record them and send them off to record companies. But this was far off. The main goal was to keep working, keep practicing until he moved from amateur to professional. Only the few make it. He thought he had a chance, because the fantasy was so certain, the idea so majestic and pure, the image of his success so vivid, and yet he knew in his gut that these same visions would cheat him in the end, that nothing would transpire from these long practice sessions or these fantasies which pushed him from one session to the next.

He loathed practicing. He preferred his freestyle sessions but even these had limitations, as they were short-lived. Keep dreaming. It was all some psychotic dream, for at the heart of the American dream lingered exactly what it had originally promised: a dream. The same musicians are awarded the lucrative record deals, the same politicians with the same myopic visions get elected, people with the same level of so-called intelligence get the same level jobs, until nothing at all changes. Reality simply operates on the illusion of change, as each generation strives to accomplish what their ancestors had already accomplished. We fight the same battles, listen to the same riffs, salivate over the same women, and ejaculate the same genes into infinity. But this can't be true, he mused. Technology changes. There are new inventions, new cures, and a host of new laws. Fashion changes. Many things change, but all under the rubric of what's acceptable, or what is feasible. For the human being to change beyond the ghosts of the past would take some higher ability or perception, not induced by drugs or alcohol, but given to the human being by the process of evolution. Could telepathy be that higher ability? Nah, of course not. How silly of him to think this way. It was all the same game, but he couldn't deny what had happened in the meeting. If only it could be true. If only these coincidences meant something...

"Noble, Noble McCloud," he heard. "Hey, Noble, you woos, wake up man..."

"What time is it?"

"About two-thirty."

"AM or PM?"

"AM."

"Jeez, Shy. I'm trying to sleep," the sheet still over his head.

"Listen, man, I need you to take a walk for a little while."

"Where? It's late, man, go to sleep."

Shylock ripped the sheet from his body.

"C'mon, man, I've got a girl coming over."

"Can't you go to her place?"

"Not tonight. Now get your sorry-ass up and out of here. You can come back tomorrow morning."

In the cold moonlight he roamed the Waspachick strip. Every so often he was stopped and questioned by the police officer on the night shift. He explained his unfortunate situation after exploring the shop windows and pondering the ballast of silence which haunted the town. Not a soul seemed awake at this hour. It was quiet and cold. The nearest all-night convenience store was in the combat zone further south. He wasn't about to put his life in danger, and besides, he didn't have a dime on him. He couldn't afford a stick of gum on his budget, which came from Shylock.

With a heavy heart he sat at the edge of the town park and looked to the sky. It couldn't get any worse. It could only get better, and when it does get better, it wouldn't be enough. Iron dividers trisected the park bench. He couldn't lie down. He sat stiffly in one of the sections. The park held memories of his mother, how they picnicked at the foot of the statue, how time with her went by effortlessly. He pushed his hands deeper into this jacket pockets. He began to shiver. He pulled his arms from his sleeves and hugged himself. If there were a point to this, he needed it now. If there were a reason for his prolonged permanence, he needed it more than any of the fantasies which buoyed him. One would think a divine hand would intercede, but Noble merely gazed at these stars unmoving, motionless, dead but sparkling with wondrous color, as though they danced with the moon as their choreographer. The silence, the cold, the creaking planks of the park bench, the occasional patrol car, and the abundance of time all denoted an intense longing for meaning and purpose within the vagrant lifestyle he had chosen for himself. Choosing this lifestyle was the final blow, but just as the universe would not bend, so he would never yield to time's marching feet.

He dozed off for a couple of hours. The police didn't bother him. He sat in the shadow of an elm tree and slept restlessly. He awoke early in the morning. It was still dark. He walked to the church. The doors were locked. He bunched up in the corner of the entrance and dozed for a few more hours. Once or twice he awoke only to shift positions. His legs had fallen asleep. A knot developed in his back. He stretched out and lay prone on the hard stone slab and avoided the sphere of light emanating from a nearby lamppost. He cursed Shylock dozens of times but knew he could not return until later in the morning. He heard his name being called over and over. He was dreaming, until the voice grew stern and demanding. He woke up to Harry's wrinkled face. It was morning suddenly, and he wiped the frost from his jacket.

"C'mon," said Harry, "I'll buy you some breakfast."

They drove in Harry's late-model Buick to the East Waspachick diner. They sat in a booth overlooking the thoroughfare which led into the center of town.

"What in God's name were you doing out there?" asked Harry while chewing French Toast.

Noble ordered scrambled eggs and sausage.

"I always wind up in these terrible situations. I have 'bad luck' written all over me."

"Elaborate."

Noble told him about last night.

"So you really are going to any length, eh? Don't worry. It gets worse before it gets better," his ruby-red polyester suit blaring.

"I mean, I was close to picking up a drink. Really close. That apartment is a bachelor pad. There's booze all around. And I would find an apartment of my own, but, as you can tell, I'm broke."

"Why can't you get a job? I mean everyone has to work. Even the richest man in America works."

"I've had bad work experiences, and my work is with my guitar now. I see what jobs do to people."

"Noble, get a job. That way you can afford your own apartment. What's wrong with working for a living?"

"I can't. Okay?" as he munched on a sausage link.

Harry ordered coffee for both of them.

"My life is with my guitar," he whispered. "One can't do it half-way or part-time. I was put on this earth to do one thing, and that's play guitar. 'Do one thing, and do it well,' is my motto. If I can't play for a living, then there's no sense in living."

"Hell, Woody Guthrie had to work," said Harry. "Musicians do have day-jobs, ya know."

"Well, I'm the new breed of musician then. You go as long as you can. It's better to burn out than fade away."

"Lemme tell you something. I know that alcoholics drink because sobriety lost its priority. Sobriety has to be the priority, okay, priority number one, because we lose what we place before our own sobriety. Play your guitar, don't get a job, that's fine. But your sobriety has to be the first priority, otherwise we lose what we put ahead of it."

"Oh, I plan to stay sober. There's no question."

"Well, you have to find another place to live if you want to stay clean. I know that if I roomed with an active drinker, I would definitely pick up. You have any family in the area? Maybe you can stay with them."

"That's also out of the question."

"For Chrissakes Noble, how are you going to stay sober and live with an active drinker at the same time? As I see it, you have two options: look for a job, or move back in with your family. You can't stay in that apartment."

"I don't know, Harry, I just don't know. I'm as close to being a bum as I've ever been. I mean, you saw me out there? Sleeping on the church steps? How desperate was that?"

"Get a job, or move back in with your family. Besides, who wants to put up with getting kicked out and sleeping on the steps of church for Chrissakes. That's no way to live."

They went to the early-bird meeting thereafter, and Noble shared of his present situation. The consensus favored Harry's idea, that he leave Shylock's place as soon as possible. Many in the meeting urged him to get a job, but Noble's obduracy was ironclad. Under no circumstances would he work, as it would diminish his artistic performance.

After much thought, Noble decided to visit McCoy McCloud. Certainly he had his reservations, but approaching him would be better than getting a job. If, however, his father turned him away, then he guessed he would have to find work in Waspachick. The thought of visiting his father didn't agree with him, but the alternative was living with Shylock.

He wondered what made sobriety so important all of a sudden. Why after one day, a mysterious day no less, did he cling to a way of life he had thought dubious and irrelevant? Noble wasn't sure himself, but it dealt specifically with the coincidences of last night's meeting, the idea that he was no longer alone with his whimsical daydreams, that these alcoholics understood what he was going through as they had once been burdened with a similar grandiosity. Sobriety, then, would improve his play, because the mysterious powers in the universe would align with his goals and visions. He couldn't escape those coincidences. They alone sanctioned his true purpose, sanctioned his determination to proceed along a tough, hard road. He didn't want to return to that old lifestyle, the misery of walking home from East Waspachick in the snow, the DWI's, and the jails. He had found instant friendship in the rooms and now a sponsor in Harry. He asked him shortly after the meeting, and he accepted. Of course his urges didn't mysteriously disappear. He still wanted a drink, but he discovered that by remaining sober, a room of people suddenly cared about him, Harry in particular. The benefits of staying sober, however, were not readily apparent inasmuch his playing still suffered from abstinence. But at the morning meeting, he was told many times that his playing would improve, that he would be more productive and more focused. He was convinced by these affirmations.

He was more interested in those strange coincidences. Harry must know something about him that he did not. Perhaps Harry knew the direction of his life, as though it had been preordained that one day, some day, he would indeed play on a stage in front of thousands. Perhaps sobriety had been ordered by the Higher Power so that it may lead him to greater things.

During the early-bird meeting he looked for signs and coincidences, but he found none. Harry wore polyester again. If he wore cotton, it would signal telepathy. But at this meeting there were no coincidences, only an outpouring of attention for Noble's predicament. He would keep coming in order to investigate Harry and this phenomenon.

Nevertheless, he was now poised for a visit to his father's place. Ivan offered him a ride, but he walked instead. He prepared a long speech for his father. He would say he was now living sober, and he would do the chores every morning without fail, that he would mow the lawn, (now that spring had arrived). He wouldn't mention his guitar, and if it came to it, he would beg. He would become the small mouse unnoticed except by the wiring and beams behind the walls. He would not make a sound to disturb him. McCoy McCloud would never know his son lived in the same house. He would keep the stereo low and his room neat. He would practice without an amplifier. He would stock the fridge with Cornish game hens and curb his eating so his father ate more and he less.

The lane heading south was a different world, an area west of the combat zone which he hadn't seen for some time. A young girl rode by on her bicycle, pink streamers waving from the handlebars. The two-story houses became one-story houses as he journeyed farther south. Budding trees lined the lane, the sidewalk loose and crumbling, the red paint on the fire hydrants peeling, crows perching on telephone wires, each step becoming more gruesome. He never expected a return to his old neighborhood, a residential subsidiary of north-end landlords.

His father was an exception. Many in the south-end didn't own their homes. They usually rented and sent their children to the high school which was supposedly one of the best in the state. Noble wanted nothing to do with his childhood. The memories of his alienation attacked him from all sides, negative images of a school-yard fight, the pretty girls who laughed at his outfits, the teachers who told him he would never amount to anything, and they were correct so far. Noble hadn't gone anywhere. He had remained in the town all of his life, as though it were a wooden box tightly tailored to his specifications. He thought he'd be buried in Waspachick. The more he sought escape, the heavier the ball which chained him to the town.

Living with Shylock was progress, but not enough to alter his dealings with the south end. The lawns were muddy. The frames of the houses were warped and sullen, uncollected garbage was stacked high in front of the driveways. A pit-bull barked as he passed. He approached his house and found to his bewilderment and shock a realty sign posted on the front lawn. The house had been sold. His father's Oldsmobile, however, was sitting out front. He looked through the windows. There was no furniture in McCoy McCloud's room. Even Noble's old room had been swept and cleaned. The house was vacant. McCoy McCloud must have skipped town, but then why did he leave the car?

Noble went directly to the real estate agency in the center of town. The agency occupied the first floor of an upscale building. Outrageously priced homes were advertised in the front window. A young, attractive receptionist answered the phones. Noble waited in a comfortable lounge chair. A wave of fatigue hit him. He hadn't showered or shaved in days. He could have slept in that chair all day, until the receptionist approached him.

"Can I help you with something?" she asked matter-of-factly.

"Yes," said Noble getting to his feet, "I'm here for the real estate agent who's selling my father's place."

"You're a client of ours?"

"Not exactly. I'm Noble McCloud. My father owned the house on 216 Overlook Lane. The house was sold, but I knew nothing about it."

The receptionist made a quick call into the back office. The reception area was merely a front to the office behind a closed door.

"Mr. McCloud, why don't you have a seat," said the receptionist. "Elaine will be with you shortly."

Noble snoozed in the chair. He felt a warm hand on his knee. A woman of his age sat in the chair next to him. Noble would have married her if she proposed.

"Hi, I'm Elaine Dyer," she said gently, "I'm the agent who sold McCloy McCloud's house."

"Nice to meet you."

"And how are you associated with McCoy McCloud? Are you a relative or a friend?"

"I'm his son. I'm wondering what happened to the house. It came as a real surprise."

"You mean, you don't know?"

"Know what?"

She looked to her feet for a moment.

And she asked again: "You don't know about any of this?"

"I'm afraid not. I left the house shortly before it was sold. I have no idea what's going on."

"Noble, if I could use your first name, your father, he, well, and I hate to tell you this. You look like such a, how would you say it, a kind man, and I'm sorry to be the bearer of such horrible news, but your father, he passed away last week, probably while you were away. The bank foreclosed on the property, and we were hired to sell the home to another buyer."

A grave silence followed. Even the receptionist on the phone fell silent. Death indeed is a part of life. He didn't know what to say or how to react.

"Would you like some tea or coffee?"

"Umm, no thanks. I guess I should be, uh, going now."

"Yes, I'm sure you have a lot to think about, and I'm sorry, so very sorry."

"Where's the body?" he stammered.

He was directed to the police precinct on the edge of Central Waspachick.

At the precinct he was told the burial had already been performed. "We can't keep the body for more than three weeks," said the officer on duty.

"Imagine the stench in this place?" The officer did, however, hand over a box of belongings. Apparently even the furniture was sold.

"Where is he buried?"

"East Waspachick Cemetery. They took him last week. I think he died of cardiac arrest."

After signing a few forms, he rummaged through his father's belongings in the town park. The park was nearly empty save for a nanny pushing a stroller. In the box he found a small bottle of gin, a wallet, some spare change, and a set of car keys. In the wallet he found thirty bucks. He found credit cards, a condom, ATM withdrawal receipts, and suddenly an old picture of Noble as a young child sitting on his mother's knee. Noble had never laid eyes on this picture before. Perhaps his father did think of him in the unexplored secrecy of his heart, the part of him buried beneath the ill-tempered surface. When he gazed upon this photograph, however, he couldn't help himself. Tears rolled from his eyes, not necessarily for his father's passing, more for the lost opportunity; the family he would never have. At least he had the car keys.

He collected the Oldsmobile and drove to Shylock's apartment. He took a long shower. Under the pricks of hot water he realized that he too would die at some point. Life was for the living, not the dead, and he contemplated all angles, that this existence was a test, or a wait-station, or a miserable hell, or a hedonistic free-for-all, or ludicrous and absurd, or a long-winded progression, or an education, or a chance to create, or all of these rolled into one. Wise men say we're not supposed to figure it out, but Noble thought he could, not due to hubris, but due to a hunch that within existence there lurks a greater meaning, or at best a reasoning which is cogent and understandable. Meaninglessness is too convenient an explanation manufactured by the lonely. Nevertheless, meaninglessness had a sound and persuasive argument, only that he wished there were a Higher Power operating in his life, that events, whether benign or malignant, happened for a reason, that an accident is really no accident, a death really not a death, that someday he would play his guitar in front of thousands, because the guitar was the only real family he had.

We live through our parents. There was nothing left but the slender, waisted pulchritude of its body and the melodies which flowed from the amplifier, his plectrum plucking each silvery chord as an expression of his empirical investigations into the deep, contentious mystery which surrounds the human being. In keeping with his original plan, Noble would practice hard and long. Once in a while he would indulge in his free-style approach, but the combination of traditional chords and free-style would produce original tunes, some mellow and smooth, some sentimental, some salacious and wanton, some political, some outright rebellious, some dirge-like and dark. At this stage he could never go back, since there was nothing to go back to, as though his history were a vast, salted field where no plant grew, where no animal grazed. His slate was clean.

In the afternoon he set out on the new adventure of making original music. He knew standard notation and tablature by rote, and he conscientiously committed every sound to bar-lines. He was shocked by this ability, a graduation of sorts, and for several hours he worked on one particular song. His confidence returned. Everything was somehow right with the world. He was contributing to the artistic flux. By the session's end, he had one solid achievement, an instrumental with eclectic moods and themes. He was proud. He hadn't felt this satisfied in a very long time, but once he stepped onto the balcony of Shylock's apartment and beheld the rooftops and the distant, solitary steeple of the Methodist church, his premature swell of satisfaction simmered. He had no family left. He couldn't live with Shylock anymore. He had an alcohol problem, and soon the nightly meeting would commence.

The evening was warm enough for many alcoholics to gather on the church steps. The faces were familiar enough, but Noble, like a true wallflower, stood on the periphery. Lots of action taking place, the in-crowd thirteenth-stepping the younger, delectable females. There were a few new female faces. He spotted Smiling Willy talking to one of them, a woman much too young for him. Scandalous, especially with Missy around. Meredith had her eyes on Skinny Leroy, and they seemed to laugh and smile together. Yep, they definitely slept together, there was no doubt in his mind. It's funny how these women at first looked repulsive, but after attending meeting after meeting, they grow attractive. This was yet another mystery, that over time the women in the program begin looking better and better, and the man who hasn't had sex for one full year (longer in Noble's case) falls victim to their overriding allure. Sure, relationships in the first year were a definite no-no, but as far as Noble could see, some alcoholics were definitely hooking up. Noble's social skills needed work. He had never been gifted in this area. (Whether or not he was gifted at anything is another matter). Naturally he was anti-social. He feared what people thought of him. Ivan and Milo soon drifted towards him. They shook hands.

"Look at all this eye-candy," said Ivan with a boyish grin. "I'm getting a prostitute if my luck doesn't change."

"Keep comin' Ivan," laughed Milo.

"Are you all right?" asked Ivan. "You look down."

"It's nothing. Just a long day, that's all," said Noble.

"Hey, you guys wanna hang out tonight after the meeting?" asked Ivan.

"Sure," said Milo.

"I don't think so, guys. I'm a bit tired."

"You shouldn't isolate," said Milo.

"Yeah, it'll lead you to a drink. You need to stay out of your own head, which is the most dangerous place for any alcoholic. Oh, by the way, did you get your living situation taken care of?"

"Not yet. My family won't take me back. I guess I'm stuck living at my friend's place. I have to talk to Harry about it when he shows up. You guys didn't see him, did you?"

"He should be here," said Milo.

"Oh man," exclaimed Ivan, "look who's coming."

They craned their necks above the gathering.

"It's Vanessa, oh man, she's looking good."

"She's hardly wearing anything," said Milo.

Noble thought she had a nice body, but other than this important attribute, she looked plain.

"She's so out of my league," said Ivan.

"Yeah. A snob to boot," said Milo.

"She's got so much money," said Ivan, and then a non-sequitur: "Debauched," with a mischievous smile.

"Ivan, get your mind out of the gutter," laughed Milo.

Come to think of it, she was looking pretty good, and the gathering swarmed around her. Noble then spotted Harry. He parked his Buick next to the church. To Noble's dismay, he wore a cotton, khaki suit, which meant something baffling was bound to happen.

Harry made for the doorway, avoiding the social scene altogether. Noble caught him before he entered.

"Harry, you got a minute?"

"Sure. How did it work out with your family?"

"Harry, my father died."

"I'm sorry to hear that. You must be having a tough time of it. But you're here, right?"

"It's going to take a little time to get my bearings straight."

"You're not about to drink over it, are you?"

"No. I think I'm sticking with sobriety."

"One day at a time. If you want a drink, have it tomorrow, right?"

"I suppose so. But the major problem involves my living situation. The house has been sold. I can't live there."

"Get a job then."

"I thought of another alternative. I have a car."

"And?"

"Well, for now I can sleep in the car and take showers at my friend Shylock's place."

"Noble, what is wrong with a decent job? What are you so afraid of?"

"This is my plan, okay? I can stay sober doing this."

"You really are going to any length, eh? Woody Guthrie never slept in a car. Him or, who's that guy? He sang 'Hello, Walls?' Died a few months ago? It's on the tip of my tongue."

Noble had no idea.

"Anyway," continued Harry, "as long as you stay away from your friend's apartment, I have no problems with it. You young Bohemians are a real pisser. Bunch of hippies. But if by any chance you feel like picking up a drink or some of that wacky-tobaccie, you get on the phone and call me immediately, is that clear?"

"Yessir."

"And don't call me 'sir.' You'll get through this tough time, I know you will. You're headed in the right direction. Trust me," and he rolled his eyes awkwardly, which was totally out of character.

When the meeting began, Noble understood why Harry had rolled his eyes. The meeting was packed, more crowded than previous meetings. Stimulation hung in the damp air, within the expressions of these alcoholic faces. Harry sat directly across from him, as in the previous meeting. Cotton was his cue, so to speak. Noble knew he had to have an open mind, but how open could he make it? This entire idea was preposterous, that two people could communicate, a tête-à-tête without speaking. His brain was filled with so much anger and pain unearthed by his father's death, and he couldn't believe this was happening, how could it happen? And why was it happening to him?

'You shouldn't worry so much,' he heard clearly, as though his mind had a transistor radio beneath its gray flesh. He looked to Harry. Harry looked directly at him and rubbed his nose.

'This is crazy,' thought Noble. 'This is not happening.'

'It's happening,' thought Harry. 'Give me a sign. Either rub the nose or scratch your knee.'

Noble rubbed his nose conspicuously.

'Good,' thought Harry. 'Now listen closely to the meeting. Remember, it's only one day at a time. If you want a drink, have it tomorrow,' and he rubbed his nose.

Noble, as a result of this, could concentrate little on the meeting. He heard maybe a few words and then drifted into confusions. Something was happening to him, and he was loaded with questions: Why me? Especially, and most importantly: 'What's the point of all this?' This new form of communication, for it to be valuable, must have a direction, a goal, an objective. But Noble was too busy debunking what just took place. Was it his imagination, or did what happen happen? A similar refrain of self-doubt, but a small part of him believed it. Anything resting on an *a priori* belief, however, without rigorous scientific scrutiny was specious at best. In essence, there was no way to prove this was happening, no way at all, and he searched for ways, and perhaps parapsychologists have tried to prove this phenomena, and shouldn't the public know about it? Yes, someone has to know, but no one would ever believe him, like the supposed efficacy of homeopathy, conjuring spirits, crystals worn around the neck, mood rings, acupuncture, psychics, tarot cards, palm readings, over-the-counter muscle enhancers, and the litany of mystical remedies permeating the fabric of traditional practices. But why him? What did he do to deserve this? Think of the possibilities: an end to mental illness, an end to violence by psychic intervention, a solution to the Prisoner's Dilemma, enhanced intelligence gathering, proper physician diagnoses, and the overall knowledge that we are not alone, that someone may understand our suffering, our struggle, our true emotions, our true intentions, our true aim to be the good people we were born to become, not the insect, but the goodness and purity of the human spirit which rests with virtue, selflessness, altruism, charity, and mercy. Imagine this? The rule of conscience permeating the problems of our nation? A nation of peace and happiness?

Noble perhaps overreacted, but when faced with the apocalypse, which really boils down to the human being and his transformation into the mindless insect, then one scurries and scratches for lofty aims, and perhaps telepathy was a step in the right direction, the evolution of the human being into a human being. But wasn't he reinventing the wheel? If this was an old phenomenon, then why hasn't anyone spoken of it before? So many questions, and if telepathy were to have a goal, then yes, the goal must be world peace, an end to violence, and the implementation of our conscience into rational decision-making. Still, the doubt lingered in the dark congregation room. He was a guitarist, a struggling musician who would sleep in his car, shower at Shylock's, and attribute this strange experience to his overactive imagination.

He was too exhausted to share at the meeting. He could have used a drink, but somehow this revelation and its cursory investigation would keep him sober and in attendance. It was all so peculiar and bizarre, but at heart he was the same guitarist, and despite these events he must stay steadfast on course and pluck the strings until his fingers fell off. What happened was unreal and should be considered thus. His guitar was real, and the sound of it real. One day he would compose the perfect opera for these supernatural occurrences.

After the meeting the alcoholics gathered once again on the steps. Noble bummed a cigarette from one the alcoholics, but he was in no mood to talk. Ivan and Milo did succeed in dragging him to the diner. His brain was tired by the time they arrived. They sat in a booth. Milo was bothered by the cigarette smoke. He ordered fries with mozzarella cheese and gravy. Ivan ordered coffee and a cola. Noble ordered coffee, nothing else.

"Good meeting?" asked Milo.

"Lots of action," said Ivan.

"I don't really feel too comfortable at these meetings," said Noble, revealing too much.

"Why, what's wrong?" asked Milo.

"It's too much of a social scene. I'm not into that game. I'm just there to stop drinking."

"Yeah, but it's good to get connected," said Milo, "get phone numbers, build healthy relationships, avoid the people you were getting drunk with…"

"Change your people, places, and things," said Ivan.

"And besides," insisted Milo, "it's good to talk to other people instead of isolating all the time. We need other people. We can't do it alone. It's a 'We' program."

"If I didn't fantasize about Vanessa all the time, I would definitely pick up a drink," said Ivan, "The Three M's. Live it and learn it. These are the pillars of early sobriety."

"Please," said Milo, "in all seriousness, you've got to reach out. Our best thinking got us here. By the way, what's going on with your apartment?"

"Basically, I don't have one. I don't even have a house anymore. I'm sleeping in my car for now. I don't have much of a choice. If I want to stay sober, I can't live with my friend anymore. He drinks constantly."

"Don't you know anybody who can help?"

"No."

"I respect that; I really do," said Ivan. "You're really working the program. I wish I could help you out, but I live with my parents."

"And my apartment is tiny," said Milo.

"I know I can no longer drink. I have my music to think about. I've been so concerned with the image of a musician: that a musician, especially a guitar player, has to drink and drug and have sex with his groupies in order to make it. It's all a delusion. I have the chance to take music to a higher level, really I do, and I don't need alcohol to do it. It's such a myth, and I can't believe I fell for it. Believe me, I have no problems with others using alcohol and drugs casually, but for me, I have a problem with it. If I turn out to be an establishment, soft, pansy-ass, sappy, sentimental rocker, then so be it, but I no longer have to play the role of the druggy artist, because I'm learning more in sobriety than I've ever learned. There are infinitely more possibilities for me. And I may be living in my car, but at least I no longer have to live a lie."

Ivan drove him to Shylock's. Noble collected his things, packed them into the Oldsmobile, and drove to the town park. He parked the car in the shadow of an elm tree. He had a half-tank of gas, no money, only his guitar without an electric current. He lived this way for a week straight, attending three meetings a day, showering at Shylock's, and relying on him for food.

He visited Shylock often, and the two were old friends again despite the previous incident. Actually, ever since Noble left the apartment, their relationship improved.

Noble's commitment to his instrument flourished. In the Oldsmobile, mostly at night when the police cruisers roamed the Waspachick strip, he practiced and practiced. He also composed new music and put these creations to paper.

At the meetings he refused to get close or chummy with anyone. He remained aloof and on the periphery. He was a bit leery about socializing. Luckily Harry wore polyester at these meetings, so he didn't have to worry about saving the world or advancing the human species. Sobriety at least calmed him. Sure, he still dreamt of one day playing his music in front of thousands. He sparred with the apparitions who reminded him constantly of how selfish he was. Perhaps they were right, but gradually they became more affable and supportive of Noble's endeavor.

He slowly settled into reality as a man without a family. He remembered his mother especially, and his father who perhaps meant well by his anger and severity. McCoy McCloud wanted a man out of his son, not a whimp or a coward. Maybe somewhere in the heavens he was proud of his only son for sticking with his dreams and his visions. His son was finally growing up, understanding the value of a dollar, and exercising discipline with his instrument.

In the heavens McCoy McCloud must have approved of Harry. Noble grew closer to him as his sponsee. Harry was often redundant in his advice. Noble earned every DWI card. The old man took him out for dinner every so often. Everything was operating smoothly, and with each passing day, Noble was more comfortable in his sobriety. On occasion he would hang out with Milo and Ivan, but not for too long. He was more comfortable alone. He had much to accomplish. His fingers extended over the wooden body, messaging the neck, his compositions inscribed into the annals of eternity, one day at a time. If he could only find a woman.

Book Three:

Alexandra

Chapter One

The Waspachick strip throbbed with students let out for summer vacation. Noble slalomed through gangs of loud, excited teen-agers posturing for summer flings. Outdoor tables adorned the coffee houses and the restaurants. Suped-up cars with subwoofers on high boomed and thumped through the center of town. Many came from surrounding townships to cavort in the heat. The winter ended abruptly, and spring lasted for only a week. Noble couldn't help but spot the wine glasses at the tables, the pints of beer, the charged atmosphere making him long for the sloppiness of a few drinks. The women who were too young for him filled the coffee houses. Even the college students looked adolescent. The women who were out of his league drank freely with their affluent suitors at the Trattoria or the Greek grotto. Waspachick women were never single. Someone always got to them first. Better stay away from them. Too young, and he could be jailed. A woman of his age, and her boyfriend would break his kneecaps.

He drank vicariously and thereby avoided the abominable hangover in the morning. For a while Noble had been riding on the 'pink cloud' of sobriety, a time when sobriety seems too marvelous, a movement from unmanageability to organization, clarity, and functioning. He found people who were interested in him, and he could play the social game with the alcoholics he met at the meetings. Nevertheless, he mostly observed these social interactions and kept his distance. On occasion he would go to the diner with Ivan and Milo, but over the last few weeks this activity tapered off until he developed a solitary routine.

He attended two meetings a day, one at noontime and the other at night. He showered and washed his clothes at Shylock's. Shylock gave him a weekly allowance. "You're my investment," he said on a number of occasions, "and when you make it big, I want front row seats."

After the evening meetings, he would shut himself off in the Oldsmobile and compose his instrumentals. It got to the point where he didn't know how to do anything else. He didn't ask Shylock about a coffee house performance. Shylock was doing enough already, and Noble was too timid to impose on him further. The next alternative involved playing on the Waspachick street corners, but he worried about the police.

Already he had received many warnings for camping near the town park after dark. Usually he drove around the block and parked in the same spot. The officer on night duty was kind enough. He warned him but allowed it anyway.

He called Harry from the pay phone next to Shylock's coffee house. He called him when he felt like drinking. This was often, and at one point Harry asked that he call collect. Noble never had enough change to finish a conversation. He saw Harry on a daily basis. Harry attended night meetings only, now that Noble's recovery was underway. "If you want a drink, have it tomorrow," said Harry repeatedly. This redundancy actually worked. Whenever he thought of drinking, he remembered this mantra, and when the morning came he was thankful he didn't drink the night before. The 'pink cloud,' however, dissipated slowly. He improved in his sobriety, but there was always something missing.

He desperately needed a woman to fill this void. The Three M's had worked through the 'pink cloud' era, but not beyond it. He was tempted to take the Oldsmobile, his guitar, and his belongings on the road. The 'traveling bug,' he called it. At times he couldn't stand being in Waspachick. A vacation from the routine would help, that or an all-out escape to the West Coast in search of this nirvana as he imagined it. But ever since his recovery, his chances of an escape were slim. New entanglements, money especially, kept him in Waspachick. Without Shylock's allowance, he couldn't eat, let alone fill up his gas tank. He could make it as far as Pittsburgh. Secondly, escape translated into getting drunk or flying along the highway only to smoke a joint, gulp at whiskey, frolic with women, have a beer and hear the band, et cetera. There was little or no excitement in his life. It had all grown so routine and dull. Sure, his playing improved, but other than this, his existence still resembled a parched wasteland. Where was the fun, the challenge insanity brought, the unpredictability, the wine, women, and song? Something was missing.

Perhaps he was too young for the serenity the program promised. Only retired people liked serenity, he mused. But the old-timers always said they wished they had found AA a long time ago. Their lives, they said, were wasted due to alcohol, as some of them drank continuously for thirty, maybe forty years. They envied the young alcoholics.

Ultimately the entire concept of AA rested on spirituality which resulted in serenity. Either surrender to a Higher Power or die, and Noble was very uncomfortable with this ultimatum.

The reasoning behind this, however, was sound. Alcoholics always try to run their lives by themselves, without any assistance, like the auteur who tries to manage the entire production. The program went against self-reliance and essentially gave this self-will up to God as the alcoholic understood Him.

Harry's understanding of God was simply the acronym 'Group Of Drunks.' The alcoholic turns over his will, because at the times when he had exercised self-reliance, the results were disastrous and catastrophic. For Noble it was the psychiatric ward. He didn't dare ask Harry where his last drunk led him. Nevertheless, the program was essentially a spiritual one. Spirituality filled the void that drinking couldn't fill. In other words, Noble's escapism, his longing for a pina colada on a beach with blonde women would never fill this void. Traveling cross-country with a joint and a half-pint of whiskey wouldn't fill it either. The salted soil of his wasteland could never be cultivated by imaginary crops. So the program also insisted that the alcoholic, after turning his will over to the care of the Higher Power, act in accordance with His divine will. The twelve steps were a plan of action. "All you have to know is that there is a Higher Power, and you're not it," said Harry. Yet Noble was bothered by the twelve steps since they all presupposed a reliance on this mysterious Higher Power, or at least steps two through twelve. Noble was not surprised when Harry said: "The first step is the only step you have to get one-hundred percent." In short, the belief in a Higher Power remained his biggest hurdle. This was due to his rudimentary perception of a Higher Power.

When he prayed, he simply looked at the sky and received no answer whatsoever. The sky, hopefully not so starry, represented this Higher Power and His deaf ear to Noble's pleas. Yes, he still wanted the cheering audience. He prayed and wished, prayed and wished, and meanwhile his playing never left the Oldsmobile. He refused to practice where others could hear him. Nevertheless, his understanding of this Higher Power was too narrow, a monotheistic conception of a God with limited powers. Aside from this, Noble grasped slowly the multifarious nature of God, that he may actually be operating through people. This led him to believe that telepathy was not associated with the supernatural, but the spiritual. He had mistakenly given telepathy a parapsychological association, like voodoo, astrology, or sorcery. Telepathy, however, was a spiritual phenomenon. It filled the void.

Still he was unsure. It could have been his imagination, but the signs were so overt, so conspicuous, so blatant and deliberate. The evidence of its existence was overpowering and unforgettable.

Harry wore his cotton clothes at least once a week. He behaved strangely on these nights-his staring, his smiling, his eyes rolling, a wink in the middle of a meeting- and gradually he rented space in Noble's mind. Even when Noble didn't physically see him at the meetings, he had conversations with him. He couldn't distinguish what was real and what was imaginary. This was the bitter problem haunting his compliance. He separated the real from the imaginary until the latter took over. Little did he realize that for the imagination to function, it must also rely on the real or the empirical. Imagination without conscience, and now without knowledge, yielded a nightmarish delusion of majestic proportions. The two sides needed to work together. Yet the telepathic exchanges humbled him.

He tried to figure the whole phenomena out, like an incredible puzzle, but he decided that the best way to attack the puzzle was to declare ignorance. 'I've tried to figure this whole thing out, and I've come to the conclusion that I don't know anything,' thought Noble. 'That's the smartest thing you've said yet,' responded Harry. These telepathic experiences kept him coming to meetings, and he had no idea where it would lead him. He had no idea who possessed telepathy and who did not. Somehow he was stuck with it, and he would not ask anymore questions as to its nature, or above all, its intent and purpose.

One bit of knowledge he did uncover: that AA could only help with not taking that first drink. Some saw it as a blueprint for life, but Noble agreed with his sponsor that AA could only help with alcoholism, not much else. Some of the old-timers talked of miracles. 'Don't leave until the miracle happens,' was but one of the many catch-phrases. The program had its twelve promises or miracles to match its twelve steps. Noble thought these promises too farfetched, extravagant, and contradictory. For instance, the catch-phrase, 'We must live life on life's terms,' contradicted with the promise, 'Fear of people and economic insecurity will leave us.' The term 'life' and 'fear' were both synonymous terms inasmuch life is all about insecurities and fears. Fear is a basic staple of life and the basic trait of the human character. Noble wouldn't dare walk too far south after midnight. And then the promise, 'Self-seeking will slip away.' Really? Impossible. To follow the program rigorously and then have these twelve promises fulfilled was the equivalent of achieving a heaven on earth. This could only take place if and only if a psychic change took place. The perceptions would be cleansed, and naturally one finds heaven. But how to carry on the task of living with other non-alcoholics was another problem. After psychically changing, does one simply wander naked along the Waspachick strip thinking he has found the garden of Eden? One would find a jail cell instead. All frivolity aside, the program required a mental sacrifice, not in half-measures, but in a total measure. Whether this happens slowly or quickly depends on the irrationality of the alcoholic. The more irrational, the quicker one finds this heaven on earth. 'I came for my drinking, and I stayed for my thinking,' he heard someone share. Noble was reluctant to throw himself on the sacrificial alter of AA. He wasn't about to permit a full psychic transformation. He knew, however, that these meetings did affect his mentality, his attitude especially. For instance, whenever he urged, he thought of 'One day at a time,' and he immediately called Harry. "Have the drink tomorrow."

Sometimes he reviewed the twelve promises. The AA philosophy encroached upon that part of him which remained, how shall we call it?, Sane? "Keep it simple," said Harry. "Don't drink and come to meetings. Don't think yourself out of the program." Noble knew that any intelligence applied to this simple program would lead him to the nearest liquor store. One essentially had to be ignorant, until the mind is utterly and irreversibly transformed. Perhaps this was a cult after all. Noble was not ready to take this leap, but he was forced to. Otherwise, a relapse would result. And besides, he was still in early sobriety.

AA was not a perfect program any more than existence itself was not perfect. Some interpreted the Big Book loosely, others closely. Harry was a realist in his approach. Therefore, AA could only help with drinking. There was no pot of gold at the end of the rainbow. The program couldn't help with financial difficulties, family woes, or the loss of a loved one. As a corollary, Harry insisted: "Things don't necessarily get better, but you get better."

On occasion Noble found himself in denial, that maybe he wasn't an alcoholic. It was just one silly mistake that landed him in detox, and as a result he had to avoid all which was at one time enjoyable. His early sobriety focused on the first step: his battle to accept his allergy to alcohol. No easy task.

Noble expected a regular meeting in the evening. Approximately thirty alcoholics were present. They hung about in cliques. There were younger women present, but the tall, good-looking, athletic men of his age cornered them ahead of time, as though they were predisposed. The women at this meeting were quite attractive. He stood by himself in a corner with a cigarette, examining these terrible cliques, or better yet, examining his own lonliness apart from them. He spotted the young woman who at one time was part of the Manhattan club scene, or at least that's what she shared at an earlier meeting. She had been cornered by Smilin' Willy and Skinny Leroy, two people he secretly despised on account of their gregariousness. Noble was better. He had better attributes than these two snake-charmers, and yet Noble could do nothing more than sip his coffee, he took it black, and suck on cigarettes, a new habit. But now these popular men worked their magic. It was either the men who did it consciously, or the women who were attracted to their wealth and status.

These two were definitely thirteen steppers, that step beyond the twelfth step which mandated trysts with women. Social climbers, these men-decent jobs, decent clothes, a good example of the Waspachick ethos infiltrating the sanctity of recovery. He could do nothing but stand and watch as these men worked with ease and heightened bailiwick, as though they had training in the art of seduction. He had rarely before felt like such a down-trodden misfit, the pariah whom no one wanted. He hated the feeling- he hated everything about these rooms, how nothing ever changed, how the women flocked to these men of better standard. The sad fact remained: that no matter how he despised these men, he wanted to become one of them, to possess the trait which won women's hearts. 'What was this trait?' he asked himself. What could win this New York City clubber, this divine creature dancing to techno, strippers in cages, flashes of colored light? And was she so divine indeed? Or was his brain bending out of shape at the sight of this woman, well along in her sobriety, ready and willing to befriend these men who played their cards just right and exposed their hand at times most propitious, at times most hurtful to Noble's self-esteem? Although he had stopped drinking, he felt so down about this entire fellowship, or this lack of one. Even Ivan and Milo subtly avoided him. They gathered in another section of the kitchen and enjoyed themselves.

'AA is not a social club,' he heard his sponsor saying. Or, 'No relationships in the first year.' Those men mingling with the opposite sex openly violated this principle. He could have curled up in a ball in the corner, or he could have run to the bar for a shot to ease the pain of these social realities. He arrived at the point where both drunkenness and sobriety led to an equal misery. No matter what, he had to stick with it, live in his car with his guitar and play lonely ballads, long plaintive progressions in the darkness and sulk and pity himself and point the finger at the heavens for consigning him to such a fate. Womanlessness. An awful state, but one to which he contributed often, like a daily donation to some senseless cause. His attitude had turned sour, a return to his roots, the same darkness which cast its shadow in the florescence of this kitchen, the smoke so thick that one, deep inhalation could collapse the lungs. This was the extent of his darkness- the concept known as womanlessness, the idea that even the pure, golden-hearted soul is subjected to intense day-dreams and fantastic excursions with a woman but in reality must do without her due to defects of character which precluded a woman's touch, her earthy bouquet, her lips, the expanse of her back. And Noble never knew how far it would go. It had something to do with madness, a dark insanity which pushed him further into himself, the curled ball in the corner devoured by the roaches, as though his own body were a corpse decrepit with the anguish of eternal life. Telepathy, he supposed, didn't fill the void as he originally planned.

All melodrama and hyperbole aside, Noble knew he must go without women for the rest of his days, and in the process he will learn to despise, ridicule, and berate all women. As a result, his days and nights will lack its most essential meaning which gives existence its value. Or so he thought, until he saw within the fog of cigarette smoke another woman enter the kitchen.

He didn't believe his eyes at first. The loneliness must be playing tricks on him, tempting him like an oasis to a thirsty man. It couldn't be. It couldn't be the woman he had met at the East Waspachick bar. How dare she intrude on his darkness, how dare she interrupt the setting of the sun, his moment of ultimate defiance against all things female. Yet she ushered in the light to a man who already declared himself dead.

Alexandra Van Deusen walked into the room knowingly, as though she had been a part of the program for years. Noble knew, however, that this was her first time to this meeting. The men conversing with the club-goer and her group turned in surprise. The entire room gravitated towards Alexandra, as she was a newcomer and strikingly beautiful. Noble had never seen her in the light, only through beer goggles. Her sun-lit hair fell to her shoulders, her eyes blue, or were they green? He wasn't sure. Her features suggested Elysium, a thin blonde face with full, moist lips. He would have sacrificed his sobriety to kiss them. Just one moment alone would do. Her lips would taste better than the most potent intoxicants. Amazing how light follows darkness, as though the two conspired in bringing a neurotic turmoil. And as the darkness left him, and her light struck the cloisters of his heart, bells sounding, the plumes of loud fireworks trailing in limitless skies- he again drifted into his preternatural world, where events and people were staged arbitrarily. Alexandra Van Deusen, and her arrival to this church of all places, stirred his soul and tinctured his otherwise gloomy predicament. He had no choice but to fall for her again. But his shyness prevented him from reintroducing himself to the woman who had twice rejected him. And wouldn't you know it, the athletic men noticed her like predators, and they seamlessly broke from the club-goer and extended their hands to this sublime beauty.

Damn. Their action was so simple, but they were the first to greet the fair Alexandra, and usually the first greeting always sets the tone for involved friendship. The in-crowd certainly punished Noble who stood in the same place genuinely awestruck by what had transpired. She put on airs as any newcomer does. She seemed unbroken by alcohol abuse. She wore a masque, a confident, resplendent facade which didn't show the slightest hint of adversity, trauma, or negligence. Her affectation placed her in the bar, talking to that greasy, long-haired guitarist, only that this was the kitchen of an AA meeting. Strange how behaviors copied themselves. She could have been drunk or high or God knows what. Noble wished to confiscate her from the likes of the in-crowd. He wanted to take her away on a long trip leading to Nirvana and then return as lovers. He even laughed aloud, and the alcoholics next to him gawked in bewilderment. His ironclad composure at once fell slack by her presence. If he owned a pair of manacles he would have chained himself to her side. He would have kidnapped her and traveled to the ocean to make love on the sand. Yes, he must do something. He must act on this terrible desire which ate away his innards, which possessed his mind, which provided an escape from darkness, only to be replaced by passion, the same passion of a lover unrequited. But first, he must befriend her, not as a would-be lover, but as a man interested only in her mind and slow recovery. This, he figured, was the only route to her heart. In the meeting he will set an example by sharing poignantly on some ridiculous topic. He hadn't shared in quite some time, and his words must suggest strong sobriety.

Every newcomer desired the next right move, and Noble would advertise his correctness and parade it like a latent talent. Of course he imagined dialogue. Yes, that's what he would do. He would ask her to the diner for coffee. What's a recovering alcoholic without coffee and cigarettes? But somehow he must pry her away from the likes of the popular crew. They talked with her freely, perhaps giving pointers. He couldn't hear what they said through the din, but he was certain that the in-crowd was again practicing that thirteenth step, and they did so deftly.

The meeting began a few minutes later in the congregation room. Alexandra sat next to the same in-crew which greeted her. Her seating arrangement stank of dubiousness and injustice. Noble could not concentrate on what was being said. He could only stare at her, wondering if she had any recollection of the two times they met. What a woman, he said to himself, and then he wondered why on earth she appeared in this way, only to be lulled by the likes of others. He couldn't believe how quickly she diffused into AA's most socially acceptable clique. No matter what anyone said, elitism ruled the world. It ruled the world of music especially. Have the right look, and the world opens its doors. Play a good guitar, well, that was a secondary consideration.

"Are there any newcomers to this group?" asked Milo, the group leader. Harry was absent unfortunately. He attended a Knights of Columbus meeting across town.

Alexandra raised her hand: "Hi, I'm Alexandra, and I'm an alcoholic."

"Hi, Alexandra!" almost a resounding cheer, the most life he had heard from this group in a while, like a winning touchdown. All eyes were upon her. Even Milo had been swayed by her beauty.

Noble refrained from sharing anything. In fact, everyone who usually shared for what seemed like hours could only mutter useless comments, short quips to which no one paid attention. Tonight was Alexandra's night, and when her turn came, the room which usually reverberated with shifting positions, coughs, the passing of the basket, the drum of fingers, all stopped as though time had ended. No one moved. A spotlight would have done better.

The other women regressed into ugliness. An aura of light bathed her and isolated her, and yet the group followed her every word like a spider hanging from its last thread. If only he could wrench her from the tall hunk sitting next to her.

Noble had heard many songs about choosing the man most reticent, shy, and altogether lonely, but within the grand hall nothing was farther from the truth. Women never choose the odd guy, the lonely man who pours all of his energies into creation. They instead go for the likes of Smilin' Willy, his height, his cellular phone and beeper, his wicked tongue, his fashionable clothes, his athleticism, everything about the man, a prime example of Waspachick and what it was becoming. This Alexandra, this lovely creature plucked from the East Waspachick bar, this incredible woman, only if she knew of Noble's desires, if only she could know of his pledge to care for her and protect her from the unruly elements of an evolving world. He would have done so instantly. He would have defied the wisdom of the stately elders who declared that a union had to be properly matched and that a poor man with a wealthy, young woman was the equivalent of social suicide, that a union could not take place between two economically disparate people, one lonely and going nowhere, the other who could land any man she desired- a doctor, a lawyer, an investment banker. But wait. Hold on. Noble latched onto an idea, a scheme.

She may still remember their conversation at the bar. He could still play the role of investment banker. Marvelous. This could work, if only he could gain entrée at tonight's meeting without those buffoons sitting next to her. Yes, he instantly recalled that impersonation from memory.

Wait, first. Waiting for access; a moment when all reasoning fails, when he walks up to her and asks her to the greasy spoon a mile away. He could drive her in the beat-up Oldsmobile, and perhaps they would run out of gas on the way, a walk together under a brilliant sky, and Noble confesses his complete infatuation over her, this terrible, stomach-turning obsession recharged, so that he could no longer pluck the strings or play a progression with any coherence, only a mountain of careless chords, illogical and unworthy for a woman such as she. He will offer the world, and yet he must swallow and bear his inconsequence over her development in the program. Must all of him somehow involve her? What was this terrible hunger, this fascination with this one woman? Normal men of his age look for something more in a woman, but a man without experience, without wisdom, look only at the facade of beauty, not the inner core which sets the relationship in motion; almost a sickness which captured his mind, and a heat which flashed with every slow heartbeat.

Now it was Alexandra who rented space in his head. He could have opened his skull and tossed his fleshy brain into a frying pan, he could have dropped to his knees and asked for divine intervention, if only she would return his desire, if only for a second she would offer her time and devotion towards him, why, nothing on earth would matter except the intrinsic meaning of walking in the park on a springtime afternoon, hand-in-hand, nothing exchanged, only the birds flapping and chirping, the breeze adding security to an otherwise blissful moment, and yet he could not escape the pressing reality: that he was as close to being a bum than ever before. Her suitors had jobs, fat wallets, vacation homes. What would a woman such as Alexandra be doing with him anyway? He lived in a car next to the town park, he played guitar to the audience of himself, he had no gigs lined up, no job, no education, only this intense obsession with this one woman.

She could do so much better with a Waspachick man. She had a chance to rise above the mulch of social misfits who eventually walked in the footsteps of the town bum. She could easily play tennis at the country club, live on the north side, summer in East Hampton, find a stability which comes with responsible, cardigan-wearing men singing barbershop melodies. Would she dare dispose of this for some no good, out-of-work, and above all else, foolish hobo, a person who could never show her the light she instantly emanated, only the darkness which racked his memories, his dreams, and his soul?

In the congregation room he could have easily fallen to his knees and offered a prayer, either for a powerful panacea to this Alexandra or an aphrodisiac which apotheosized him beyond any Waspachick man. His prayers never worked before. Why would they work now? Always these long wish-lists to his Higher Power. A perfect world commences, and the Higher Power shows the tragedy of war; one minute a woman walks with him in the park, the next minute she's gone. Not even an unctuous genie could fulfill his wish-list, and he would have given anything for a simple conversation at the diner. Yes, he must be bold and fortuitous and forgo the disapproval of both his sponsor and those in the kitchen who looked askance at this attempt at wish-fulfillment.

It would look too obvious. Already the in-crew had taken her hostage, and they did so subtly. Her turn to speak came, and the room fell silent.

"Hi, my name is Alexandra, and I'm an alcoholic."

Her words slipped into tears. She wiped them away with her long fingers. She could no longer contain her emotions, and as she cried, wouldn't you know it?, Smilin' Willy of the in-crowd massaged her shoulder, oh yeah, like he had to be the one comforting her, like she selected him to rub her down. Nevertheless, Noble hung on her every word, as though it were astringent cleaning his pores.

"Hi, Alexandra," chimed the rest.

"I don't know what I'm doing here," she cried. "This is my first meeting…"

"Welcome," said a few.

"And I've had enough. I don't want another drink. I'm so close to committing suicide right now, and if I didn't come to this meeting, I would have easily done it, and I need help. I don't want to drink anymore. My life is so screwed up. My boyfriend, well, he's active, and we're breaking up soon, and I want a drink, and I don't want a drink at the same time. I'm miserable but also afraid what my life will be like without alcohol. You guys are so lucky, and I don't know what to do about my boyfriend. We're living together, and he drinks too much. My whole life is a wreck, it's all a wreck…"

And throughout her sharing, Smilin' Willy messaged her back. He did so effortlessly, as though he were meant to caress the space of skin where neck and shoulder met. Noble remembered the AA aphorism well: 'get 'em while their shakin'! He could do nothing but watch as the lion claimed its prey and withdrew to the den. If he had nerve, Noble would have ended it immediately, but he had no control over the lion's wandering paws, her doleful eyes appreciating every maneuver. She found friendship without even trying, and Noble knew he must penetrate the clique which had taken her captive. He must wait until the meeting's end and wait for the right moment in the kitchen where he will introduce himself a third time, perhaps even give his phone number, but wait- he no longer lived at Shylock's. He couldn't give out Shylock's phone number. He would somehow have to get hers. He must do it, or else risk forfeiting all of his chances to the super-clique.

Milo asked that she stay a little while afterwards and get phone numbers from others in the program, preferably women. He also mentioned that if she were to stick with it and work the program, things would get better. "This too shall pass," he said.

After the meeting, the kitchen adjacent to the congregation hall filled quickly with both people and cigarette smoke. Groups of people talked, everyone but Noble who stood next to the coffee pot and the stale, half-eaten cookies. He looked for Alexandra. Smilin' Willy conversed with her. The nerve of him. Maybe if he moved closer he could spark a conversation. He inched to the other side of the room. No one said a word to him. He got close enough to hear their discussion.

"...sobriety is so much better," said Smilin' Willy.

"It really is," said Skinny Leroy.

"It's always tough in the beginning."

"I don't know. I just don't want to drink tonight," she said, most likely surprised by all the attention.

"You don't have to drink tonight," said Willy. "Hey, listen, why don't you come with us to the diner. You don't have to drink tonight if you don't want to."

"Oh, I don't know if tonight's a good night," she said while glancing at her watch.

"It may help," said Skinny Leroy.

"Well, okay. Want to meet at the diner in East Waspachick?"

"That's perfect," said Willy.

Noble had heard about enough. He moved in tightly, almost barging into their conversation. But before he had the chance, they vanished through the back door, thus dismantling his strategy. Alexandra took one look at him and hurried out with the in-crowd. Soon, others left, and Noble stood in the kitchen alone with Milo.

He helped clean the kitchen, and then Milo left. He was alone
suddenly. He disliked the idea of returning to his car. He didn't know where
he could go. He liked the idea of having coffee at the East Waspachick diner.
But wouldn't it look odd, sitting by himself, being noticed by the flock which
carried the fair Alexandra away? But he had to see her. He couldn't go
through the night without her. Sure, he had nothing to offer. Yet he craved for
her presence. He must play the fool in order to get her. He must at least try,
or even fight for her, and then let them talk, call him names under their breath.
Let it come.

He arrived at the East Waspachick diner only to discover they were
nowhere to be found. He must have missed them, precious gasoline wasted.
He did spot a few familiar faces from the meeting, but no one invited him into
their booths. He sat at the counter, ordered black coffee, and smoked a
cigarette every five minutes. He believed that Alexandra Van Deusen
interrupted his creativity. He had been doing so well. In the darkness of the
car he had progressed, and somehow the presence of this creature shattered
his will to play. Never had he been so acutely frustrated. He couldn't play this
night, even if someone paid him. He could only contemplate.

Living in his car wasn't as easy as he figured. But he had to live for the
moment, the moment when a woman intrudes upon the heart despite the
barbed wire and alarms which secure it. The worst cases of loneliness, he
reasoned, are those which are sanctioned by the self. Somehow he played a
heavy hand in this. He urged for a drink, another suicide mission which would
do him in for good, because he couldn't stand one more instant without her.
From the first moment he saw her in the East Waspachick bar to this moment
when her absence left indelible footprints on the floor and a fragrance in the
air, he had always, well, he could never 'love' another. How he hated the
term: 'love.' Whenever he had loved, no one returned it. Whenever he
designed methods to capture love, it sank before christening. What a laugh,
this concept known as 'love.' He hated the word. He would live only to spite
that word which left him barren like a crucifying wind. Love was but another
fantasy fed by delusion. If such a state existed, it had nothing to do with him.
It caused pain, not the bliss it promised. The musicians sung of it, the poets
dreamed of its ultimate power, and yet 'love' never materialized.

Noble prayed for it, he wished for it, longed for it, hoped for a sliver to
fall from the heavens. He did not love this Alexandra. How he needed her
though. If she only walked in and took a seat next to him for a little while.
Who was she kissing? Whom did she love? Why did he hear that same, tired
refrain: 'it was never meant to be,' with resignation, as though 'love' had its

own plans, its own strategy which eschewed Noble McCloud. The philosophers, the artists, the musicians especially threw the term around loosely, as though it added bliss to their lives, when its tenets and precepts belied all objectivity and truth. Love had nothing to do with truth. The truth is loveless and bleak, a man suffocating at a diner for which he had wasted precious gasoline, staring into the black, syrupy crud, and ordering another cup to keep him company.

It was good that he stayed. The popular crowd, along with Alexandra, walked in and seated themselves noisily at the tables. They lit their cigarettes, and Noble caught side glances of Alexandra. She smiled and laughed periodically, putting on airs. They seemed to be having a good time, their chatter mingling with the clanks of silverware, crockery, and glass. He wondered what had taken them so long. He then strategized. What could he do to penetrate the fortress which surrounded her? He could have scaled the immense wall, supporting himself on the cracks of the surface, never reaching the top. This Alexandra never cared for him from the beginning. It was a love without hope, the bird-catcher who lets his flock escape only to see them circle the Squire's daughter who passes by. Noble concluded that he was a doomed man, the kind who imagines things which are never there, only to realize the profundity of nothingness after an entire lifetime of self-deception.

We only see what we want to see- her eyes looking his way for an instant, her smile, her smooth milky skin touching his. Perhaps this Alexandra had hidden feelings for him already, feelings which needed release. What did she think of him? The evidence proved that she felt nothing, but in Noble's mind, she avoided him only because she liked him.

Beautiful women often have twisted minds, he reasoned. Perhaps Alexandra cared for him, but somehow couldn't express her feelings. This gave him some hope, and when unrequited love and hope are amalgamated, the result is a delusion. Hope overpowers the dismal reality. We keep hoping for these feelings to be reciprocated; we involve ourselves in imaginary mind games. We over-think and over-analyze, and ultimately we play the fool by exposing our hand when the woman in question hasn't even been dealt yet. Could she ever think of him in the same way? Notice here how Noble turned an impossible situation into something possible. He was too consumed to review the evidence. Yes, she really did think of him, regardless if she blew him off at the Laundromat or kept company with the in-crowd. It didn't matter, because women love these games, and they can play more adroitly than the most ingenious of men. And Noble sensed he could play this game better than Alexandra, a game which took on the characteristics of an emotional roller-coaster, not for Alexandra of course, but for Noble alone, since it all took place in his own mind. Conceivably, he could be sitting at the counter, and she could be staring at him, regardless if she could have any man she wanted. What power in the hands of unattainable women, the power to transfigure a serene man into a desperate fool.

His heart surged while overhearing her laughter. He could have clawed his heart from his chest and dropped the bloody muscle in front of her. An endless and haunting obsession, so visceral that all other considerations of normal existence are disposed of, and nothing but her image energizes the mind, these endless questions which never have answers, only speculations on whom she loves, whom she takes home after a night at the diner, whom she kisses when her lips become her most formidable security and defense. Then he thought of letting her go from his mind. Let her go, find another woman. But how to let go of a woman who has, bit by bit, penetrated those clandestine cloisters which his mind itself has protected from himself, the emotions never felt, delicacies never tasted, spaces of skin never touched, fragrances never inhaled, perceptions never experienced.

There are other fishes in the sea, he thought, why should this one be so important? Dismiss her from the psyche, avoid seeing her, don't give her the pleasure of small talk, don't listen to her when she cries during the meeting. Forget her. But how does one forget if not through patience, for only time stanches wounds so deep, and until time heals and calms, he was stuck at the diner, ordering another coffee, chain-smoking, turning his head and finding her in a fit of laughter over some joke Smilin' Willy had told, perhaps blushing when she mentioned an old lover.

He returned to Waspachick and parked along a side street off the strip. He climbed into the back seat and took up his guitar. He tried an old melody, but his fingers released an alien tune which made little sense. He strummed chords, he picked each string, he slid along the neck, but nothing worked. He thought he could easily make music from these unrequited feelings, to imitate his own turmoil with his art, as though the strings could paint Alexandra, summon her laughter, mimic her weeping, and preserve her deepest aspirations.

After an hour of fiddling with the instrument, he grew tired and instead lay in the back seat, wrapped himself in a blanket, and dreamed of his next encounter with her. Playing the guitar seemed less important. He must never let her know. He must hide this lingering fascination, keep it close to his heart only to be released in the darkness of the sedan. What more could he do but wait until the next meeting and pry her away from those vultures.

The night was quiet and still; only a few passing cars. He couldn't get to sleep, because her beauty invaded him from all angles. He tried a variety of positions, all of which didn't work. He had questions, many of them. She had a boyfriend, an alcoholic boyfriend, yes, someone loving her. She lit up a room when she walked through it, her blonde locks caressing her shoulders, her blue-green eyes searching for company. How on earth would Noble McCloud win her heart when she wanted nothing to do with him? He must strategize again. He must think up a plan. He would write her a song, a long instrumental with crescendos and decrescendos describing a torrid love affair.

A love song would never work. Too antiquated a method. Romance died out a long time ago. She would be more embarrassed than flattered. There must be a route to her heart. Perhaps she held a vision of the perfect man, the Waspachick man. Her man was wealthy, a body like Michelangelo's *David*, competitive and pugnacious, obsessively protective, and somehow a sense of humor and nonchalance which made light of serious circumstances. Her man could have any woman he desired, but chose Alexandra above the many applicants who fell before his feet. They could worship each other as individuals who had surpassed natural selection, as creatures beautiful to others but outsiders unto themselves. They would live together, marry, and have Waspachick children who continued the tradition of pulchritude, as though anything other than beauty was inhuman.

Alexandra deserved a man of high caliber, a man of fat paychecks and silk suits. Love took a back seat to financial security and gain. The love that Noble possessed would never win her. As one grew older, one's love required expression through material items- the wedding band, the new shoes, the bottle of perfume, the shopping bags filled with nonsense. Love is then hidden like trinkets in an attic. A kiss no longer works, a sigh and a shudder no longer make a captivating melody. Instead of partners, they become a team, as though the world deserves a good conquering, and every human a slab of meat which tastes like chicken. Love must fit in somewhere, thought Noble. It can't be some strange cannibalistic feast. Maybe Love had its own time and place, like a rain after a drought. His heart filled with love, but never once was this love requited, which made him question whether this was love at all. It was a hunger. Love had to be a greater phenomenon, never a crisis which caused pain and lament, but a pool of deep water on a dry river bed. Only time, patience, and avoidance will end the infatuation, but a deeper love never heals. It defies time and mocks patience. It withstands the challenge of seasons, forbidden fruit, logic and reason, even alcoholism. It encourages sleep rather than insomnia.

And in the car Noble couldn't get to sleep. He wished for a sedative, perhaps alcohol, anything to erase her visage, her body stretched next to him in the coldness of the car, radiating a warmth, those blue-green eyes seeking the depth of his love, and in his mind he breaks out the guitar and thumbs a simple song which alleviates his intense longing, a desire which the corrosion of time may never wreck. There are complications, however. They can't live together in an automobile. He must provide for her, but he has nothing, only a guitar, a canteen of water, and an obsolete car.

He had structured his days exclusively for his guitar, and wouldn't ya know it, he received from the heavens exactly what he wanted, an isolation with his instrument, for he thought he would never need anything else. And suddenly a woman occupies his thoughts, and he can't get rid of her. It used to be that women, as a collective, beleaguered him. But in the car, the hallucination of one woman made the rest disappear until he could see nothing else but this one woman, as though she were the answer to his suffering and downward plight, as though all other women didn't matter.

He came to the conclusion that he would forever be alone. He could scream, and no one would hear him. He could walk along the strip, passing the housewives with shopping bags, teeny-boppers in denim bell-bottoms, patrons visiting Waspachick's restaurants, and he collapses on the sidewalk from grief, and no one cares. Perhaps AA wasn't a good idea. He could have used a drink to fill the emptiness, but drinking would merely compound the problem. He would encounter the same emptiness, but in the psych ward where it all began. Wasn't there any escape? All was going so well.

He got out of the car and paced the sidewalk. Insomnia irritated him. The town was quiet. The lights buzzed. Air conditioners rattled on full blast. He could have yelled into the sky at those same stars which never winked but stood frozen in the dark blue, and he could have driven his car to another town, and then another, farther away from the agony she alone provided and he alone could never abandon. Forget about her, he thought. Forget she ever walked into the congregation room. But if he forgot her, then who would fill this terrible emptiness? Yes, the emptiness which haunts the man who understands the injustice, absurdity, and irrationality of the universe, one man with a guitar in a bubble, his own sphere of influence protecting him like a car bumper from women who strolled hand-in-hand with their boyfriends, like a visor which rendered him blind to feminine beauty, like an antibiotic to the virus of unattainable women. Such a bubble would be wonderful. If only time would grab his spirit and propel him towards forgetting, filling the emptiness with permanent distractions. But no, he needed more from Alexandra Van

Deusen, her body next to his, his hands along her arms and legs, skin like butter, her lips like wild strawberries.

He must let her know. A secret admirer, yes, from afar, totally discreet, under the guise of helping her through the early stages of sobriety. Of course. This was the answer. And what of the guitar?

He could always play at night, and practice once in a while during the day, but until this matter was resolved, she alone would fill his thoughts and painstaking attention, every bit of conversation a dialogue played with a serene mask, while underneath lurked a calculating animal who could survive only if she loved him. A good plan indeed. There was hope. And the bright star above winked, and the moon smiled, and the universe was no longer absurd. He will follow her to these meetings, befriend her, and then unleash upon her the torrent of his love. He was now the investment banker, living in the North end.

He crawled into the back seat of the Oldsmobile. The guitar gleamed by the small interior light, but he hadn't the will to strum it. And isn't unrequited love the purest form of love, a love which exists in the mind, so intense that one is driven either to decisive action or to the misery of never knowing the result of such decisiveness? Wisdom steers us clear of these traps. We know by experience to ignore the signs, the signals which barely tell us to stop or to go, and most of us know ahead of time, most of us understand the buried wisdom of walking away and letting a delectable freedom reign over these entanglements.

It passes, reasoned Noble, while reaching for a more comfortable position. It really does pass, and once it passes, unrequited feelings become those which ought to be avoided, such that one must work hard, terribly hard, to avoid them. It starts when you see a woman as beautiful, and then the mind intensifies its vicious hold. Yes, Noble prayed in the car for this predicament to end without the emptiness at the point of rejection. He wanted that freedom one feels when the object of his desire has lifted from the heart and released into the midnight skies, returned to those same stars which instilled the vision of her, those blue-green eyes hiding her secrets, those signals which say stop but go, no but yes, friendship but proceed, please, proceed until he is nothing but a man eviscerated by an infatuation. Finally, time. 'Oh time,' thought Noble, 'heal me, for I never asked for this, or did I?'

He wrestled with the concept of Love, which was the last concept he wanted to engage, for it had always tricked him. He had heard that true love is found when both partners share the same feelings. When love is a one-way street, love is less than true and falls into the substrata of obsession. Yet if a man has never driven on Love's freeway, the cars on both sides colliding and compressing into a snarl of chrome and aluminum, then the current definition of Love remains open to new but guarded interpretations. He wanted nothing to do with women, because his love would never be as true as that shared by the couple walking along the strip, hand-in-hand, skipping and laughing in an idyll all their own.

Love rarely visits the man who stands alone. It may touch him as a malady from time to time, and when it hits, it consumes every moment, as though nothing matters but the object. It did not fit into his model, his ambition, his structure, as though obsessions and infatuations pushed away the truer forms of love in favor of a sweet misery, the same catharsis which comes from self-pity, a suffering which is sweet but also destructive, as it alienates him from the collision where both share love equally. Ironically his yearning for Alexandra pushed her farther away. He falls for her so badly that he doesn't have the chance to love. He stays within his automobile in the darkness and wishes for his fortunes to be reversed, but somehow he feels more at home in the darkness, because misery is familiar, the abuse routine, the punishment gratifying. It was a cycle, he determined, which ended as it always began- in loneliness. Perhaps this is what was meant for him- one man in an ocean, standing alone as the waves wash over him, wave after wave of unattainable women. Loneliness, then, is not such a terrible state. Within it he can play his guitar until the strings shivered and snapped. He could create and produce and one day nab the record deal, his ship coming to port, loaded with free-wheeling women hungry for him, and then the tables would be turned, and he could offer his revenge by breaking hearts. He must stand alone, because he knows no one else and understands his vulnerability. He stands alone, not by bravery, but by cowardice.

Serenity. Something he touched but now had been lost. All of that intensity returned. The melodrama, the suffering, the child-like gravity of every moment over one, haunting infatuation.

Chapter Two

He awoke the next morning in the throes of a dream. He fell from a precipice into a rocky valley. His heart lunged as he leaped from this height, and as usual with dreams of this sort he awoke before hitting the ground. He hadn't dreamt of falling for many years. He awoke in a sweat and wondered what the dream meant. Perhaps he was losing control, that the pink cloud of sobriety had dissipated amidst the whirlwind of Alexandra. It left him in a distasteful frame of mind. This is an understatement. He awoke urging for a drink.

The interior of the car didn't help matters. His muscles were sore, and his neck ached with a crick. This was no way to live. He never knew he could sink so low, yet he believed his homeless situation would lead to better times, as though suffering were a rite de passage of any great artist. Why one had to suffer flew beyond his comprehension, but he reasoned that every entity must suffer in order to change or grow. He no longer thought in terms of the insect, for he didn't have a job anyway. He thought the pursuit of this lofty aim, this vague ideal called 'art,' transformed the insect into the true human being, and yet he saw no evidence of this. If anything, he became more of an insect, caged with his guitar, as though the instrument were his only connection with humanity, and through this instrument, he could one day do what? Yes, he knew exactly what it would lead to, that one word which motivated him beyond any perfunctory conversation at a roadside bar: Women, the point he reaches when he attends a party and all the women know his name and engage in reverse obsessions. Some may claim that for all women to obsess over Noble McCloud would lead to infinite complications. Probably this smashing young bachelor would be emasculated in his sleep. Noble's quaint rumination, however, was pure bliss and pleasure. His desperation was that strong, and he hoped Alexandra would fall for him. But how?

She's the type of woman every man wants. Again, Noble exaggerated and generalized. Men have many tastes. They look for different attributes. Some want blondes, others brunettes. But let's consider the conception of beauty in Waspachick. The conception was so narrow that when a beautiful woman passed, there wasn't a man on the strip who did not turn his head, hang his mouth, wander up her supple legs and into her heart-shaped, well, Noble was getting carried away, but the point proved enough. Traditional beauty outweighed avant-garde beauty. When a woman who is beautiful knows she's beautiful, ceteris paribus, she will appear beautiful, because she wants to appear beautiful. Sure, she will claim an adherence to pseudo-feminist ideologies, but she reinforces her beauty by looking so good. Certainly she refuses to appear ugly. Waspachick women of acceptable standard flaunt what they have and claim the opposite. Noble thought he understood this pattern well, as the real feminists, who Noble found aesthetically ugly, were far away on their own Amazonian planet. That's not to say that Waspachick women didn't use their minds. They did, but only to appear beautiful. This was the extent of their misplaced, misdirected capacities. The ultimate woman on the Amazonian planet understands her subjugation to the male gaze. This made an ugly woman infinitely more beautiful. But remember, this was Waspachick, and such an ultimate beauty, he decided, would never be found here. It's as though Waspachick had not evolved beyond its original zygotic ineptitude. He was forced to comply with the high standard of beauty which made a few women beautiful and the rest, well, ugly. Alexandra, then, was more a concept than a woman. She represented this narrow conception, the ninety-ninth percentile of beauty, and many may think him guilty of placing a woman up high on the proverbial pedestal, but this woman, to a man so inexperienced in the ways of the opposite sex, can never avoid this deification. The moment when a concept supplants the reality of menopause, ovulation, water retention, premenstrual syndrome, the ethic of care, wrinkles, breast cancer, osteoporosis, even pregnancy, the more deviant the subjugation; the more pressure on the woman to comply with the Waspachick standard. As a result, the woman in Waspachick-reality gets breast implants, lyposuction, electrolysis, nose jobs, permanents and hair-weaves, until there is nothing left of her but the concept and her failure to live up to it. So much for Neo-Platonism.

This put Noble in a tough spot. Was his obsession based upon a concept? He mulled over these inanities and came to no definite conclusions-only that he wanted Alexandra, and he would do anything to get her. It was obvious that she knew of her own beauty which made his situation even more hopeless, and he hated everything about the town, its snobbery, its haughtiness, and perhaps its women? No, he could not hate women, but a few bad apples ruin the bunch. In the stuffy Oldsmobile, he fought against this hatred. There was no way he would succumb to the misogynist impulse. It was morally uncouth, sinister, and regressive. Of all the influences women fueled his art. He believed a woman, somewhere (or 'nowhere'), waited for him, and he wouldn't be satisfied unless and until this woman revealed herself. Somewhere down the line, a good woman waited, and for now he would endure this child-like obsession. Perhaps obsession is too strong a word, but he couldn't call it anything but an obsession. That's what it felt like- a sweet misery, a pain and anesthetic simultaneously.

He visited Shylock at the coffee shop, which was a mere block away. He dodged the mid-morning cars. Several customers quietly read their newspapers, and he could see through the wide window that Shylock was busy at the espresso machine. Nevertheless, he needed an ear, and Shylock was the perfect candidate.

"Hey, it's Noble, Noble McCloud," sang Shylock, "where have you been all my life?"

"Hullo, Shy."

"Why so glum?" as he banged espresso grounds.

"Shy, we have to talk."

"Uh oh. Can this wait 'til later?"

"Not really."

Shylock removed his kelly apron, and they took a seat at their familiar table.

"Shy, I need a woman."

"Tell me something I don't know."

"No, I mean this one woman I saw last night at the meeting."

"How old are you?"

"I've got the emotional maturity of a five year-old," he said resignedly, "but stop patronizing me."

"I'm sorry. Obviously this is serious, but then again, it's always serious with you."

"I know," said Noble, unable to shake his glumness.

"Well, why don't you ask her out?"

"It's not that simple. A) She's beautiful. B) She's surrounded by men all the time. C) In AA hooking up before a year is not advised. D) She has a boyfriend already. E)…"

"Okay, you needn't go any further."

Noble's spirit soared when Shylock conspired.

Shylock continued: "I've never seen you like this, because you're not drunk, and it seems like this woman has been…"

"…making me miserable?"

"Exactly. It's time for action."

"I agree. I'm sick of being the one who always gets looked over."

"That's the attitude. Be angry, really angry."

"I'm angry all right. She'll be at the evening meeting, I know she will. She'll be talking to the popular gang."

"Noble, let me put it plainly. You've always taken rejection too hard. You've always been too shy around women. That's your nature, and it's hard to say if a young boy can overcome these natural defects. And I mean 'young boy.' You take rejection too hard. That's the young boy in you. But inevitably the young boy must become a man. Do you get what I'm saying?"

"Not really, but continue."

"Noble, this is not a perfect world. Sometimes our intentions are pure, but the actions we take are impure."

"This world is in no way perfect," said Noble in call-and-response.

"No way is this a perfect world, and a boy can never accept the consequences a man must accept and face. You have always been the 'nice guy,' the quiet passive, peace-loving, friendly type, and only a boy can get away with that in this world. You let people walk all over you. I'm not being curt, I'm simply stating facts we both know. You get embarrassed easily. It's gotten to the point where you're afraid of women, because somehow you take it so personally when they look at you funny."

"Yes. Certainly. Absolutely…"

"And one day, Noble, you've got to literally take those blows, because the gain at the end of the bout is extraordinary. You may get laid for once in how many years?"

"I can't even remember, it's been so long, but go on."

"It's time for a radical change in attitude. You can't be so sensitive when it comes to women. The way you're headed, you'll probably turn gay, or you'll marry the bottom of the barrel. If you want this woman, and obviously you do, there has to be a change."

"I'm ready."

"No. You're not. Noble, what do you think about when you ask a woman out, and she says no?"

"I feel terrible, horrible."

"See, you have an inferiority complex. You think every woman who rejects you is superior than you, when the opposite is the case. The only way you feel superior is when you exercise control over those few people, normally me, who have some emotional attachment to you. In other words, you are superior to your close friends and inferior to the strangers who look superior. But this is another matter. The point is that you need to reverse this trend. You must be superior to strangers and equal in your treatment of your friends."

"I'm not sure I follow you."

"In other words, you must exercise your superiority over the woman of your choice and the men who try to get into her pants. This nice-guy, beautiful-loser mentality will never work. Sure, you're broke and all that, but you're, you're, you're…"

"An artist?"

"Precisely. You're a talented musician who has snubbed the rest of the world to play rock 'n roll, if that's what you play, and everyone else is beneath you."

"Like little rodents and insects?"

"Exactly. But even more beneath you is this woman. See, no one says it, and if these women were asked, they would deny it, but women want to be led and controlled, I shit you not. They want that masculine machismo, bravado, Old-Hemingway survivor's instinct. You fight for a woman. That's the only way you win her, and if she eludes you, you take her by force. It's the only way."

"Shylock, I think you're overreacting."

"Am I? Let's look at the facts. I got laid the other night. I've slept with dozens of women in that last few months. And am I that good looking? Not really. It's all attitude. Let's look at you. You don't have a job, you live in your father's old car, and you don't have a woman. You haven't had a woman for several years. I'm telling you man, you need to change."

"But can a man rise above his boyish defects?"

"You mean can a boy rise to the level of a man?"

"Yes."

"For you, it will take practice. I mean, imagine yourself at the age of forty. Nice guys do finish last, Noble. I can't understand why you don't see this. Change, Noble, it's all about change. You're too sensitive."

Shylock gave him a cup of coffee on the house. Noble thought these things over and knew he must submit to Shylock's definition of a man in order to get the woman of his choice. Shylock had proven his success, and his advice was heeded. This is not a perfect world. A kind, gentle man has no place within it, and if he must fight, he will fight. He could no longer avoid conflict and confrontation. He went to the noon meeting buoyed by this new outlook. If he were to get Alexandra, he must not merely persist annoyingly, but simply take what was his, like a settler fighting over territory.

He did share at the noon meeting about his urges in the late morning, and he concluded that he drank to escape the pains of becoming a man. Harry wasn't there, surprisingly. Noble could have used his perspective on the woman situation, but he instantly recalled what Harry had always said on these matters: "Under every skirt, there's a slip."

Noble mentally prepared for the evening meeting. He planned every step. He must get Alexandra while she stood alone in the church kitchen. If she were talking with the in-crowd he must infiltrate their ranks.

After the noon-er, he did go to the diner with Ivan and Milo. They rode in the black Japanese sports car which reaked of gasoline. "It's probably someone else's car," said Ivan en route, clearly in denial. His car was on its last wheels, and Noble could sense Milo's unease. Ivan's constant smoking could have caused an explosion. The East Waspachick diner was nearly empty, and Milo's unease, which was his general mood since he suffered from both anxiety and depression, loosened a bit. The kids from the high school who usually swarmed the diner were noticeably absent. This eased Milo's anxiety. He ordered a large plate of cheese fries with gravy. Ivan ordered potato skins. Noble ordered coffee. For all the garrulousness that had once occupied these mid-afternoon excursions, they were quiet, almost bored with themselves, until Ivan, who loved to 'stoke the fires' of conversation, mentioned Alexandra Van Deusen.

"New meat for the sharks," said Ivan.

"Definitely," said Milo.

"You guys think she's good looking?" asked Noble, feigning ignorance.

"See, my strategy is to let the women come to me," said Milo," and more often than not, they do come."

"She's so unattainable," said Ivan. "Watch how people start thirteenth stepping her. My guess: she'll be taken by the meeting tonight."

"I thought she has a boyfriend though?"

"Yeah," said Ivan, "but her boyfriend drinks, or at least that's what she said. Even Phinaeus was looking at her funny, and when Phinaeus looks at a woman, you know something's not right. She's the kind of woman who turns a gay man straight, or a straight woman a lesbian."

After the diner, Noble isolated in his car which sat stationary along the town park. He rolled down all the windows as the heat hung motionless in the interior. He was determined to complete his fifth instrumental. He worked vigorously, despite the many distractions of the town park, especially a couple necking on the lawn. He had Alexandra in mind, and the instrumental reflected, not the opportunity of capturing her, but an articulation of his despair after being rejected by her. A tender adagio, his fingers along the neck slurring the notes, almost graceful in its execution. Yet a fire lies beneath this tranquil surface, as his fingers soon pluck briskly, a furious arpeggio, and then another tranquil dolente, accenting each note with a haunting sadness. At anytime the instrumental would erupt from its frustration into an agitated rant of tremolo picking, but Noble exercised patience. He did not give his anger away, until the listener, whomever she may be, understood the full meaning of his desire, as though it were a fire spanning the length of human history, spanning the length of the neck, the strings vibrating, the note trilling, but patience. Yes, patience is required. The listener must be suckered by the pianissimo and then jolted by the truth of a crescendo so unbearably loud and chaotic that it leaves her stunned and gasping for more. He repeated

the tranquil refrain, a heavy and ponderous succession of chords, and when
the initial mood was spent, he plucked faster and louder, muffling the strings,
sweat dripping from his face, a furious and sustained jam which bespoke of
his intense anger, the idea that the gentle-hearted could never last within a
world of egotism, a world of self-interest, but he did not continue this tempo
for too long. One must come to a conclusion, that the only result involved the
acceptance of tragedy, as though someone close to him died for no apparent
reason.

His free-style approach proved more enjoyable, simply because it was
carefree and pleasant, a toying with the instrument, and he tried to have fun
but noticed a recurring trend. Most of his instrumentals seemed too explosive,
perhaps melodramatic and exaggerated, or the same point pounded into the
ear of the listener. And in many instances he believed he had listeners, like
Harry for example. Parenthetically, If Harry had access to his thoughts, then
shouldn't he understand his melodramatic tendencies? Possibly. Anyway, his
instrumentals were never happy. Why couldn't he stop this petulance and
simply get over the old Noble McCloud, the young boy who saw his mother
eyes open and lifeless in a pool of blood? That was the past, and this was the
present. One day at a time, and here Noble borrowed from the program. He
should live in the present. For some reason, though, the intense visual and
histrionic images of past events, negative and destructive, would never leave
him alone. It's as though these thoughts were involuntary thoughts, like
involuntary heartbeats or respiratory breathing, images and sounds which
wouldn't go away.

Memory is such that we never perceive the event as we first
experienced it. The memory grows into a bathtub full of blood, his mother
limp and blue, her veins popping through her skin, her weak blue eyes, the
ends of her hair dipping into the maroon pool, her breasts sagging just above
the bloodline. It's one thing if Noble deliberately recalled this image to evoke
a cathartic pity, but this was not the case. Ever since the event, he had fought
to purge the image and sound of his mother, her entire history, and with his
father gone, he could finally bury the sounds, especially, the racket in the
living room, the crying, and the shouting. But his parents wouldn't stay six
feet under. The deceased composed a horrific symphony, this never-ending
dirge calling him to do nothing but, finally, grow up, to stop torturing himself
for the sake of providence, and get on with what the scroll ordained, the
sentence for which no crime is committed, this sentence for being human.

It was a mood. That's all it was, and he needed a walk to suck in the
afternoon air and expel the mood, the melodrama, the passionate misery

which no listener would buy. Feedback and distortion without structure would work in some towns but never in Waspachick.

The strip teemed with bored housewives, baby strollers, African-American nannies, sport utility vehicles, the police cruiser stationed at the intersection, the dizziness of instant summer and its promise of fewer clothes, beach vacations, and pedophiles on the lookout for middle-schoolers in heat. Where was Phinaeus anyway?

He wandered the strip like a transient. He stuck out like the town bum whom actually smiled to him as he passed the park benches, as though the weathered, avuncular bum knew something Noble did not know. Soon the disability crew from the apartments above Shylock's coffee house loitered the park benches. He was about to call Harry from a pay phone, but gave up. A man is really alone unto himself, and a boy even more so. Aside from this epiphany (and epiphanies, contrary to popular belief, are not always pleasant), he formulated what he termed 'The Alexandra Plan.'

This comprehensive plan took all factors into account. But no matter how intricate the plan, the bottom line remained: the courage to walk up to her and take her from Smilin' Willy, simply grab her mid-sentence and pull her to his motorcycle behind the church and rumble to unknown frontiers and emerge victorious from the barren plains, as the mutual ride seals an everlasting bond between the two, a secret only the two of them share, not the gradualism and turbulence which defines popular romance, but an understanding between them, like being trapped in a room together for one full year, chained to each other, stuck together until they have little choice but to love. Or maybe the popular romance. She walks along the Waspachick strip oblivious to the sharp, angular sedan which darts through a stop sign, and Noble pushes her out of the way only to injure himself, a light contusion, nothing more, and Alexandra is so grateful that she instantly falls for him. Or she is bothered by a stalker and calls upon Dick McCloud, private investigator, and at the moment when the stalker lunges at her, Noble barges through the door, wrestles the one-eyed man to the floor, and thus wins her undying affection. Or perhaps a whimsy which struck a chord closer. Noble plays his instrumentals along the street corner. It's raining, the sustained drizzle accompanied by periodic sneezing and coughing. The strip is deserted, only he sees in the distance a European sports car taxiing towards him. It's the only car on the road. It stops, and the windows hum down, and it's Smilin' Willy in the driver's seat, and Alexandra on the passenger's side.

"Play something," barks Smilin' Willy.

"Honey, be more polite," says Alexandra as she playfully slaps his arm.

"Hurry up, we don't have all day," he barks again.

Noble plays in the wind and down-pouring rain his own original tune, and by the end of it, the rain has soaked him, both of them are impressed. They never expected such vitriol from a six-string.

But Smilin' Willy tosses him a copper penny, and says: "Only an idiot would play in the rain," and peels away towards the North end.

The cold rain pelts him, but he refuses to leave. He simply stands poised with his six-string, scratched and battered from years of dedicated play and abuse. He stands and waits until his fingers burn on the frigid ridges of the bass string, and he plays repeatedly the same instrumental, forcing himself, and pushing hard towards the goal line, until he spots the same car drifting from the North end. The car lumbers in front of him. It's Alexandra.

"Y'know, hypothermia is really prevalent this time of year. Why don't you hop in? I'll buy you some coffee in East Waspachick."

Earth to Noble...Come-in Noble. He finds himself staring into a store-front window. Elegant lettering reads: 'New York, Sydney, Tokyo, Bal Harbour,' and other distant locales. A middle-aged woman smelling of a strong political bent walked in. What the heck?

Noble followed her. The saleswoman greeted the Thatcher look-alike cordially while avoiding Noble who sat on one of the sofas. He looked at the sales tag and reasoned that it cost more than his living quarters. But as far as the saleswoman bothering him or shooing him from the store, he waited like an official from the Equal Opportunity Commission, and if he were harassed, why he'd approach a reputable law firm which would add media coverage until South end protesters lined the strip, and the fashionable chain-store were run out of town. He expected harassment but instead received its equivalent. He was ignored, even after the Thatcherite said goodbye. The specter of discrimination hung palpably in the perfumed environs, a subtle class superiority with an occasional stare by the saleswoman, bored, it seemed, from an afternoon of doing absolutely nothing. Ironically, if a job were to open here, Noble would feel right at home. He departed the store and meandered to Shylock's coffee house.

"This town's got some attitude," said Noble, all miffed.

"And why shouldn't it?" asked Shylock. "It's only one of the richest towns in the county, in the state for that matter."

"Well, I'm a member of this town and deserve some respect, damn it."

"Oh, no. You didn't do one of your protest things again?"

"No. I walked in as a customer, and the salesman blew me off."

"Noble, what did we spend twenty minutes talking about?" asked Shylock angrily.

"What? So now I'm the one to blame, right? Like I did something wrong? Why do you take everyone else's side but mine? You always take their side, as if I'm always wrong."

"What was our discussion about? Just tell me."

"I did exactly what you told me. I walked into that store with dignity, and I was blown off."

Shylock stretched over the counter. The coffee shop was empty.

"A man, Noble. A man also accepts what he is not. You're still playing the little boy who doesn't have enough change to board the bus. Look at you. Take a good look in the mirror. You haven't shaved in days. Try a shower every day. You'd be surprised. I'm not trying to insult you, but seriously, if I were the merchant, I wouldn't wait on you either. If you want service with the way you look, you could go to the crack houses on the South side. Maybe I was wrong this morning. I just fed you the attitude of a man. You've got to realize that a man also understands realities. You look like a goddamned hermit."

Shylock slapped his keys on the counter and said calmly: "Listen, go to the apartment, take a long shower, we're talking soap, deodorant, the whole nine yards, look in my bedroom closet and pick out something. It'll be a little loose on you, but damn it Noble, this can't go on. You're not Peter Pan or some great legend, Noble. You are a man without a job. I wish I could get that through to you, man, but you never face up to it. Sure, you're an artist, and by now you got to be talented and all, but this is reality. Say it with me, R-E-A-L-I-T-Y. Again, Re-al-ity. Okay? Wake up. You're not a boy. A man, Noble, a man, and a man shouldn't rely on anyone but himself. In order to make this woman attracted to you, you must show that you are self-reliant..."

Shylock continued in this manner, and by the time Noble left the coffee house, he was rejuvenated, a jump start surging with the hormones of manhood itself. He even cleaned out his car. No short order. Days of pastry wrappers, cigarette boxes, cans of ultra-caffeinated soda leaking on the floor mats; his car only a fraction of the size of his old room.

At Shylock's he shaved twice, he showered so long it nauseated him. He applied gel to his shaggy locks, even lotion to his arms and legs. He slicked his hair back, and then he selected a pair of khakis and an oxford shirt, in keeping with the town dress code. He viewed himself in the mirror from all angles, surprised that the previous 'boy' became the 'man' Shylock spoke of.

The kitchen of the church buzzed with social activity. Noble had arrived later than usual. The gathering out front moved to the kitchen. Even Harry, in cotton, talked jocularly with his fellow old-timers. Noble kept himself aloof. If Harry saw him all dolled up, he would have foiled his plan. Of course Harry would have interpreted this as an early sign of relapse, as the wisdom dictates: 'Relapse occurs before one picks up the first drink.' The kitchen was peopled enough for Noble to hide behind circles of conversing alcoholics in the hopes of finding Alexandra buried within. He tried to avoid the attention, but Ivan and Milo found him swiftly, as though they had tracked him beforehand.

"Aren't we looking spiffy," smiled Ivan, offering his hand.

"It's like you're another person," said Milo. "Are you all right?"

"Yeah. Just thought I'd look a little nicer around town."

"Hey, I beat an expert, a master, and lost to a grand master today. I won twenty bucks," said Ivan.

"Good for you," smiled Noble, searching for Alexandra and indifferent to Ivan's achievement.

He excused himself for coffee and wandered the periphery. He spotted Smilin' Willy, and he thought he saw, yes, there in the thickest part of the gathering stood Alexandra, her plucky nose inclined towards Willy's height. She looked so plain in contrast to Noble's attire, but her coquettishness made her all the more desirable. Naturally Noble burned with envy, but the plan was merely at stage one: locating her and keeping her within an observable distance.

The implementation of stage two then went into effect: measuring the relationship Will and Alexandra shared. They seemed so chatty and undisturbed by those around them. They were into each other, it seemed, or was it Alexandra's affectation? Did she act this way towards every man? He saved the other stages for after the meeting, and in the meantime he concerned himself with Stage Two. They were already interested in each other, and with Willy's thirteenth-steppin' reputation he probably crossed the line and succeeded in some indirect manner- his hint of cologne, a dental cleaning, Retin-A, an extra hour in the gym. Compared to Smilin' Will, Noble lost Stage Two, and this defeat ushered in the despair, until he heard: 'We don't compare someone's outsides to our insides. We identify. We don't compare.' Unmistakably Harry's hard-lining. His wry, sardonic baritone hit him in surprise, only, Harry stood at the other end of the kitchen, staring at him fiercely.

'You were supposed to call me this morning. What happened?' heard Noble in his brain.

'Jesus, Harry, not now,' thought Noble.

'This is not some cotillion. We are here to get sober. I know what you're up to,' and he gave him a sign.

'What on earth could you mean?' thought Noble.

'I wasn't born yesterday. No women in the first year. You know this already. It takes the focus off our own recovery.'

'Some things are more important. Don't worry, I have my priorities straight.'

'Do you remember that night?'

'What night?'

'I told you to never forget how you were feeling the night I took you to the Emergency Room.'

'Harry, we don't have to get into this,' thought Noble. 'Believe me, I'm comfortable in my sobriety. Nothing's wrong.'

'Watch out, Noble. Time to be careful. You're takin' your will back.' Harry rubbed his cheek and exited to the kitchen.

Stage Two led easily into Stage Three, the mass exodus through the side door to the congregation hall. Noble positioned himself directly behind Willy and Alexandra, eavesdropping on bits of conversation. They were in their elementary phase. Willy mentioned his sales job, and Alexandra said: "I was considering a sales position at one point, but then I said no way. I had to drop everything."

Stage Four: seating arrangement. Willy was flanked by the core 'in-crowd' of Meredith, Missy, Skinny Leroy, and the extra women who looked good apart from the halo Alexandra radiated. In these meetings, the alcoholics usually sat in the same places. A shift in seating was not surprising but noticeable. The closer one moved to the in-crowd, the more noticeable. Then he remembered Shylock's advice. A man, damn it, a man. Stop pussy-footing around. One must be the shark, the tiger, the eagle swooping upon a frightened prairie dog and carrying her off in his talons. He wasn't about to steal anyone's seat, but the women surrounding the in-crowd were expendable. He found a seat next to Meredith, her frizzy, reddish hair crimped and scented. Noble could have planted his lips on her right then and there, but he kept his focus on the deity at the center. Meredith looked at him and smiled libidinously, but she quickly flung her head- an invitation followed by condescension.

The beginning of the meeting led conveniently into Stage Five, which was listening carefully to what Alexandra shared. This could be used for after the meeting, when he would spark a conversation with her, pretending he identified with what she shared. The discussion went around the room. The topic, once again, was 'powerlessness.' Noble heard the sighs of disappointment when this topic was chosen. He joined in. For some reason the meeting's leader loved this topic.

Noble didn't care what anyone shared. Harry shared the same 'have it tomorrow' pedagogy, and when the meeting turned to Noble, he said: "I'll just listen tonight. Thanks."

Meredith always sounded good. She sounded like a woman who really worked her program and cared nothing about the social aspects, which was completely false. She spent most of her time chasing Smilin' Willy who said he was traveling on business tomorrow. This was indeed euphony to Noble's ears. He listened to Willy further. He would be away for three days, and where he went Noble didn't care, only that he would get a crack at the fair Alexandra for seventy-two wonderful hours. He relaxed a bit after hearing this tremendously good news.

"Hi, I'm Alexandra, and I'm an alcoholic."

"Hi, Alexandra!"

"I'm working on the first step, since I'm a newcomer, and I've had loads of help from the people in these rooms. I am powerless over alcohol. I know that now. I'm also romantically involved with someone who drinks, and he really got angry about my going to meetings. We had a fight about it last night. From my understanding, I have to give myself completely to this simple program, and I'm having a tough time doing that. I don't want to go back to where I was. I want to be a woman of dignity and honor like the program promises. I'm urging all over the place, and a few people have called me, these old friends who are wondering what's up with me, and I don't know what to tell them," and she started crying, and Noble found pleasure in this unexpected turn, "...I don't know what to do anymore. My whole life is falling apart. I don't know who I am anymore..." At this point, Willy messaged her back. "...And I just want all the pain to go someplace, but it never goes anywhere. It stays with me, and even though I'm living with this person, I've never felt so alone before, like no one in the world understands me, that no one in the world has been through what I'm going through. I'm asking myself whether this program can help someone like me, because I'm so confused. I was near death because of alcohol, and I don't want to go there again, really I don't. Thanks for letting me share," and she wiped her tears with her slender fingers. Willy's meaty paws moved to her far shoulder. Perhaps she would sleep with him tonight.

The meeting soon ended. The remainder of the meeting focused on Alexandra. "It gets worse before it gets better." "Don't leave before the miracle happens," was another statement. Noble planned Stage Six, and he rehearsed it dozens of times.

Even after sharing in this manner, Alexandra bounced back and chatted with Willy in the kitchen as though nothing happened. Noble floated from one corner to the next, waiting his turn. He was prepared to become the man who pulls the woman away by her hair. Finally, after checking himself over, he entered the feeding frenzy with the mindset of a shark. But once he interrupted their conversation, the sensitive boy returned, and he stammered:

"I really identified with what you shared," said Noble.

"Thanks," said Alexandra smiling, the type of smile which said get lost so she could continue her talk with Willy.

"Really, I mean it. I've been experiencing the same problems. I'm Noble McCloud, by the way. Noble McCloud," and he offered his hand to both of them.

"Where are you from, Noble?" asked Willy.

And to think he was a human being as well.

"Waspachick. Yeah, I live on the North side."

"Really?" asked Alexandra excitedly. "Whereabouts? I also live on the North side."

"Well, you know, up on the hill pretty much. The Heights, in fact."

"I also live in the Heights," she persisted. "What road do you live on? Maybe we're neighbors. I'm on Bower Lane."

Thank the Higher Powers she specified a street. Noble had never been to the Heights.

"Oh, I'm only a few streets over," he said.

"Where? Chestnut Street or Victoria Terrace?"

"Closer to Victoria Terrace."

"Wow. You must give me your number. It's comforting to find someone from the same neighborhood," said Alexandra.

"Well, I'm from out of town," said Willy, still smiling.

"Oh yeah? Whereabouts?" asked Noble.

"East Waspachick."

Noble finally beat Willy. He was the man emerging from the ashes of boyhood. He was making headway all of a sudden, which led into stages seven, eight, *ad infinitum*, because these stages all led to her bedroom, and he envisioned this moment, the two of them frolicking in a queen-sized bed, the earth moving, the clouds of heavenly providence colliding, and then just as suddenly:

"Your phone number?" she asked.

Noble gave her Shylock's number unthinkingly. But a man must accept the consequences of his actions, and he knew what Shylock had meant by manhood. Lie and lie well. Or was it a misinterpretation?

As they exchanged numbers, her chit worth more than all the diamonds in South Africa, Meredith barged in.

"Diner?" asked Meredith.

"Yeah, why not?" said Alexandra. "Noble, you wanna come along?"

His heart fluttered, and on the verge of accepting her invitation, he thought about transportation. He certainly couldn't show up in his clunker.

"I'll pass," said Noble wisely. "Maybe some other time. But I will definitely call you."

"I look forward to it," she said.

The in-crowd took off, and after waiting for a few minutes, avoiding Ivan and Milo in the process, he bolted to Shylock's coffee shop.

"Are you freakin' nuts?!" yelped Shylock after Noble informed him. "The Heights? You told her you lived in the Heights?!"

"So what? I got her number," as he waved the cherished chit in front of him.

"My God, Noble McCloud. You really did yourself in, man. But at least you got her number, man," and he gave him a high-five. "Good for you, man, only, how could you give her your number? You don't have a phone."

"Well, Shy, I gave her yours."

"You what?"

"I thought it'd be all right."

"Oh, no. Don't involve me in your schemes."

"C'mon, Shy. Work with me here. Don't you see what's happening? I have the opportunity to be friendly with the girl of my dreams, and you're the one who got me there. I couldn't have done it without your help. Can't you see? Friendship will lead to a relationship, a relationship will lead to romance, a romance to sex, and sex to marriage. It's all part of the plan."

"Aren't you getting ahead of yourself?"

"These things are possible, Shy. Finally I'm on the right track for once in my life. The forces of Athena are working with me. The heavens have answered my desperate cry for help, and I have her number. You should have seen the look on that guy's face when she gave me her number. I'd pay a million bucks for a snapshot of his face. East Waspachick's for losers, man. He doesn't have a chance. The power's in my hands now. Oh Shy, finally after all these years, I'm winning, and you're coming along for the ride."

Shylock clearly didn't share his excitement.

"And what am I supposed to do if she calls?"

"Tell her that you're my executive assistant."

"In what venture," he asked incredulously.

"We own an investment banking firm."

"Damn it, Noble, don't get me involved in this."

"Shy, I have a chance with this woman, and you are obligated to help me. If you don't, I'll be ruined."

"You're already ruined."

"C'mon, Shy. This is the new and improved Noble McCloud."

"It's true. I've never see you this happy before. I guess I'll have to change the answering machine greeting."

"Clothes. I need clothes."

"Noble, remember what we talked about? A man has to rely on himself. It's all about self-reliance. Suddenly you're relying on me more and more. I don't like it one bit. You should have just told her the truth, for both our sakes. And what are you gonna do when she finds out?"

"Let's worry about that later."

He skipped to his automobile across the street. He immediately made for his guitar and notebook. Although his practice session was long and at times difficult, he had produced a tune of incomparable beauty, happiness, and hope. There wasn't an angry or depressing note in the piece, and after committing it to bar-lines, he played the tune over and over. For the first time, he wished someone could hear it. He had stumbled upon the ultimate purpose of his music- to make his listeners feel good, not angry or depressed about the collapsing of the world around them, no longer the bird's-eye view of existence, but looking at events laterally, as a participant in life's affairs rather than the gloomy individual alone, afraid, and dubiously cynical. A new turn for Noble, and he knew this and celebrated in due fashion by playing his new creation into the wee hours of the morning, playing for Alexandra and the many children they would have together. In Noble's view, this was indeed a possibility, and once again his expectations were grandiose. Nevertheless,

he realized that his dreams aligned themselves with the dreams of many
Waspachick villagers- the home on the North end, the stunning wife, and a
couple of children. This vision did not diminish his fantasies but
supplemented them. After a hard evening playing to thousands in the
amphitheater, he journeys in his limousine to the North end. Alexandra
prepares his favorite meal of Cornish game hens with mashed potatoes and
vegetables. He sings a tune dedicated to his children, and they laugh in
delight, and afterwards he adjourns to the bedroom where they make
passionate love until the early morning. He watches the sunrise and
determines that life is not a sentence but a gift each and every human being
deserves.

Chapter Three

On the next day Noble woke up just in time for the noon meeting. He
had slept in his clothes, actually Shylock's clothes, and he groomed himself in
the rearview mirror. Although he was generally disheveled in appearance, he
looked better than previous mornings. Being clean was a novel experience.
The attitude of cleanliness carried the day, and he hoped it would endure. He
made plans to call Alexandra immediately after the nooner, but as he
approached the church he was surprised and shocked to see Alexandra sitting
on the wide steps.

His heart jumped. He wasn't about to spoil this opportunity. He tried
playing it cool and calm, but he couldn't hide the anxiety which pushed him
from the edge of the supermarket to the entranceway of the church. He
clenched his fists several times. He took long deep breaths, as her attendance
was totally unexpected. He would be the hero or the goat, and in his mind he
heard a thunderous applause, as though a small universe howled inside his
brain. He had an inkling as to how his Higher Power operated. The Higher
Power had given him a small taste of His omnipotence, and naturally Noble's
head exploded into an anxiety which pushed him closer to the woman who
conversed with no one else.

She waved innocently, as though she had been waiting for him. A bead
of sweat trickled from his brow. Calm and cool. He couldn't resist turning on
what little charm he stored away for special occasions. This was the first of
these occasions.

"I didn't expect to see you here," he exclaimed, almost a shout which
drew attention from the light gathering.

"Yeah," she said, "I didn't think I'd make it."

"No work today?"

"It's my day off," she laughed. "As a matter of fact, I've had many days off lately," a lilt in her voice.

"It's my day off too. Well, that's not altogether true. Most of the time I'm working at home. Ain't it a dandy what modern technology can do these days?"

He wished he didn't sound like such a farmhand, but Alexandra giggled anyway. He took a seat next to her and smoked. She also lit up, and Noble performed an award-winning rendition of the young wealthy businessman and alcoholic, a man who wasn't bound to any petty schedule. He traveled the world making business deals in Osaka, teleconferencing with his associates in Hong Kong (despite the Asian contagion), and he was doing fine money-wise. His pleasant, cautious manner made it seem this way.

"You're awfully young to be living in the Heights," she remarked.

"Is that unusual?" as he imagined how he looked to her.

"Well, when the mean age is over fifty, I think that would constitute a very peculiar living arrangement."

A touch of Waspachick snobbery in her tone, the hidden code of Waspachick's elite. Too much television helped him here. He commanded the role as the understudy who gets his big break by poisoning the lead. The Stanislavsky Method. How would it feel losing a billion in equity and still having a couple billion to do nothing but attend AA meetings and ski Aspen? And of course there's all those fall fundraisers for the museums one never sets foot in. He determined the summer was meant for, yes, his summer home in East Hampton. But he played it cool. The rich and successful hide their wealth as skillfully as they exploit the worker.

"Well, I don't always stay here," said Noble. "I go away a lot, but meetings tie me to this town. One gets so bored in this tiny village," he said as urbanely as possible.

"Yeah, our family goes away once in a while. At least once in the summertime."

It begged the question: "Where do you go normally?"

"We have a place in Hilton Head. My dad loves golfing there, so we always make the trip. I'm going in July."

He had no idea where Hilton Head was and didn't care. He commanded the flow of discourse, edging her out with movie-mogulish East Hampton and his beach house.

"So you live with your family up in the Heights?" hoping to seal the victory before being nabbed.

"I live with my boyfriend."

"How old is he?"

"He's thirty-five. But the relationship is dissolving really quickly. It's so tough living with someone who drinks constantly."

"Maybe you should move out," hinting she should move in with him.

"I'm thinking about it. My sobriety has to come first. I know that now. Everyone in the program has been helpful. I'm more confused than I ever was. It all came crashing down. I really hit my bottom, and I'm only twenty-three. I really fucked up my life this time. My family doesn't trust me. It got so bad, and my boyfriend doesn't understand, no one seems to understand me."

"Believe me," consoled Noble, "the first days are always rough, but you'll rise above it," and he used Smilin' Willy's rub of the shoulder. He hadn't touched a woman's body for several years. He was sexually aroused.

"What makes you so sure?" as she looked into his eyes.

"I don't know if you're aware of this, but we who live in the Heights have an old saying: 'We live in the Heights for a good reason.'"

She looked perplexed and said: "I've never heard that one before."

"Don't worry about a thing," smiled Noble. "It's tough in the beginning. We all had to go through it. Each and every one of us. Soon we'll both look back on this and marvel at how far we've come. Just wait it out. One day at a time. Use the people in these rooms. You should call me too. If I'm not there, my assistant will take a message. Be strong, and slowly the miracle will take shape. You have to trust this program."

"Noble?" she asked dolefully, "You want to get some coffee after the meeting? I know you're probably busy and all, but I can use some company this afternoon."

Noble paused. He remembered Harry's words: 'Alcoholics take hostages.'

"I had an appointment for this afternoon, and my car's in the shop, but I'm sure I can make it to the diner, but you're driving, since I walked here."

"Deal," she smiled sweetly, and they went inside the shady congregation hall.

Mostly old-timers attended the meeting. Milo led. Ivan was missing in action, and the meeting commenced somberly. It gave Noble time, not necessarily to plan his next move, but to assess the magnitude of his deception. He remembered his own formula: the imagination without conscience leads to a nightmare. This was indirectly related to his deceit. He had become absorbed in his role, and he would tread carefully. He knew where this was leading. The look she gave him, her sweet, blue-green, captivating eyes inviting him into her confusion, as though they validated his own decrepit, deplorable existence. No matter the success of this scheme, he made a promise under the heavens that someday he would let her know of his dishonesty. He didn't believe, however, that he would get very far anyway. She needed a friend, not another lover who resembled, at least in status, the boyfriend she lived with already. Again, he jumped far ahead, assuming they would make love in the town park at the stroke of midnight when the sniveling police officer made his rounds. The look she offered convinced him that an affair would soon commence. He was certain of it, only, these delicious prospects were tainted from the outset; a relationship based on a preposterous fabrication. How he got himself into these situations he wasn't sure, but if the love of another woman were the ultimate achievement, a heavenly and sublime gift, then wouldn't he have to lie and cheat and steal and plunder in order to achieve this love? Wouldn't the man have to fight, even kill to arrive at this love? Hyperbole again, but Noble had never loved before.

His feelings towards Alexandra certainly resembled it. He loved her from the first day she rejected him. He loved her when she walked into these sober rooms. He loved her when she cried, he loved her as she sat across from him, listening to the old, toothless drunk who talked of God and His everlasting presence. Love ought to elevate consciousness, he thought, but he was ashamed of himself. He needed her, but not this way. He had gone on for too long denying love. He used to think the word a farce, a scam, a fraud, a menace, a twisted falsehood. But in the congregation room, he had a shot at this same elusive concept which every Waspachick North-ender took for granted. Perhaps he should throw in the towel and forget about Alexandra, avoid her at all costs, return to his self-imposed exile in the Oldsmobile and compose the tired rants of rebellion, frustration, melancholy, and self-pity. He could have easily continued these rants against the oppressive world, but he reasoned that once a lonely man is touched by this condition, he may never return. 'Grab it when it comes your way,' he thought. Escape was no longer necessary. He found the end of his journey in Alexandra's visage.

"Tsk, Tsk, Tsk. And you were doing so well," he heard behind him.

"He had it goin' for him, and he shot it straight to hell."

The apparitions in the congregation hall. He thought he had won them over through his diligent practice of program principles, but they were clearly disappointed.

"What the hell do you want me to do?" fired Noble lividly.

"Take it easy," said the idol, "but you've really crossed the line this time."

The idol pointed to Alexandra and asked: "Is that what you want? To ruin the woman? She asks for your friendship, and you blow it up into a question of 'love?' Lemme tell you something. Love is a lie if you proceed like this."

"You're settin' yourself up for the big fall," said the mechanic. "All those months of hard work, and in the end you'll break her heart."

These words resonated. In a small way, however, he felt superior because of this possibility, the idea that he would break a woman's heart, instead of her breaking his. This fed into the manhood motif, that men must break hearts in order to remain men, and the women to remain women. It's been this way for centuries, and to turn all sweet and sensitive would deny his ego and his prospects for love.

"We've warned you,' said the idol, and they disappeared.

Their anger usually took on these short visitations as opposed to their long, drawn out, and supportive discussions. Noble was thankful they vanished when they did. It was inappropriate of them to trample upon his ego which had never seen this much inflation. And he looked to Alexandra, her blonde hair flaxen and parted to the side, her face slim and supple, her nose a cute little button, and her body the epitome of all he had longed for. She would have never pegged him for a man of the Heights, that mythical place to which a Southerner never traveled but only heard about, and the reason for never discussing this area of Waspachick before was due to Noble's total inaccessibility to this area. His imagination, it seemed, also had limits, and by involving the Heights in his scheme he was near certain of obtaining the prize. He couldn't forego the opportunity to walk with this woman along the strip, showing her to the saleswoman who had ignored him earlier.

"My car is in the shop, so thanks for driving," said Noble as he slid into the leather seat of her sports coupe. Impressive. Fully equipped with digital CD player and other accouterments. Noble made sure not to rave about the car. He kept quiet, his eyes popping from his skull, a sweet fragrance wondering from Alexandra's limbs as they sped towards East Waspachick.

He could have driven with her for hours, the top down, a groovin' tune on the radio, the breeze tousling her hair, the hum of the engine, and the beauty of this one woman who not long ago seemed unattainable. But this was not a dream, but the pressing reality begging him to stay cool and composed before cracking.

Holding the door would seem too romantic. He forewent this impulse, because technically this wasn't a date, merely a meeting of two addicted personalities. Even the waitress served him with more pluck. And soon they were sipping coffee and chain-smoking such that a detox from the diner would soon prove necessary,

"How long have you been in Waspachick, Noble?" she asked.

"Oh only a short time. I just bought the house a couple of months ago. I needed a break from business, and of course the alcohol. Have you been in town long?"

"Not too long. I was up at college in Boston, but alcohol and drugs, y'know, I had to leave the whole party scene. I'm glad I left it. It was something I really needed to do, and some of the things I did up there were just outrageously terrible."

"Well, you don't have to go back there if you don't want to."

"I don't plan to, but some of the things I did will forever haunt me."

"Where did you go?"

"Terrible places, absolutely terrible, it was a nightmare..."

"I meant to college."

"Oh, Radcliffe, but I hardly spent much time there. Most of the time I was in the bar, or in someone's apartment doing lines."

"Cocaine?"

"I'm a certifiable coke-head, but don't mention that to anyone."

"I won't, don't worry. I'm a good keeper of secrets, and besides, all of us went through rough times. That's our disease. We always want more and more. It's not uncommon to be cross-addicted."

"Yeah," she said again with a touch of Waspachick urbanity, "but I hear that most alcoholics don't want druggies invading their meetings."

"I wouldn't worry about it. I think you underestimate people in the program. Just don't drink or drug and go to meetings. Keep it simple."

"Well, I keep my substance abuse to myself, unless of course, I trust someone enough to tell them."

"You can trust me," declared Noble. "I know what it's like."

"What's your story?"

"I went to school in," not Harvard but the other one, "in New Haven for a little bit. Got my bachelor's and my business degree."

"Yale?'

"Yes. Spent a lot of years up in New Haven. Got my degree in the I.B.M. program."

"I.B.M. program?"

"International Business Management, and then I started my own company which does work for other financial firms, contracts, litigation, foreign investment, that sort of thing,"

"You must have traveled a great deal."

"Tokyo, London, Paris, Bar Harbor..."

"Maine?"

"We had an office up there. A clearing house so to speak, but I don't want to weigh you down with all the technical jargon. It's basically a worldwide, long-term capital investment firm. It's going quite well, although I'm seriously considering leaving and pursuing what I'm most interested in."

"Which is?" she asked.

"Music. I'm thinking about pursuing my music full-time."

He knew he won her with this admission. The wealthy business man leaving his work for the artist's life. She smiled and said:

"I once dated a guitar player."

Noble knew this well and hoped she wouldn't recognize him from the night long ago. It seemed years ago, but they were both drunk, and he quickly spoke of his artistic ambitions. The more he veered towards honesty, the better.

"I play the guitar myself," he smiled, "and I've been practicing hard, really hard, and I've been composing some of my own music."

Her features glowed with renewed interest. He discovered he really didn't have to lie, her blue eyes shining and radiating like a child unwrapping a Christmas gift. Their eyes met, but Noble quickly turned away. A real man would stare into the endless blue of her irises, but he stared into his cold coffee instead. The signals were overt, their chemistry colliding, and he had to make a move, but how?

"Let me ask you something," she said. "Do you like playing the guitar, or do you love playing it? Do you really have a passion for it?"

Truthfully, over the last few nights he enjoyed playing, and this was an extraordinary occurrence. Prior to Alexandra, however, he despised the process. Sure, he had a passion for it, but the act of creation itself taxed the mind so heavily that a practice session received a satisfactory evaluation if he didn't destroy the instrument on the pavement. A low threshold.

"I love it, and I hate it," he said.

"Which means you take it seriously. It's the mark of a true artist."

"You think so?"

"I know so. Believe me, I've known a lot of talented musicians, and they all say the same thing. Most of them can't stand it, especially the composers. It drives them looney."

"Really?"

"Oh yeah. I know you're coming from the financial world, so you're not too experienced in the ways of the artist, but most people I know love their art passionately and at the same time hate it."

"I've hated it. I wonder why I even continue."

"Because you're in tune with the frustrations of creation. It's never easy. When you first begin, sure it's wonderful, but over time, the frustration factor increases. Why do you think most artists commit suicide, or resort to drugs and alcohol? How do I know this? Because I've dated many artists. I dated a painter once who worked for years painting his canvases black, pure black, and afterwards he'd slice the canvas apart with a butcher's knife. This was a guy who had his own show in SoHo."

"I knew the process was tough, but I can't fathom a guy ripping apart his paintings."

"Imagine sleeping with the guy? That was an experience in itself," she laughed.

Noble melted in his seat.

"I take it you know many artists?" he asked.

"Painters, sculptors, musicians mostly," she said, "and they all reached a similar fate. It was either a slow suicide or a quick one. They all boozed, snorted, injected, you name it. That's why I had to leave the whole scene. After dropping out of college, I lived with a friend in SoHo, and then I saw it all- the drugs, the sex, the alcohol. That's what they do, and they end up like Basquiat, all of them Basquiats waiting to happen, and they don't care, because it's fashionable for them. They don't see what they're doing to themselves, but if they do it artistically, hey, they don't care."

"Please go on."

"Not much more to say about it. I could have died in that apartment. The only thing I know about high ceilings after that adventure is that I could have hung from one."

"I'm sorry. I didn't mean to..."

"Oh, don't. I've come to terms with the things I've done, and they're not pretty."

"One day you will enjoy an artist's work from a sober point of view," said Noble. "Sometimes I miss the insanity, but if we don't change, we

ultimately die. I can't go back to that old way of life. Believe me, you'll one
day learn to appreciate sobriety. Your life is much more…"

"Boring, lifeless, insipid?"

"It seems that way at first, but believe me. It gets better."

"I'd love to see some of the stuff I saw when I was totally whacked
out," she looked into his eyes again.

"You can. Give it time. Everything seems boring now, but you'll learn
how to appreciate those things to a phenomenal degree."

"I've got an idea," she said primly, folding her hands and sitting up
straight, "why don't we see an exhibition this afternoon?"

"Where?"

"I know of this gallery in SoHo. We can make it before closing."

"Alexandra, I mean, I hardly know you. We just got here, and as the
program instructs, we should avoid people, places, and things. It's not a good
idea to visit your old haunts. I know that I can't, because it will lead to a
drink."

"I don't wanna go by myself," she pouted.

She was obviously set on going, and Noble hadn't seen Manhattan for
many years, and his upper lip twitched, his mask crumbling. He should have
avoided her, but the thought of leaving Waspachick behind thrilled him and
made her even more attractive. An escapade with a deity. How could he turn
this down? But first he must play the part of dutiful alcoholic.

"Alexandra, I think you want that old life back. How many days do
you have?"

"Three, maybe four."

"It's not a good idea."

"But I'd be going with someone who's sober, and it would reinforce
our sobriety. Believe me Noble, if you're a serious artist you have to
familiarize yourself with other artists. There's nothing in Waspachick except
commuters and suburbanites. We can't isolate ourselves from art which is
what SoHo's all about. C'mon? We'll be back in time for dinner."

They rode along the highway with the top down and the music grinding
and thumping lucidly through the digitized stereo. He had never heard this
strain of music before. It reflected Alexandra's acquired tastes, these
outlandish, foreign instrumentals which bespoke of an artistry much higher
than his own traditionalist bedrock. The affluent musicologists must have
found merit in its oddity, its careless, formless movements pushing it further
into obscurity, the type of tune which is never played on the major radio
stations, an eclectic, technological mesh only the city-dweller could tolerate.

But as they glided closer to the city, he vaguely understood how this music found a niche. He compared it to the Manhattan skyline, for example, which towered futuristically above them. Less was more, these steel and glass structures refracting the sun's iridescence. Every nook and cranny of horizon was occupied. The helicopters and airplanes streaked across the azure, the cars inched towards the tollbooths, a chaos which achieved a mysterious order by an invisible hand governing the populace.

"There's nothing like the city," said Alexandra, her hand on the gear stick. "Anything from Waspachick is culture shock," she said knowingly. "Just keep an open mind about SoHo."

They flew down the Henry Hudson parkway, then the trafficky West Side Highway into the slanting streets of Greenwich Village. The city never stopped or ended. It was in perpetual motion and expanding like a gassy nebula. Everyone moved and made noise as though powered by a glowing furnace at the center of the earth. The livery services, the pedestrians walking dogs or waiting at bus stops, the traffic lights, and the street merchants unwound his provincial perspective. He couldn't handle the onslaught of liberation. Every pedestrian represented a complexity which overstimulated his perceptions. He had thought himself so important, but at these sights he grasped the interrelatedness of the construction men jack-hammering an avenue, a popular song wafting from a car interior, and an old woman caning herself across an intersection.

As they journeyed farther South, it got downright bizarre. They parked in a garage and walked into the thicket of SoHo. He likened it to landing on a forbidden planet, the life forms clad in black, a neighborhood where a business suit was inappropriate, and the women in particular looking alike, sounding alike, rushing from gallery to gallery, he presumed. Even SoHo was not immune to look-a-likes. The uniform of black, bell-bottomed stretch pants with high platform shoes ruled the inhabitants like an artistic ordinance. Nevertheless the blackness designated them as cultured and lofty, and Noble appreciated their commitment to the artistic ideal, this anything-goes mentality as expressed through their collective fashions.

He knew, however, this entire scene may unsettle his artistic principles derived from hours upon hours of practice in the Oldsmobile. Maybe he was seeing too much. His mind was irreversibly altered. He had grown accustomed to his solitude, and no matter the innumerable insults he hurled at Waspachick, he at least knew it well enough to dislike it, to poke fun at it, to suffer from its haughtiness so he may one day exact a revenge. But his indoctrination into SoHo life, although perfunctory, challenged him: either enter with an open mind and allow the experience to change him and affect his music, or simply cling to his narrow-minded principles which translated into tormenting labor. Either way, he was confused, and his mind raced.

"I haven't been here for six months," said Alexandra.

"I don't know what to think. Everyone's so, well, active. It's alive, this whole area is alive."

"Don't tell me you've never been to SoHo before?"

Noble almost forgot. He was a man of the world.

"It's been a long time, that's all. I haven't been in this area for several years, and this is my first time sober."

"I'm going to show you the inside of SoHo."

"Remember, we have to stay sober."

He wished he could have said this with more force.

"We're not here to drink, Noble. We're here to see some art, that's all. You shouldn't worry so much. You're acting like you've just seen a ghost."

She pressed his hand as they walked. They veered off Broadway and headed down Mercer Street, her hand still comforting his anxiety. They walked along the cobblestone street, passed the buildings of medium height. Narrow entranceways and enclaves led to artist studios. The block seemed reserved for painters and sculptors, even dancers. Each step brought him closer to those who toiled as he did. He held her hand tightly, and they came to a narrow doorway. They walked up the staircase and entered a gallery.

To his delight it was free of charge. He didn't have a dime on him and would have hated explaining his pennilessness.

He couldn't relax. Every one of his facial features, every step, every word had to win her, and so far the act worked, only that he was devoid of a personality, almost afraid to show it, for she may think him incompatible.

The gallery itself was situated in a vast space, almost vacant with enormous windows. On the walls were propped various pieces of amalgamated junk. The gallery played soft classical sonatas barely perceptible to his ears. The artwork seemed composed by the trash of civilization, compact and self-sufficient but exuding the complexity of an overwrought symphony.

"What do you think of this work, Noble?" asked Alexandra, probing his artistic depth.

"I've never seen anything like it," he said. "It's quintessentially urban, but it achieves a contemplative stillness. It reflects somewhat what I've seen so far: the mechanization of our society. The piece lives and breathes, though it's only mangled metal and industrial scrap. In a way it mocks itself by pretending to be living, when really it's defunct."

He was proud of his analysis, but Alexandra simply said: "Interesting," as though she hid a more correct and learned interpretation. He didn't press the matter but continued shuffling from one piece to the next pretending to identify deeply with each. When they came upon their fourth piece, they were interrupted by an ebullient voice from behind.

"Alexandra? Alexandra, is that you?"

Noble thought the woman beautiful. Dark rings circled her eyes. But he couldn't handle two women at once. His strategy was tailored for one woman only.

"Natalie? Natalie how are you?" said Alexandra.

They pecked both cheeks, and Alexandra introduced him. The fates mandated a threesome for later in the evening. Once again he was aroused.

"Where have you been? Where's Michael? I haven't seen both of you in ages."

"We're living in New Jersey."

"Arghhh, New Jersey?" she grimaced.

"Tell me about it," agreed Alexandra. "At least I'm much healthier than before. Not so strung out."

"Listen, you have to drop by tonight, really you must."

"Oh, I don't know," said Alexandra, "we do have to be getting back, and I have my friend with me. Noble, would you mind if we stopped by one of our old hang-outs? It won't be for long."

"Old hang-out?"

"It's nothing. It'll only take a few minutes. We'll be in and out. Plus, you do want to see the inside of the art world, don't you?"

"I guess."

"Well, it's done," said her friend. "We'll meet down the block in a couple of hours. It'll give me time to straighten up around here."

"And we'll have enough time to get a bite to eat," said Alexandra cheerfully.

"How do you know her?" asked Noble as they studied an oversized installation by the same artist. More junk except on a wider scale.

"She's a friend of a friend. We hung out a lot before I moved to New Jersey."

Noble was suspicious, and how dare she introduce him as a 'friend.' This was the woman he planned to marry, and she hid her superiority with a clever grin, as though Noble were ignorant and oblivious to higher art forms, which he was.

In keeping with Shylock's philosophy, he must assert his manhood to win her. Any woman who felt superior to the man would dump him and make love to another man who made her feel inferior. Basic Waspachick theory, but in no way could he assert his manhood on her turf. Her wider experience gave her the edge. He could have mentioned the beach house in East Hampton, but this would be a non-sequitur. He tried to say something smart about the installation.

"It represents the modern hassle of the industrial age," he decalred.

"It's a post-modern piece, Noble," she retorted. "It borrows heavily from classicism and creates an object d'art which sternly criticizes its antecedents. And, by the way, these pieces aren't defunct. They breathe life into a world where art is of a secondary, if not tertiary importance."

So much for superiority.

"But let's eat. What are you in the mood for?" she asked.

"Alexandra, silly me, I left my wallet at home. I didn't think of bringing it."

"Don't worry, I'll buy, but you buy next time. I get to choose."

He didn't know if there'd be a next time, but it lightened the load. She approved of him, and this was enough, although his curiosity ran wild as to what she saw in him. Holding hands and soon dinner implied a romantic interest, but it was hard to tell, since he had faired miserably with the artwork. My, how mesmerizing she looked when she stuffed his analysis down his throat. How much longer he could sustain this performance while assailed at every turn by high culture? He had been dormant, wrapping himself within himself, as though he were the only thing worth caring about. He had never known the pleasure of caring for someone else. The apparitions were right in their harsh judgment, that he had been self-centered, narcissistic, and egotistical. He even cared for these welded pieces of scrap metal hanging on the wall and of course Alexandra who thrived in her own element. Her features were utterly sublime, such that the junk on the wall and her feminine beauty were blatant contrasts.

She continued looking at the artwork one by one, dancing along the parquet floor. At the final piece, a towering confusion of junk, Noble could not take his eyes off her, his ears capturing every sonorous note of her in-depth commentary which he could not translate. Pure gibberish, but tonally a feast which made his heart cry, her voice so very cultured and finely tuned, and he fought his blatant staring, his ears reveling in her melodious pedagogy, as though Noble were a *tabula rasa* and she a divinity sent to restore his dignity and permit a flood of emotion which drowned the one-way obsession and irrigated a mutual affection sanctioned by the Amazonian planet.

"Noble, why are you looking at me like that?" she asked.

He did not hear her the first time, as his epiphany was all-encompassing. He knew this woman was the one he waited for, that the earlier days of misery and loss were a divine conspiracy so that he may stand in front of junk and look upon her. Only, he should not show it. Yes, he must remain the man. Don't crack or it's all over. Again, her mysterious, flirtatious lilt suggested a full knowledge of his kind without much effort.

"Uh, I don't know," he said, dumbfounded.

"Noble, we're here for the artwork," as she pointed to the massive wall of scrap metal.

Women do know everything. Their knowledge is infinite. She was clearly amused by his overt attraction. He wanted to explode in confession, to tell her the exact truth. Honesty, however, would drive her away, and he kept his mouth as tight as a hatch.

"Let's get some dinner," she said. "We have a long night ahead of us."

They dined at a small sidewalk café a few blocks from the gallery. Noble was afraid of eating, since his manners were shoddy, but throughout the course of the expensive but sparse dinner, he subtly copied Alexandra's manners. He rehearsed the performance ahead of time. He had calmed considerably, and he hoped to rescue his financial role to add a touch of authenticity. Alexandra enjoyed this dinner. The black-clad pedestrians reinforced and reinvigorated her former, wilder life. Noble fed into it. He asked questions to keep her rambling.

He asked: "How has the art scene changed in recent years?" or "Who's your favorite sculptor?" or "How much are those pieces worth?" This gave Noble the wherewithal to expound upon financial matters, although he strayed from the point. For example:

"Our clients are also art collectors. Big names: Victor Van Gogh, William De Koonig, Picasso, even more contemporary figures like Augustus Rodin and Da Vinci. They really make us rethink our industrial values."

Alexandra thought his sarcasm hilarious, only Noble was dead serious.

"Seriously, Noble," as she poked at her salad, "when do I get to hear your music?"

He was reluctant to touch upon this subject, but since shop-talk and the environs coalesced, he aligned himself with honesty: "I'm giving up on the financial industry. My real work is with my music, and I'm almost ready to let someone else hear it. I can't procrastinate any longer. My ship's gonna come in. It has to. I know it will. But I'm not sure how to proceed. I guess the first step is studio time. I need to make a recording of my songs, or land a gig somewhere. I'm thinking about playing in the town park, putting my hat on the grass, and playing for the common man."

"Why do you care about the common man? You live in the Heights. You ought to be a staunch conservative."

"Let's just say that my ancestors came with nothing but the shirts on their backs and a nickel in their pocket. I want to bring my music to the masses."

"A Marxist in principle but a libertarian in practice? Jeez, Noble, your finger's in a lot of pies. I understand, though. My analyst says creative people usually have split personalities."

"Really?" he asked in surprise.

"Certainly they do. They have problems integrating different personalities within their own identity."

"I don't understand."

"Take a musician, such as yourself. He grows up absorbing information. He's fascinated, not with himself, but with others. He has the ability to distinguish between different personalities. One of his school friends may be funny. Another may always complain. Having a good ear, he listens to all of these voices, and innocently, he tries to incorporate them into his own personality, but he can't, although he tries. He is unable to digest this information. He holds it in his mouth and regurgitates it in the form of music. His music reflects the personality types he's absorbed- a chord reflects humor, a strum suggests complaint, and the jam takes him on an adventure. It's sad though, because the musician can't integrate these different moods, and he ends up confused about his identity or his place in the world. He's not sure if he's the comedian, the whiner, or the adventurer. He can't cope with those who are more integrated than he, because they are predisposed to society's norms. The musician then feels inferior to those who exhibit a stronger identity. He's the outlaw who roams. He can't connect with any one person, because he's three people at once. Naturally, he takes to alcohol and drugs to escape this dilemma, that or he is forced to use his imagination to determine what's appropriate, social conventions especially. He is so bitterly alone that his imagination takes off, and when confronted with a real life situation, he can't respond properly. He feels like he's being taken advantage of. Paranoia escalates. He gets fearful of others but clings to something he can control- his music, and after doing it for an extended period of time, most likely with the aid of drugs and alcohol, it turns out he can't do anything else. He winds up poverty-stricken and marginal."

"Does it get any worse?" quipped Noble.

"In fact it does, because if the musician is knowledgeable about past trends, he knows traditionally the great artists have suffered the same. With this knowledge, he thinks he's doing the right thing as the other artists did before him. He doesn't even know of his own demise."

Noble thought this utterly preposterous and said calmly:

"I have to disagree with you."

"Okay," she laughed, almost in relief. "What exactly do you disagree with?"

And then a silence. She propped her chin on her fist and waited for his rebuttal.

"First of all, you paint a very bleak picture. It doesn't have to be that way. At least it's not that way for me. I'm perfectly content playing the guitar. I enjoy it."

"Are you sure?"

"It's not always easy, but I'm content as I said. You're view is so bleak. I don't see it that way at all. An artist doesn't have to have a split personality in order to be a great artist. Anyone can play the guitar whether one has a strong identity or not. It's like you're arguing for a natural talent, that the guitarist has to be born a guitarist, that he has to have some developmental problem, which is not the case at all. It takes practice. Practice makes perfect. A man doesn't automatically become a guitarist. It takes practice, just like anything else. And what is 'great,' really?"

"It's good you believe that, but honestly Noble, I've seen artists come and go, especially around SoHo, and a talent, or a gift for playing the guitar or creating post-modern works of art, is necessary. That's just my opinion. I've seen many artists come and go, and hard work doesn't count for much without natural ability."

It was clear she relished putting Noble on the defensive, as though it were a game, as though she were digging for the root of his philosophy only to uproot it and rebuild her version in its place.

"...It's not realistic, Noble," she continued, "and I hate to burst your bubble, but it doesn't work that way. Some people learn quickly and get it. Others learn slowly and never get it. I didn't invent the system..."

"We'll agree to disagree," said Noble angrily.

They finished their dinner in silence. She paid the check with a credit card. She placed the gold plastic in the leather folder without looking.

"Listen," she said, "I didn't mean to…"

"Don't worry about it," said Noble.

"I used to have ideals like you. I know what it's like to work really hard, but it's true only the few succeed. Any artist should know this beforehand."

They strolled along Mercer Street and Alexandra slipped her arm into his.

"You're not angry with me, are you?"

"Why should I be angry?"

He was angry. It seemed like he had nothing else but his guitar, and this slowly drifted from him. He could do nothing else but play it, and the thought of not succeeding suddenly came into full focus. He was no longer the man who felt but an engine who played hard, unable to control what it produced. While playing, he divorced himself from his instrumentals and allowed them to flourish without understanding their meaning, as though he had little choice in their efficacy, only that he must produce like the machine he was becoming, each hour with his guitar more dreadful than the first. He understood, as they walked beneath the sunlight towards a place only Alexandra knew of, that the guitar can't solve the world's problems let alone his. It cannot master the unsolved riddle of relating all of his experience within a set of chords. No one would ever understand him completely- his dreams, his motives, or his aspirations. Hence his definition of success had to change. A sold-out arena wouldn't do any longer, the groupies wouldn't do. Success, instead, concerned how well a listener could understand and thereby empathize with his experience.

His definition of success didn't change in a matter of minutes. He still longed for the sold-out arena, but he at least came to a more proper conclusion of what music, and art in general, must do: to communicate the breadth of existence and hopefully guide the listener's interpretation towards the truth which hides underneath. Perhaps this was too controlling a definition, as whimsical as his daydreams. Nevertheless, he stumbled upon this vague, new, and frightening idea- that he should play the truth. But there are only a few convenient truths. Broader philosophies graze its borders, never quite hitting a universal certainty. The truth, in essence, was deeper and richer, open to an abundance of interpretations, infinite in scope, and troubling to those who seek its treasure. He wasn't ready for it. He couldn't distinguish between the reality and the fantasy, as though his entire existence was a confusing ball of lies.

"I'll keep going no matter what happens," he said finally.

"At least you have money. It makes it a lot easier, doesn't it?" as she rested her head on his shoulder.

Rush hour soon startled the quiet Mercer Street, and they had been strolling for some time, looking into the enormous windows and narrow entranceways. It seemed as though the area and its inhabitants placed more importance in the night hours than the day. Working gave them money to buy the necessities, and at night they diligently made their lives worthy of the highest art. He couldn't believe Alexandra had taken kindly towards him, despite their disagreement. He had urges to kiss her on the sidewalk but wasn't sure if she liked him as a friend or as a lover. He didn't take the leap necessary, as she may flee into an alleyway and head to Jersey without him, leaving him in the megalopolis stranded without any money. He played it cool, his speech laconic, his performance resolute. They came to the end of the street and turned around.

"Where are we going tonight?" asked Noble.

"We're going to a bar," she said, "but don't worry. We're not there to drink. We'll be in and out. I haven't seen my old friends for a while."

"I don't think it's a good idea. You're only a few days sober."

"You'll be there, right?"

"I guess, but it's best to keep away from places which may trigger us to drink."

"Oh, Noble, you shouldn't worry so much," and she gave him a kiss on the cheek.

"What was that for?"

"Because you came with me."

"Oh."

But he couldn't be happier. He could die and go to heaven now, and his days would have meant something. A simple kiss unlocked his essential meaning, and in his grave he would at least smile. Amazing what a kiss from a beautiful woman can do. He would take her wherever she wanted to go, only that they shouldn't drink.

He remembered the principles of the program, that he was powerless over alcohol, and that his life had become unmanageable, that he landed in detox due to his predilection for the drink, that he should keep his memory green, that relapses occur before a drink is ever picked up. But how could one stay sober when drinking and drugging were as prevalent in music and painting as the products themselves? One would have to reinvent himself in order to stay away from these two baffling predicaments, and it had gotten so that he was afraid of alcohol and what it might do to him. Jails, institutions, and death. Yet Alexandra was so joyously happy, and he was so filled by her keen interest in him that it balmed the bite of the twelve dismal steps which sucked the life from every musician, every artist for that matter.

The bar itself didn't have a sign over its doorway but scaffolding and a security guard out front. The velvet rope was pulled, and they were permitted to enter. He had never seen a place like it. It sure as hell beat the East Waspachick bar which he likened to a fetid saloon of local malcontents bent on a rumble after closing. For one thing, the ceiling was at least three stories high with a wide dome of glass. The place was filled with people wearing black clothes and eating dainty appetizers, sipping wine, and conversing. The din was substantial, and some even took pictures, the flashes striking from the center. Noble thought for a second that they may be taking snapshots of him, as his music was well-known on an alien planet in a galaxy far-removed.

He quickly regained his senses. The bar area was long and also quite crowded, the liquor bottles propped on florescent shelves of mirrored glass, like the Manhattan skyline. From the middle area where the tables were kept, two women waved. He recognized the same woman from the gallery; He forgot her name.

They squeezed between the tables, and Alexandra kissed each of them on both cheeks. They were very attractive, waifs almost, and they were clad in black evening dresses. Alexandra introduced him, and instead of the usual handshake they kissed him as though he were an old friend.

The women ordered a bottle of wine, and Alexandra a seltzer water. Noble ordered a diet cola. He didn't pay much attention to the conversation but engrossed himself in the scene. He had little idea what to say as his apprehension towards the bottle of wine and the liquor on the shelves tempted him. He excused himself and headed towards the bathroom, but this didn't help matters. The bathroom was located on a high plateau where even more black-clad people sat and conversed. He looked for the men's room and found instead a lounge where a woman applied lipstick. He went to ground level and searched in vain for the men's room. He even went into the small kitchen where they prepared the tiny appetizers on fine china, but still no men's room. The workers, with whom he found a familiar connection, directed him upstairs. So up he went a second time and found the same woman, also in black, applying blush to her sunken cheeks. Behind her stood a row of cubicles. Their doors were made of liquid crystal, it seemed, some reading 'occupied,' some 'vacant.' He was about to ask for directions until a man exited one of the cubicles. It dawned on him delightfully that the bathroom was unisex. The woman applying makeup didn't share in his amusement, but another young man, an African-American, laughed with him.

Things change and for good reason. It brought him a step closer to the opposite sex. The lounge was equipped with a soft leather sofa, and he could have hung out in the bathroom for several hours, only that it would look a bit ridiculous. He returned awestruck by the lounge, awestruck by the entire scene as though he were a child again. Sobriety had reduced reality into simple pleasures, while those who drank needed more advanced pleasures, a deluge of entertainment, a carnival after the drudgery of their jobs. He remembered, however, that he was a man of the world, and he shouldn't let the unisex bathroom distort the act. He had been to a unisex bathroom where? Oh yes, in Paris.

As he approached the table, however, he was aghast to find Alexandra sipping red wine. He too felt like taking a drink or smoking a joint. He quickly pulled out a cigarette. He was a man of the world and appreciated the artistic temperament.

"I see you're drinking again," announced Noble.

"How perceptive," she said and then continued the discussion she was having.

"…and his opening did so well," said one of the women, "and he really misses you…"

"Yes, he does," chimed the other.

"When you moved to Jersey, we didn't know what to do. We had no way of getting hold of you. The old gang's got to get back together."

"Jersey is such an armpit anyway, you really should move back to SoHo, girl."

"I think I'm going to," after gulping the wine. "It beats Boston too."

"You guys met up in Boston?" asked Noble, hoping to participate.

"Yes, Noble," sighed Alexandra, and they continued talking as if Noble weren't there. He reasoned a drink would loosen him up and allow him to converse more freely. Sure. He was a man of the world hobnobbing with women of the world, Radcliffe women no less. But he was so bewildered by their condescension that he couldn't chat, his tongue in a vice. Instead he sat quietly and obsessed over the bottle of wine, a priapic centerpiece.

He did manage to blurt out: "It's getting late, Alexandra. Shouldn't we be heading back?"

He said it too softly, and their conversation continued, a highbrow gibberish only pampered women uttered. He wished Harry were around to guide him. He imagined talking with him, using Harryisms like: 'There's a guy in these rooms I used to know named Joe Colt. He's been sober for twenty-six years. One day he says to me: 'Harry, I don't think I'm an alcoholic.' I thought he flipped out. But he looks at me and says, 'but I know, sober is better.''

Clearly, it was decision time, and he would have left immediately, but he had no money to return to the safe arms of Waspachick, the security of his simple world, his Oldsmobile, his guitar, the meetings, even his grumpy sponsor. He had seen too much and heard too much. He was actually homesick while the art world pressed on with its gossipy din, and although Noble thus far had played a stellar performance, one worthy enough for an award, he knew he must either leave or return to the drink and wind up in jail.

"Alexandra, can I borrow like, say, five bucks for a pack of smokes?"

"The cigarettes here cost six dollars," said the same woman who worked in the gallery. Natalie, her name.

"Fine, how about six bucks?"

Upset that her conversation was interrupted for the third time, Alexandra begrudgingly gave him a ten dollar bill. He asked again:

"Maybe we should leave, Alexandra."

"I'm not leaving," she said.

He knelt beside her and said forcefully:

"Listen to me. We're allergic to this stuff. It's important that we leave before you tie one on. I don't want to ruin the fun, but remember when you told me you're entire life was screwed up? Remember all that pain and misery? Well, there's still time. We can get back to Waspachick before anything else happens. These people aren't your friends. They wouldn't want you to drink if they were your real friends."

"Who are you to decide who my friends are?"

"Listen, you're a little tipsy, but you don't have to get drunk. I know this place appeals to you. It appeals to me too, and I would love to drink with you, but I know I can't, and somewhere you know that you can't either. If you want another drink, have it tomorrow. It's as simple as that."

The two women opposite him sneered. Alexandra filled her wine glass, toasted the women, and downed it all in a single swallow.

The two women clapped and laughed. Humiliated, Noble exited the busy club. He used the money for a subway token and a bus ticket to Waspachick. Finding the Port Authority, let alone a subway, was not easy, but eventually he boarded a local uptown train. He gazed upon the passengers of all colors, all shapes, and he had never felt so utterly alone and insignificant. He was one grain of salt in an infinite sea, one particle of dust on the subway linoleum, and yes, he did long to be with her, drinking and cavorting with those who monopolized the artistic flux and the trends, these same personalities who were photographed on the society pages, the bar and its towering liquor bottles, the avant-garde answer to a bathroom, the artists at the end of the bar sucking down martinis, he wanted to be a part of the current, as this was his definition of success- to be photographed with beautiful women, to drink alcohol without having to be accountable and responsible. But it became the fantasy which went wrong, as though he barely tasted the things he always wanted to taste only to be pulled away at the last moment.

And then there was Alexandra who he thought he loved, but love, as the pinnacle of all thought, would never materialize, as Alexandra became yet another daydream, and he cursed himself for even thinking he could have had her in his arms, serenading her from his Oldsmobile as the night temperatures dip below freezing. He was so close, and instead he settled for a long bus-ride via the New Jersey Turnpike, the wetlands overshadowed by refineries and factories giving way to the small, sagging towns before the final stop adjacent at the Waspachick town park. Although it was early in the evening, he crawled inside of his Oldsmobile, wrapped himself in his blanket and fell asleep without thumbing a single string.

Chapter Four

He didn't expect to see her again. And when he awoke in the Oldsmobile, his muscles sore, his scalp numb from resting against the body of his guitar, he offered a small prayer that she may find her way back into the shade of the congregation room instead of in someone else's arms, which he presumed, she could have very-well fallen into last night. While praying, he looked to the ceiling of the Oldsmobile in skepticism and disbelief. He doubted his modest appeal would be answered, as our most needy and heartfelt prayers are often unanswered, despite the best of intentions, and perhaps there is a reason for this. If our prayers were to be answered promptly with the charge and brilliance of electric conductivity, they would screw up our lives rather than help. God, he supposed, was not a genie, and if He were, we wouldn't wish for anything but our own aggrandizement. But he did wish Alexandra returned, if not now, then later.

Many in the program talked of a miracle happening, and that one shouldn't leave before the miracle takes place. He needed a miracle that morning. He didn't think it too presumptuous to pray for Alexandra's return.

He couldn't understand how his prayer was a greedy wish to a Santa Claus guiding his reindeers through the twilight. Whenever a prayer was unfulfilled, recovery labeled the prayer a greedy wish, and when a prayer was answered, the wish became an act of divine providence, a euphemism for a wish by an alcoholic with more maturity. The Higher Power never gave him what he wanted, but what he needed. Well, he needed her. It wasn't too much to ask.

For Noble's Higher Power, as he understood him, He, She, It, Whatever had limited powers and was imperfect. The proof was incontrovertible. Ask the five year-old child of a Tutsi refugee, or a Holocaust victim, or an ethnic Albanian is Kosovo province, or any man, woman, or child who suffered or died for the high crime of being innocent and having simple prayers which were ultimately ignored. Noble reasoned that if a Higher Power, in keeping with basic monotheism, accepted the praise for his good deeds, then perhaps he should share some of the blame for his cruel, irrational, often glaring miscues. Again, ask the rape victim. But the immediate response must be that the devious Lucifer had a hand in altering innocent minds into criminal animals who refused to embrace the All-knowing Creator. Those who do not accept God, fall to the Devil. But it's hard to say whether or not the Tutsi child, naked and starving, the bones in his back more prominent than the skin wrapped tightly around him, ever had the opportunity to embrace the All-knowing, ever-present Spirit in the sky. Hard to say if the paunchy man stealing rice from under the child was somehow forced to steal by the Snake. If the human being can admit to himself, finally, that man and womankind are controlled by both bipolar forces, then perhaps monotheism, or any theism for that matter, will become one of the most laughable theologies ever to cross the intellect, as absurd as the Twelve Gods bickering on Mount Olympus. But Noble wasn't about to change the face of religion. He was too confused as it was. He knew his concept of a Higher Power stemmed from immaturity and ignorance, even arrogance. He did know, however, that the program's solution to this mess, the Higher Power mess, fell short of satisfaction.

Again, the reasoning was seductive: that the alcoholic had tried to run the whole show by himself, and this led to alcohol abuse. Since the alcoholic had failed using his own methods of self-reliance, and since he had executed his self-will and thereby failed almost to the point of death and disaster, then he somehow has little choice but to rely on a power greater than himself. Otherwise, he would end up drinking again.

But this presupposes that no other factor but his own will, or his own ego, guided him into drinking, that he had ruled out God entirely before deciding that a belief in himself was the only option available and an option which was greater than God's will. They say that one contradiction ruins the entire theory. Noble thought of a priest who drinks alcoholically. The reasoning also presupposes that a power greater than himself will end his alcohol abuse. In turn this suggests that a Higher Power has far better intentions for him than his own. Subtly, alcoholism and self-reliance complement each other, and each is given an equally harsh treatment. The reasoning that one drinks because one's will is weak is the foundation. The actual choice to turn over this self-will to the care of a God is never mentioned. Nit-picking aside, the major issue involved choice. The program reasoning assumes the alcoholic chooses to drink until death or disaster, because he simply wants to. He, in essence, chooses to become an alcoholic, he chooses an inflamed liver, the gout, and wet-brain. Noble heard in the rooms that the specter of alcoholism is rooted in the inability of the drinker to stop drinking. If this is the case, then he's drinking, not by choice, but by some other force. So then why is his will taken away, if he does not will alcoholism? It's not the case that alcoholics purposely choose to death and disaster. And if the alcoholic does not will alcoholism, then wouldn't it seem peculiar to submit to this 'other force?'

The program placed all of its answers in spirituality while pretending that this was a logical option. Noble wasn't swayed by its logic anymore, because it wasn't logical, only persuasive. The founding fathers understood the alcoholic inside and out, but perhaps they went a bit too far. Considering one in thirty-two alcoholics in the program actually succeed in never touching the liquor again, the spirituality doesn't hold many drinkers for long. Noble admitted that a pure form of self-reliance doesn't do much good either. A compromise, then, between self-will and the will of a Higher Power may work, and this, he guessed, was the route contemporary AA was taking. The self doesn't know it all. Either does a self who relies only on a Higher Power. But wouldn't it be nice if a Higher Power were omnipotent, compassionate, kind, and loving? But Noble believed 'cruel' and 'brutal' were also undeniable traits.

There was an important codicil to the program of recovery, luckily. A big one. Noble could understand the Higher Power as he wished. It could be a candle, a tree stump, a Heavenly Father, or even a group of drunks in the congregation room. This lent a flexibility to recovery. But to turn over his will and his life to the care of this Higher Power, well, even his Higher Power would laugh.

Sure, Noble was pissed off. He didn't notice the forces at work when he pulled out of that SoHo bar without drinking. He was more conditioned than she, the sobriety-speak rammed into him, the quotations, the maxims, the steps, the philosophy, the stories, the nicotine, the caffeine, the diner, the Serenity Prayer, the Grapevines, the Big Book, the phone numbers, the congregation hall, the wide eyes when a fellow said exactly what Noble needed to hear, and his old life losing its ground into another oddity unbeknownst to him. And meanwhile, the dank interior of the Oldsmobile, the strewn clothes, and the guitar, which he decided would be the Higher Power of his choice.

"You're gonna think yourself right outta this program, and right back into the bottle," said Harry to Noble over breakfast the next morning.

Noble told his grumpy sponsor what had happened the night before.

"Seriously," said Harry, "you're not supposed to think. You're overcomplicating a very simple program. Don't drink and go to meetings. This is what I order you to do, and if you don't do it, you will end up where I found you. And don't expect me to give you any more of those damned DWI cards. You will go to meetings at least twice a day. You should have never, and I mean never, put yourself in that situation with a woman who has only a few days sober, you big dummy. And stop playing that damn rock 'n roll crap. Woody Guthrie never played that garbage at all hours of the night. If you wanna see art, go to a detox center. Those drunks are all works of art, lemme tell ya, they're great works of misery, frustration, loneliness, and bankruptcy, because that's what drinking does to people. We aren't a bunch of God-freaks. You should know better. Unless you're queer, there's no reason why you should be in New York City."

"Harry, I think you're overreacting," said Noble, trying hard to avoid his steely blue gaze. Harry wore a three-piece, gray and polyester, and Noble was relieved by this.

"It's a simple program in a world of shit," said Harry, "and if you complicate it like that, the blame will fall on you. The program doesn't fail; you fail. Plain and simple."

They ordered coffee after finishing their breakfast, and Harry pulled out a filterless cigarette. Noble could think of no one but Alexandra. Harry caught him staring out the window.

"What's wrong, Noble? It's like you're on another planet."

"It's nothing," he said.

"If something's on your mind, best to dump it, 'cause that's what I'm here for. Is it the girl?"

"I just don't know anymore. This whole sobriety thing. I mean, I go to these meetings every day, and my attitude, it's my attitude which tells me that I shouldn't attend these meetings anymore. I see the same faces, and I'm sick of seeing these faces. It's not that I resent anyone in particular, but something says to me: 'hey, I don't need these meetings anymore,' and in comes the woman of my dreams, and we really hit it off, and I thought my life was getting better, y'know, and I'm sick of these meetings. I'm sick of these cliques, and I'm sick, I guess, of being sober. I can't say if things have gotten better, because they haven't, and well, I think I'm in love with her, Harry. I think I'm in love with Alexandra, and I've never been in love with anyone."

"Oh boy," said Harry as he reclined.

"I don't know what to do about it. I guess I'll have to forget about her."

"Under every skirt, there's a slip. How many times have I told you? Keep away from the women in the program. First of all, most of them are certifiably insane, and second, you take the focus off yourself. From now on, stick with the men, and more meetings will help your attitude. The second that you think you've had enough of the program, the second you should get to a meeting. Without meetings, we drink. You ask anybody who comes back after relapse, and they'll say the first thing that led them to a drink was not attending meetings. Meetings are our medication for an incurable disease, and sometimes we don't want to take our medications. I know for sure that on some days, I frankly don't give a goddamned for a meeting. But if I want to stay sober, I know I have to come. And you do want to stay sober, don't cha?"

"I just don't know anymore, Harry. I mean when I first came in, I was so happy, but now I'm just going through the motions. My heart's not in it."

"This too shall pass. Things don't get better, but you get better. This program doesn't help with life's ups and downs. It doesn't help a poor man become rich. But I know what it can do: it keeps us from the first drink. It keeps us out of the hospitals and the jails."

"I'm tired, Harry. I'm really very tired of everything."

Noble attended the noon meeting but didn't share what was on his mind. He couldn't say openly that he fell for a woman in the program and was suffering due to its consequences. The words he heard were similar to the day before, and the day before. He wasn't about to drink. Urges had left him, but he couldn't help but feel down and gloomy. The other shoe fell, so to speak. The words of the meeting were merely vacuous and vapid, nothing which related to his situation. But the topic of "progression," hit home.

The drunks discussed their bottoms. The domineering theory held that the first drink leaves them where they last left off, and as they drink they approach new bottoms worse than their first. They called their bottoms 'boxes,' how they'd wind up in the 'box' again. This was the insanity of the disease, that the alcoholic will drink in spite of knowing where he or she will end up. One guy's 'box' was the dark enclave of his basement, another found his 'box' in an auto accident, another in a prison cell. Noble could only think of an escape, some flight to a place where alcohol was served twenty-four hours a day. He couldn't take sobriety anymore. The people at the noon meeting seemed so content with themselves. They were so happy and delighted. Their brains were captured by the message, and he resented everyone because of it.

Even Ivan and Milo were doing well. Ivan announced he was celebrating a year of continuous sobriety which merited applause and pats on the back. Noble, on the other hand, was totally detached and had little or no reaction to Ivan's achievement. He had kept his distance from Ivan and Milo for the past several weeks, to the point where socially he was alone. The drifter, the rebellious alcoholic fighting against a program which tried to help him, and he would go down in flames just to spite every one of these happy, brainwashed imbeciles who spoke of light, courage, hope, and ultimately their own joy. He simply wasn't like the others. He was, in fact, better than these old-timers who spent thirty or forty years drinking their families and jobs down the drain. He believed he was unlike these people, that no one in the rooms shared the misery he went through, and the meeting dragged on until his mind burned and he had to message his brow to keep it from burning and overworking itself into the box he built especially for himself. The last thing he wanted to do was ask people for help. There was nothing more degrading than asking another alcoholic for help when they wore their spiffy little smiles. He manufactured his own misery in this manner and hated everything about the program since it confiscated and thereby ruined the only part of his life truly enjoyable: drinking whenever and wherever he damn well pleased.

He did, however, attach himself to Ivan and Milo after the meeting. He congratulated Ivan with a firm handshake. How Ivan stayed sober for a year, he didn't know. One day Noble wanted to tell his own story, but he dismissed this thought. He was too nervous, and he had turned down qualifying before. He didn't like talking to people.

Ivan did invite him out to the diner, and Noble accepted. Milo also came along, and the old gang was together again, a unified front against the other Waspachick drunks who invaded the meetings only to hook up with men and women and vanish upon getting laid. Noble decided he resented everyone, himself and the world, and if his arrogance didn't change, he would be gulping down a beer and a shot at Greely's tavern where his father must have died.

They rode in Ivan's car, the classical music on full blast. It must have been Mozart, but Noble had no idea. They sat at the diner, and they both suspected something was really wrong with him. Noble denied the charges and sipped on his coffee and smoked every five minutes, his body warm and his mind still burning. The sooner he forgot about Alexandra the better. According to Ivan and Milo, word had surfaced that they were seeing each other, which Noble denied. He didn't want to talk about it, only wished that he could fly away and never return. Milo said:

"Y'know, Noble, no one's keeping you here. It's not like anyone's chaining you to your seat. You've got to focus on the positive."

"Yeah," said Ivan, enlightened by Milo's words. "You're doing so well. We don't want to see you leave. You've been around long enough to know that if you go out, you'll have a belly full of booze and a mind full of AA. That's hell right there."

It's as though Noble didn't have a choice any longer, that the program prevented him from taking the first drink. He had heard so many terrible stories, such that drinking was impossible. "Drinking is not an option for me," said Ivan, "and it's good to have you back. You've been isolating, and you're attitude is shitty." Tell him something he didn't know.

For the remainder of the afternoon, Noble worked on a couple more songs which added to his repertoire. Most of his instrumentals were fraught with suffering, with the exception of the earlier two which were uplifting and positive, the same two songs inspired by Alexandra. Nevertheless, the tunes he composed during this session were angry and rebellious, each chord loud and relentless, each strum harried and ugly. His mind burned so badly that he needed his old lover back, not Alexandra, but the whiskey. It had carried him through difficult times, and the more his frustration burned a hole in his brain, the more he longed for the dark amber, warm and strong, gushing through his system. Caffeine and nicotine were never good substitutes. Either was composing very angry melodies. Even the guitar was no longer a release. One may argue it never was. But Noble wasn't about to give up believing that his ship would come in, the large record deal handed over by a man in a metallic tie. But he could not count on these things anymore. Something needed to happen which was not happening already. In one lousy night he had returned to the same person he was with the whiskey, only worse. He was unhappy and a dry drunk.

He didn't want to see Shylock either. He missed the way things used to be, not that their relationship changed much. Noble was still a free-loader. Shylock was still a charitable donor. But there was a time when the two of them couldn't live without each other. He guessed he branched out. But he wasn't about to confess that his encounter with Alexandra turned out to be an abominable failure. He already knew what Shylock would say about it. 'Be a man,' he would say. 'Stop being so sensitive. There are plenty of women looking for a good lay. Men move on. They don't fall in love. The women fall in love, while the man cheats on her.'

After the brief diner visit, he slept in the back seat and opened the window a crack to aerate the fetid interior. He listened to the radio, every song a sad reminder of the two days of bliss he had lost. As Ivan mentioned, a drink was not an option. 'If you want a drink, have it tomorrow.'

He did wake up in time for the evening meeting. He was sweating, and he wiped his brow with a bath towel still damp from a ground-breaking shower a couple of days ago. He walked down the strip, passed the town park and the town bum who sat on a bench and smoked. The disability crew was also about. Noble wondered how long it would take before he too inherited their lowly positions. Escape was impossible. They knew him well. At least they knew he had been living out of his car.

The evening was warm and humid. Kids from the high school bottlenecked the ice cream shop. He yearned for a simpler time, when the evenings rolled along uninterruptedly, but after a careful reflection, his evenings never really rolled smoothly anyway.

He sat upon the church steps with a dozen or so alcoholics. He didn't want to know their names. He was content with having to look at them night after night and not utter a word. He wasn't sure if Harry would attend, but by the time the meeting began, the dark, candle-lit congregation room filled to capacity. He guessed these other drunks needed a drink as well. He sat away from the in-crowd, their faces shiny like ripened apples. It made him sick to see Smilin' Willy conversing with Missy, whom he had learned through Ivan, had problems with bulimia. Willy was supposed to be on a business trip. His mind wandered to the anorexic in detox and how crazy she was. Harry's rule rang true, that everyone in the rooms was certifiably insane, including him. But as this thought draped a negative pall over the meeting, he was grateful and confused when Alexandra tiptoed in during the reading of the preamble.

Her skin had paled considerably. Dark rings encircled her eyes. She kissed Smilin' Will, Missy, and Meredith before taking her seat with the in-crowd. Although she didn't look in the greatest shape, she was still beautiful. Her hair was disheveled, and she wore little makeup. She was as white as a bloodless corpse, but even her troubling features sustained her beauty. She smiled, as though nothing had happened the night before. She too acted the part of the debutante at a single's ball. In keeping with the latest fashion, she was strung out while still attractive. Only certain women could pull this off, but in the same vein, only certain men like Noble could find her this stunning at her worst. Nevertheless, she took a seat, and the meeting commenced.

Soon Alexandra shared, and her sobbing tale of last night's events gave Noble a sadistic pleasure and satisfaction. She cried through most of her story, that she had snorted cocaine and drank nearly a gallon of wine before passing out at a friend's apartment in SoHo. She also apologized to Noble indirectly, that she should have listened to his advice. While she shared, she was comforted by Smilin' Will who rubbed her thighs and Meredith who messaged her back. She didn't look at Noble at all.

Although Noble felt at ease, her crying did make his heart sink, not in pity, but in genuine grief for her pain. Alcoholism and drug addiction, he considered, are much more serious than the social aspects of the program, although the young people don't realize it. When a beautiful and wealthy young woman balls her eyes out, there is a certain satisfaction, not necessarily due to vindictiveness or class bias, but an understanding that she is no different than any alcoholic or drug addict. She too has a heartbeat, and maybe she hasn't worked a single day in her whole life, but she still cries and feels pain. Bars of gold are really no different than bars of iron. When a beautiful and wealthy Waspachick woman falls, certainly there's a delight, but when a fellow alcoholic slips, there is a part which needs to comfort her. Perhaps Smilin' Willy wasn't such a womanizer, and Noble reconsidered his initial resentment towards him. If Alexandra sat next to him, he too would do the same.

She cried through the duration of the meeting, and Noble still loved her. He wasn't sure whether or not to approach her. Maybe she needed her friends, and Noble was uncertain whether or not she wanted him in that respect.

Once they were all outside, however, Alexandra approached him. She didn't say anything, only stood there in the lingering sunset, and she again cried and fell into his arms.

"I'm sorry, Noble, I'm so sorry," between sobs, "I didn't mean it. I didn't, I didn't..."

"There, there," as Noble hugged her and stroked her hair. "Please don't cry. Please, it's okay. Everything's going to be all right, don't you worry..."

He held her for a long time, such that her tears soaked through his collar. He didn't expect this and felt ashamed for his delight earlier. She was a dove with a broken wing, just a little nervous, and he kissed her cheek and hugged her some more. He didn't realize how pig-headed he was, how selfish he had been, as though there were layers to his selfishness he had yet to peel.

"I should have stayed with you, Alexandra," he said, "I should have never let you stay in that place. I should have pulled you out of there. That's no place for an alcoholic to be in. I should have seen the signs..."

"No, don't say that," she sniffled, "don't blame yourself. You did the best you could."

She asked him to the East Waspachick diner, and Noble accepted. They were friends again, after a good long cry. They drove in her sports sedan. Noble pretty much blew off Ivan and Milo, as she blew off the in-crowd whom had plans to see a movie in the center of town. They sat at a table overlooking the parking lot. Alexandra cried intermittently as she told Noble exactly what occurred in the SoHo night club:

"I don't know what happened. I pretty much blacked out, or browned out, because I do remember some of it. I started drinking the red wine, and at first it was a thrill, it really was, and I drank until I was fully loaded and drunk, and it felt wonderful. But then, remember those bathroom stalls upstairs? Well, next thing I knew, all three of us were all laughing. They emptied the vial out onto a cosmetic mirror, and we snorted, each of us, these big fat lines, and we also had a threesome..."

"In the bathroom?" asked Noble, flabbergasted.

"Yeah, that's what we usually did, and I remember being in the bar, drinking more, and snorting more until all of it was blurry. We went to a night club down the street, and we did even more. We couldn't stop snorting, and we drank even more wine to the sound of a DJ playing hip-hop, and it was all fine until these guys tried to pick us up, and after that I don't remember much, only that we didn't go home with them. We went to my friend's apartment. She was having a party of her own, and I snorted more and drank more. The coke kept me up, but once it was all gone, I think I passed out at her place. I distinctly remember this guy unbuttoning my blouse and having to fight him off. I could have been raped last night, but I was cognizant enough to say 'no.' I woke up this morning on the floor, my face in the carpet, and thinking to myself: "What have I done, what have I done," and I admit that I've never felt so terrible in all my life. I knew from that point, I learned from that point, that I am definitely a drug-addict and an alcoholic, and that I need sober people in my life, there's no question. I just wish we never went into SoHo last night. Say something, Noble."

"I don't know what to say."

"Noble, you must tell me what you think of me. Isn't it just awful?"

Noble rubbed his eyes and sat speechless for a minute or two.

"A threesome?" he asked finally.

"Is that all you can think about?"

"It's not that, it's just, well, Alexandra this is your life we're talking about. This is life and death, and it's obvious you're not taking this seriously. What were you thinking? Or better yet, what the hell was I thinking? I should have pulled you out, but I didn't know you well enough, and when I got to a meeting this morning, I thought I'd never see you again, really, I thought you'd never make it back, and I was so down about it, all day, I was in a real shitty mood, because I couldn't stop you, and I should have stopped you..."

"Noble, there's absolutely no reason why you should blame yourself. The fault was all mine," as she reached over and caressed his hand. "You shouldn't blame yourself for my actions."

"I'm sorry, I'm sorry I didn't discourage you from going into the city. It's a trap."

He wasn't sure whether his own words were scripted or genuine, but her milky hands, wholesome and supple, charged him, and he was egged on.

"No, no, you mustn't blame yourself. It wasn't your fault," she said.

"I just wish you'd take the program more seriously, and attend meetings, and do the things the program suggests. What I think of you doesn't amount to a hill of beans. It's what you think of yourself. Is that what you want out of life? Snorting coke in the bathroom and then having a threesome with two women you hardly even know? I mean, you have to stop doing these things, if you wanna live. I'm just sorry I wasn't there to stop you."

"There was nothing you could have done."

The caressing of his hand alerted him to things unappealing about her, because he knew he had captured her. Call it a Flaw Detection Device canvassing her features. There had to be something wrong with her. Perhaps her breasts weren't as large as he preferred, or the fuzz on her upper lip was too bushy, or maybe she was putting on weight, or her paleness without makeup, or anything to preempt his moving deeper into her. He had never seen a Waspachick North-ender up close, and he tried unsuccessfully to find a flaw. He instead drowned within her soft, blue-green eyes. That's not to say she was flawless, but to Noble's gaze she exhibited a flawlessness beyond his reach, and knew that her overtures were a little too good to be true.

"I've learned my lesson," she said. "I'm an alcoholic and an addict. I know that now."

"Go to meetings. Ninety meetings in ninety days. And if at the end of it, you don't think the program is right for you, then go back out there, and it'll refund your misery."

Harry mentioned this constantly, and he hoped he got it right, the way he would say it.

"You always have the right things to say. That must be the Bulldog in you," she smiled.

He didn't catch the metaphor.

"I guess so," he laughed, not sure why he was laughing.

"So, what's there to do tonight?" after sitting in silence. How quickly she became her old self.

"I don't know," said Noble. "There's the movies, I guess, or there's the coffee shop on Waspachick Avenue. Or there's the bowling alley. Hey, have you ever been bowling before? Let's do something fun. Sober fun. We have the right to have some fun, don't we?"

"If you're from New Jersey, you've definitely gone bowling," she said. "How about it?"

They rode further east to a town which straddled the New York/New Jersey state line. They listened to Noble's favorite station which played tunes he grew up with, strong bluesy rock. Alexandra was excited enough, and they pulled into a crowded parking lot brewing with teens and local college students. The bowling alley itself thumped with popular music and kaleidoscopic lights, a disco ball which speckled the ceiling in a pointillistic decadence, even the occasional strobe which made the bowling ball leap from one end of the alley to the other before colliding with the pins. Each time she knocked a few down, she danced in glee and laughed like she were a little girl on her first outing. Noble was generally phlegmatic, since the volume of the music precluded any conversation, but Alexandra beat him two games out of three.

He was interested in her enjoyment, not in the bowling itself. He fell for her all over again, and he did his best to conceal it. He was only a friend, and that's how he would play it until she initiated something beyond it. From the looks of things, he was doing well and smiled so much, his face twitched on occasion. It was too dark to notice. They bowled into the late hours, and for once in a long while, Noble was happy, but as is the case with him, he suffered from uplift anxiety. He was so happy he found it too strange. Even the popular music was appealing, and its meaninglessness made sense, no small feat for a man who at one time hated the stuff. He discovered that popular music was meant for young couples in love, and perhaps there was a time and place for it. He was totally enraptured by her energy, if only she knew the truth about him, that at heart he was a liar like all the men she had kissed, and no longer did a mystique surround the Waspachick woman. Alexandra was her epitome, and to think of all the years he wasted criticizing her kind and running away from her kind, instead of being himself, only that he wasn't himself. He was an investment banker and entrepreneur educated at Yale with a mansion in the Heights, and he badly wanted to admit his deceit. But why ruin her fun? The night before proved so miserable for her, that fun was the only alternative.

He remembered the apparitions, and he foresaw the scene unfolding, but it was his turn to bowl. A gutter ball, to which she pouted and then messed up his hair. He could have bowled for forty days and forty nights. He didn't know how to lead, only to follow and bow obsequiously, and especially run away, far away to the California shore, but suddenly she appeared, and there was no longer a reason to run, or to look at things from a bird's eye view and combat the brutality of innocence robbed and youth plundered, but there existed some meaning to this grand puzzle, and she was it. He could not deny that her presence changed him from the beast he was becoming to the man he was about to become, but he again played it cool and assumed nothing.

"Ahh, I haven't had that much fun in the longest time," she said on the way home. "I took you three out of four."

"Beginner's luck," countered Noble. "I thought I'd go easy on you."

"Please. I beat you fair and square. I should have an infomercial my bowling's so good. 'How to beat Noble three games out of four.' I'd make tons of money. Hey, how about this idea," she laughed, "why don't you come to my place for a cup of coffee? I can make good cappuccino."

"But you're boyfriend? Won't he be there?"

"Nope. He's away. Won't be back until tomorrow. We could go to your place of you want."

"My place is under renovation, and besides, I wouldn't mind seeing where you live."

"Good, then it's settled."

Nevermind they had had at least five cups of coffee from the meeting and the diner combined. What's another cup?

They sped through Central Waspachick and up the dormant strip. Noble spotted his car along the park and was thankful to be away from it. He was a bit nervous as they ascended the winding road for a good five miles into the mythical section known to all as the Heights. He had no idea where she was going, but when old stone walls girdled the road and the occasional gateway led to other roads, he knew he had reached the forbidden place. Cool and Calm. Breathe in, breathe out, and don't crack. The Heights was his home, and he too owned a good deal of property. They pulled into a gravel road which ascended still for a couple of miles. Alexandra flicked on the high-beams, and soon the trees fanned out to an open field mowed properly and protected by wooden fences. Up ahead stood a Dutch manor home with floodlights accenting its stucco nutmeg walls. He had never seen a house so large, only on television, and at the sight he froze, unsure how to react. The Aryan race did win the war after all. But he tossed this cynicism aside and blended into his role.

She parked in a five-bay garage. Another car sat in the darkness, a sport utility vehicle no less. The boyfriend, he assumed, was away on business. Noble too should have been away on business. He never knew these properties were so far apart. She had mentioned they were neighbors. He assumed a South-end block, or basically a city block, but the spaces between these residences were miles apart.

"Well, here we are," she sighed while turning off the engine. "C'mon up."

He followed her through a side door and climbed a small staircase. They entered a space larger than the congregation hall of the church; thick, plush carpeting, a hand-woven Pakistani rug, leather furniture, paintings on the wall, wide windows, high ceilings, and yet another floor above them with the same square footage. He had no idea people lived like this. The mythical Heights hid palaces of this sort, and one would never know it from down below. A grandfather clock, glass end-tables, and even more daunting, a baby grand piano. How old was her boyfriend again? He dare not ask.

She made cappuccino in the kitchen area. He could hear the frothing machine, and he sat in a leather couch which swallowed him in comfort. The copper pot hanging from the utensil rack exceeded Shylock's monthly allowance and even the blue book value of his car. Cool and calm. Breathe-in, breathe out. He boarded in properties like this all over the world, and by the time she sat next to him with the cappuccino, he was so relaxed that he nearly forgot about the coffee.

"I must say, this place is beautiful. I really like what you've done with it," said Noble.

"It's nothing compared to Victoria Terrace."

"Well, every home has its charm. When did you move in with him?"

"We've been going together for a year or so, and once my parents got sick of me, I went to SoHo, and I met Michael at an exhibition, and we connected, so I moved out, drunk and high, and here I am."

"You're ready to qualify," he chuckled. "He deals in art?"

"He's a collector. What do you think?" as she pointed to the paintings.

"Very nice, although I'm all thumbs with art."

"This I already know," she smiled, "but don't worry. I like you for the clothes you wear."

Noble had worn his Oldsmobile clothes and had forgotten to change into Shylock's stylish attire. Shit.

"See, that's what I like about you," she continued, "you're so diverse, even eccentric," (or mentally ill depending upon one's position on the ladder). "I mean you're full of contradictions. You're really down to earth, and yet you're cultured and mature. You're not like the other men I meet, all of Michael's friends. No one would ever know you lived on Victoria Terrace. It's like you identify with the poor. You must have strong values."

"I guess so. Yale didn't change me much. I'm a down-to-earth kind of guy."

She laughed: "See, you did it again."

"What?"

"Oh you're charming all right. I bet you have tons of girlfriends, oh I know. A man like you doesn't stay single for long."

"But I am single. Honest."

She moved closer to him, the cappuccino untouched, her arm sliding behind him.

"This place is very spacious," said Noble, trying to change the subject.

"I'm sure you've had your share of girlfriends."

"There were a few, but I haven't found the right one yet."

He was so close he could taste her lips pressed upon his, but remembered she was still active, and to kiss her now would be taking advantage of her at a vulnerable point. She must make the first move. He could have been in kindergarten where his artlessness with the opposite sex first began. He could have easily kissed her, but waited for a sign.

"Well, I'm sure you'll find the right one," and she moved in even closer.

"It's getting late," he said nervously "Maybe I should go home."

"You can sleep here. We have a guest room upstairs."

"Alexandra, I don't know. Won't you're boyfriend be home soon?"

"He's not coming home until tomorrow afternoon."

"Alexandra, what are we doing here?"

"We're talking, that's all," she smiled. "Tell me about your guitar. How's that coming along?" as she placed her hand on his thigh.

"I've written close to ten songs, and pretty soon, I'll have enough for an album. I've got to get a recording studio, cut a demo tape, maybe play a gig or two. A friend of mine works at the coffee shop, and I'm gonna ask if I can perform there."

"I'll hold you to it, and I'll be there. You can count on it."

It was too late to walk back. The cops would have pegged him as a burglar fleeing a botched job. He decided on sleep.

Alexandra showed him to a large guestroom upstairs. She kissed him goodnight, a peck on the cheek. He undressed and slid under the cool, pima cotton sheets. He hadn't slept in a comfortable bed since his late father threw him out, and the bed was unparalleled to any bed he had ever slept in. He immediately fell asleep but was woken up later in the night. Alexandra called him from the doorway. No, this was not a dream or one of his fantasies. Her silhouette stood in the light glowing from behind her.

"I can't sleep," she said, and she crawled in beside him.

"It's okay," said Noble, too exhausted and comfortable to think straight.

She cuddled close and kissed him. Noble didn't think of the consequences of their lips connecting. Making love to her was the closest he'd ever come to ecstasy, and the gruesome quality of the guitarist's nights, alone and afraid in his isolation, led to an inspirational energy to which only those who have been with a beautiful woman can attest. Their sex was by no means perfect, but they were so good together that Noble finally felt his love towards her, rather than the over-thinking and over-analyzing which comes with obsession. She gave him a door, and he pried it loose to find a meaning he could never intellectualize, a link to a garden where they played and danced among blooming flowers, the trickle of water from the nearby creek flowing into the infinite, her body pressed to him over the plush lawn, her hair falling around him.

The mind doesn't make the man. The mind has its limitations. It's more the case that a woman makes the man. All of those nights of intense isolation and dutiful practice, for what? He found what he was searching for within her, and in the same vein, she discovered the shy, innocent, misdirected boy and catalyzed him into a man complete and knowing, confident and secure. A guitarist alone can do nothing, his fingers paralyzed. He may toil, blister, and complain, but alone he can never find the essential meaning which becomes the foundation of his quest. And in those dark nights, alone, he pushes strangers away, only to long for one who may understand him. His ears are deaf to the euphony of a woman's call. He refuses to listen. He only plucks and strums within the cocoon of his inexperience, and so the music he makes fails. He hears only his own voice as though it were the only sound worth listening to, and he gets lost within his own thoughts, the typical madness which isolation and obduracy bring. Only a woman can cure this madness, not that he would practice any less diligently, but the woman adds to the tone of his productions and aids in the stable mentality making the chords ring true. He cannot shut himself to the society of which he is a part. He cannot disassociate himself from that single strain of euphony and harmony gasping and moaning from within her. He meets and engages the voice with his deft fingers in the hopes that music can be made, and more often than not, the collaboration exudes an eternity no man or Higher Power may tarnish through the blows and abuses of time. They are young and venerable simultaneously, and their love translates into elegant symphonies which strike the universal heart. Yes, their love-making was that good, and they made this music deep into the night, until the rosy-fingered dawn.

They collapsed into each other's arms glistening with sweat. Noble couldn't think as he used to. Yes, he would even find employment to support them both. Yes, he would carry her away, and they could explore the regions of each other. It would take the rest of his life, but this was the woman he could never lose to another man. He must persist. And what of the act, the role of multimillionaire businessman? He could never let her know until she fell for him completely. Noble had already fallen. For Alexandra, it would take some time.

"How did it feel?" she whispered.

"I've never felt like that before."

"Like what?" as she stroked his hair.

"A man, Alexandra. You've made a man out of me, and this isn't my first time. Alexandra, I hate to say this, but I have to. I think I'm falling for you. I think about you all the time, and when you're not around I'm terribly

sad, and when I'm with you I'm so happy, very happy, and sometimes I think
I don't deserve to be so happy."

"Why don't you deserve to be happy?"

"I don't know, but I don't deserve a woman like you. I know that.
You're so beautiful, and you're so smart, and maybe we better stop seeing
each other for a while."

"You deserve to be loved by me."

"Do you?" asked Noble.

"Do I what?" she asked.

"Y'know."

"No I don't."

"You don't," he acquiesced. "Well then I guess I'd better be going."

"Wait. I'm missing something here."

"You said you don't love me."

"No, Noble, I didn't know what you were talking about."

"Do you? Love me? And if you don't, it's no big deal. I'm sure you've
slept with others, and I guess this is just a fling, and I guess…"

"Shhh," as she put a finger on his lips, "you think too much. You
shouldn't think so much."

Having her in his arms was enough of an answer for now, and he slept
for a few hours.

In the late morning he dressed and told Alexandra he was going home
to check up on the renovations. He walked to Shylock's coffee shop and told
his friend about the events.

"Allrrright Noble!" yelled Shylock patting him on the arm. "You did it.
You did it, man. Congratulations. And with a woman from the Heights? Rarer
still to sleep with her. You're a fuckin' champion."

The bright sunshine filtered through the dust of the coffee house. A soft
jazz piano played in the small room. A customer sat deep into the interior,
reading a newspaper.

"Shy, I hate to say this, but I'm in love with her."

"You're what?" asked Shylock sharply.

"I'm in love with her."

Shylock withdrew from his tasks at the espresso machine, and they sat
at their usual table overlooking the calm strip.

"Have you lost your fucking mind? Have you been drinking again?" as
Shylock peered into his eyes for signs of inebriation.

"No, Shy, I'm not drunk or high, but I think I'm in love with her."

"Jesus, Noble."

"What the hell was I supposed to do? You think I wanted this? I never asked for it, really I didn't. It's out of control, this whole thing is out of control."

"Well, what the hell did you expect? You wanted this to happen. You wanted a woman. Now you're in love with her? Bullshit. Don't sit there and tell me you didn't want this. You wished for it, and now you've got it."

"Let's not live in the past, Shy. What the hell do I do now?"

"It's easy. You dump her. You've had your fill. It's time to cut her loose and continue with your life."

"I can't do that," shook Noble, "I can't dump someone I love."

"Remember what I said? A man, Noble. A man. Men don't fall for women, especially on the first lay. You've got to cut it off, or else you'll wind up in a worse situation. A lie can't last forever. She's gonna find out."

"There must be a way."

"When you become a billionaire, you mean?"

"Work with me, Shy. You don't have to criticize me."

"I'm sorry," he sighed.

"I can't dump her. I would feel so terrible."

"Lemme tell you this, Noble, and this is my opinion. If you're not going to dump her, you have to tell her the truth. Face it, man- you're broke and homeless, and you grew up on the South end. You live in your car for Chrissakes. It's not natural that you're going out with a woman from the North end, not even a North-ender, but a woman from the Heights, which is like the North end of the North end, am I right?"

"What are you getting at?"

"This will never work. You and she, together, will never work. That's your future, and once you realize that, then you can take steps to get laid and not have such a huge emotional attachment afterwards. I'm telling you this for your own good. It's not natural. It's like a black man falling for a white woman and getting laid in the Jim Crow South. It's not going to happen. Blacks go with blacks, whites go with whites, poor goes with poor, and rich goes with rich. A South-ender with a North-ender will never work, and was never meant to work."

"I can make it work," said Noble excitedly.

"How?" asked Shylock incredulousy.

"I can say that I'm leaving all my riches for a life with the guitar."

"She won't believe you'll give away your fortune. No one does that. Either you tell her the truth or cut her loose. It's the only way."

"I can't. I can't do it. I'll have to lie until she falls in love with me. That's the only way. And because of it, I need your help."

"Why do you always involve me, man?"

"I need clothes. Nice clothes, and you're my assistant if she calls."

"How long do I have to put up with this?"

"And also Shy, can you get me a gig here, playing?"

"You mean with your guitar?"

"Yes," announced Noble with an upsurge of optimism. "It's time for Noble McCloud to spread his wings. I've worked long and hard, and it's important to give myself back to my listening public. This is my time. My ship has come in, Shy. Finally, I'm goin' places. I'm in love with the woman of my dreams, and she, I'm sure, will see me the same way, but she must hear me play. That's when she'll be hooked. Things are happening. I've taken the risks, and they're paying off. And you're coming with me for the ride."

Noble reached over the table and hugged him.

"Wonderful," muttered Shylock.

The one customer looked from behind his paper, shook his head, and continued reading.

Chapter Five

The Waspachick strip in the summertime throbbed with students and visitors from surrounding townships who came mostly to dine in the restaurants, which were established only a few years ago. Noble recalled a simpler time, when the strip was sparsely dotted with a gas station and hardware store. In two decades, the strip had become a popular spot for both yuppies working in nearby Manhattan and also the kids in sagging denim who peopled the town park. Automobiles clad with mirrored chrome hubcaps, radios blaring, cruised the strip with the more conservative SUV's. These cars cruised for women, while the SUV's crawled close to the shops and hunted for the latest lawn ornament. Noble's car was stationed in the same spot for months without so much as a ticket or a break-in or a theft. When he heard from Shylock the town council voted to put up parking meters along the park, Noble displayed not the slightest disdain. He was so content with the way things were going, with Alexandra and his guitar, that Waspachick during the height of summer seemed magical. Alexandra soothed his escapist tendencies.

He would have rather remained in Waspachick than bolt to the shores of California. They hung out together constantly, and stayed sober together.

They met at every meeting, and when her boyfriend left for overnights in the big city, he stayed with her in the Dutch manor home. His lies, however, were wearing thin, as Alexandra wondered daily where he worked and why his BMW was still in the shop, and why she couldn't at least see his property on Victoria Terrace.

To the first curiosity, he said he took a break from investment banking to pursue what he truly loved: his guitar. She accepted this. The BMW in the shop warranted a bigger fib. It turned out that Noble had asked the mechanic to sell it for him, and the proceeds of the sale would go towards a Range Rover, or a Lexus, or a car which definitely kept pace with the Waspachick standard. Selling the car would take time, which brought him a step closer to settling Alexandra's curiosity.

The biggest and most daring fabrication involved his Victoria Terrace property. In conversations with her, he stalled and stalled again, changed subjects countless times, and hinted that he no longer wanted to stay there. He would sell the property, put the proceeds of the sale into a bloated trust fund which would dole out thousands of dollars a year towards the non-profits helping the sick and the poor. He shifted focus from his fictitious wealth, education, and status onto the wild dream of playing his guitar without the burden of wealth, almost like voluntary poverty but with a guitar. Alexandra should have investigated these claims, but due to her youth and emotional dependency upon the older Noble, she bit her lip and thought nothing wrong with his master plan. She understood artists, and Noble fed into this understanding. She believed her initial assessment: that Noble was an eccentric and wealthy Waspachick villager, the costumes courtesy of Shylock, the money to dine her once in a while also courtesy of Shylock. Shylock's friendship, by the way, wore thin during this week or two of extravagant spending, but he had never seen Noble so happy and content. Noble even introduced him to Alexandra, of whom Shylock remarked: "She's a knockout."

Keeping a woman of this caliber was not easy, but Alexandra did fall in love with him. She was a bit miffed how Noble never played his instrumentals for her, but again Noble stalled and beseeched her to wait until the coffee house performance. Noble's happiness ought to contrast sharply with his original view of the working world as insectaries, or of all Waspachick villagers as condescending, pretentious snobs. He was now a part of them. He was influenced by Alexandra's values. The Dutch manor home also shifted his general outlook of the town he desperately wanted to leave a few months ago.

He got carried away with the act on many occasions. Alexandra mentioned in passing that she attended Saint Paul's school for secondary education. Noble said he went to Saint Bartholomew's, a well-known church in East Waspachick. When asked about his childhood, Noble said he grew up in bucolic Vermont, but when Alexandra insisted on a weekend trip there to visit his family "of good stock," Noble said they had since moved to New Hampshire. Why couldn't they visit New Hampshire? "My family moves around a lot," replied Noble.

After a week or so, Alexandra told him frankly that she felt "shut out" of his life, that he was not up-front and too elusive in all his affairs, and there were some trust issues involved. Noble calmed her with the scheduled coffee house performance, as though after the event, everything would be made known, as though beyond it glowed a mutual nirvana of letting her into his life.

There were only two people in Waspachick who knew of Noble's deception: Harry, his sponsor, and Shylock, his best friend. Ivan and Milo grew suspicious, but they were kept in the dark. Noble avoided them as the rumor mill within the program spun and spun on its own indefatigable energy.

But the tougher issue concerned the joy and ecstasy Noble felt when he saw, visited, and made love to Alexandra. He had never felt so complete before, as though a large chunk of himself fell into place. Up in the Heights, they took long walks on her boyfriend's property, and they made love in the grass, the summer sun hovering over them. They had long discussions about their future together. Alexandra assured him she'd leave her boyfriend after the coffee house performance, at which time Noble would get honest. His plan, thus far, was working. She had confessed her love, and she sunk her hooks deeper into him, to the point where they couldn't fathom being apart. This may seem farfetched for such a short time period, but their innocence and naiveté in the matters of love hurled them into a righteous codependency. Alexandra loved easily, and Noble was inexperienced with relationships. A good pair. He yearned to be truthful, but he had grown so accustomed to lying, that he sacrificed his conscience to be with her. He could feed her his half-baked lies and still live with himself. He had captured the quintessential Waspachick woman, after all, and he wasn't about to let her go. This added to his scheming, which he always coordinated with Shylock, who reluctantly spent money on them. Noble preached to her the ideal of the simple life unencumbered by wealth. She had her doubts, but when she realized at a meeting one night that sobriety was the divine gift they shared in common, sobriety then became a cementing bond and the impetus for deeper confessions of their mutual love, despite his preaching on the simple life.

But it's not the case that Noble spent all of his time with Alexandra. He would say he had some business to attend to and retreat to the Oldsmobile, and on nights her boyfriend returned, he stayed in the car and practiced until his finger joints ached. He completed his coda and then rehearsed each instrumental to perfection, adding an accent here, a trill there, an allegro burst of tremolo picking to finish a particular piece. He was no longer driven by the same fantasies of escape and flight to the cheering amphitheater, and this diminished his drive, quelled his ambition to some degree, as bliss without an artists anger or internal conflict is a curse, or so he believed. He tried familiarizing himself with the earlier rage and frustration before Alexandra dropped into his life, the period of meaninglessness, and luckily he had committed these notes to paper. Otherwise he would have never recreated the vitriol of that dark period. In fact, the former work struck him as maudlin. Those days were far removed from the confidence and completeness with which Alexandra filled him. Yet, he knew he must play these dark instrumentals and include them in the performance.

He decided on set lists and rehearsed at all hours of the night. During these sessions he missed her and longed for her company. Relationships, as well as early recovery, also have 'pink cloud' periods wherein romantic explorations are new and exciting. It was in this period that Noble's coffee house performance was scheduled. He wasn't so jealous of the boyfriend up in the Heights due to Alexandra's refusal to sleep with him. She made this clear many times, and Noble prodded her on the subject until she proved her devotion. Naturally her devotion was at its early stage, and perhaps she had some manipulating to do herself. One can safely say, however, that Noble deceived her much like the method actor deceives his audience. He acted exceptionally.

Harry, on the other hand, was so upset with Noble that he, at one breakfast, yelled at him thoroughly. He did not necessarily care about the relationship, only that it would at some later time affect his sobriety. It took the focus off himself. At several meetings Harry wore cotton, and mystical telepathy took place. Noble was still uncertain about this telepathy business but really didn't care. He had what he always wanted, and slowly but surely, his sobriety ranked below Alexandra and the guitar on his list of priorities, and this is what troubled Harry. To his sponsor's ferocity, Noble replied in his usual manner: "Harry, I think you're overreacting."

Nevertheless, Noble was in love, and like the sweet chord which elevates expectations to untold heights never before reached but instead visualized in the mind's eye, those many acres of lush lawns and wildflowers swaying in the mid-afternoon breeze, making love to a woman of exceptional beauty and culture, so his dream manifested itself into a reality greater than his prior visualizations. To touch her strawberry lips struck sensuous notes he never before heard, those moans and gasps as he entered her, to the intimacy of lying in the grass and talking of a future open wide and ready to embrace them. He could have held her until the world ended, until the breeze which cooled their hot skin ceased to whisper. He never understood how reality could far exceed his most daring fantasies. He hated leaving her after making love, but he returned to the Oldsmobile and practiced ruthlessly.

For three weeks at summer's peak, Noble continued in this manner. He had never before known of a happiness this great. He concluded it was the blessing of sobriety, the reward from a past rooted in anguish and cruelty. He would never again doubt or underestimate the value of his existence. He would never allow the cynicism and the reproach for the idyllic town pollute the rhapsody of its shops, its housewives, its women, its haughty attitudes, and strange charm. It boiled down to this one gig at Shylock's coffee shop. And he was prepared. He invited Harry, Ivan and Milo, Shylock, and of course, Alexandra.

Chapter Six

The night before the performance, Noble and Alexandra held each other in her boyfriend's bed. They had just finished a round of love-making which lasted into the early hours of the morning. The stillness of the early hours permitted the soft shrill of crickets beyond the bay windows, which gave a sleepy, moonlit view of the oaks girdling the Dutch manor home, her skin as soft as Turkish silk, her blue-green eyes asking him questions without uttering a word. They held each other in the stillness, and Noble could have died under her body, and his existence would have made sense. It would have had a value beyond his rudimentary understanding. He was once a man of impressions, but as a result of the woman in his arms, he recorded every detail of her breathing, the way her body rose and fell atop his, her blonde hair tickling his chest, her lips tucked into his neck, her wide, smooth back rising and falling, rising and falling...

"I'm not tired," he whispered.

"Me'neither," she said. "Are you nervous about tomorrow?"

"I never knew it would come to this. It's funny when a person's dream comes true. It feels so weird. I can't believe it's real."

She kissed him and said: "Does that convince you?"

"I don't know if I deserve to be so lucky," he continued. "I've been so selfish, Alexandra. So very selfish. I used to hate the world so much that I wanted nothing to do with it, and my mother and my father fought a lot in our Vermont home. I hated them for that, and I hated this town, I hated everything. These past few weeks, I'm learning how to love, and it's different, and Alexandra, I do love you. Really. I love you."

"You think too much," she said while kissing his neck. "Did anyone ever tell you you think too much?"

"There are many who are unhappy, the whole of their lives they scratch for a decent home and their families, and they pray, and it never happens for them, and I've always identified with them, the ones who never amount to anything."

"It doesn't make sense, Noble. You've accomplished great things. You're highly intelligent, you're successful and artistic, and a phenomenal lover, and you have me, Noble. I don't see why you shoulder this incredible guilt. It's like the whole world's on top of you. You feel guilty for being successful. I can't understand it."

"Would you still love me, if I gave it all away. Just sold everything and traded my old life for a life of music?"

"I thought we already discussed this."

"I need to hear it again. Please."

"Yes, Noble. If you left your wealth for music, I'd still love you."

"Even if I were broke and out on the street? It's funny how no one loves the town bum, that old man who sits next to the pharmacy? What if I were him and you were you, and you walked by with your boyfriend? Or how about fifty years from now when I'm playing my guitar on the street corner, and I'm in rags, filthy rags, and my face was loaded with whiskers, and I played a tune no one liked, and then you walked by with your husband, fifty years later, would you still love a broken-down old man like me?"

She sat upright and turned on the table lamp.

"Why are you always testing me?" she sighed. "Why must I always jump through rings of fire or walk on hot coals? It's like you're testing me to see how much I care about you, and you ask me repeatedly, and each time the scenario gets worse and worse. Why do you insist on torturing me? I told you again and again, that I'm leaving my boyfriend. Why do you keep bugging me about it?"

"I'm doing it for a reason, Alexandra."

"Then tell me. You don't tell me anything. You're always so vague, and at first I thought it mysterious, almost exotic in a way, but ever since I fell for you, I feel like you're hiding things from me."

"Like what?"

"Like you're entire life, Noble. Why can't you let me in? Don't you trust me enough? And we go these meetings together, and your talk is evasive and lofty. You're never specific about where you're going, what you're doing, who you're seeing. I mean what am I supposed to think? Maybe you're seeing another woman, or maybe you're really married?"

"I swear to you, I'm not seeing another woman, and I'm certainly not married," as he put his head in her lap.

"Then why won't you answer my questions? You're almost like a politician in your answers."

"Trust me. Please, trust me."

"How can I?"

He kissed her thigh and moved up her stomach, then to her breasts, finally to her mouth. He reached over and turned off the lamp.

"If you weren't so good in bed, I'd definitely leave you," she whispered.

They fell into bed again and made love until daybreak. The glowing orb breaking through the foliage cast its orange light across their bed, and they were too exhausted for Noble's routine getaway into town. He said he met Harry in the mornings, all in accordance with precise planning. He would attend the morning and afternoon meetings, and finally adjourn to the coffee house and play his heart out. Because he had frolicked through the night, as continuous love-making tends to invert the sleep cycle, he was too tired to move and fell soundly asleep, until of course, he heard the downstairs door slam and heavy steps shuffling up the staircase. He shook her a second time and then a third time, but to no avail, and before the door opened, he rolled from the bed and pulled himself under it. He pulled his clothes underneath with him.

The box spring sagged from above as the boyfriend sat on the vacant side of the bed, his pant-legs visible.

"I'm losing you, Alexandra," said the muffled voice. "I know I've been away a lot, and we've had our problems, but I'm here to work them out. I don't want to lose you, honey," as he lay next to her, the box spring squeezing Noble's head.

"I think it's too late for that," she said drowsily.

"I know I've treated you badly, honey. I'm here to make things right between us. I've been a jerk, a really big jerk, and I've even stopped drinking. I swear, I won't touch another drop."

"It's not only your drinking," she said, "it's your lies, the many transparent lies you expect me to believe. I know you're seeing someone else. Don't insult me by sitting there with your dopey expression and denying it. I'm not an idiot. I know you're seeing another woman. The trips to the West Coast were never for business, were they?"

He paused for a minute before coming up with an answer. Under the bed, Noble also waited. After the performance he would tell her, after the applause and many compliments by those in the audience he would confess his deceit. He no longer wanted to lie. She had already fallen for him and would have to accept him.

"No, they weren't," said the boyfriend, "and I'm sorry, but you became so cold and distant. We stopped making love, and you went to those damned AA meetings which divided us even more, and I couldn't handle being so far removed from your life. We've worked hard to build this relationship, honey, and it's worth salvaging, if you want my opinion. I swear to you, I'll change, I won't drink anymore, and we won't involve my friends, in fact, we never have to see them again. I'll never go astray again. Please, Alexandra."

"It's too late," she said. "I'm sorry, Michael, it's too late. Our relationship ended a long time ago, and at one time I did love you, but not anymore, and it's not your fault. It's the way things worked out. You lied to me too many times, and I stood by you while you saw other women, but not anymore. It's over, and besides, I'm seeing someone else too."

"Do you love him?" he asked wearily.

"Yes, I love him, and we're moving in together. I'm sorry. Nothing you can say now will help us. It's over, and by this time tomorrow, I'll be living with him."

The boyfriend shifted positions, which squeezed Noble's head even more.

"How about one for old time's sake?" he asked.

"I'm sorry, Michael."

He got to his feet and said formally: "I'm conducting some business in town, and by the time I get back, I want you and your belongings out of here," and he slammed the door on his way out.

Alexandra breathed a sigh of relief, and Noble slid from underneath the bed, the sheet wrapped around his naked body.

"You're here?!" she exclaimed.

He jumped onto the bed and kissed her passionately.

"Then you heard what I said?" she asked.

"Every word, every last word, and I love you, Alexandra, I love you, and I always will."

"When can I move in then?"

"All in due time. Tonight after the gig we can live together."

And they made love a third time, after the boyfriend was out of the house.

Alexandra and Noble both attended the morning meeting at the church across from the supermarket. Harry was present. He wore a cotton khaki-suit which indicated the mystical thought-exchange. Noble couldn't stop his thoughts from springing to the forefront of his brain, as he exploded with thoughts of his 'love' for Alexandra, a term he had never thought possible, and with each snippet of mental dialogue, Harry overtly rubbed his nose, or grazed his cheek, his pale blue eyes fixed on him throughout the meeting. Harry was definitely angry with him. Noble hadn't called for several days, and Harry communicated his worry and anger.

'This is not fun and games,' thought Harry.

'Yes, I know, Harry, but please, I'm involved with the girl of my dreams,' thought Noble.

'And what happens when you tell her the truth? You're supposed to be doing the next right thing. Have you read any of the literature yet?'

'No. I haven't had the time.'

'Bullshit, Noble. You're headed for another relapse, you and she both.'

'No need to worry, my stringent, nicely-dressed sponsor. I no longer need to drink after tonight when I perform my collection for all my friends, you included.'

Across from him, Harry rolled his eyes, and the meeting for a few minutes continued without incident, until he heard from behind him the two apparitions, the idol strumming his guitar, and the auto mechanic polishing the carburetor.

"Is this the way you want it? After the gig, you'll let her know?" asked the idol.

"The sooner, the better, if you ask me," said the mechanic.

"No one's asking you," fired Noble angrily.

"My friend has a point," said the idol. "What makes you think she wouldn't accept you for who you are? You used to be a damn fine musician.

Now look at you. A liar and a cheat. It used to be that you were so dedicated to your music, and it seems you've left it for a woman."

"Is it gonna be your music? Or the woman?" asked the auto mechanic, finally finished with his carburetor and admiring his work.

"I can have both, can't I?" asked Noble.

"It doesn't work that way," said the idol. "Either you're a dedicated musician in love with your guitar, or you assimilate into the rest of society, find a job, get married, and reduce your overall musicianship to a hobby. Are you prepared to make music a hobby, Noble? Are you prepared to leave your guitar for her?"

"I never thought of it that way," said Noble after having pondered this carefully, "but if it came down to the choice of having her or becoming the musician I always wanted to be, why I'd choose my guitar just to play it for her. Is that so wrong of me? I love her, and I don't understand why I have to choose. I wish I could have both. I don't understand why I can't have both."

"That's all we needed to know," said the mechanic.

"Our work is done here," said the idol. "You're learning, Noble."

"Wait! Wait!"

And the two apparitions melted into the dim of the congregation hall, as Alexandra squeezed his hand under the table, and the meeting commenced like nothing happened.

He wasn't so worried about his choice. After all, the apparitions were only figments of his own imaginings, and hopefully he would avoid the sadness of making a choice. He thought he could have it all, although he did admit his guitar was further from his mind than before. His grand deception took center stage, and after the coffee house performance, he could settle down with his music and make love to Alexandra, whom he presumed would stay with him in the Oldsmobile, because she had nowhere to go. By the grip of her hand, he knew he had landed Alexandra, and the admission would make her angry and upset at first, but ultimately she would yield and accept his true identity.

At the meeting's end, Noble made sure Harry would attend the gig.

Harry said knowingly: "I hope you know what you're doing."

Ivan and Milo also said they would attend, and they wished him good luck.

"Break a leg," said Ivan.

Alexandra returned to the Heights. She had packing to do. Noble, for most of the afternoon, isolated in his Oldsmobile and rehearsed for several hours. He knew the tunes by heart and found that he could improvise a little, giving his music more fluency as opposed to the rigidity of articulating each note. The relationship with his guitar had changed. He no longer held its body like the lifesaver in a turgid ocean. This worried him, but overall it was a blessing. Many musicians die with their art. Alexandra, in essence, saved his life, as the guitar was always too fickle a companion. It could surprise him on occasion when a chord followed another just right, or when a flawless jam caught a resonant riff, much like a rope-tow which pulls the piece along to its bitter conclusion. But other than these intermittent, lackluster joys, most of his sessions were battles with misery, despair, frustration, and exhaustion, a deep exhaustion. In the Oldsmobile he rehearsed through the afternoon, missing the noontime meeting. A weighty exhaustion overtook him, and after a final rehearsal, he napped in the back seat with the guitar in his lap.

He awoke with a start. He checked the time on the radio. He had just a few moments to shower and dress himself nicely for the groundbreaking gig. He was nervously excited, a skip in his step, as he waved to Shylock in the window.

He approached the counter with a boyish grin, as though the world had declared him sovereign, and Shylock his humble counsel.

"Where the hell have you been?" asked Shylock. "I haven't seen you for days, man. You don't call, you don't stop by. What the hell has gotten into you?"

"Don't worry, my good friend. You're buddy has been just fine."

Shylock leaned over the counter and whispered: "How is she? It must be good, right?"

"Picture it as good, but astronomically better."

"Jeez, Noble. I'm impressed. Very impressed. You've been so upbeat lately. It's like a New Noble McCloud. You're confident and comfortable, like a man ought to be."

"Listen, Shy, I meant to tell you this earlier, but I've been saving it for the right moment, and it's as good a time as any to tell you how much you've meant to me these past few months. I mean, all of this, my love life, my guitar, my art, it's all because of you, man. You were there when I needed you. It's like your my brother, Shy, and tonight when I knock 'em dead, it's all because you've been my best friend. People don't have friends like you. I wanted you to know before I go on tonight."

Shylock looked to his hands for a moment and then said softly: "Thanks, Noble. I'm always behind you, no matter where you go or what you do." And after a few moments more: "Hey, enough of this luvvy-dovey shit. C'mon, get your ass to my place, take a shower, get your ass all dolled up for tonight. You're gonna rock 'em Noble McCloud. Let it ride. And by the way, my boss, the owner, will be here tonight. He thought music in the joint would draw a lot of customers, and he's thinking about featuring other musicians too. I really sold him on it. Believe me, by the time you perform, this uptight town will get a real shot in the arm."

"I have it all planned out and timed perfectly," said Noble. "Three sets: *Darkness*, *Light*, and *Alexandra* with breaks in-between. I'm ready to go, Shy. All my friends will be here, and you know what they say, 'a man can't be a failure if he has friends.' Oh, and one other thing, if Alexandra calls, tell her I go on at eight sharp. I'll get the amp from your place. See, Shy, it works, everything works. With a little faith and help, we get along. I'll be here by eight o'clock."

'Slow down,' he thought, as he hurried along the bustling strip. It was a Friday night, and he looked forward to a long, hot shower to calm his mood. He had loads of time, but hurried anyway, the excitement giving a nervous tingle to his fingers which he clenched into a fist. Breathe in, breathe out. Relax. Nothing but time to stand under the hot, prickly spray and mentally prepare for an astounding night. He had little reason to rush, but he hurried towards his preternatural success as the stars had preordained.

The gig was one performance out of many. This wasn't the end-all gig. After the first, the others to follow would become easier and less fraught with the nervous anxiety itching his fingers. And after he climbed the slope to Shylock's apartment, he was out of breath, an anxiety pounding on the inner walls of his skull. Maybe he had taken this too far, and he realized he may snap from exhaustion at any time. But he pushed. He climbed the small set of stairs and made it to the apartment.

He stood in a trance under the nozzle. He cleansed every part of his body. He chose a coal-black suit with a matching tie from Shylock's closet. The apartment was a subtle reminder of the whiskey. But that was his old life, and returning to his old life was not an option. Sobriety did allow its miracles, and he quickly dismissed the stinking-thinking. He checked himself in the mirror several times, and when his reflection exuded a polished perfection, he returned to town and collected his instrument which he wiped down with a damp towel. He tuned the instrument until each string warbled to his exact specifications. He even offered a small prayer, a thank-you note to the Higher Power whom he had previously misjudged and ridiculed. He was finally ready.

The coffee shop in the waning sunlight swarmed with customers. A sign had been posted in the front window advertising Noble's performance.

Many sat outside and enjoyed their caffeine on the benches which Shylock had arranged. Noble smiled to the onlookers. The far corner had been set up with a microphone and a small amplifier more powerful than Noble's ten-watt gizmo. He arrived fashionably late. His friend's all sat together at a table facing the strip, and he greeted them warmly. He hugged all of them, even the embittered Harry who chewed him out earlier, his cab-yellow polyester suit contributing to the carnival which Noble had hoped for. But more than any one person in the room, he was profoundly moved and uplifted by Alexandra's presence. She looked radiant, all decked-out in elegant black attire.

"Mr. McCloud, I'll have to fight off all these Waspachick women if you ever look this good again," as she straightened his tie and brushed his lapel. She kissed him and caressed his cheeks.

"You'll be fine, okay? Don't think so much."

Shylock introduced him to the crowd. Noble plugged in, checked the tuning, and finally was ready for his performance. Once again he was stricken with an anxiety not uncommon to an amateur's virgin performance, but with Alexandra smiling and encouraging him, with Shylock's boss giving him the go-ahead, he began his first set, and a dark ominous morbidity settled over the audience. Midway through his second instrumental, Shylock approached him unexpectedly. Noble cut the piece short and ended with a low, off-key bass chord.

"Hey, Noble, listen man, the boss says enough with the dark stuff. All the customers are leaving. Can you move ahead into the light stuff, just for a change of pace?"

His friends, even Ivan and Milo, nodded in agreement.

"Okay, Shy," he said, "I'll play the more popular tunes. My upbeat stuff."

"Yeah, and you're doing fine," as he gave him a thumb's up.

Noble began his *Light* set prematurely, a shift in mood, but the first instrumental was so long and loud and nonsensical, that Shylock, in the midst of Noble's tenacity and deep concentration, interrupted him a second time.

"Noble, my man, can you play something a little more, shall we say, upbeat, a little happier, and with less aggression," and then Shylock whispered in his ear: "It's the boss, man. It's driving customers away, and he doesn't like it, so play something familiar, okay?" and he gave him a pat on the arm. "You're doing fine, just jazz it up a bit."

Embarrassed, he glanced at his row of friends who smiled weakly like a group of dejected scouts tired from hiking in the rain. He noticed how the earlier crowd that mobbed the joint had taken their business elsewhere. Harry stayed and listened. He sat as cold as a stone, as though he were in an AA meeting. Ivan and Milo, their mouths hanging, sat speechless and awestruck like witnessing a dead corpse hanging from the ceiling. Alexandra smiled sadly, not expecting Noble's music to be this terrible.

But he played selections from his last set, the *Alexandra* set, and he engrossed himself within the first instrumental of this set, hoping it would revive the audience. During the piece, Noble couldn't help but overhear Shylock arguing with his boss, a paunchy Waspachick business owner bedecked in gold chains and bracelets. The arguing between them grew heated and obvious, and it took great pains for Shylock to approach Noble a third and final time.

"I'm sorry, Noble. I'm really sorry. It's not my decision."

He stood within their silence. The coffee house had turned silent with the exception of the espresso machine whirring. His heart sank, and in his humiliation, he unplugged the guitar from the amplifier, removed the sling from his shoulder, and ran onto the vacant street, the guitar in his hand. Alexandra chased after him in the darkness. She caught him at the edge of the park trying to run away. She nearly tackled him to the ground.

"Oh, Noble," she said out of breath, "It's only one performance. It's only your first time. Many don't get it the very first time. It takes time, Noble. You didn't have to run out like that. Those people in there care about you, and I care about you."

"Alexandra, you just don't understand," he panted.

"But I do, I do understand. I know you've worked hard for this, and it failed, and so what if it did fail? There'll be other opportunities. You can't just run away, because you failed once. It takes many failures. Believe me. I understand. I know the routine. One failure doesn't mean you stop playing. It doesn't mean you give up."

"You don't understand," he kept repeating, catching his breath.

"Then make me understand. I want to understand. I love you. Nothing will ever change that."

"I'm not the man I appear to be."

"So what? I'm not the woman I appear to be either, but this is only a temporary setback with your music. I believe in you, you've just got to believe in yourself. That's what counts."

"I've always been a failure, Alexandra. That's why you don't understand. I've always been a failure at everything I set out to do."

"But that's not true. It's not true at all."

"Believe it. I try hard, I work hard, but I never really achieved anything."

"How can you say that? Sure, you may have failed at your very first performance, but how can you say that you're a failure at everything, Noble? A total failure?"

He lay on the cool, moist grass, his guitar next to him, and Alexandra cuddled close above him. He gazed at the stars and wondered if his dark period equipped him with a universal truth. He hated what he had done, and in many ways, he hated himself for doing it. He hated having to tell her the truth.

"I am a failure, my sweet. You fell in love with a failure, and I'm not just saying that."

"Noble, I think you're overreacting," she whispered.

"Remember when I said that if I left everything for my guitar, you'd still love me?"

"How could I forget? But don't talk this way. We've got our whole life ahead of us. We'll do it together. Don't give up now."

"I deceived you, and I lied to you."

"How? Stop doing this to yourself. Stop doing this to us."

"I never finished college. In fact I don't live up in the Heights..."

"Why are you saying these things? Why are you torturing me like this," she cried.

"Damn it, Alexandra, I don't have a home up in the Heights, and I never went to Yale, and I'm not a wealthy business man..."

"No, Noble, No. Why are you making things up?"

"I'm not. I'm telling the truth, and I hate the truth. I hated it so much that I deceived you, but I'm not deceiving you anymore. I don't have a car in the shop, I don't have a home in the Heights, and I don't have a job. I'm from the South-end, Alexandra. Just a plain-old South-ender with silly dreams, full of silly dreams, and you would have never wanted me as a South-ender. You would have never loved me if you knew the truth. I didn't mean to hurt you, because I'm in love with you. But it's all a lie, all of it lies, and I lied so well that I even deceived myself. To think I could have a woman so beautiful, so smart, so gifted as you. To think I could have been a musician. I never meant to hurt you. I loved you so much that I had to lie. But you've changed me. I'm more of a man because of you, and that will never change."

She wiped away her tears and regained her sense of place. She was silently in shock, but gradually, as a sophistication came to them, it finally made sense. She smacked him hard and ran into the night, her figure blending with the darkness, until she disappeared.

"Please, dear Lord, forgive me," muttered Noble. "Please forgive me for what I've done to her. Alexandra, you said you'd love me...."

Chapter Seven

The smack still stinging, Noble started up the car and crawled around . the block. He parked in the darkness, opposite the Methodist church, its stainglass windows illuminated. He didn't want sympathy from anyone who heard him perform. Although he loved Alexandra, he knew it couldn't last, and considering his deception, perhaps he had known this all along, that a woman so stunning in beauty and intelligence was never meant for his lips.

He shut off the engine, and the quietness of the block, removed from the throbbing summertime strip, caused him, in his loneliness, to reflect upon his failures, both with the guitar and the woman who slipped through his fingers.

He fought the urge to cry, but he found himself sucking air, and his eyes welled up. He reasoned that it was good to weep every once in a while, as Odysseus wept every now and then. And the guitarist, Noble thought, finds good reason to weep once in a while, simply because it is always a struggle, and only the few survive, or appear to survive. It's not the case that the guitarist sits on a stack of wealth and drinks or smokes his life away with voluptuous women on each side before entering a sold-out stadium. It's often the case that the true guitarists are never even heard by most listeners. Yes, the ones who slave over their instrument in the hopes of capturing the appropriate and precise sound which elucidates the web of experience, and that web astounds the listener with a complexity not unlike his own. That the guitarist must play and play on, despite the tumultuous relationships, the divorces, the minimum wage jobs, the many rejections, the child on its way, the rent unpaid, his clothes threadbare, his stomach empty, and his fingers stricken with soreness at every joint, yes, the guitarist, through all of these trials, must endure. This is the bottom line, and such an endurance may bring him to both love and hate his instrument. It will bring him to his knees. He (or She) loves it when it cooperates and hates it when the chords do not reach their expected potential. And at times, he may smash the instrument on the pavement, knowing full well that this one wooden, inanimate object got the better of him, that it has succeeded in confusing and frustrating his plan for a musical permanence in which perceptions and attitudes are changed as they rise to meet the higher consciousness any form of music must establish and propel.

There are times also when the guitarist has but one listener amongst the sea of many: himself and himself alone. Noble believed that the guitarist must somehow have faith in the instrument despite those who shun him, despite those who simply say 'you should stop playing. It's a natural talent, and only the few make it anyway, so quit while you still have some time left. Be realistic.' But the guitarist knows full well, in a fit of laughter or the swell of silent tears, that he cannot stop, that he cannot end this relationship with his instrument. And not ending it does have a price, as everything has a price. He may fail resoundingly. He may be booed from the stage in humiliation, such that his confidence shakes, and he loses faith in those artistic merits he spent many years achieving and many more dreaming about. He may also lose his family, make few friends, and love but a few women. Regardless, the playing continues, and ultimately the guitarist succeeds, only this success is never measured by the applause he receives, or that fabled record contract he signs. The guitarist succeeds only within his own heart, and he or she will bask in this success, if and only if he can dust off those eroding strings once again, and play but one more time for a conclusion he can never see, a dream he will never achieve. In turn, the guitarist must understand his plight and embrace it, only to thrive, as we live but once, and the opinions of others mean nothing compared to those of the self, not to mention that one significant other, his guitar.

Yes, no matter how riddled with punishment the scroll, no matter how the mind of the guitarist burns, he pushes ahead, and though he may despise his poverty and his loneliness apart from those who seem to know it all and live happy lives, he should also know that those same people who appear so content and fulfilled had also, at one point, striven to achieve his same height but failed, and thus discontinued the struggle. If the guitarist is to succeed, he must never stop, and in turn he will cope more effectively with the sleazy hotel rooms in which he stays, the dank and gloomy bars, and the coffee houses which give him a cold and cruel reception. His success, then, is not determined by objective successes, but what he does during times of failure. Should the guitarist ever abandon his instrument, he alone will know the specter of his failure, and he will never be able to live with himself.

Thus, pick up the body, no longer as glossy as he remembered it. He cradles the neck and presses the strings and continues all over again, because he will neither tolerate nor accept his own failure. He will go down unsung, unremembered, and penniless, but he will go down playing. This is the only mark and artistry of the gifted guitarist. He plays not for his own existence, but for the sound it engenders. When he is a minority of one, and those closest to him insist he stop producing those horrendous riffs and jams, this is where he shines. In his supposed rejection, he finds the gem of opportunity. And to that guitarist who is lost and afraid, also learn how to smile, because ultimately, we hear you.

Noble would have given up his fantasy for the real thing. Instead of playing for the world, he would play for her, a continuous serenade, as he imagined it. Noble often thought in extremes, and whether or not he was right is debatable at best. If he could hold Alexandra just one last time, one more kiss, one last exploration into her before he played, he would have given away, not his guitar, but the love he held towards it. But the damage was done, a damage as palpable and salient as the muggy interior of the Oldsmobile. He wanted a drink. Whether or not he took a drink is another story, but he gave the engine a rattle, calmly put the car in drive, and lumbered down the crowded Waspachick strip. He intended to head out on the bare highway into the glorious night where most of his music was made. He would head towards a place where his music was accepted, in the hopes of finding another Alexandra. He only got as far as East Waspachick, though. He ran out of gas.

The End

Acknowledgments

The author wishes to thank his family without whose guidance, generosity, dedication, and love for their son this publication would have never been possible.

The author also wishes to thank those in the program of *Alcoholics Anonymous* for their input, support, and inspiration.

Finally, the author wishes to thank *First Amendment Press* for its commitment to this novel and for its pursuit of freedom of expression for the many writers it plans to publish and are also overlooked by established publishing houses.

Please visit *First Amendment Press* online at www.fapic.com for the latest on Harvey Havel's second novel *The Imam*, which will be published in March of 2000. If you would like to send us your comments by e-mail, please e-mail us at fapic@msn.com.

FAPIC Order Form:

Please rush the following books:

***Noble McCloud, A Novel* By Harvey Havel**
Quantity?_____@ US $25.00 each (Shipping and Handling included).

***The Imam, A Novel* by Harvey Havel**
Quantity?_____@ US $25.00 each (Shipping and Handling included).

(NJ Residents please add 6% Sales Tax)

Name:_____
Address:_____
_____
City:_____State:_____
Zip Code:_____
Email:_____

Make check or money order payable to:

First Amendment Press Int'l Co.
38 East Ridgewood Avenue
PMB 217
Ridgewood, NJ, 07450-3808